HANK

&

CHLOE

HANK & CHLOE

JO-ANN MAPSON

HarperCollins*Publishers*

Grateful acknowledgment is made to Wenaha Music Company for permission to quote from "Rock and Roll Girls" by J. C. Fogerty. Copyright © 1984 Wenaha Music Company. Used by permission. All rights reserved.

Grateful appreciation goes to the following people: Mark Secor, DVM, Officer Jeanette Chervoy, Peggy Darnell, Phyllis Barber, François Camoin, Leslie Ullman, Alexis Taylor, Rich Linder, and Alejandro Morales. I also acknowledge a great debt to many fine texts on mythology, and in particular to Alexander Eliot's inspiring and poetic *The Universal Myths*. Special thanks to my literary agent, Deborah Schneider, who held unwavering faith in my work, and to my editor, Janet Goldstein, who gave Hank and Chloe first-class lodging.

HarperCollins books may be purchased for educational, business, or sales promotional use. For information please write Special Markets Department, HarperCollins Publishers, Inc., 10 East 53rd Street, New York, NY 10022.

Designed by Claudyne Bianco

ISBN: 0-06-016943-5

For Valerie Mason Brannon,

who taught me to ride horses,

and Stewart,

who taught me how to love

As in the choice of a horse and a wife a man must please himself, ignoring the opinion and advice of friends, so in the governing of each it is unwise to follow out any fixed system of discipline.

G. J. WHYTE MELVILLE, *RIDING RECOLLECTIONS*, 1878

Sometimes I think
life is just a rodeo,
the trick is to ride
and make it to the bell.

JOHN FOGERTY, "ROCK AND ROLL GIRLS," 1984

CHAPTER

1

Answer the door after midnight and you might as well set a place at the table for trouble—Chloe Morgan's first thoughts when the knock came. Hannah, her shepherd, let out an initial throaty growl from her nest of blankets, then thumped her tail in the dark for the all clear. Tugging the horse blanket from her bed, Chloe padded barefoot across the rough plywood floor.

Rule one: You were damn careful out here in the middle of nowhere. Hugh Nichols let a select few live in the slapped-together shacks on his two hundred acres; he'd be damned if he'd sell out to developers so they could fling stucco around his land. But when it came to just who got to stay and who didn't, he was mercurial. You did nothing to make him question his decision. Few of the shacks had electricity, but Nichols had tapped into the county water, so it wasn't all that bad. Rig up a hose and you could take a cold shower. If you wanted to read after dark, you could light a hurricane lamp—oil wasn't expensive. Living here was safer than the streets had been, when she'd lain awake in her truck till dawn, fearful of every noise. Each night since she'd moved here, she said a silent prayer of thanks for the roof.

So far the county had left them alone, but she wasn't naive enough to think it would last. Who knew? You did what you could and then you moved on.

She walked quietly through the dark and rested her cheek against the plywood door. "What do you want?"

"You got a call."

The voice was Francisco Montoya's, who lived nearest to the pay phone and the main house, where Nichols slept off his legendary drunks and fought with a series of women he believed were after his considerable bankroll.

Bad news could always wait. "Tell whoever it is to call back in the morning."

He tapped louder now. "Chloe, you got to wake up. Mr. Green from the college. His mare is foaling. He asks for your help."

She cursed softly to herself. "Okay, Francisco, thanks. Go on back to sleep." Naked except for the blanket, twelve hours' work under her belt and only two hours' sleep, she wanted to go back to bed and the respite of unconsciousness. Earlier, the night air had smelled like rain and her truck tires were showing steel. Now Phil Green's mare was giving birth. So what? Did he want her to share in the joy of it? She despised foaling—the utter mess it could turn into, the way owners got stupid with pink or blue birth announcements, and all that crepe-paper nonsense. Too often she'd seen tiny hooves lacerate the vaginal wall, an ignored infection rack fine horseflesh until death came like an awkward blessing. The heartbreaking view of twins haunted her still—she'd sworn off all that—simply tried not to think about it and get on with her own work, teaching people to ride. But Phil was a good friend. He hadn't begged—he never would.

Out her only window, she watched the reflective stripes on Francisco's jacket dim as he trudged back up the hill to his own place. Home was an old tow-along silver Airstream, complete with electricity he'd jerry-rigged off a truck battery. Constantina was pregnant again, and their four-year-old daughter, Pilar, was just out of County Med with a winter bug that had turned into pneumonia. Out here a lot of things could level you, but Francisco and Constantina were illegals. They lived in fear of illness. The expense and the lack of proof of citizenship were more nightmarish than enduring the sickness. Once in the hospital, anything could happen. Social workers didn't help any, separating everyone. So they took care of each other out here, circled their wagons when there was trouble, recycled scrap aluminum, fed each other's animals when money was tight.

Hannah sat obediently by Chloe's side, snapping at some unseen insect. She had slim pickings in winter. Chloe shut the door, lay back down in bed for a minute, cursing motherhood, winter rains, the night in general. Then she got up, threw a pink sweatshirt over a denim miniskirt and found her tennis shoes, the only pair of footwear dry enough to be of service.

"Go get in the truck," she told the dog, and Hannah flew out the door, down the fire road, and into the bed of the old Chevy Apache, her bent tail folding beneath her like a flag at dusk. The truck started on the second try, a good omen. Chloe drove out of the compound without her headlights so as not to wake any more of the squatters than she had to.

Forget reason and plausibility, there were times Chloe swore she heard voices out here. Not babbling or devil tongues, human voices. Once she figured she wasn't crazy, she decided maybe they belonged to people who had died long before, whose very lives had been erased by time and progress, but who weren't quite done speaking their piece. On nights like these when she drove through the canyons in darkness, half asleep, on the watch for deer crossing, she heard them the clearest. *Hermana, hija....* They called her back from swerving off the highway, kept her awake. Tonight they were saying, *La yegua sufre . . . tocala....* She kept the windows rolled up and didn't stop for anyone. You didn't need a newspaper story to learn the wisdom of the road—everyone was suspect—everyone had an agenda. But that didn't stop her from stealing sidelong glances at two hitchhikers, noting their hopeful grins, the echo of others who seemed to single her out, speak to her. *¡Date prisa, por aca!* She would have liked the company of another warm body, even if they never touched or spoke. Just someone along for the ride. Like Fats had been, Fats Valentine. *Stop it.* Her life was singular now, since his death.

There, past the junction at Cook's Corner, as she waited for the traffic light to turn, she watched two bikers stumble out onto the tarmac. That character with his thumb out—his face held an echo of Fats's smile. Probably dangerously drunk, his liver halfway to cirrhosis. The other guy had the jutting brow of a Neanderthal and probably a survival knife to match every outfit. Forty years ago, he might have been an immigrant orange picker, his overalls thick with the labors of a night spent smudging, hope suffusing the weariness in his bones as he rounded another row of trees in the glistening frost. But the trees weren't there anymore, were they? A whole town surrounding the giant, nearly new university had sprung up like concrete circus tents. Still the words whispered in her ear, the breath faintly erotic as it tickled her neck flesh: *Nunca seremos vencidos. Este niño representa mi sufrimiento, y mi esperanza. . . .*

She shook her head drowsily and in the distance before her saw the freeway, a trickle of moving cars. Stay awake, she commanded herself. Phil Green needs your help. No good for anyone if you fall asleep and crash someplace like Irvine. You think the city fathers would name a street corner after you? No way, sister. Scrape you up like the rest of the trees and pour concrete for a new foundation.

But under the hard shell of highway she felt something else press against her tires. Preremembrances she could not possibly know, yet did. The faint outlines of roadhouses from sixty years ago shimmered before her eyes like heat mirages. She heard bits of tinny music from an old upright that had traveled the plains in a covered wagon, losing a few strings to the desert animals who thought they might make fine nesting material. Old music, simple, prim love songs asking permission to court and woo. People who weren't there. Visions. The result of some kind of brain irregularity you developed, deprived of sleep and adequate protein? All she knew was they had to do with the earth somehow, a past so charged with promise that it couldn't quite give up its grip on the present. Not that it was unpleasant; she never felt lonely. She saw them shimmer in those heat mirages; they were in serious desert now, land not in the least fertile, no longer preoccupied with rain but resigned to the stasis of hot waiting. All those faces—what did they want to tell her? Didn't the people coming west sense that they'd never leave? Why not go back to what they knew? A certainty of weather, seasons that descended like ritual? What promise drove them on? Was any struggle worth it? *To stay alive. Bear children to increase the tribe.* Some notion. Underneath that notion another surfaced, equal in weight: Someday they would each have to give up with grace.

It was raining hard now, the water hitting her windshield at an angle. The wipers were just about useless. She slowed down to help the old tires gain purchase on the slick highway. It was a twenty-minute drive to the junior college. A couple of hours might go by in an instant, seeing to that mare. She craned her head out the window to see if it was clear to change lanes. She hadn't brought her work clothes. She would have to drive back home, hopefully have time for a quick nap, get dressed for work. She worked at the Wedler Brothers Café from six to three-thirty, its sole waitress, but Rich didn't need her in until nine today—a miracle. He'd been promising to break in a new waitress for a relief shift, and after several who quit in their first hour, he'd found one he swore was a jewel: Lita. Whatever kind of name that was, Chloe hoped she would work out, didn't have those fifteen-inch-long fingernails or a penchant for the color black. If she smoked the same brand of cigarettes that would be nice. They could bum off each other.

She exited the freeway at the old Fairview Road, driving past all the sleeping houses in the subdivisions. Used to be that this road led straight into the fairgrounds. The extra-wide lane was designed for horse trailers and cattle trucks. They held a swap meet here every weekend now—cars and hundreds of vendors forming an outdoor mall. This was the last stretch of county to be paved over and civilized. Slowly the college was following suit, phasing out whole departments that seemed impractical and leveling anything that resembled the California style of architecture in favor of blocky, two-story brick buildings. She drove the back way through the service roads and parked in a handicapped slot near the Agriculture building. Outside her car she was immediately drenched—the rain's signature to the storm. After it quelled, she whipped wet hair from her face and hustled toward the lighted barn. Inside, after nodding hello to Phil, she straddled the prone chestnut mare, her skirt hiking up nearly to her crotch.

"Well?" Phil's face was pulled tight. The trouble light hanging from a nail on the barn wall flickered across his damp forehead.

"I don't know anything yet." She checked pulses, gum color, respiration. "How long has she been prone?"

"A couple of hours. I thought she was just getting comfortable. But then I couldn't get her back up. She's not going to make it, is she?"

"I'm not a vet, Phil."

"But you've been around this before. I can handle it. Tell me."

Chloe smiled, stretched her hand over the horse's neck to give his shoulder a pat. He sighed with relief, and immediately she felt sorry she'd given him any kind of gesture that could be mistaken for hope. Truthfully, it looked like no good; the mare was nearly beyond fighting, committed to lying down and apathetic when Chloe goosed her. With all those textbooks, all his telling students how it's done, had Phil missed the early signs of trouble? Not likely.

She stroked the mare's muzzle and her hand came away bloody. What the hell was that about? She wiped her hands in the straw and cedar shavings.

"I waited too long, didn't I?"

"Probably had nothing to do with it."

"So?"

"Phil, this is a grace time. What we do is call in a vet, stand here, and hold a hoof."

"And watch the lights go out."

"Maybe." She stepped over the horse and took his hand. His calluses nearly matched her own. She wished she could erase his pain, but it was beyond her, beyond just about anything short of a miracle. Cross fingers, she said to herself. Pray.

CHAPTER

2

At 6:00 A.M., Henry Oliver, Hank to his friends, "Yo, Professor," to the current batch of students who pegged his class as an easy A, buttoned his best shirt. It was an Irish cotton Henry Grethel, requiring both the judicious attention of his dry cleaner and the use of his only pair of cufflinks—silver buffalo nickels, handed down from his maternal grandfather, who'd died just before Hank's mother was born. The shirt was too expensive for a junior college instructor's budget, and he'd walked away from it as soon as he'd seen the price tag—a whopping seventy-nine dollars. He didn't spend foolishly. But later on, he'd gone back. He wanted it so badly he hauled out rationalizations, telling himself it was practical in the long run—high thread count, the beige color neutral enough for any season, formal or casual occasion. Dining in the peninsula's better restaurants, slow dancing to big band music—the shirt would perform up to its price tag in time. Today he wore it to act as a pallbearer.

William "Hoop" Hooper, one of his father's golfing buddies, had died of something, but at just this moment Hank couldn't recall what it was. Probably a coronary, or maybe it was the inevitable cancer. His septuagenarian parents had a burgeoning cadre of recently deceased friends. Henry senior and Iris had finally sold their bayfront home and were renting a one-bedroom unit in World of Freedom, a retirement community in the inland hills of Laguna. Much as he disliked the idea of the two of them in this holding pattern, he had to admit it made sense. The complex served three meals a day and had medical staff on call. Funerals came with the territory, Hank supposed, just as able-bodied sons were enlisted to assist at them.

Now he stood by the other men, in the properly somber posture, waiting for the end of the eulogy. The pug-faced minister appeared determined to embroider layers on each fact of Hoop's life as if he were waxing the moon by hand. Hank glanced over at Hoop's widow—Ella?—in the front pew, dressed in navy and white. She held a dry hand-kerchief and looked up, puzzled, as if perhaps she had accidentally ended up at the wrong service. She cleared her throat loudly, twice, and the minister looked up, faltering for a moment. Then he launched into what Hank recognized as your classic "death-on-a-higher-plane" crescendo. He threw in a little "God Bless America" motif, cashing in on Hoop's World War II service and the current trouble brewing in the Gulf. That, of course, was the trouble with Christianity. Soldiers of Christ never quite made the leap from the service of the martyred Jesus to per-form any significant service of their own. It fell under the heading of your everyday loss—ordinary. Hank knew several dozen myths on death, but his personal favorite involved a tribe of Malaysian pygmies. They had the right idea. First, a week-long walk as one left the body, cer-tainly enough time to get used to the idea of doing without it. There was, of course, no escaping unpleasantness with the other spirits. They broke one's bones, and then that rather unfortunate business with the eyes. But weren't skeletons and sight unnecessary baggage in the after-life? In the end the departed soul was encouraged to drink its fill from the *mapic* tree, whose flowers were not perfumed petals cupping a center but full human female breasts where a man was allowed to drink until sated while dreaming of rebirth. He smiled slightly at the thought of Hoop lapping, guzzling, calling out to Hank's father, "Christ, Henry, hurry and get up here!" But the only human voice saying anything at all was that of the minister's forced awe: "the mystery of it all!"

Hank bet that in half an hour, tops, the man of God would be back in his rectory kitchen, eating glazed doughnuts and counting out his gratuity. Hank would be in his office at the college, grading a few papers and counting the time until he would go home and grade more papers. Which of us has a better grasp on things? he wondered. We're both sorry mortals, groping in the darkness. His smile twitched beneath his mustache and he wished he'd eaten breakfast.

At forty-two, reminders of his own mortality came to him on a daily basis—the twinge in his lower back as he stretched out on the carpet to execute his fifty morning push-ups was now part of his morning routine. He ate fruit now instead of pastry on his coffee breaks, tuned the office radio he shared with Asa Carver back to quiet stations that gave extended global news reports, and took the weather seriously. Peaceful, maybe sedentary. He wondered when this gradual shifting of gears had occurred. Even as he took his cue to lift his portion of Hoop's casket with the others, the task seemed numbingly familiar, not unmanageable at all. Inside, a man's life was reduced to the simplest of definitions. Dismissed, beyond grief. We get used to it, he thought, and wondered briefly how he could work that notion into one of his lectures.

Iris sent a determined smile Hank's way as he stepped from the altar toward the pews. His mother's gray hair was wound into a heavy coil atop her head, secured with silver combs she'd had since she was a young woman, teaching school on the reservation in Page, Arizona. The funeral rated high on Iris's list of important events, Hank could tell, because she was wearing her turquoise squash-blossom necklace. The necklace appeared only on the most monumental of occasions. *I'll wear it to your wedding*, Iris had promised, *and someday give it to your wife.* But of course, there had been no wedding to wear it to. A Navajo man had made her a present of the necklace in exchange for teaching his son to read, the first reader in his family. How little Hank knew of his mother's life. Slight alarm prickled his skin beneath the good shirt and jacket. She'd had a bout with cancer a year ago. The surgery permanently subtracted ten pounds from her frame and subdued her merry laugh to a cautious smile. He'd driven her to chemotherapy once, when Henry senior's car was getting new brakes, but otherwise the details of her illness had been kept from him, the same as he had been shielded from most unpleasantness in childhood. Oh, they insisted everything was *fine* now, just dandy. As if she had never had cancer at all. But it could recur.

Henry senior made an exaggerated gesture toward his own extremely paisley necktie. Hank deduced that this meant his own was hanging awry. Christ, what did his father want? For Hank to stop, balance the casket on his hip and straighten his Windsor knot? He tried not to frown, but he felt the heat of annoyance flood his cheeks. Such trivialities seemed to obsess his father, who couldn't quite leave behind his life as an administrative civil servant. *It's all a snap, son, if you just follow the rules.* And when there are no rules, Dad, what do we do then?

Hank understood why his mother had spent a lifetime in her husband's shadow. For the same reasons, Hank had completed the rank of Eagle Scout, had served for years as acolyte while his chums were shunning church, trying to pick up girls. The necktie, which he intended to rebury in his closet this evening, was a twin to his father's—a Christmas gift—and one of five decent ties he owned. Both Hank and his mother knew from experience it was much easier not to fight Henry's wishes, just to smile and slowly step to the left whenever possible. Iris had dabbled here and there: substitute teaching, the Literacy Guild, where she still enjoyed teaching others to read, but since the cancer she had withdrawn into a world with narrower boundaries. Though the complex offered countless activities for aimless joining, she sat in the living room of the apartment, needlepointing doe-eyed animals for throw pillows, Henry never far from her side. One hopeful sign: recently she'd ordered Henry to wallpaper the kitchen in hair-raising stripes—fuchsia, lemon, a tangerine shade worthy of a macaw's lunch. *Cancer.* The syllables were designed to shock. But Iris endured with a Republican's blindsided confidence: "President Reagan did just fine and I will, too."

Hank couldn't explain the childish counting of footsteps he'd done from the altar to the polished hearse waiting outside. . . . *thirty-nine, forty, forty-one, forty-two.* His age—a number as random as stars in the sky, but disturbing. When he stepped away from the hearse, his parents were by his side. His mother pressed his shoulder. He took her hand.

"Thank you for helping, Hank," Hoop's widow said at the curb, touching his sleeve lightly. "You're such a gentleman to lend a hand. Wasn't the minister insufferable? And why Hoop wanted a sunrise service is certainly beyond me. He never got up before nine unless it was for a starting time. I guess the rain took care of the sun, anyway. We're having a breakfast back at the complex after the graveside. Join us?"

"Of course," Henry senior answered for all of them. "We'll be with you as long as you need us, dear."

Hank shook his head. "Gosh, I'm sorry, I can't." Emily? He'd blanked out on her first name, and it wouldn't do to screw up now. He forged ahead with his practiced condolences, taking care not to press too hard on the small bones of her arthritic hand. "I'm afraid I have a seminar I have to teach. My students count on me. I hate to let them down."

"Of course. You go on."

He kissed her damp cheek in celebration of freedom. His father lifted a hand to protest, but Hank was already slipping through the crowd, moving carefully past the aged bodies toward the rain-wet parking lot. He waved to his parents, his palms outstretched in a "what can I do?" gesture, tapped his watch, and made his escape.

Of course it was a lie. He had time to drink a cup of decaf from the widow's good china. He could eat the bakery croissants and the sturdy quiche, stand around for an hour, listen and smile while friends and acquaintances reminisced, making sense of their lives. Henry and Iris's boy—*Professor* Oliver—a master's degree. Upright, dependable, though his necktie is a little crooked. Teaching is a noble profession these days, isn't it? Oh, yes. Prattling on about those wonderful ancient myths in an arena of determined business majors. And all for a subsistence-level salary. *You get used to it.*

As he gunned the motor of the seasoned Honda, it occurred to Hank that during his entire career of teaching at the junior college, nearly all his work, save for final grades and one impassioned grant proposal, had been done in pencil.

CHAPTER

3

Invoking the gods would do no good. The stench of death had moved in, suitcases and all, perfuming the old school barn. Chloe's legs were damp, chilled gooseflesh. Bits of shavings clung to her skin as she knelt and studied the laboring chestnut mare Philip Green had gotten her out of bed to examine.

A sleeping horse—no overt signs of disaster to the layman, but that unbalanced, nonscientific feeling prevailed. Phil had kept her posted for the last three weeks on every imminent sign. One day he had come into the café at lunch hour and shouted, "Chloe, her teats waxed!" and Rich had poked his head out the cubby where he received the orders, answering, "More than I ever got her to do, buddy."

He'd done a textbook preparation: spread new cedar shavings, purchased the requisite bottle of iodine for the umbilical stump, laid out assorted syringes and vials of tetanus antitoxin on a clean towel, standby antibiotics—all purchased on Chloe's suggestion from State Line Feed and Tack, where you paid nearly what the vets did, semi-wholesale. He had fifteen-dollar scissors and a hot-pink halter and lead rope—hoping filly.

All that insurance, and Chloe would have bet her tip jar that the mare wasn't going to make it through the birth.

The trouble with the mare was complicated, signs she couldn't read. For the last fifteen minutes she had been popping football-size clots. Chloe broke one open with her finger to study the fibrin. It was clumped and stringy, like unripe grapes. Further, it smelled rank, as if it had traveled from a deeper source of infection. She settled herself down, sitting cross-legged in the cedar shavings, taking the mare's head into her lap. Nothing for either of them to do but wait for the vet.

While she waited, she stroked the mare's face, feeling her facial bones beneath the thin hide. The school barn was neat, tidy, worn down from the passage of animals over the years. Chloe studied every plank and tool hanging from the walls. This was the nineties, no more Future Farmers were graduating from the school. Agriculture and husbandry were being phased out of the curriculum, and Phil's horse was the sole equine occupant left. Her foal would have made two, a beginning. It was still raining, slower now, the washed street smell thin underneath the cleaner thrust of heaven-driven water. The thrumming on the tin rooftop soothed them both. Phil had his head in his hands, his bald spot glinting in the flashlight glow. Outside, the thinning school herd of Herefords grazed the half-acre pasture. Chloe heard them lowing in the dark, wondering about breakfast. Cows were fools—fresh manure factories. But she admired the unlikely picture they made standing behind the fence alongside the boulevard. She heard the freeway traffic's high keening in the distance. Early commuters to LA, aiming to beat gridlock. She ran her palms across the mare's cheek, feeling for the pulse she'd kept a mental tally on since she'd arrived. The mare sighed at her touch, and a small rattle followed the outtake of breath. Chloe moved her hands down the rib cage now. Not much muscle there, but what could you expect, off the racetrack in Caliente, bred out of God knows what kind of nightmare? Phil shouldn't have bought her at all, let alone in foal, but he was like a lot of new horse owners, couldn't wait, swayed by the two-for-one idea of pregnancy. The foal was still viable, moving against her hand, struggling to find a way out. The mare coughed, and her nostrils filled with blood. Here we go, Chloe thought. Was there one orifice left that hadn't bled?

Phil looked up. "I've pretty much bitched this, haven't I?"

Chloe wouldn't let her face reveal anything. "You call the vet again?"

"His exchange said they'd find him. They said—"

"Oh, piss on those ˙answering service people.˙ They're all drug addicts or nineteen-year-olds. You call back and tell them Chloe Morgan says if Gabriel Hubbard can't get his sorry ass out of bed, he's going to regret his entire life not to mention his practice."

Phil smiled, showing even white teeth. "You know, some of us spend our whole lives just working up to a 'pardon me.'"

She stuffed the last clean towel under the mare's bloody hindquarters. "Hey, that's not my problem. We're losing this mare. Make the call."

He left the barn, locking the stall door shut behind him as if he expected the mare suddenly to bolt.

Answering service, my ass. Gabriel Hubbard was out catting. Good vets were rare and passionate—it might take years before you found one who knew his trade and possessed the instinct that elevated him beyond able. Gabe was that. His talent was as gracious as love at first sight and just as undependable in the long run. He might be the best, but he wasn't going to get here in time to save Phil Green's mare. Oh, he'd mop up, be sure to send out his bill, but the mare was the knacker's.

Phil returned, shaking rain from his sleeves, popping the tab of a Diet Pepsi. "They said the same thing."

Chloe leaned over the mare and took his offer of a hand to pull her to her feet. "Phil, you called me for an honest opinion. Well, the truth is, things look iffy as hell."

"Iffy."

"You want a word, that's mine." She swallowed a warm sip of soda from the can he held out. "Phil, you teach the husbandry classes. Press a thumbnail into her gums. Her capillary refill is a pretty clear indication of internal hemorrhaging, even if she wasn't bleeding from every goddamn place we can see. Look at her. She's not even fighting. If you've got a shotgun in the barn, you might want to take it down and load it."

His weight shifted from one boot to another in the cedar shavings. "Don't think I could do that."

"If Gabe doesn't show up soon, I guess I could do it for you."

"My foal?"

"Mother Nature's giving you a strong nudge here. Letting things alone might be the wisest idea we come up with."

She watched the tall professor's face empty of hope. He crouched down, stroked the mare's neck, then buried his fingers in the long mane hair. Years ago, when they'd first met, he ran the 4-H youth project on horsemanship in his spare time. Over the years he'd been responsible for sending her students, a select few, those who had the spark it took to make a good rider. He'd been there when Fats died, offering help she couldn't bring herself to accept. Now he led pack trips into the Sierra Nevada so people who had the money could photograph the few remaining herds of mustangs. Twice this year he'd conned her into lecturing to his classes, a sort of "blue-collar" authority on horsemanship, and for her time he'd slipped her twenty-five dollars that she knew came out of his own pocket. His wife was a hefty redhead named Sally, who pretty much dedicated her life to keeping Phil happy. So their kids didn't make the honor roll. They said "please" and "thank you," and looked Chloe straight in the eye, none of this metalhead nonsense that seemed to have infected the rest of the teenage world. Phil Green had a heart, and he wasn't afraid of the contents. Trouble was, sometimes that kind of thing came back and slapped you, whereas vets like Gabe got hard. She wondered how human doctors weathered the agony that came with telling bad news. It seemed like it was the idea of loss that bewildered people into begging for respirators, anything to maintain a semblance of life. Heartbreaking shit, but so long as the chest lifted, technically life was present. When it quit, you shook hands with your grief, got on with things, or you lost your mind. It all depended on which side of the fence you stood.

"All right," she said. "I'll give it a shot, but the odds aren't in my favor. Just so we both know that going in."

Phil nodded. "I understand."

"Good. Go call that goddamn vet and tell him to get down here, that he's got about five minutes left to be a hero."

Phil pressed his arms around her shoulders. "Thanks, Chloe."

She brushed him away. "Don't say that. Later on you might hate me. Get me a clean rope, and let's see if we can find your baby's legs."

Gabriel Hubbard, DVM, pulled up half an hour later. He was wearing a tuxedo and reeked of champagne.

He chuckled at Chloe's rope. "What in Christ are you doing, a rerun of 'Wagon Train'?" He took off his jacket, threw on a cellophane sleeve, doused it with lubricant and drove it up inside the mare to his elbow. He rotated his arm, checking the foal's position. "Sorry I'm late."

"Oh, spare us the details," she said, absently coiling the rope in her hands.

Phil hovered nearby. "Anything?"

"Wish there were some contractions to fight around, Phil." Gabe withdrew his arm and stripped off the glove with a snap. "Total inertia. This baby's not moving."

Chloe said, "So shoot her with oxytocin."

"I'm getting to that. Jesus, when did you graduate from A & M?" He found a vein, administered the injections, then lifted the bound tail and studied, shaking his head. The mare's heaving sides labored in a guttering shudder and stilled. She was gone.

"Fuck that," Hubbard said, letting the tail drop. He nudged her heavy side with his boot tip. "Goddamn quitter bitch. Phil, if you want me to try and save this baby, I have to get mean and I have about ninety seconds to do it."

Phil made a sound, not comprehending.

"Do it," Chloe urged him. "Whatever it takes, so that this day doesn't end in a double disaster."

"Kneel down and brace her side, Chloe. I need something to lean against."

"Already there."

The sound of the scalpel slicing through flank flesh echoed through Chloe's eardrums. She clenched her jaw as the scrape of the vet's pliers separated layers of muscle. Hubbard worked quickly, making an oblique incision across the uterus, and the crumpled foal flopped forward, suddenly relieved of the pressure that had held him captive. Blood spilled over the amniotic sac and splashed up onto Chloe's chest. Her pink sweatshirt clung wetly to her breasts. She pawed at herself uselessly with her free hand. The smell torqued her gut, threatening to make her vomit the Diet Pepsi.

Gabe slit the sac and hooked his fingers into the foal's nostrils to dislodge the mucus plugs. He gave the foal a little massage, and it came alive, blinking startled eyes.

"Colt," he said. "Come on, baby, breathe for me."

With a choking squeal, the horse sucked air, looked around in panic, and struggled unsuccessfully to free himself of Gabe's hands. Hubbard handed Phil a towel. "Looks like you're going to be Mama for the time being. Towel him down."

Phil knelt. He took the towel from Chloe. "It wasn't popular to go into the delivery room when Sally had our two. Don't quite know what I'm doing here."

Chloe placed her hand over his. "Just rub him gently. Let him get to know your feel. Dry him, that's right. Then we'll work on getting him standing."

The colt's eyes glistened against the dark wet muzzle. He looked to Chloe like a bathroom rug thrown over an armature. Furred bones, done up hastily, folded like a backpacker's idea of saving space. He had a classic mule head, ears still bent to the skull from all those months inside. She watched as Phil placed his hands beneath the breast and hindquarters to lift him to a standing position. All three of them took a good look at the feet, fetlocks touching the ground. Wonderful, she thought, a bad job all around.

Phil sighed.

"Don't the two of you go out drinking just yet," Hubbard said. "This is fixable."

Phil tried his best to whistle, but it came out reedy, bagpipes at a funeral. "How?"

"Nowadays you splint, cast, exercise," Hubbard said. "He'll come around with some work."

And barrels of money, Chloe thought.

An hour later, when Gabe had completed his examination, he

clapped Phil on the back. "You didn't come out empty-handed after all. It's Miller time, cowboy."

The colt pitched forward and whinnied, making his first exploratory nudge at the dead mare's flanks. His impossibly long legs buckled, and Chloe did a quick save before he fell headlong into the mutilated back end of his mother. Lamblike cries sliced through the barn.

Phil shivered. "Gets to you."

"You're just worn out," Chloe said. "Not to mention drenched from the rain." Her own heart knocked at her chest wall.

They watched the jutting head poke into his mother's side, harder now, questioning. Each jab dislodged another gelatinous clot from the mutilated vagina. Hubbard prepared the antibiotic and tetanus injections and asked Chloe to hand him a third syringe for vitamins. "There's a colostrum farm in Chino," he told Phil. "I'll give them a call and order what you need. Pricey stuff, but you can't get on without it. Meanwhile, you can try milking out the mare. Chloe can show you. I'll finish up and see if I can scout you up a lactating mama."

Phil reached into his Levi's for his checkbook.

"Put that away," Chloe said. "Dr. Hubbard can get his check in the mail in thirty days like the rest of us."

Gabe chuckled. "That Chloe, she's a punisher, all right."

Chloe spread her jacket underneath the mare's teats. She sent Phil to fetch sterile jars from Dr. Hubbard's truck. For a moment, she sat there, adrenaline flooding her skin with infinitesimal tingles. An average birth took as few as ten minutes, the longest, maybe an hour, tops. They'd been here most of the night. The mare's eyes stared up, recording nothing. Morning was beginning to flood the barn. In a shaft of sunlight, a particle of cedar shaving caught in the shifting air, fluttered down, and settled on the open eyeball. Without thinking, Chloe delicately picked it away. The colt butted her with his mulish head and whimpered.

Hubbard said, "Hey there, little guy. Be choosy who you imprint on."

"Nice party, Gabe? Too bad you dirtied your tux. Guess you'll have to buy a new one."

"Don't you start in on me. It was for a worthy cause."

She snorted. "Your wife's tennis bracelet fund."

"No, actually it was a benefit for the homeless. Seems like it's up to working folks like us to lend those poor bastards a hand. Maybe I'm not telling you anything you haven't already heard."

Chloe bit back the "son of a bitch" that erupted from the core of her being and wanted more than life to brand his forehead. Gabe had helped her out a little over a year ago when she'd gotten in over her head, deep. Despite paying back the money, there seemed to be no repaying the debt. If she snapped at him now, she'd only regret it later. He was an ex–Green Beret and he knew more about fighting than she could ever hope to. Simply put, there was no territory he considered neutral. He knew anatomy, not just the animal world, hers. Since she'd started saying no, she'd been on the receiving end of many a well-aimed verbal dart.

She sat back on her heels. "Let's just get through this, Gabe. What do you say?"

"I'll set some time aside to give it some thought."

She watched him iodine the cord stump. The colt already trusted his hands. He wasn't just good, he was the best when he worked at it. This baby would not only make it, but he'd see to shaping up those legs personally. As they said in the trade, he was a leg man, and she trusted no one else when it came to her own horse, Absalom, who suffered from navicular disease.

"You're handy," she said.

He smiled at her, fingers working almost of their own volition. "You should know."

"Christ, you never, ever, ever quit! Thank the Lord I'm not your wife or I'd probably be in prison by now for murder."

Phil opened the stall door and stepped inside. Chloe took the half-dozen jars from him, only to see him reach down to stroke the mare's neck. It was already stiffening. He pulled his hand back as if he had touched flame.

"Guess I better call somebody."

"Let Gabe take care of it."

Phil bent his head and scrubbed at his eyes with the back of his hand. "How do I say good-bye?"

"You just say it."

Chloe looked to Hubbard. *Do something, dammit.* The vet fastened the foal halter around the baby's head. "Chloe's right, Phil. Get it over with. Walk away. Here's an idea. Go make your calls. Sally, whoever. Then send me over six of your best students and we'll do a necropsy, take care of things, and give them some hands-on experience in the bargain. You go get some sleep."

"I don't think I could sleep."

"Bet you a beer you can. Go on, both of you."

Chloe took Phil by the shoulder and led him out of the barn into the tentative light of the new day. Sun shone improbably through the rain, washing the brick buildings. Cars were starting to fill the parking lot—grounds staff, those diligent few students arriving for the early classes, the unlucky faculty, trudging blindly toward the coffee machines, a small herd of lean athletes headed for workouts.

"Come on," she whispered into the crying man's ear. "You look like a guy who could use a cup of coffee."

CHAPTER

4

J anuary rain fell outside the faculty office building. The sky delivered it at a noisy slant, scrabbling against the luckier offices that bore windows. Hank's had one. Hank's office mate Asa said they weren't windows at all, but "visual strips," something akin to a glass Band-Aid, and he wanted no part of them, thank you very much, Hank could have the window view.

Hank stepped carefully over the puddles forming on the slick cement outside the secretarial offices. He was an untenured professor of Folklore and Mythology and taught three classes each semester. In his free hand he held his mail, collected for him by Karleen, one of the mailroom employees.

She'd handed it over personally with a mascaraed wink and then held stubbornly on to her end. "Come over tonight. I can rent a video, and we can both forget to watch it." She paused meaningfully. "Again."

He pressed his lips together to project a reasonable facsimile of a smile. *Karleen*. That solitary lapse of judgment on his part was turning into a canyon of regret. "Papers to correct. Maybe another time."

"You keep saying that."

"I do. And my students keep turning in papers."

She frowned, let go of his mail, and spun away, her dangling plastic airplane earrings circling the clouds of her pink lobes.

His other hand firmly grasped the sturdy handle of an army-green collapsible umbrella he kept in the glove box of his Honda. Southern California be damned—there was always the possibility of sudden change—earthquakes, chemical spills, even rain like this could turn nasty, give you a cold in no time.

He unlocked the office door, closed it behind him, and sat down at his desk in the unlit office. It took a few moments for his eyes to adjust to the darkness. He listened to the rain knife at the walls, shivering slightly as he removed his good shirt and hung it on a hanger, then placed the hanger tip in the handle of the file cabinet. While he buttoned up the comfortable oxford cloth he'd brought to teach in, he stared at the good shirt's creases and noticed how they mirrored his slight chest muscles, as if the heart of him had stayed behind, huddled inside the wheat-colored cloth.

"Time to get to that ark you've been planning, Noah," Asa Carver said as he stood in the doorway shaking his imitation Burberry coat dry.

"Pardon?"

Carver switched on the light. "Two by two, that sort of thing. Wake up. Find a visual strip to peer out of. *Lluvia*. Rain."

Hank blinked. "It's just spitting."

"Then it by God slobbered all the way up to my wheel wells on the boulevard of apartments."

Southern California architecture was one of Asa's pet peeves. Of Hank's town house in Irvine he'd said: "Behold, the Emerald City, if you like living on a movie set. Tell me, are the boulders wire and *papier-mâché*?"

Hank took nothing Asa said to heart. Asa taught Medieval English and spoke fluent Spanish, so his position at the school was not quite as threatened as Hank's—if budget cuts continued, they would simply make him teach composition, ESL classes. People could live without the myths, the old stories, but they needed to learn where the commas went. Asa was recently married for the second time, swamped in post-honeymoon libidinous bliss, only occasionally screwing his ex-wife on the side. The ark business was merely a variation on an old subject. All through his divorce from Claire, Asa repeatedly urged Hank to pair up. "Even chromosomes do it. I want you to be happy, man."

"I am happy."

"No, you're not. You can't possibly be happy until you're thoroughly messed up by a woman."

"Like Claire?"

"She'll do as well as any."

"Maybe I should marry her."

Asa's face had gone rubbery for a second, and Hank had to laugh. "That *was* a joke."

Hank liked Claire. He never told Asa so, but she reminded him of Laurel, his first love, technically once his wife. The marriage, a Tijuana brainstorm, both of them sappy from cheap margaritas on Easter break their senior year, ended four weeks later when she walked out and had the whole business annulled. Twenty years had passed, but Hank remembered her when he saw shapely calves, when he looked at his female students and felt an ache that was difficult to put to rest. It had happened so long ago that he no longer mentioned it to people—why bother, when it took longer to explain than it had lasted? He kept quiet when he'd unlocked the office those predivorce mornings and found Carver asleep on the secondhand couch, the lanky coed destined to be the second Mrs. tucked beneath his arm. He wouldn't venture to give advice where he had failed.

Carver grumbled, "Okay, gods. This is Southern California. Claire and I were going to play tennis today." He shook the rain from his watch. "No rain for two years, and now this. Care to explain yourselves?"

Hank leaned back, and his swivel chair creaked in protest. "I don't know, Asa. Rain, the obvious portent of doom. Maybe the gods are trying to tell you to cool it. For example, in film, rain is a signal of deep shit to follow."

"How deep are we talking? Usual six inches?"

Hank smiled. "Well, gosh, I haven't measured lately. Why *did* you get married again?"

"Because I am in *love*, man."

"Love."

"Bethany is. . . " He kissed his fingers and sighed. "I shit you not."

"So why screw it up playing tennis?"

Carver shook his head. "You just wait, Oliver. You sit there so pompous, so immune, but your time's coming. Some Valkyrie is going to storm into your life and grab you by the short ones. There is no cure for the sting of Cupid's arrow."

"Romance died a natural death along with the Industrial Revolution."

Thunder cracked outside as if to underscore Hank's words. Both men jumped slightly, and Asa Carver laughed, a hoarse, dry cough. "The official word from above," he said. "The gods are busy fashioning a woman from a bolt of lightning. They do not want me to play tennis this afternoon. What the hell. I can knock off early. Bethany's trying to impress me with home cooking. Can I endure a few bites of *Gourmet's* latest Tuscan recipes?" He pinched his abdomen. "Solid muscle, thanks to my rejuvenated sex life. A man who works out has room to indulge."

"Believe it or not, your sex life is not my sole source of entertainment."

"Trying to tell me something?"

Hank picked up several papers and let them drop to his desk blotter. "Office," he said. "Work. Paycheck."

They bent to their desks and left each other alone. Asa owed Hank fifty-seven dollars, dating back two or three years. Penny-ante poker, where he habitually borrowed and lost. Hank wouldn't ask for it, but he also would not play poker with him anymore.

Over Hank's desk hung a dog-eared poster stating: "It will be a great day when the schools get all the money they need and the Air Force has to hold a bake sale to build a bomber." Over Asa's were yellowing page proofs from articles he had published in little-known journals, partially obscured by five-by-seven glossies of Bethany on their honeymoon. She was twenty-two years old, sunburned hot-dog pink, wearing the style of bikini that Hank thought most closely resembled dental floss. Sometimes Hank would get up from his desk to look at that picture, trying to see what it was about her that had caused Asa to irrevocably alter his life. She was thin, not beautiful in any Breck-girl classic sense of the word, but the low-slung hips and pouty lips implied a portentous sexuality that threatened to act like heroin on whoever dared take a taste. She looked like any one of a thousand students Hank had encountered over the years: woman-child trying out the poses, working her lures in her mother's high heels and rouge. When they finally met "formally" at that absurd church wedding, the guests on the bride's side were all young and high-pitched, the men hooting, the women flushed and envious, jockeying anxiously for the bouquet. The guests on the groom's side were spare in number and much too eager for the open bar.

Directly across the narrow hall that separated the faculty offices, Philip Green's door stood open. The tattered brown easy chair the agriculture professor usually occupied was empty. Carver had dubbed Green "Cowboy" after he'd bought the mare and finagled keeping her on the school pastures, those three-odd acres as endangered as their own positions here at the college. The mare's name was Cassiopea, and she was a five-year-old chestnut thoroughbred who'd run the track in Caliente until she'd bowed a tendon. Phil was thrilled with his acquisition. He told them over and over, "I got her for five hundred bucks. That's *nothing*." And then he'd discovered she was in foal, and spoke of this discovery as nothing short of providential. "Ten bones he names the baby Jesus," Asa kidded, and even Hank had to laugh. Phil did go on.

The hallway skylight darkened with cloud cover, and Hank spoke without looking up at Carver.

"You suppose Phil's horse is okay? All this damp can't be terrific for Mama, not to mention Baby."

"Foal," Carver muttered. "His cowboyness would shit a biscuit if he heard you use the incorrect terminology. I wouldn't worry. Undoubtedly he's bought the creature little jammies with feet in them. Down in the barn tucking her in."

"Probably."

From their office on the second floor, they could hear the cattle feet of the students down below in passing, bits of conversation echoing as classes changed and they moved from building to building. Later in the day, students would hover in the alcove, making plans for the evening, arguing about politics, often giving each other the low-down on the professors themselves. Hank generally kept an ear peeled. As he marked a passage fraught with generalities and circled half a dozen misspellings, a male voice sharpened. *Please.*

"Show time," Carver said, scooting his chair back.

"Aw, come on, Eileen. Why the hell not? It's not like I haven't done my share of kneeling down for you."

"Because, Guy, I, like, find it revolting. Totally."

"Way to go, Eileen," Hank said. "Hold the gate."

"Whose side are you on?" Carver protested. "Guy wants his blowjob, that's all. Probably deserves it, too."

"Eileen's a nice girl. Doesn't do windows, either."

"She's spoiled rotten," Carver insisted. Daddy just bought her a new BMW with leather upholstery. Guy deserves his turn." He yelled out the window, "Give him a break, Eileen! You did it for me and you loved it!"

The voices went silent. Hank shook his head. On the paper before him, a student had dismissed the *Odyssey* in one terse paragraph as "this sort of boring story, you know? But it could be a totally radical flick if Peckinpah got hold of it."

The sound of bootheels shot up the stairwell.

"Eileen's coming to get you, Asa."

The stairs outside the office creaked and a distraught voice ascended.

"Dammit, Chloe. I keep going over it in my mind, but—"

"Look. It's over. Nothing you could have done."

"Maybe a uterine tear. Early on in the labor."

"Stop torturing yourself. Nobody could have known."

Asa scooted his chair back and mimed to Hank, "What gives?"

"It's just—" Again the words broke off jaggedly into the clamor of grief, and Hank recognized them as belonging to Phil Green. "So damn sorry."

"Look at it this way. You learned a lesson about buying horse bargains."

The woman's voice was a whiskey tenor. She could have sung

along with Willie Nelson, Hank thought. And Phil, well, this morning it sounded as if he could have written the lyrics.

"You and Hubbard did all you could. My fault for not having her vet-checked in the first place."

"I really think you ought to consider giving that baby away, Phil."

"Why? Hubbard says if we splint the legs, there's every chance the fetlocks will straighten."

"But you don't know what you're getting into."

"So I'll learn."

"It's a full-time job."

"You can help me."

"No. I won't do that. Not with an orphan."

"Orphans make it."

"No!" The woman's voice rose an octave. "You have no idea what it can be like. You'll both suffer, and the horse ends up confused as hell and chock-full of vices. Jesus, look at me. I can't go to work like this. I'm a bloody mess."

"I think I've got a sweatshirt in my office. Come on."

Finally they rounded the corner. Hank craned his neck to peek out the door. Phil Green, all six feet four inches of him, stood in his office doorway holding on to the back of a soaking wet blond in a pink sweatshirt that was covered in equal measures of rain and blood.

"Trouble?" Carver piped up.

"Take a look for yourself."

Phil waved, but the blond's back was to them now. "Cass dropped early. We were up all night with the vet." He cleared his throat. "Looked like she might come around, but then she went all shocky on us and hemorrhaged." He snapped his fingers. "Just died, like that."

Carver whistled. "That's terrible news, Phil. Really sorry to hear it."

Phil's grimy hands patted the woman's back. "I even had the miracle worker on the job, but that wasn't enough."

She made a sound of protest and tried to pull away.

Phil grasped her shoulder. "You guys had better congratulate me or I'll start crying again. I guess I'm a proud father, reluctantly. We delivered her colt."

Hank said, "Sure. Congratulations. Anything we can do?"

Phil tried to laugh. "Not unless you happen to have a clean shirt." He looked at the hall clock. "I have to give a lecture in ten minutes."

Hank got up from his chair and retrieved the funeral shirt. He wasn't all that keen to lend it—it would be miles too small for Phil—but the gesture was called for, and this way he might get a better look at the woman. "Sleeves will be short," he said. "Roll them up, and it'll get you through your class."

"Thanks, Oliver, but—"

Hank cut him off. *"De nada."*

But instead of Phil taking the shirt for himself, the woman intercepted it. She stripped off her bloody sweatshirt and let it fall to the office floor before the three men. Well, in truth, Phil, who was facing her, did look away, but Hank didn't, not at first, and he felt reasonably certain that Carver was taking this freebie as well. No nonsense of bra to hinder the view, either. A muscled vista of freckled skin shone in shades of ivory and peach, contrasting with the drab hallway. As she swung her arm into the sleeve, Hank caught a brief glimpse of left breast, a pale half-moon a little wider than the span of his hand that swung maddeningly out of sight into his shirt. There was a scar, too, underneath her right shoulder blade. Had to be at least eight inches long. Pink stitch marks fanned out from it like a centipede's legs, a hasty repair. Then it disappeared as she gathered the shirttails and knotted them around her waist. She wrung out dishwater-blond hair in one hand and turned to go, confronting their gaping faces for a moment. Her eyes were brown.

She stared at Asa's smarmy grin. "You got to be pretty hard up if that got you off."

Then she picked up the bloody sweatshirt, balled it, and handed it to Hank, giving him a half-smile born, he was sure, of an earned disgust with all men. "What do they do, pay you double to room with this jackal?" When she smiled, a chipped front tooth was exposed. Down the staircase her footfalls sounded slightly, and then she was gone.

Phil took the sweatshirt.

Asa laughed. "Interesting morning thus far, boys."

They exchanged guilty smiles. Hank took a deep breath. "So. Vet think the colt will make it?"

"Touch and go, but yeah. Thanks for asking." Phil waved, a flaring of long dirty fingers as he slowly descended the staircase, each cowboy bootheel knocking against the risers. "Think I'll cancel my classes and get on back to him. I'll keep you guys posted," he called up.

"Do that," Asa said.

Hank stared for a moment at the bloody swash across his hand.

Carver let out a hoot and punched him in the shoulder. "Better shut your jaw, Oliver, you'll catch flies. Just who do you suppose that was? The war-torn Valkyrie come for your heart?"

Hank didn't answer. He wiped his hand on the student's paper in front of him. Here's a little something else about The Odyssey.

Carver laughed until his breath was emptied. He took a gasp. "Man, are you going to have dreams tonight."

Suddenly cold, Hank reached for his jacket. He felt the subtle ache of serious change beginning in the marrow of his bones, shrewdly working each cell. She had his shirt.

CHAPTER

5

Raw skin chafed beneath the shirt she'd taken from Phil outside his office. What the hell was she thinking? She'd taken her sweatshirt off in front of those men. The faces were a blur—the one with the mustache—he was cute, the way he looked down, pretending he hadn't seen. They couldn't know the stench of blood seethed in her pores, that nothing on earth could make her feel quite as claustrophobic; she would have marched naked in a parade rather than endure the smell. A few tears puddled in her eyes, and she admonished herself. Crying will do you a hell of a lot of good. Next time, have the foresight to slap on a bra when somebody gets you out of bed after midnight. Plans were always what you made *after* you blew it. Now she'd have to work her shift at Wedler's braless, her nipples growing sore with each swipe of rag across the greasy formica.

She hadn't expected to pull an all-nighter. Or that Hubbard would arrive so unforgivably late, or that the mare would cash it in. That was a puzzle. The baby—well, maybe he would follow his mama, and Phil's problem would be just one more gaping wound waiting for the stitch of time passing to heal it up.

Ordinarily she relished walking under the dripping, forty-foot eucalyptus trees, breathing in the just-washed, cough-drop smell of their seedpods, the tail end of a good winter rain washing her face. The college campus was like a well-tended park without the stock of crazies that tended to gather in a green place. The student parking lot was a sight to behold: all those cars lined up in ranks, mostly new models. The money in one aisle alone could set you up for life.

Students rushed past her, their backpacks stuffed full or arms lugging notebooks. They were all talking, too, as if they had so much to say there might never be enough time to say it in between classes. The idea of attending college seemed to come naturally to them. A few sleepier students staggered by her into those automatic-opening doorways, just like the supermarkets. Some of the students grasped striped coffee cups from the vending machines. She and Phil were going to get coffee. That had been part of the plan, but somewhere between the barn and his office, time had butted in and reminded them they both had jobs to attend to. She felt the pocket of her skirt hopefully, seeking wayward change. Nothing. Her wallet was in the truck, tucked into the glovebox. Well, ten minutes and she would be at work, where coffee was free for the taking. Rich Wedler threw in ground vanilla bean he stored in canisters of sugar. He thought it was that touch alone that kept the customers coming back. But it wasn't that. It wasn't even his cooking. Wedler's was an old-time diner, different specials daily, but basic cooking with none of this nouveau art-on-a-plate nonsense. Coffee was fifty cents, a plain hamburger alone $1.75. Lunch for $3.75, and you'd go away full. For Chloe, it was free, and her one meal a day. She'd learned to wait.

She threaded her way through the horticulture gardens, snagged an orange off a dwarf tree, peeled and ate the sections as she took the long way around the barn to her truck. Chicken-shit detour, but she didn't want to set eyes on that colt, listen one more minute to his pitiful cries for a mama that was by now piecemeal under Gabe's scalpel.

Motherhood. You waited all those months and put your body through irreversible agony. For what? Chloe had never seen her own mother, not that she could remember. Thirty-three years ago babies weren't the commodity they were today. The deal was *not* to get pregnant. Nobody was out there with lawyers and thousands of dollars, hoping to snap up your mistake. Briefly, she considered her oldest fear: that there was some grotesque history to her file that the courts and the orphanages had kept hidden from her. Sometimes, on a slow afternoon at Wedler's, she might sit with the *Register* and read one of those stories about natural mothers reunited with their given-away babies. Instant kinship. A mass of missed Christmases made up for in no time. All those happy endings. Was it like that for everyone? She never tried to find out.

Even without dwelling on the subject, many times she had dreamed about her mother. She was never the one with the monogrammed stationery lightly scented with Chanel, with the soft hand that caused a deeply buried memory of comfort to surface. She was a *thing*, obese, barely recognizable as a woman, who had slaughtered dozens of babies on her way to state prison. When the dream-Chloe introduced herself to the refined lady in endless strands of perfectly matched pearls, the lady would smile apologetically, pat her hand, softly insisting there'd been a mistake. Then she'd point to the harpy in the muumuu and say she was the real one.

She spit out the last of the orange—it was green and tasted bitter—and found a trash barrel for the peelings. The stupid mare was to blame for bringing all this foolishness to the surface—she and the rain. A good night's sleep would refresh her. It was best to discard such thoughts. They were like credit card come-ons. Before long, all the nice talk was out the window and you were getting pay-up-now-or-else phone calls. Everything was best done alone, pay as you go. She was who she was, singular, standing here laced into her own two shoes. She could take inventory from now until next week and this day, with all the awful truths counted out before her, would have to be lived through, loss or gain. Nobody had chosen her. She had traversed the court system for years, entered and left more than twenty foster-care situations before the age of seventeen. When the men started coming into her room at night, breathing beer into her face and poking fingers under her nightgown, she'd hop out a window and hitchhike back to Orangewood, bang on the glass doors until a security guard let her in. And there were the times that she failed to live up to the Kate Greenaway dresses and dead daughters whose void she was supposed to fill. She'd heard it countless times from more kinds of mothers than there were molecules to air: *Chloe Morgan, you are not an easy child to love.*

Maybe not. But I'm living proof that you can get by *without* love, and that most of us do. The difference is, I'm honest about it.

She tucked all that into an envelope and sealed it up after she went to the Gilpins at age sixteen. They were different. They fed and clothed her, gave modest advice, were patient when it came to wresting kindness from the hard child she'd become. Eventually, she saw that in their own quiet way, they admired her. It wasn't that they couldn't have kids of their own; they'd had three.

When she tried to run off from them, bull-headed over a ten-o'clock curfew, Ben sat her down and told her some things. It was a baseball scorecard between them and God, he said: God, three; Gilpins, zip. Vietnam, car accident, and leukemia, respectively. A run of bad luck. We just got lonely, that's all. Won't you keep us company? Chloe tried to believe she wasn't there to replace any of the photos they had on top of the piano. She understood that if she ran away from them, God's score would up another point, take all hope out of these two gentle human beings. So she stayed.

Her truck was parked under a larch tree. Even from a distance, she could see there was a yellow ticket on the windshield. The truck had at one time been that Aqua-Velva blue popular in the early fifties. Now it was mostly Bondo and welder's-torch gray, save the white fender she'd picked up last month in a lucky junkyard foray. English riding spurs hung off the rearview mirror, the chrome catching sunlight. She and Ben had taken apart and put back together the engine of this truck so many times that she knew its every idiosyncrasy.

But Ben was dead now, Margaret living with a sister in Florida.

Hannah, her white German shepherd of indeterminate age, was not in the truck bed. Chloe felt panic bubble into her throat. The dog had run off before, and it had taken Chloe weeks to locate her, bribing shelter attendants to set her free. Please, not this on top of everything else. The dog sat up in the passenger side of the bench seat and groaned, stretching her front legs and thumping her bent tail. With every beat, damp white fur flew.

Chloe retrieved the ticket and tore it in half, threw it into the trash, and cupped her hand around a match and lighted a Kent 100. She eyed the wet dog, who was trying her best not to leap from the truck and lather her with glad kisses. "You are a bonehead," she said to the dog. "I told you to stay in the bed." The dog quit panting, cocked her head, and looked penitent. At once Chloe opened the door, bent over, and gave her a fierce hug.

"Morgan, your hair looks like creamed shit on gravel. You living in your car again? You're not wearing a bra. How many fucking times do I have to tell you? Trying to drive me insane. You and every other female on the face of the earth."

Chloe ignored Rich Wedler, who studied her from the supply room where blue-and-white Smart and Final Iris labels winked cheerfully from gallon cans. She sat on a fifty-pound sack of flour, sipping her coffee and looking out the screen door into the alley. The borrowed shirt hung on deer antlers above the pay phone. She had tucked a new Wedler Brothers Café T-shirt into her denim skirt, and tied a clean apron over that. It looked enough like a uniform to get by.

"Those shirts are for the customers. I'm docking you five ninety-eight plus tax."

"I'll wash it and put it back. When's the last time somebody asked to see one? Purple and green. Who thought up your color scheme? Stevie Wonder?"

He flung a spatula into the sink and turned on the hot water full force, causing the dish soap to hiss into furious bubbles. "Say it was my grandmother, Chloe. My dead grandmother thought it up and even as you slur her memory she writhes in her grave."

She laughed. "You don't have any female relatives, lizard boy. You hatched under a rock. What's today's special?"

Rich wouldn't answer. His olive skin darkened to a husky sunburn when he was angry. Coal black hair stood out from the back of his head bound in a two-inch-long ponytail, thick as an Indian woman's braid. He wore Wedler Brothers T-shirts seven days a week, and slim-cut Levi's that hung on his bones like drapery. At least he had no tattoos.

"Roadkill," he finally answered. "I ran over a crow out back in the alley and tossed it into the black bean soup. Let's try it out on Hannah."

At the sound of her name, the shepherd lifted her head in the doorway.

"Go back to sleep," Chloe said. "Say you quit scheming to murder my dog, Wedler. Stick to the weapons you know. Home fries and gravy. Slow death by saturated fats."

He wagged a slotted spoon in her direction. Suds trailed down his arm and disappeared into his T-shirt sleeve. It would be hot, Chloe reasoned; dishwater didn't cool that fast. But Rich wouldn't pop a bead of discomfort if it meant showing her he felt pain. "I'm warning you," he said. There was a sound of crashing crockery from the dining room.

She stubbed her cigarette out in her saucer. "Warning me what? That you're going to replace me with nimble Lita?"

"She'll be okay once she gets broken in."

"That's if you don't drive her to quit."

"Out of here," he said. "Out of my kitchen."

The Wedler Brothers Café was a cult hangout that served more than one master. In the early mornings, they fed truckers and fishermen, regulars Chloe knew by name and menu preference. A little later, frustrated telemarketing salesmen fed on farmhand's breakfasts, the poor man's Valium. Much later, kids from the junior college filtered in and out, the second generation of hippies who'd grown up on their parents' Grateful Dead albums, the metal-heads dressed predominantly in black, pins through their ears and, in one unforgettable case, through the cheek and nose, connected by a silver chain from which dangled tiny silver skulls. What the hell do you do when you get a head cold? Chloe wanted to ask the girl, but didn't want to lose her tip. They formed a community over food, ordering greasy sides of bacon and grits with those meadow-in-a-box herb teas or sugar-free soda.

Chloe got them what they asked. Wedler's had a truly gifted lunch menu—nine kinds of soup daily, generous sandwiches on homemade bread Rich kneaded with his own hands. Lunch was often standing room only. The whole business ended at three, when Rich would emerge from the kitchen and tell everyone it was time to go home. Every couple of months the diners drew up petitions requesting longer hours and dinner menus.

Rich patiently delivered them the same speech: "If I was planning to serve dinner to make a profit, I'd be down on the peninsula selling alcohol to drunks in boat shoes."

"It's your wallet," Chloe always said, shrugging.

"Success is a phase, Morgan. Tomorrow? Who ever knows? Even stock markets are transient."

Through every bank deposit (which he didn't trust her to make), Wedler remained convinced that at any moment the café would go under. The city was talking redevelopment somewhere down the line; where would those petitioners be when *that* shit hit the fan?

In the back of her mind, Chloe thought maybe Rich should give lithium a run for its money, but might a positive attitude turn him ambitious? Would he start making her wear a hairnet and some rank poodle skirt like a fifties throwback café? Put in a jukebox and drive the customers to the nearest McDonald's?

Two gray-haired seniors sat down at a window booth. They looked expectantly toward the kitchen, and Chloe scanned the room for Lita. The new girl was nowhere, so she took menus over and grabbed a coffeepot on the way. The woman was striking, mid-seventies, wearing a turquoise necklace. The man was a little older, his face scarred in places. He stared hard at the television screen mounted above the counter corner. Rich had it set on an exercise show featuring spandex-clad ladies performing suggestive push-ups.

"What a pretty necklace," she remarked to the woman. "Coffee?"

The woman pressed her napkin into a stray crumb that decorated the tabletop. "Do you have tea?" she asked, staring mid-chest, where Chloe could feel one chilled-to-erection nipple poking the first E in Wedler's. Christ, it was Monday, forever, all over the world.

"Six kinds herbal, plus Lipton's."

"Lipton's."

"You take cream?"

"Is it fresh?"

"Well, we don't have old Bessie out back, but it's the real thing."

The woman gave her husband a little slap on the arm. "Dear, if you can peel your eyes away from that screen you might want to order."

He loosened his tie and gave the spandex ladies a farewell glance. His favorite form of exercise, Chloe figured. Guy could probably bench-press 180 with his eyelids, if it was female tonnage.

"Decaf, sweetie," he said.

She thought she could size up appetites fairly well. "We've got homemade biscuits and gravy to just about break your heart," she told him. "How about an order of those to tuck alongside a cheese omelet?"

For a moment he looked hopeful. The wife with the necklace didn't have to say a word. "English muffin," he muttered.

"Coming up."

Rich caught her arm as she opened the refrigerator to get the cream.

"Today you be nice to my fucking customers," he hissed.

Chloe sighed and shut the stainless-steel door. "And those that are celibate?"

He stumbled back to the kitchen, bawling Lita out for cutting the carrots at a Chinese angle. "You want everyone to expect the vegetables to be cut nice from now on? Just cut them regular!"

Chloe sighed and bit her lip. She told the old couple, "You have to excuse the cook. He's cranky until about three o'clock. Let me get you something else. Fresh berries? We have some strawberries that were just delivered this morning."

"No, thank you. Just the cream."

The woman took a sniff of the pitcher before she poured.

"That's right," Chloe mumbled. "Always best to check for dead mice."

"Young lady, we've just come from a funeral."

"Sorry." She served the elderly couple their snack, then stood behind the register staring out at the boulevard, watching the wash of color change as cars sped past. She thought of the dead mare again, her shoe-button eye staring up at nothing, not seeing the rotting rafters of the barn, the human faces trying to will her back, or the troublesome colt who had sent her south in the first place. By now, if Gabe had wrapped his legs, the colt might be up and running, thrilled with the freedom having legs offered, even such iffy legs as his. When his stomach reminded him something was missing, they'd plug him with formula, but when he needed the warmth of his mother's flank, where would he go?

The necklace woman signaled for more hot water. Chloe nudged Lita. "I've already insulted them," she said. "Your turn."

Lita, short, mousy, closer to forty than she'd told Rich, was determined to please. "So sorry to hear about the funeral," she said, fingering an amethyst crystal on a leather thong that hung down between her breasts. "Try to think of your loved one as taking a long nap. Can't hurt, can it? I mean, nobody's actually proved heaven exists, have they? When you get right down to it, a nap's pretty darn close to heaven, isn't it?"

Chloe watched Lita ring up their bill. "Good job with the carrots," she told her. "Keep it up."

Kit Wedler showed up just before three, when Lita had gone home with a headache and Chloe was wiping tables and filling up bottles of Cajun hot sauce from a plastic gallon jug. Kit was wearing a lavender pantsuit designed for a woman who had worked long and hard to top a hundred and fifty pounds, not a five-foot-three thirteen-year-old who regularly pored over the pages of *Sassy* magazine.

"Hey, Chloe, *hate* that shirt."

"Thanks, I hate it, too. Why aren't you in school?"

Kit ignored her question. "Seen my dad?"

"Out back arguing with the produce man. Trying to rook him out of his measly profit on the tomatoes. You'd better not be cutting school again."

Kit helped herself to a large Coke. It wasn't Diet. "I swear to God, I'm not cutting school. It's 'teacher preparation' day."

Chloe screwed the last lid down on the hot-sauce bottles "Your dad might fall for that story, but not me."

Kit added a hefty scoop of ice cream to her glass and topped it with six maraschino cherries. "Guy, you, like, don't trust anybody, do you?"

Chloe wiped up a splash the Coke had left on the counter. "I trust Hannah."

"Come on, Hannah's a dog."

"Don't let her hear you talk like that. She thinks she's a goddess."

Kit sat down Indian-style on the wooden floor. "Honest, Chloe. They let us out. They're supposed to, like, *require* all this extra time to plan lessons and shit. I guess that's why they about run you down on their way out of the parking lot." She waved hands in front of her face, miming cars with them. "Honda madness! It doesn't matter. I hate school anyway. Geeky boys sticking their tongues down water fountains. I am *sure*."

Chloe sat down on a counter stool. "School's got pluses. It taught me where the apostrophe goes. How to divide. I can figure out why I bounce checks and recognize the possessive errors on billboards."

"Whoopee."

Hannah slunk in and butted her head up under Kit's hand.

"Don't give her any ice cream; dairy's bad for dogs."

"Jeez, I wasn't."

"And don't let Rich see her in here, either. He'll start in on the Health Department and her fleas."

She gave the dog a fingerful of float. "No way. Look at her cool, thick fur! She'd like, make an *extreme* winter coat, if it ever snowed here. Hannah doesn't have fleas, do you girl?"

"Only because they all die of thirst on the hike in."

Kit stirred the float with a straw, then set it down on the floor. Hannah crept closer until Chloe cleared her throat, then the dog laid her head down and pretended to be sleeping. "Chloe, what color's your pubic hair?"

Chloe set her order tablet on the counter. "This weird tan. It used to be blond, back in high school. I guess when you get old and decrepit, it darkens. Why?"

"Mine's just this awful red," she blurted, fighting tears.

"Red's number one, kiddo. I'm jealous."

"You're just saying that."

"Am not. Why, just this morning I took a poll of all the male customers. 'Guys, what's your preference?' I asked. They all said the same thing—fire-engine red—what? You don't believe me?"

"Duh," Kit said.

Chloe leaned down and played with Hannah's collar. "Do you get teased about it in gym?"

Kit nodded. The tears were spilling down her cheeks now.

"There's more important things to waste tears on. What can I do to make you happy?"

"Nothing. I want jet black, like everyone else has."

"I don't have jet black."

"You don't have to take showers in P.E., either."

"True. I suppose you could try dyeing it."

"No kidding? Would you help me?"

Chloe undid her apron and tossed it into the trash can filled with soiled linen. She folded her arms across her breasts, more to support their weight than to hide them. Rich's daughter. He'd gained full custody when her mother took off for India to console the exiled Bhagwan after the Oregon commune failed. Now Bhagwan was taking his long nap in the great universal oneness, and who knew where Mrs. Wedler was? Since that time, Kit had added poundage to her frame each month the same way some girls wear scores of clinking bracelets from the wrist to the elbow.

"I don't see why not. We'll do mine too. I hope the drugstore has a stomping big selection. I think I want hot pink. My favorite color. And if there's any left over, we'll do Hannah up, give her a big old racing stripe, right down the back."

Hannah lifted her head, studied their faces, hightailed it for the back door. Kit wiped her face on a napkin and looked up at Chloe. "I wish you were my mother."

"Think it over, Kit. I'd embarrass you to death, whipping all those snake-tongued girls in your gym class."

Kit tried to smile. "Yeah, probably. But they deserve it."

CHAPTER

6

He might as well have been reading them model airplane instructions; he was dying up here along with Eurydice and her poison snake. Those students who weren't drawing pictures in their notebooks or filing their nails were nearly asleep despite Orpheus's lyre and his grief. Sometimes, no matter what you did, it just went like that. The teacher who took it to heart would end up jumping off a building, so Hank didn't take it to heart. He stopped talking, waiting for them to notice the silence. A few of them stared up blankly; the note takers looked irritated at the break in established rhythm.

"My apologies," Hank said. "I'm not fully with you today. Earlier this morning, I drew the lucky task of pallbearer at a funeral. First time for everything, so they say. It's funny; I've been standing here for years discussing the myths that explore death and never felt frightened of my own mortality, but it's different when you and a few other men are hoisting a casket on a one-way trip."

Larry Kolanoski, the lone surfer who favored the back row, tossed his head back, whipping sunbleached hair from his red-rimmed eyes and said, "Yeah, it's heavy, dude."

Laughter, some groaning. The majority responded to any admission of human emotion on a teacher's part as unthinkably absurd. Their disbelieving faces would rather be out living life, even on a cold and rainy January day when the surf was lousy, than sitting here listening to a middle-aged man ramble about his own mortality. A great deal of mileage would wear on those faces between now and forty, but there was no way to explain that to them. They wouldn't believe it if it were engraved in stone. It had to surprise everyone, and surprise each of them differently.

"Actually, Larry, a casket's surprisingly light, when you consider the weight of a man in his seventies who lived fully and died suddenly. That's the eerie thing."

"So, is class canceled?"

Hank dismissed it all—the blond formica desk chairs, the putty-colored walls, the stained blue carpeting school budgets were scheduled to replace next year after they decided which teaching contracts not to renew. He focused on Cora, an elderly woman who enrolled in his courses every semester. From her information sheet he'd learned that she was returning to school after a forty-year hiatus. When Hank was having a bad day, he often spoke only for Cora's benefit, allowing the others around her to dim out. "Sorry, Larry. Departmental funding willing, we'll be seeing each other for the next three and a half months."

"Bummer." The boy sighed and laid his head down on the desktop, where it would no doubt remain solidly planted for the next hour and a half. Who knew why he was here? He worked nights. His father bribed him to stay in school with a hefty allowance. Was there now a major in surfing?

"Okay," Hank said. "Let's see if we can jump forward from the river Styx to my funeral again. No river there at all, not even so much as a fountain, come to think of it. Let's look at it in terms of modern myth. It might be fun to write out a few of our own."

A collective groan rang out. Actual work? Hank ignored them.

"First we'll set the scene. This man begins a day of his well-deserved retirement in the ordinary manner. Thoughts of death aren't even near his conscious mind. He's more concerned about his golf score. Then it happens. He feels the stab of pain shoot down his left arm and in the brief span of consciousness left to him, he realizes he's dying. What sorts of mythic encounters can you imagine? Anybody?"

His shier students grinned and gazed down at their notebooks. *Don't call on me, please. I only took this class because Andrea told me it was an easy A. What do I know about dying?* Several of the males stared boldly back as if this was no game in which they intended to participate. He allowed the requisite thirty seconds, then pointed to Kathryn Price, the blond freshman from Texas. She might not have an answer, but she was gutsy and jumped right into any discussion. And listening to her cornbread-soft accent was not in the least unpleasant.

"Me? Oh, shoot, Mr. Oliver. How can I guess what an old man might think?"

"You have brothers, uncles, a father?"

She frowned. "Six brothers, unfortunately."

"Go from there. Use your imagination."

"Well, first off, I think he'd be pissed at all the things he didn't do, like maybe climb a mountain, or clean his rifle, maybe kiss his wife that morning, or at least get to ride his horse one last time. Yeah, I think he'd be sorry for all the stuff he meant to do, but didn't. And then I think he might be mad as hell."

A dark-skinned hand shot up, didn't wait for acknowledgment before speaking. Carlos, new this semester. Methodical papers that verged on the poetic. The kid needed to be at the university, not piddling around the junior college. "Sir, do you think the manner in which one dies makes a difference?"

"Give me a little more to go on, Carlos."

"Well, I agree with Kathryn. Anger's no bit-part player in life. The recent events in the Gulf—people dying in savage circumstances—do you think—"

William Strauss shook his wrist, braceleted with several thongs and what looked like spiked dog collars. "Did you, like, hear what they did to the people over there? Drilling holes in their kneecaps? Raping grandmothers? Isn't that sick?"

Hank took a measured breath. "It certainly isn't healthy. Will, all of us appreciate your interest in politics, but we've got a lot of ground to cover here. Can we stick to the subject?"

"But a heart attack's so boring! Couldn't he die having his skin ripped off by a vulture?"

Kathryn swiveled to face Will. "You really ought to see a therapist, William."

"You're all the therapy I need, baby."

"Oh, grow a conscience!"

Hank suppressed a smile. Were all Texas women like that? Maybe he should fly down to Austin for spring break. "Let's try to make everyone happy here. We have an ordinary death, a man in his seventies. But it's no ordinary event to him. We'll try to address Carlos's concerns, and to appease William, let's imagine that possibly the heart pain feels like a vulture is ripping off his skin. We've established that he might feel regret and anger. Now let's throw in an observer. His golf partner? No, too easy. What if we place an animal there? How about a coyote, wandering onto the golf course, looking for something to eat?"

"Yes!" William shot out. "Tired of eating housecats from the Big Canyon tract! Make him rabid!"

Hank could see William Strauss approaching orgasm from the potential horror of the situation. Perhaps he would have been better off sticking to poor Orpheus—guileless musician whose only mistake had been looking back, not trusting that the woman he loved would follow—letting the students sleepily finish out the hour. But he forged ahead. "No to the housecats this time, Will. You might consider the idea that death is not so jarring in the animal world. On a daily basis, most creatures see it, certainly nondomesticated creatures. They're almost instantly recycled, whereas man is not directly returned to the earth. Animals in the modern world exist in several categories: as pets, pests, curiosities, and to feed man. Vultures, and we're talking the garden-variety type, eat the flesh of dead animals. When the bones are left, smaller animals go after those for the calcium. Eventually the whole mess filters down into the soil and grows grasses, berries, what have you, to feed other animals. And the whole business starts over again."

"Gross," Kathryn sang out. "I won't need my lunch money today except for a pack of Rolaids."

"But why is it unsettling to humans, Kathryn? Are we so insulated from death that we simply ignore it?"

She looked away for a moment, and her voice softened. "One summer I saw a girl drown in a Dallas swimming pool. Just dove in smiling and didn't come up till a lifeguard dragged her. She was blue, with purple lips and her arms and legs all limp. I was maybe six years old at the time."

"But you never forgot it. Did you go to her funeral?"

"No, but half the town did. Mama said I was too young."

"That's my point. So we come full circle to my funeral. When man, useless, really, save for his consuming, exits this world, does there have to be a send-off ceremony to salve the anxiety the living feel? Is that the function of a funeral, much like the one I attended? Maybe its roots are ancient appeasement for this break in the order. In ritual, such as my walking along with the other men lifting a part of the casket, the participants willingly suspend reality to ensure release of the soul. In reality, all I did was lend a few muscles to move a box from one place to another—the church to the hearse—but the myth I participated in involves brotherhood, a willing suspension of disbelief, a certitude that maybe it required my living hand to help his body pass from one world to the next, that unseen world we all expect as a reward for good behavior. The survivors see the funeral as integral in the final journey of the dead, cyclical, respectful." Most faces were on him now, listening. "But maybe most of us are feeling like Kathryn. Deep down, we're scared. I wonder if any of you could participate in such a ritual and not be forced to confront your own mortality?"

Gentle Cora was filling her wire-bound binder with copious writing. God alone knew what she made of this day's lecture. He could imagine her evaluation: *Mr. Oliver is a very nice man and he dresses neatly, although he doesn't often wear ties. Sometimes I think he gets off on tangents, however, and wastes valuable class time with personal reflection.* Maybe she was going to turn him in to her pastor, heathen Henry Oliver, the soulless community college professor. The female students looked around themselves uncomfortably, and the men were frowning. Only William Strauss frantically waved his hand, looking to Hank as if he had given this subject entirely too much thought. Hank simply would not call on him again today. Encouraging the imagination of this primal young man was touchy business.

Larry Kolanoski sat back up and rocked the legs of his chair. He was grinning. He flicked one finger upward, and Hank nodded in his direction.

"Mr. Kolanoski returns to us."

"Is this, like, one of your personal stories, or is it going to be on a test?"

They laughed like hyenas. Even Cora was smirking, her tight, lipsticked mouth twitching at the corners. Slackers. He assigned them six chapters on the underworld and dreamed up a paper on the spot. "Gods using animal forms," he said. "Compare and contrast with what we've discussed this morning. Your own version of Coyote assisting our nameless dead golfer into the netherworld."

It wasn't in the syllabus, and they bitched. Seventeen more papers to read, but the caved-in expressions on their faces more than made up for it.

"Stop your groaning. Look in your textbooks. It's fascinating." He fanned pages and chose an example at random. "Morrigan, quite the quick-change artist. In her lifetime, she took the following forms: an eel, wolf, heifer, raven, and a mortal woman as well."

The minute hand clicked over to the six, and they stood rapidly, as if an alarm bell had rung.

"Double spaced. No onionskin!" he called out as they exited. He knew he would be successful if one-fourth of them actually took the paper seriously. He wondered for possibly the billionth time if he was teaching them anything other than how to waste an hour and a half.

Phil Green was fitting a rubber nipple over a glass jar as Hank approached him in the school arena. Someone had expertly bandaged the colt's legs and outfitted him in a jaunty new halter with brass buckles that shone brightly against his small face. Hank admired the baby's determination as he yanked at the nipple and butted Phil's legs. Intent on draining that bottle, he seemed to be unaffected by his orphan status.

Phil turned his face toward Hank. "What do you think, Oliver? Any chance he'll grow into these bones?"

"I'm no expert," Hank answered. "But he looks determined. Say, about my shirt. Any chance you'll be seeing that girl in the near future?"

Phil shrugged. "Hard to tell. She comes and goes, sort of like this rain we're having. In the spring I can usually cajole her into lecturing to one or two of my classes."

"Actually, I was hoping to get the shirt back a little sooner than that."

"Sure. I'll try to hunt Chloe down for you."

"Chloe?"

Phil slapped his milk-splattered hands on his jeans, and the sudden gesture sent the shying colt off into a stiff-legged canter that flung him into the dirt every fourth stride. The men stopped talking and watched the colt. Phil said, "Chloe Morgan. She used to break horses for Stroud Ranch before they got into land development. Worked with the legendary Fats Valentine, last of the old-time trainers. They were getting top dollar for some time, quite the team. She fell completely apart when he died. Nearly bought the farm, from what I heard. She still keeps a hand in, but I doubt it will ever be like the old days."

Centipede scar, tough mouth, the peach skin. "She have a telephone number?"

Phil chuckled. "If she does, odds are it's disconnected."

"That was an eighty-dollar shirt, Green."

"Eighty dollars? What's it made of, the Shroud of Turin?"

"Probably a few threads of it."

Phil Green snapped his fingers. "Come to think of it, I heard her say she was waiting tables at the café on Newport Boulevard. You know, the one with the striped awning. Next to a waterbed store or a Ticketron or something. They're only open for breakfast and lunch." He captured his colt, struggled unsuccessfully to attach a lead rope to the halter. "Sorry about the shirt, Hank. We were both a little goofy from all that blood." He shook himself. "I'm still a train wreck, to be honest with you. Worse comes to worst, I'll reimburse you for the shirt."

Hank waved his hand. Phil couldn't afford it, and he didn't want that. "You've got enough to keep your hands full here. What the hell. Tomorrow I'll eat breakfast out."

"Great idea. Say hi to her for me—and tell her I said thanks."

The colt whinnied and sprang across the muddy dirt of the arena, very much full of himself. His soiled bandages didn't slow down his investigation of the world newly opened to him. He bent his nose low to sniff the earth his hooves raked up. When a crack of thunder left over from the morning storm sounded, the colt pinned back his ears and shot past them at a dead run, farting all the way.

Hank laughed.

Phil smiled for the first time that day. "Guess we'll call him Thunder," he said. "It's best when they name themselves."

That evening Hank watched the news recap on CNN while grading papers, a departure from his usual routine of MacNeil/Lehrer. Tonight his concentration was broken by a dozen idle worries. The last straw was the report on the dwindling ozone layer. All-too-distinct videotape of clear-cut rain forests, both aerial and close-up shots. There was no wilderness left. A rather formal translation of natives' views narrated the segment, which he loosely translated for himself: *Selfish white American pigs are to blame. How are we supposed to feed our children?* The ramifications of the planet heating up magnified until it was impossible to take student thought seriously. He shut off the TV, went upstairs, stood under the shower until his skin felt pleasantly blistered, toweled dry, and brushed his teeth.

He'd bought the town house mainly to shut his father up. It was "time he invested his money," according to Henry senior, though Hank liked renting the old Victorian on the west side of town. In the mornings he could smell the ocean breeze, though he had no ocean view. On Halloween, he usually ran out of candy feeding assorted ghosts and witches—kids who moved on to better neighborhoods before they grew up. He'd biked to the college in good weather.

The town house was brand new—no history to it. It was connected to four others, floor plans flipped every other one, but essentially the units were carbon copies of one another from the fake exterior stucco-adobe to the color-coordinated vinca plantings along the curving walkway. "Get an end unit," his father insisted. "Better resale value." One flaw of the end-unit design plan was that the master bedrooms butted up against each other, Hank's to the bedroom of newly-wed neighbors who seemed determined to break all known records for conjugal frequency. He towel-dried his hair, listening to their cries inching inexorably toward climax, the woman's voice jumping an octave and shortly thereafter, the man groaning as if he were moving a piano. There you go, everyone had the requisite good time. Hank continued to listen through that timeless interval of peaceful aftermath, so deep it seemed as if you could drop a stone into it without ever hitting bottom. Secretly he hoped death was like that thick silence, but it wasn't a concept he could easily articulate with his students. He imagined the progress of the man's hands tracing his wife's cooling skin. For a small portion of time everything was quiet, eyes washed clean, muscles slackened with exertion. But any minute now they would start in arguing, softly at first, then working into a torque that ended with slamming doors. They did it so often he had come to view it as part of their afterplay. No words he could make out, nothing serious, just two people used to living alone learning to compromise by verbally beating the tar out of one another. He got up to shut the window and inhaled the rain-wet scent of the grass. Over the top of the parking structure and in the distance, he could see the outline of Saddleback Mountain, the two humps dipping in the middle to form the saddle seat. The night sky was puffy with clouds, a deep blue gray broken by wispy shadows. It was never dark enough to see stars due to the well-lighted master plan for the community of Irvine.

That woman who had his shirt—Chloe—one of the personas of Demeter—wasn't she the "green" one, the caretaker of young crops? But that was the books talking, and Hank had seen her—she was a living, breathing woman. Still, what an odd name, old-fashioned, perhaps a diminutive of Clothilde? No telephone. From Phil's intimations he'd gathered she lived marginally, almost hand to mouth. How did a person get to that point? Phil had said a horse trainer named Valentine. Were they lovers? Probably. She was out there tonight, somewhere quite different from where he was, he was certain of that. Maybe she was already in bed, tangled in sheets, turning now on her belly, the shoulder blade with the scar exposed. It wasn't a scar one could easily identify, not an operation, perhaps a childhood injury. It looked rough, as if something had been torn away, as if she had been dewinged like some troublemaking angel who was summarily demoted to earth. But an unlikely angel, this woman. Not shy. That momentary swing of breast. He shouldn't have looked. In her brief encounter she'd accomplished something he'd never been able to—she'd shut Asa's smart mouth. If she were married, surely Phil would have said so. She wasn't married. She had to be a singular unit, living life simply, he knew it. Waitress. He supposed it was proof of his inherent sexism, his weak spot for waitresses. But the ones who weren't nineteen and giggly were generally earthy and primal, wise in nature. When one smiled and stood by your table, her weight sunk into one hip, asking, "What is it you want?" he always felt a distinct loosening in his gut and the desire to answer truthfully. *I want to eat something good. I want to walk in beauty. I want to die inside of a quiet, loving woman. Can you get me those things?* They had to know there was power in food. Whoever fixed your meal owned a part of you.

He got into bed. He smiled in the dark, bemused at late-night stirrings in his loins from this conjured fantasy. When he'd slept with Karleen, with other women, too, they were forgotten an instant later, nothing they said or did drew him back. He was careful not to lead them on with false hope. He knew when they were satisfied, and what they expected from him, but no magic made him remember them.

There were HIV posters in the faculty restrooms now, not just the students'. And what about that rumor about Alec in the art department testing positive when he wasn't even gay? This wasn't the sixties, which was probably where the whole nightmare had begun. Well, fantasies couldn't kill you.

He turned into his pillow, gave it a friendly punch, and shut his eyes. Still, that swell of breast.

CHAPTER

7

C hloe held the wet borrowed shirt up to the morning light outside her single pane of wavery window glass. All but one of the bloodstains had come out under her diligent laundering. It took gentle soaking and repeated blotting rather than scrubbing to lift the blood from the delicate weave. Just a faint orange tinge near the third button remained, nothing a day outside in the sun wouldn't cure. She worked the arm of the pump again, splashing icy water onto the shirt in her secondhand basin. She wrung it out by hand, then went behind her house to hang the shirt on a line between two scrub oaks.

The sky was chambray blue, shot through with faint gray clouds moving eastward on the horizon. Yesterday's storm had moved on to pound the desert senseless. She wished she were somewhere outside Blythe, watching the transformation take place when that dry earth received the damp blessing. Everything would bloom, from the tall-armed cacti down to the smallest of grasses, and for a few days it would be smorgasbord time for all the animals.

She stood still for a moment, her face lifted to the 5:30 A.M. air and the quiet of the canyon. The intoxicating aroma of damp trees and wet rock, the song of a single jay competing with the knee-high creek running at full force tempted her to grab a couple of apples and take off on an all-day hike. Deep in the box canyon, her small shack was tucked into the hillside, its back wall taking advantage of the landscape, almost like a dugout. The chimney for her woodstove—fifty bucks from the Santiago landfill—was patched with bright metal. Hugh had bought a load of propane tanks, dragged them in, meaning to outfit everyone with heat, but they were still unattached and had been for months now. Big on ideas, Hugh was, but when it came to screwing in the nuts and bolts, you were on your own. Her place was smaller than the others, but the location had advantages. After three gravel roads into potholes that sucked and bit tires, the most skillful explorer would throw in the towel. She wasn't often surprised by visitors. There was a back path up from the main house, but only those who lived there knew about it. She could go for days and not see any one else from the community; the others kept their kids close by and didn't let them wander out this far, fearing county agents more than they feared mountain lions. She unsnapped two clothespins from the line, secured the borrowed shirt, and whistled for Hannah.

Across the creek the shepherd yawned from her crow's nest on sunny rocks.

"Up and at 'em," Chloe called. "Time to go to work."

The dog laid her head back down on her paws.

"Last chance to change your mind or here you sit until supper-time."

Hannah seemed to be intent on studying the leaves and insect life the water sent downstream toward deeper pools.

"Suit yourself, Hannah. Don't waste the whole day. Catch us something for supper—a fish would be nice."

Letting the door bang shut behind her, Chloe dried her hands on a stolen towel from the Wedler Brothers Café. She plunged her hand into a dusty five-gallon jar that sat on the floor, fished past assorted rocks and pennies to extract a receipt that still smelled faintly of the pickled chili peppers originally housed there. She counted the wad of folded money for the second time that morning: $350.87. It was enough to get her saddle out of hock from Wes's Feed and Tack, which had been its home for the last three months. It was her best saddle, a Hermès, the only one she'd ever owned that wasn't second- or thirdhand. She'd won some major shows on it, gleaned countless ribbons and a few cash prizes, enjoyed her longest run of luck. The money she'd gotten pawning it had saved her from starving, and now it would be hers once again, come full circle. Lessons. Absolutely. Shows? Maybe. Definitely the Swallow's Day costume parade, a little fun couldn't hurt, for Christ's sake. With that saddle, she had no doubt, the good life would start all over again.

Wes was at his shop early; deliveries. She caught him just as she'd hoped to, surrounded by bales of sweet-smelling alfalfa and stepping distractedly over bright yellow sacks of calf manna. His marmalade cat sniffed through the goods while Wes tallied the count onto a beat-up clipboard.

"Thieves raised my cost again," he told Chloe when she threw the truck into park. "Look at this stuff. I swear the farmers save all the good hay for themselves, send me shit, and charge double." He spit juice from his Skoal wad onto the cement floor of the warehouse. "If you don't look like a goddamn angel after these everlasting numbers. Where's your mutt? I saved her some biscuits."

"Wanted to stay home and take a nap."

"She's healthy?"

"Current on her shots and getting regular meals."

"And you?" Wes had no patience for those who didn't look after their animals. Chloe'd heard him blister Hubbard once or twice herself, when he'd disagreed with the vet's course of treatment.

"You won't hear me complaining. Wes, I'm here to make you a happy man."

His watery blue eyes crinkled in delight. "Finally going to marry my old ass—wait till I tell Chester and the boys."

She waved the money. "Even better. I came to get my old seat out of hock. It's only because you were kind enough to hang onto it for me that some little rich kid isn't using it."

He set his clipboard down and walked over to the Chevy, reached inside, and turned the key off.

"Dammit, Wesley, you know how long it takes me to get this thing started."

"I'll give you a jump later. Now you come on out of that heap and get inside. We're going to have some cowboy coffee and a little chat. Don't you argue. Just come along."

He turned without waiting to see if she was following, and she could hear the door shut inside the warehouse, the one leading to the shoebox-size office and the showroom. She sighed and followed after him. The smell of coffee was strong and bracing. Wes had her cup already poured. He nodded toward the secretary's chair for her to sit down.

"I've really got to go. I got a job now. I'm making it."

"Now you listen here, Chloe. If I had two I had me three hundred offers on that saddle for twice what you paid for it. You can't touch new leather like that for under two grand. Why don't you let me sell it and make you some decent money? It's not like you're competing regular."

She stared into the brown surface of her coffee. "That's so, but I'm thinking I might start up again."

"When?"

"Anytime now."

He was kind enough not to laugh. "Chloe, darling, it's time you faced up. You're a grown-up now. There's work to be done, and bills to be paid, life to be got on with. Not a whole lot of time for ribbons, let alone come up with the purse. Fats—"

She raised a hand. "Closed subject."

"Okay, sorry. I did promise. But let me pop you into one of these new Wintecs. Take it at my wholesale and keep half your money right there."

She hissed. "What kind of leather comes so cheap? Monkey's ass, I suppose."

"Hell, it ain't leather at all. Some kind of wetsuit material like the surfer boys use. Horse sweats it up, you hose it down. After a couple years you just throw the son-bitch away. Disposable."

"Disposable?" She took a sip of the coffee. Double strength, it hit her system like a jolt. "Just the kind of nonsense I'd expect from a Republican."

He chuckled, then coughed. "Your color sure does come up when you're ticked off. You can't blame me for trying to take care of you. An old man like me needs a challenge to keep him young."

"So take up backgammon."

"Looks like I might have to. Come on. We'll go get your saddle."

She abandoned the coffee to the desktop. It was littered with ledgers and invoices. No computer age for Wesley McNelly; he did his numbers by hand. Across the showroom floor he led her past expensive clothing and gift items; nearly everyone who could afford to keep livestock in this county was wealthy enough to stock up on geegaws. She admired the shining array of bits and breathed in the heady scent of new leather emanating from the bridle stock. Past all the new saddles was his limited stock of used ones, broken-down Courbettes that weren't worth the original price the day they sold, one gloriously tooled Mexican leather job featuring a thistle-and-acorn design, and another with a flawless basket weave that never varied from its path. Trouble with that was, tear it down to the tree and you found yourself staring at a bunch of old Mexican newsprint and masking tape.

"Here we go."

She felt a shiver traverse up her spine when she saw it. Wes laid one hand protectively across the seat and smoothed the stirrup leathers. She reached out to run her fingertips over the grainy leather surface. He'd cleaned and oiled it without asking, kept it dusted and looked after as if it were his own. The weight of the old stirrup iron felt as promising to her fingers as a gold ingot. She smiled, wanted to say thank you, but words wouldn't come.

"Marry me," he whispered in the hush of the morning. "You can stay home and watch those fuckin' soap operas and work yourself up a new layer of fat if that's what you want. Or if you want to keep busy, you can help out here. I got a big old house out there in the canyon and some sorry excuses for children who don't deserve to inherit. We could close up shop, buy a motor home, drive to Vegas and have a fling, spend every last dime together."

She studied his weathered face and steely gray hair. He was younger in heart than half the men she knew, and kinder than most of them put together. Was that a good enough reason to sign yourself over to another person's bed for a lifetime? She looked down at the saddle. "If I ever was to say yes to anybody, Wes, I suppose it would be you. Bless your heart. Keep taking your vitamins. I'll be back."

He shook his head and pocketed the folded money. "I won't spend this for awhile," he said, "just in case you think better of it."

Wes slung a fifty-pound sack of carrots into the truck bed, followed by another sack of four-way grain, a square one of A & M, and two twenty-pound sacks of Eukanuba for Hannah.

"Take those back, Wes. I don't have the money to pay you."

He wouldn't meet her eyes. "Mistake on the invoice. They shipped me some extra. No skin off my back. Feed the jughead horse and pamper your mutt. Dogs'll keep you going, honey. All that love. Now get out of here so an old man can make a buck. Drive safe, dammit."

Seven miles back up the hill and she was in the canyons again. She had, if she didn't dawdle, twenty-five minutes at the stable to turn Absalom out before leaving for work. Mud splattered her wheel wells, and the truck shimmied in the dirt road. Damp hens scrambled across the road in front of her, one of them confusedly leaving a tan egg along the side. The pipe stalls were humming with bobbing heads, all the horses fidgety, counting down the time to breakfast. In number seventy-two, the dark bay thoroughbred shifted his weight from hoof to hoof, his muzzle grazing the top rail of his stall. She parked the truck on the angle of the hill so that if she had to, she could start it by popping the clutch. Only her rubber mucking boots saved her jeans from the muddy manure. She walked carefully between stalls to her horse. In black marking pen, she'd lettered onto his trough *Media la comida en la noche, por favor.* He did tend to fat. He whickered softly, deep in his throat, his lower lip trembling in anticipation.

Without saying a word, Chloe slipped him a snap of carrot and in the same move haltered his massive head. She led him down the breezeway to the open arena gate. Inside, the sandy surface was whipped to a stiff froth, rainpocked and swampy where the drainage was poor. As soon as he was shut inside and she had removed the halter, his quiet flesh transformed into engorged muscle, breaking away from her hands into a full gallop. Damp sand sprayed up behind his hooves like the wake from a speedboat. She shinnied up the fence, hugging the rail to watch. He made long circle after circle, his muscular sides blurring past her, glittering like wet silk.

There was nobody else around to see. The stablehands were asleep in the few trailers that dotted the grounds. No other riders were there; rain discouraged early morning workouts. Nobody to observe the grace of the running horse or document the wide smile of the woman watching him. Nobody saw when his forelegs caught beneath him, heard her intake of breath or noted the recovering stumble that kept him from falling. When the subsequent limp emerged, forcing him to slow his speed to a trot, only she was there to observe it, catalog the progressive symptoms, and compare them to the last time. The bute wasn't working like it used to. She would have to call the vet, listen to Gabe's philosophy of euthanasia, how a quick blue needle was a whole lot kinder than the slow shadow of age, no matter how she padded his time with fresh hay cubes and molasses. Gabe couldn't help, it was a decision she'd have to make alone. No one else witnessed the singular moment when he came to her unbidden and laid his massive head in her lap

Winter of last year, when her bad cold settled down into chronic bronchitis, there was no apartment to go to, no place to get warm or rest. She was living in her truck, taking showers at the junior college, growing numb. She hadn't wanted to count up her debts. After Fats, they just *were*, like breathing; bills that somehow had accrued and seemed to be bent on taking her inventory one by one, paring her stock from seventeen head of horses down to one, causing her to pawn the last of her tack for less than a quarter of its worth. When it was gone, the bills remained. Sleeping with Gabriel Hubbard, DVM, was the closest Chloe had come to lying down for money.

She'd taken that two-day job working the rent string for the coyote hunt at Coto, currying up and cooling down for mostly drunk weekend riders, and managed, in between coughing spasms and white-hot chills, not to pass out. Once she and Fats had ridden the hunt themselves, merrily galloping around the acreage in pursuit of coyotes, the

Western equivalent of foxes. Those green to the hunt were riding in earnest, determined to win whatever this prize might be, but the more experienced riders ran for the sport, jumping low fences and hedges because it was permitted. They played cowboy poker, drawing cards for their hands at various checkpoints, betting like the fools that they were, fueled by beer. Now she worked here, and tried not to look too closely at the riders. By the end of the day she would have fifty bucks to show for it, fifty bucks to dole out by the dollar to her debtors, and if she was lucky, enough left over to feed Hannah and maybe herself.

Gabe rode up on a chestnut gelding. "That cough sounds nasty."

Busy checking the girth gall on an obese palomino, she didn't bother to answer. The tough little horse could go again, if this weekend Little Joe with the Rolex would quit hammering his barrel with those fancy six-inch spurs. She shoved sheepskin under the cinch strap and slapped him on. "Go easy on him," she wheezed. "He's done this before. He knows where to go without all your kicking."

"Yee-haw!" the cowboy crowed, and she shook her head.

Gabe was still there. "Hell, that guy's almost too drunk to ride. If his horse doesn't buck him off, likely he'll fall off of his own accord."

She stared up at Gabe. The mirrored sunglasses he wore reflected her straggly hair in a fish-eye warp. "You need a new horse already?" she asked, then sat down hard in the dirt, so dizzy she nearly went all the way over.

He'd grabbed one arm and pulled her right up behind him on that monstrous Circle Y roping saddle, galloped her over to the clubhouse. Over two mimosas he'd bought and made her finish (*the vitamin C will boost your immune system, and the alcohol will purify every cell*), he made her an offer: Crash at my office.

"No way."

"Look, Chloe. Everyone knows what happened. Fats left you holding a bag of rattlesnakes. Drop it. Let somebody help you out. Just until you get back on your feet again. What do you say?"

He'd taken her there that night, shown her the back room with the simple cot. "Sleep here. It's dry, and there's a heater. Just be out by seven-thirty when I start seeing patients, and don't make long-distance telephone calls."

"Who am I going to call?"

"Maybe one of those 900 numbers, I don't know."

Then he'd taken her back to one of the examining rooms, picked her up, and sat her down on one of the examining tables. With his stethoscope, he listened to each side of her chest, pausing at the lower lobes more than once. "How long have you had the fever?"

"Week or two."

"Hmm."

"What the hell does 'hmm' mean? Am I going to live?" She half wished he'd tell her no.

"If you do what I tell you, you might."

"Here it comes."

"Hey, I take doctoring seriously." He went to the locked refrigerator and readied a syringe of ampicillin. "Drop your jeans. This hurts a lot less if I shoot it into fat."

She rolled to the side and unzipped her pants.

"Jesus, you don't have a lot of fat back here to spare, do you?"

The pinch of his fingers, then the sting of the needle. It made a good focus for all her troubles. One tear escaped before she willed the others back inside. She yanked her pants back up, lay back against the chrome examining table that smelled of Lysol, which couldn't disguise the undertone of terrified-animal pee. The metal was cool against her cheek. She heard a beagle howl from the kennel section.

"Chloe, baby," Gabe uttered hoarsely as he climbed on top of her.

"Cut it out, Gabe. Get off."

"I can't help myself."

"Sure you can. Concentrate on the fact that I'm contagious."

"So I'll just give myself a shot. I can't help it. You're so goddamn beautiful, every time I saw you with Fats I just wanted to kill him so I could take you home myself."

Don't. Don't let this happen. But she was tired, cold, hungry, and too sick to listen. It had been a long time since any man had held on to her, wanted to make love to her. Fats had more passion for the bottle than he did for her. Her arms lay against her sides until Gabe gathered them up, one in each hand, drawing them above her head, holding her down in mock surrender. He liked that: being in charge. Vital clothes fell away, snaps loosening, buckles hitting the linoleum. The chrome table chilled her fevered skin. She shut her eyes and thought of Fats, the way he liked her up on top of him, the times he wasn't too drunk to finish the job.

"I'm going to fuck you," Gabe breathed into her ear, and he was right about that, there wasn't any other word for what they were doing, right here, twice, from thirty minutes after midnight until somewhere near two in the morning, with patient Hannah waiting outside in her truck—Hannah, three days without any supper and food samples right here for the taking on the counter.

Gabriel. Was his mother thinking archangel when she named him? Chloe didn't like him, didn't want to like what he was doing to her, but goddamn, he knew so many ways to coax the flesh into response it just happened despite what her mind wanted. In the Cleveland National Forest she'd once seen him coax trust from a wounded mountain lion some asshole ranger had fired on, probably the first time he'd ever fired a gun in his life. Gabe sweet-talked the lion until it was calm, then with one well-aimed shot, dotted its skull like a bull's-eye target, though he could have tranqued the cat and stitched him up again. She hadn't forgotten that. No, he had no trouble at all kindling Chloe's desire, no matter how deep she had buried it beneath her grief for Fats.

When he'd come to deliver Phil's mare, she remembered that first time. She knew full well Gabe took her to bed because he wanted to see if he could get away with it. He didn't need to get laid. There were plenty of other women who thought him a demigod. He had a tennis-playing wife, twin daughters in an Arizona boarding school, twenty acres here, and a condo in Palm Desert. That new king-cab Ford truck every year and a half meant he had money to burn. Chloe knew she was a minor distraction.

For three months they carried on, the sex never enough for him, she trying her damnedest to keep it a formality—the kind of nuisance a houseguest puts up with accepting the invitation—but eventually Gabe got to her, forced her back into her ghostly skin until he honed every nerve ending and all their spectacular responses. There were other men she'd slept with that she didn't love, she reasoned, and Gabe was careful, always using a rubber, though he agreed she had such infrequent periods she probably wasn't fertile. He was married, but only in the most general sense of the word. After awhile that didn't bother her. What did bother her was the way she began looking forward to hearing his truck pull up, how just the sound of his key in the lock made her internal motor kick in. Here she'd vowed never again after Fats, and things were starting to get complicated. She'd quit eating all but one meal a day then, the free one she took at Wedler's, and put the money she usually spent on food against bills Fats left behind. Nickels and dimes, the credit companies said. We need more than a gesture. Then she'd taken the Hermès to Wes McNelly, and he'd been very businesslike, talking "temporary loan, just to tide you over."

She'd let Wes introduce her to Hugh Nichols down at the Swallows Inn one night, and to a backdrop of country music on the jukebox, she listened to his tirade against the land developers. She agreed, they were all bastards, and Hugh took a shine to her, bought her a beer. He had the one shack available, but it was trashed from the previous tenant, so if Chloe wanted it, it was up to her to clean and repair it.

"I can stand a little mess," she'd told him. They shook hands. Wes nodded and lifted his glass to her; Hugh was his friend. That same night she left Gabe's back room the way she'd found it; the army-green blanket folded over the stained cot.

She had not been the first and would not be the last girl to pass through this office. His belt still had plenty of space for notches. Probably hers would be forgotten in a few weeks; he wouldn't even miss her. She'd been wrong. Gabe was furious. She didn't blame him; that was the way of men, they needed to be needed. Even Ben Gilpin, father of three dead children, had found time for the occasional bowling alley beauty. When she'd seen her foster father in the bar of the Kona Lanes, somehow her heart had tightened down a notch, though she wanted not to blame him—you took comfort where you found it.

Hers was here—in Absalom—the dark horse who suddenly lifted his head from her lap and took off across the arena like a colt. She let him make a full lap, then whistled from her perch on the fence. The old horse rolled in the sandy dirt, groaned and struggled to his feet. Wet sand fell from the planes of his shoulders as he jogged to close the distance between them. His bright eyes and alert ears spoke of years of mutual training, but the bond went deeper than that, and she knew it. "Come on, mule," she said to him. "This is your lucky day. Carrots for breakfast."

CHAPTER

8

After imagining her face for twenty-four hours he half expected the real thing to be a disappointment. His mother would have called it plain and honest; his father wouldn't have noticed her at all. One could call it ordinary. The quick brown eyes that darted from customer to kitchen weren't doelike or so remarkable as to inspire metaphor. She did nothing in the way of makeup to hide the smattering of freckles that canopied her nose. No lipstick either. When she smiled, the chipped front tooth was exposed. It wasn't a knock-'em-dead kind of face, but it was alive, animated, utterly without pretense. The bones beneath the skin did a classy job on the flesh. Her skin seemed lit from someplace deep inside; she looked happy in the small restaurant. Confident, untroubled.

Hank's stomach rumbled at the smells emanating from the kitchen. Freshly baked bread and frying bacon—how long had it been since he'd smelled those? Both Chloe and the other waitress, the black-haired, bespectacled woman who wasn't smiling, and who wasn't as quick no matter how hard she tried, were hopping, filling orders. He'd hoped for the security of a booth and the armor of the sports page, but there was only a single swivel stool at the counter. He sat down. The spicy scent of cinnamon buns hit him full strength—four trays' worth, fresh from the kitchen. Chloe stacked them into a tall metal cart. Maybe he would order one of those, though he usually didn't indulge in pastry. The caramelized sugar glistened. Damn the counter. The small, lopsided stool with the ripply Naugahyde squealed each time he turned to look at her. She was everywhere at once, it seemed.

It wasn't much of a restaurant. Chalkboard specials, wall-mounted television in the corner, one old photograph of the town pre-1940 in a cheap wooden frame with a crack in the glass. Plastic roses that looked as if they could use a good dusting nestled in bud vases on each table covered with an eye-piercing mustard yellow oilcloth. Four ceiling fans kept the hot air circulating. The creaky floorboards dipped in places. The rest of the town was undergoing massive rehabilitation; Hank wondered how the café and the small row of shops alongside it had escaped development. Health-food stores came and went, little shops offered T-shirts and tourist fare, and restaurants like this one had drawn him inside when he lived on this side of town. He'd felt an immediate part of the community. This morning the diner was filled to capacity. Hank could see other customers waiting outside, even though the January air was chilly enough to require jackets and scarves. A quick head count: the thirty-odd customers were nearly all male, nearly all of them watching the same show he was—Chloe Morgan. She was friendly with everyone, knew many of the customers by name. If I pursue this woman, Hank thought, I will get fat. I'll just ask for my shirt, drink a cup of tea, and walk out the door.

"Hey, toots. How about a refill over here?"

An older man in a business suit sitting at the end of the counter wagged his empty coffee cup in the air in Chloe's direction. Hank watched her reaction. Just as quickly as that face could open, so could it close, taking the light with it and retreating to a cold corner. Pride wouldn't allow her to falter, however. Her cheekbones held up even under the blush of the slur. Those bones—what was it about them?— an orthopedic man would probably fall in love with her X rays.

She poured the impatient man's coffee. "Here you go."

"About time, doll."

"Sorry. We're a little busy this morning." She smiled at Hank. "I'll be back to take your order in a minute."

"No hurry." He watched her cash a day laborer's check and count the money back to him in Spanish. Her accent was reasonably intact, but her grammar, good lord, could blister paint. The man didn't seem to care one way or the other. He took out his cracked leather wallet and showed Chloe a photograph of a baby.

"*Mi hija*," he said.

"She's cute. *Bonita.*" She handed him his wallet and a cinnamon bun, wrapped in a piece of wax paper. "Adios."

Hank watched the diminishing cinnamon rolls get doled out onto other plates. His chances of ordering one were not looking promising. On the television in the corner, he watched the sports recap—miracle—Arizona, after all these years, was coming back from the dead. Now Chloe stood opposite him, only the counter between them. Her back was turned; she looked just as well-put-together from that angle. He watched her firm behind strain against the denim skirt as she measured out fresh coffee into the tall coffee urn. She wiped her hand on the dish towel tucked into her skirt and turned to face him. "I'm telling you, sit quiet in this place and you'll go hungry. You should have thrown your napkin at me or something. What'll you have?"

"What are my chances for one of those cinnamon rolls?"

She leaned across the counter on her elbows. "We're officially out of them until tomorrow morning."

"Why are you whispering?"

"Because if I say so out loud, half the people in here will walk out and the other half will start a brawl."

"They're that good?"

She nodded. "One of the county's best-kept secrets."

"Bran cereal, I guess. With skim milk."

She sighed and set down her order pad. Behind her, the cook was ringing the library bell like a madman, and there were others waiting to have their orders taken, but she ignored all of that and faced Hank. Up close, she smelled of Ivory soap, the bars he used to carve into blocky animal shapes as a Cub Scout.

"Let me get this straight. You got dressed to come all the way over here for breakfast and you're going to let me charge you three-fifty for something you could have eaten at home in your skivvies?"

"Well, generally I use a bowl."

She flushed. "Have you looked at the menu? We cook here. Live a little. Order up."

"Eggs, bacon? That kind of thing?"

"Eggs, bacon, biscuits, gravy, sausage, omelets, homemade everything you could dream of."

"That stuff isn't supposed to be very good for the heart."

She smiled, the chipped front tooth catching on her lower lip. "Name something in life that is."

"Clean living?"

She laughed. "More die of heartbreak than heart disease, I'm willing to bet money."

Hank watched as she stretched her arms above her head and twisted her neck to the side to stretch out the kinks. He could hear vertebrae releasing in little pops. He couldn't get his neck to do that. It just stayed stiff, and the muscles hammered at him like coiling wire when he got tense. "So tell me what to order."

"This one time," she answered, "I'll put together a breakfast for you. But next time you order it yourself."

"Sure. This one time."

She pencilled the order, clipped it to the rotating chrome spinner and sent it back to the kitchen. While she was there, she picked up four more plates and went across the room to deliver them, having forgotten him already. It was a living, but what a way to make a living. She had strong arms, Hank noted, and that was her saving grace. Her shoulder muscles were visible through the cotton material of her T-shirt, and they were developed. Not sinewy, exactly, not body-builder material like those gleaming amazons on the cable network who looked as if they could crack ribs with one serious squeeze, but significant parts contributing to the whole of her attractiveness. He looked at her calves. They had muscular definition. Maybe she did lift weights. In a gym in one of those spandex leotards. Wouldn't that be nice? He unfolded the newspaper and tried hard to be interested in Charles Keating, but Mr. Keating's shenanigans couldn't hold a candle to the waitress.

His breakfast arrived in parts. Buttermilk biscuits and a cup of gravy on one plate. Next, five sizzling circles of what looked like homemade sausage—one bite and he could tell it was—then plain scrambled eggs on another. She tossed three packets of marmalade down and poured him a tall glass of juice.

"Papaya," she said. "You don't look like the coffee type."

"That's right. Actually, I quit coffee because it made my heart race." He turned, but she was halfway across the restaurant, filling ice-water pitchers; three empty ones hooked on her fingers like a string of trout. He took a bite of biscuit and sighed. My arteries are screaming for mercy, he thought. Well, let them. What would she choose for him if he ordered lunch?

The cook came out of the kitchen and grabbed her shoulder. In his hand he held an order. He shoved it in her face.

"Just what the hell does this say?"

She brushed his hand away as if it were a spider. "Short stack, over easy, coffee and orange juice."

"How the fuck am I supposed to read that cat-scratching?"

"I guess you just have to ask me if you can't."

The cook ripped the order from her hand again. "Learn to goddamn spell!" Then he retreated back to the kitchen, and Chloe was gone, through the back of the restaurant and probably out a back door. Hank craned his neck to see where she had gone and the other waitress came up.

"Need coffee?"

"No, thanks. I'm fine."

"If you're sure?"

He was quite sure he was sure. Hank looked down at his silverware. He felt heat spreading throughout his face, across the back of his neck. There was no cause to come down on her like that, but the cook gave every impression of doing just that on a regular basis.

He finished his eggs, slowly.

She came back, smoking a cigarette, her eyes red rimmed as if she'd been crying. Behind the counter, she took one last drag of the cigarette and stabbed it out into an ashtray. She fanned her face with the order pad and glared at Hank. "Just what in Christ is your problem?"

"I beg your pardon?"

"Ever since you walked in here you've been staring at me, and I want to know why you're looking at me that way."

"In what way?"

"Like I owe you money."

He pressed his fingertips into the biscuit crumbs on the small plate. It would be gluttonous to ask for seconds, but they were so good he could have eaten a dozen. "You don't owe me money," he said.

She unfolded her arms. "Well, thank God for small favors."

"You obviously don't remember, but the other day, at the college? That was my shirt Phil Green gave you."

"Oh."

"Right," he continued, extending his hand, hoping if she didn't want to shake it she might just take hold of it for a moment. He wanted to feel her skin, make contact. "Hank Oliver," he said. "Folklore and mythology—the college? Phil Green thinks a great deal of you, incidentally. I apologize if I was staring. Hell, I *was* staring. I just came to see about my shirt. You do have it?"

She took his fingers for a moment, then let go.

The city employees at the large booth were screaming for coffee. The other waitress was busy at the register, peeling the paper back on a roll of quarters.

"Wait," she said, then bumped away from the counter with two coffeepots.

Hank sipped his juice. Papaya? The flowery taste made his tongue tingle, each tastebud standing at attention. It was interesting how attractive she became when she was off guard.

"All right. Don't panic, but it's not here. I only took it home to launder it. You know, to get the blood out."

"Blood?"

"I guess there was still some on me after Phil's horse. . . It all came out, good as new. I'm terrific with stains."

"But it's not here."

"No, it's at my house."

Hank waited a moment. "Why don't you give me directions, and I'll drop by tonight to pick it up."

He felt her hesitation, felt her studying him: the crewneck sweater from Land's End, the shirt collar folded inside—straight arrow on the surface. He knew his red mustache was graying. He looked older than his years. Who from the real world wanted to tangle with a second-rate academic? There was no defense he could offer. He'd grown used to it; outfield in softball, nobody's best pal, someone women confided in but never fell for. He'd only used one of the marmalade packets; he wasn't entirely self-indulgent. He wore no wedding ring. But to this woman, was that proof of anything? Maybe all men were potential assholes, like the cook she worked for. Especially if they bought expensive shirts and weren't forthright about asking for them back.

She shook her head. "I don't think that's such a great idea."

"Listen, what do I have to say to convince you I'm harmless? Insured. Bondable. A pacifist. Every election I vote, my candidate loses, from McGovern on down."

That made her smile.

He sat back, shoving his hands into his pockets. "I'd like the shirt back, and if it isn't too odious an idea to you, I'd like to see you again. Outside of this place. Not that it's a bad place, just somewhere else, where you can have someone else wait on you for a change."

Her smile disappeared. "You mean like a date?"

"Yes. No. Whatever you want to call it. It doesn't have to be a date, per se." He was stammering like a fool now; she'd never say yes.

She let out a long breath and gave him a smile. "Well, what can I say? Tuesday has sure got Monday beat all to hell."

She ripped a ticket off her order pad and drew him a map on the back. "I won't be there until after seven o'clock," she said. "I have another job after this one. You'll have to wait for me at the gate, too, because my landlord goes mental about strangers. And the roads aren't terrific, so don't go past the gate, promise? And you can't stay too long, either, because I'm busy."

"Anything else? Permission slip? Résumé?"

"You current on your tetanus shots?"

"I have no idea."

"That was a joke."

He fumbled with his wallet, drew out a bill, and handed it to her. He got up and walked stiffly to the door, leaving his wounded dignity trailing behind him like soiled kite string. A date. Not a date. What in Christ was he thinking? He could feel the tips of his ears, steaming red sirens that shrieked his insecurity aloud.

CHAPTER

9

ich came out of the kitchen and stood beside Chloe. "So I'm an asshole."

She sighed and cleared Hank's dishes into a basin beneath the counter. "Don't try to get on my good side."

"You could sue me."

"Rich, the only thing I hate more than working for you is assisting the legal profession in any way at all."

He laid his head down on her shoulder. "Forgive me?"

"Give me a raise and I might."

He lifted his head quickly and snorted. "Give you a raise. I should fire your ass, close this joint, take all my money and send Kit to a fat girls' camp. That's what I should do. That's the only thing that makes any sense."

Chloe scooped up the money from the counter, looked down at the bill in her hand and howled.

"What?"

She grinned and wagged the fifty-dollar bill in Rich's face. "That skinny professor doesn't know it, but he just left me a forty-four-dollar tip."

"Money," Rich said. "Don't come crying to me when you find out it's counterfeit."

* * *

"How did you manage to convince my dad I needed riding lessons?" Kit Wedler asked, her chubby hands locked in a death grip around the reins. "He's intensely chintzy. Once I saw a moth fly out of his wallet, I shit you not."

"Carefully applied guilt." Chloe adjusted the curb chain on the Kimberwicke bit. Hard-mouthed Elmer wasn't going to take this one for a ride, no sir. "It never fails. And don't cuss."

"Why not? You do it."

"Kit, when you're as old as I am, you call me up some Sunday and we'll discuss it. If you find life as disappointing as I do, then you have my permission to cuss eight ways to Sunday." The child was dressed for the game, outfitted in stiff new blue jeans, her feet stuffed into a pair of Rich's old cowboy boots, and trying not to show her terror over the horse. Her flame red hair wisped out from the yellow schooling helmet like a baby's. Thirteen. She *was* still a baby, but all her extra poundage wasn't exactly baby fat. She kept her green eyes fixed straight ahead, staring into nothing, and jabbered a mile a minute.

"Have you heard that new song by Guns 'n Roses? It's way cool, but I kind of don't like Axl Rose, especially since I heard he pierced his nipples. Wouldn't that hurt? And besides, who would see it if he was wearing a shirt all the time?"

"Drop your stirrup so I can adjust the length. It's a little too short for you."

Kit didn't move.

"Kit, drop your stirrup."

"I can't."

That was true. Her leg was frozen solid with fright.

"Sure you can." Chloe stepped back and turned her head away to light a cigarette. "Kit, if you want to learn to ride, you have to trust me."

"It's not that I don't trust you."

"And trust the horse."

"In English, this substitute read us this poem about a girl getting thrown and breaking her neck. Like they say, shit happens."

Chloe took her time and blew a perfect smoke ring. Shit indeed happened, unpredictable and everlasting. "This gelding is twenty-seven years old, honey. The only place he goes fast is to sleep."

Kit still didn't believe her. "Bullshit. What about that senator that got crushed, or that guy who limps around here feeding the goats?"

"If you're that sure disaster's right around the corner, you have no business being up on the horse. Dismount."

"Well, maybe I could try it. Maybe."

"I'll just go over here and finish my cigarette. Let me know when you've made up your mind."

Chloe went to the railing of the arena fence and climbed up. She could see Kit's shoulders squared up around her neck, the tremble in her double chin. Any minute now, there would be a flood of tears and the lesson would be over before it began. She tapped her cigarette ash into the sand. Somewhere along the way, maybe one of her hip mother's interludes into communal living, thank you, this little girl had been badly scared by something, not necessarily horses. But getting on the back of a thousand-pound beast was one way to bring it to the surface. Whatever it was, she had to wait Kit out. She smoked her cigarette slowly, enjoying each breath.

Kit hung her head. Chloe climbed down from the fence, stepped back up to the saddle, and reached to stroke the gelding's neck. He nickered with pleasure. "Old Elmer," she said. "He's a fool for neck scratches."

"Chloe?"

"Bend over just a little and pet him."

"Are you sure you've got me?"

"Absolutely."

Kit moved her torso forward, and the leg in question slipped an inch. Chloe quickly slid the buckle down three holes and stuck Kit's toe back into the stirrup and stepped back. "Now ask him to walk."

Kit looked down the broad buckskin head with its scraggly, chewed brown mane. "Okay, you can walk now."

The gelding cocked a rear leg and dozed.

"See?" Kit wailed. "What did I tell you? This won't work. I'm fat, clumsy, ugly as a dog's butt. Forget the whole thing."

Chloe flipped her cigarette into the damp sand and heard it sizzle. Any more rain and this arena would be soup. Her mended boots could barely keep the dampness from her toes. "I can see you don't speak horse." She tapped the riding crop she was holding against her boot top, and Elmer perked up. A lesson horse from age twelve on, he knew the cues. He'd come to the stable nameless and overweight, lazy enough to sleep through Chernobyl unless someone stood in the ring holding a riding crop. Three hundred bucks later, Chloe had saved him from the dog food people. She never regretted it; she could put a baby on his back, turn him loose in a field of cranky diamondbacks, and he'd step quietly over them, one at a time, deliver his rider to his chosen destination without so much as an errant footfall.

She pressed Kit's heel into the gelding's barrel. "We start with lesson one. This tells him he's got the green light." Next she made a kissing noise. "That tells him to step on the gas."

They moved forward. Elmer was wiser than he looked. He knew who he could fake and who would call him on it. But the two of them were moving forward, and Kit was starting to get the smile back.

"Chloe! Look at me! I'm making him go! I'm riding!"

Chloe stood back and watched them circle the arena. If you were a doctor, sometimes you got to walk into the waiting room and tell the people, yes, she's going to make it, and if you were a teacher, maybe there were times you saw the concepts sink into the gray matter, but a riding instructor only had moments such as this one, where desire to master overcame fear, and she savored it.

"I'll never ever walk straight again," Kit moaned as they shut Elmer into the geezer pasture. He stepped lively on the walk back, smelling the cubes of alfalfa awaiting him and hearing his buddies call out greetings.

"Soak in your dad's hot tub when you get home. You'll feel it a little tomorrow, so that's why you have to ride again on Thursday."

"No way. Look at my legs. They're already starting to bruise. I wonder if this could get me excused from P.E.? You think? We're starting soccer. I fucking hate chasing a ball around on the grass and not being able to use my hands. How senile. I wonder who thought that little game up?"

"Brazilians?"

Kit waved her off. "Oh, who cares. I hate all school, really, just P.E. more than most. It is to die, Chloe, when you're a new kid, not to mention a whale."

"Don't talk like that about yourself."

"Why not? It's true. Hey, how do you know my dad has a hot tub?"

"He invited me over once."

Kit's green eyes gleamed. "Were you guys like, you know, dating?"

"Give me a break. He was having trouble with the filter and asked if I would take a look at it."

Kit stepped aside to let the stable goat pass. "How cute. Does he bite?"

"She. And yes."

"How come you know about stuff like that?"

Chloe smiled. "Sexing goats? It's not difficult."

"Ick. Pipes and drains, you know what I mean. I thought that was the main reason to get a boyfriend. To keep from having to snake hair out of clogged sinks and overflowing toilets by yourself."

Chloe and Kit pressed themselves to the pipe stalls in the breezeway to let a truck pass through. It was dusk now, darkness settling in down low to the ground like tule fog. Bright yellow light fractured the dark in places where the stable lights weren't burned out, casting impossibly huge shadows of horseflesh against the metal barn. She knew the silver Ford F-350 well enough by its dents. One in the right rear panel had been put there by her own horse, when Gabe made the mistake of trying to float Absalom's teeth without tranquilizing him first. He never had body work done, just turned the truck in every two years and let it get beat up all over again. It was past suppertime, but a vet's hours never ended.

"News flash, Kit. Having a penis doesn't automatically earn you a degree in plumbing. My foster dad showed me the basics. Handy stuff, it stuck with me, that's all."

"So if you choose a boyfriend, you can kind of eliminate that requirement?"

"Something like that. Let's go polish up your tack."

"It's so sad."

"My tack? I beg your pardon."

"That you never got adopted."

"Past history. Don't worry about it."

"My stomach's growling. Why can't we get something to eat first?"

"Because you take care of your tack first. If you don't, you'll forget about doing it later, and when you need it most, it'll fail you."

"Well, that's boring."

"No, it's responsible. Besides, the only food to eat around here is hay cubes and Cokes. You can wait a little while. Your dad will be along here any minute to whisk you off to a real supper."

"Right." Kit toed the mud. "If he remembers."

"He won't forget."

Kit pointed to Gabe's truck. The driver's door was open, the interior light shining down on his face. "Do you know that guy?"

"Yes."

"Well, look at him. He is a fox. A *major* fox."

"And old enough to be your grandfather."

"Still."

"Forget it." Chloe switched on the porch light outside the barn office and filled a bucket with water from the hose coiled near the steps. The icy chill splashed her hands, and she shivered. She unlocked the storeroom that abutted the office and gathered supplies. "Here's the sponge and there's the soap, Kit. Have at it."

Kit took one last look at Gabe, sighed, and set to work, rubbing the skinny slab of Fiebing's like a fiend. Her father's lumpy army-green down jacket made her look like a kosher dill; she'd work up a serious heat if she kept the pace up. Maybe the down would act like a sauna, sweat a few pounds from her. Chloe had hopes that the riding would take hold of her, urge her away from the comfort of food. Kit's red ponytail was tousled, and she reached up to brush stray hairs from her face. Despite the neon green bow and the tough talk, the reaction to Gabe's drop-dead good looks, Kit was still standing on the edge of childhood, looking across the chasm, not quite ready to cross over. They worked together in the quiet, the soft whooshing of the sponges darkening the leather. The familiar feel of the well-used tack beneath her fingers was as unconscious to Chloe as if she were a master knitter working on an afghan. She knew every spot where she'd stitched up tears, every bridle she'd managed to buy back when she'd sold the lot after Fats died. She took a can of Brasso down from the storeroom shelf and polished the nickel bit, not because it needed it, really, but she wanted Kit to see that she also took care of these things. Thirty feet away, Gabe Hubbard stood by his truck, a trouble light fixed on a chestnut Arab gelding who'd evidently gotten himself torn up good in some barbed wire. She kept her eye on him while Kit chattered. Nobody could stitch like Gabe. Every now and again, the light caught the arced needle and it flashed like a firefly.

"Tell me about your mom," Chloe said.

Kit sighed dramatically. "Wilhelmina *Premabodhi* Wedler. What's to tell? She changed her name from Lucille so many times I forgot what to call her. She told my dad she was tired of sounding like a Chuck Berry song, whoever that is. *Premabodhi* is Indian for the guru's head chick, or something equally gross. Now she lives at the commune, wearing robes and shit, lighting incense and praying to a million Indian gods I never even knew there were. Supposedly she wants to become an acupuncturist, but she used to groom dogs and work as a cashier in the Albertson's. I used to love to go shopping with my dad and see her there in her red uniform. She'd smile at the customers, and bring us day-old stuff from the bakery. I thought someday I might get a job there and work with her, you know, like a team, but everything changed."

Kit's face screwed up hard, lower lip caught between her teeth. Chloe stilled her polishing rag and set the bit down on a picnic table. "You're an interesting person, Kit. And you've got potential as a rider."

"I do?"

"That's what I said."

The face relaxed, then grew cautious. "Like potential the way some totally handicapped case has potential? That kind of interesting, huh?"

Gabe was leaning inside the driver's door of his truck now, writing up the bill, probably adding in at least fifty for the late call, Chloe would bet money. "Hardly. For example, you're the only thirteen-year-old redhead I know with jet black pubic hair."

Kit laughed. "Not to mention entire pelvic region! God, think we could sue Lady Clairol for failing to mention that?"

"The box said it would wear off in six weeks."

"Six weeks! Six weeks is for-fucking-ever!"

"I realize that," Chloe said. "You don't have to cuss."

Chloe watched Gabe Hubbard send the bewildered owner of the repaired gelding off with his considerably lighter checkbook. He turned and started toward her and Kit—probably he'd been watching them the whole time. They were sitting close together on the arena railing, sharing a Diet Coke, waiting for Rich to arrive. So far, he was forty-five minutes late.

Gabe hooked one bootheel over the lowermost rung of the fence. "Got some bute in the truck. I figure you're just about out of the last batch."

He looked at her soberly, the old lonely soldier routine. Cynthia was probably on a ski trip in Aspen with friends, and he was feeling abandoned. Christ. So he sees me and thinks I'll do for the night, that old song. Well, I'm not going to follow the bouncing ball. Chloe shook her head. "Dr. Hubbard, meet Katherine Wedler, Kit, as she prefers to be called. She took her first riding lesson today, on Elmer. Got him to lope."

"Whoa," he said, extending a hand. "You're home free if you can get that animal to engage all four legs at the same time. Nice to meet you, Kit. Mind if I borrow Chloe for a while?"

"Chloe minds."

"Come on," he wheedled. "Be nice. Here I was going to offer to take a look at Ab's legs for free, and you're biting my head off."

"For free?" Chloe slid down off the fence. "Remember, I have a witness."

They walked up the hill to the pipe stalls, Gabe on the left, Kit in the middle, Chloe keeping to the outside.

"Thought you might like to know that Phil Green's colt is coming along. Strong-willed little monster. Legs are shaping up."

"A baby?" Kit squealed. "Can we go see it?"

"That's great for Phil, but I don't really care to hear about it, thanks," Chloe said. She undid the latch of stall seventy-two. In the dark, Absalom's eyes glittered with fear. "Here, now," she said softly, pressing a hand to his muscled throat. She blew softly into his nostril and he quieted. She snapped a lead rope onto his breakaway halter. "Good boy. I promise, no shots."

Gabe pulled his truck up and switched the trouble light back on. While Chloe held on to the rope and muttered quietly to the horse, Gabe ran his hands down the horse's forelegs. "How did he fare on the three-times-a-day routine?"

She shrugged. "A little better, I think."

"Bute's hard stuff. He can't stay on it forever."

"Stay on what?" Kit asked. "Is this your horse? Is he sick? God, he's as big as Black Beauty. Is he a stallion?"

Chloe didn't answer.

Gabe went to his truck again and returned with an amber jar, which he pressed into Chloe's free hand. "Bear in mind all we're doing here is buying time until you make a decision you can live with. Time might run out before you do."

"Goddammit, I know that, Gabriel."

"Gabriel," Kit said. "Is that your full name? Did you know there was an angel named Gabriel? I learned it in Catechism. My mom was Catholic for about three months one time."

"No kidding." Gabe looked evenly at Chloe, and she stared right back. He got into his truck and pulled the door shut. "Don't forget, Chloe."

"Jesus," she said. "How could I?"

Gabe drove out of the pipe stalls and circled around to the main road toward the highway. Rich Wedler honked from his low-slung Triumph as he passed the outgoing truck. January be damned, he had the top down, the tape player cranked up, the Byrds playing "I'll Feel a Whole Lot Better." When the truck sped past, spraying his car with mud, he gave it the finger.

"That's my dad," Kit said. "Mr. Congeniality. Well, at least he finally remembered. Are you really going to make me ride on Thursday? What time?"

"I don't know." Chloe bent her wrist to check her watch. It was eight-fifteen. Eight-fifteen. Why did the time nag at her? "Oh, my God!" She unsnapped the lead rope and coiled it over her arm. "Kit, I have to go."

"Where? Don't you want to go out to eat with me and my dad?"

"Can't. I was supposed to meet someone at seven."

She sped through the canyon, tires screaming on the slick asphalt. What if he'd gotten tired of waiting at the crossroads, gone in and met up with Hugh? He wouldn't do that, would he? Hugh would give her hell, maybe even ask her to leave. It had been foolish to say yes in the first place. There were no cars on the gravel road as she jockeyed the transmission to make the steep grade into the box canyon. Oh, hell, why hurry? He had probably given up after the third dirt road, desperate for a streetlight. She slowed down, made the last turn possible before the road became impassable, thanks to the last rain. Here was a car, though, an old Honda, right front wheel stuck deep in a rut that had evolved out of the last storm. She braked and cut her engine, got out, and buttoned her jacket up to her neck. Cold tonight—the temperature must have been down to forty. She could see her breath in the night air, and the tips of her ears stung. Rich was crazy to ride with the top down. He'd get pneumonia or worse. She looked around. Nobody here. Then, faintly, she heard Hannah barking and took off in that direction in a slow run; it wouldn't do to break her ankle over a treed raccoon. Branches flew by her. What in Christ had she treed? God, she hoped it wasn't a mountain lion. They didn't usually come out this far, but she'd seen them on the ridge, mornings, and noticed their tracks near the creek where they came down to drink. Maybe Hannah had wounded something. Might have to go for Francisco's shotgun. She pursed her lips and forced a whistle.

The white dog gave it up and bounded to Chloe. rubbing her back up under the outstretched hand. "What are you up to?" Chloe whispered and squinted up into the trees, into the V of branches. "Oh, Hannah, Hannah. Bad dog." The sight wasn't funny, but she had to pinch her cheeks to keep from laughing.

It was that biscuits-and-gravy, papaya-juice, forty-four-dollar-tip, want-my-shirt-back-tonight professor from the college. It was him, all right. Here for their date, wedged high into the oak branches. The car had no doubt gotten stuck, and he'd grown tired of waiting, thought he'd walk a few yards to find her in a cozy cabin, kettle of tea simmering on a pot-bellied stove. Someplace to warm his hands. Well, surprise. He was beyond shivering, the cold racked him in great shudders, and his face—a white mask in the darkness—looked angry enough to spit tent pegs.

Chloe took hold of Hannah's collar. Now that her mistress was home, Hannah's enthusiasm for the stranger dwindled. She licked Chloe's hands before Chloe pushed her away with a stern command, "Stay." Hannah sat down.

"You left out the part about the dog, didn't you? What in God's name is she, half wolf?" His voice shook. "You going to chain her up or just let me die of frostbite?"

"It's all right. I have her now. You can come on down."

CHAPTER

10

Sorry about the tree business. Hannah doesn't take to strangers."

"That's the understatement of the century." Hank let go the last branch and sat down hard in the damp humus. Assorted sharp sticks and stones poked at his backside, but he was so cold and numb that the pain hardly registered. Good old terra firma after a miserable near hour: he could have made courtly love to the ground, he was so grateful to be on it and still retain ownership of his testicles. He massaged his ankles with fingers that felt like blocks of wood, trying to urge the blood back into the needles-and-pins flesh.

"You should have stayed in your car. I told you to."

"I was afraid it was going to sink in the mud. And you know what? It did." He stared at this woman he'd been so intrigued with at breakfast. Muddy boots, heavy denim jacket, and snarling beast at her side. Premature senility, that's what it was, just like his Uncle Robert, who had to be institutionalized at fifty. "You didn't tell me I was going to have to earn a merit badge finding your house."

"You didn't ask."

He shuddered with cold. "Can we go inside, just until I get warm?"

"Sure." She smiled and bent down to let the dog lick her face. He despised it when people did that. The teeth on that animal were designed specifically for tearing. It was a wild place out here. God knew what the hound had hunted down and mangled for the sport of it. Undoubtedly, she allowed the feral creature to sleep in her bed as well. This was not an attractive woman. This was brief infatuation riding the spongy tissue of the penis.

Another chill jolted his frame. Chloe reached out and took his hand, rubbing it between her palms. She blew warm breath into his trapped digits, choked off a laugh.

"You find this amusing?"

"You have to admit, it looked damn funny. Hannah had you treed like a possum."

He snatched his hand away from her and jammed it into his pocket. Disturbingly, it now felt much warmer than the other one. "If you don't mind, I'd like to call a towing service. I have classes to teach in the morning."

"I don't have a phone," she told him. "But I can make you some cocoa to warm you up, then drive you the half-mile to the phone, if you like."

He clasped the two halves of his torn sweater together.

"Would it make you stop glaring at me if I told you that I have a tow hitch on my truck? We can get your car out."

"Thank you. I'd appreciate it."

Hannah sniffed his pants leg. "She knows you now," Chloe said. "I'm going to let her go."

She released the dog, and the white shape bolted away from them through the dark. They followed her until they came to a—what the hell would you call it?—a cabin?—a shack? It wasn't a conventional house, more like a large shed you might store equipment in. It had a plywood/cedar motif, all twenty by twenty-four or so feet of it, somewhat patchwork in approach, including an old billboard advertising Stroud Ranch Homes, but it looked sturdy enough. A metal chimney rose through the slightly hipped roof, and there was a screen to catch any stray sparks—had it been lit, of course. It wasn't.

"This is your place?"

"I know it wouldn't win any beauty contests, but I was watertight the last three storms, which is more than I can say for half the new homes around here."

"True," Hank conceded. All that stuff in the newspaper about the million-dollar homes sliding down toward Pacific Coast Highway had made the front page for close to a week. "Who built it?" he asked.

She stopped short. "Some guys I know. Why?"

"Just curious."

"I redid the roof myself, though. Plus rigged the woodstove and the chimney."

He followed her up a rocky path, his anesthetized feet painfully returning to sensation with each step. Eighty dollars for a shirt that seemed determined to cost him a hell of a lot more than money. He silently thanked his father for bullying him into finishing the rank of Eagle Scout; if he hadn't earned all those merit badges he wouldn't have been able to climb the tree at all, let alone save his sorry ass from the white jaws of death this woman kept as her familiar.

"Come on in. With this yuppie gizmo, it doesn't take that long for the water to boil." She pointed to a butane-fired single-burner cooker set atop a crudely fashioned plywood-and-cinder-block counter. "My one extravagance."

She turned a transistor radio low, some twangy country station specializing in broken-heart ballads in between beer commercials. *Coors Light, it's the right beer now!* That shit-howdy tastelessness he somehow expected. No electricity. Well, of course not, were they within five miles of a telephone pole? She lit an oil lamp with an Ohio blue tip and set the flickering glass sconce on an upended orange crate. There was a sofa bed, turquoise vinyl, pulled out to bed length, covered with an opened sleeping bag and a chevron-patterned Mexican horse blanket that had seen better days. Someone had nailed a rusty horseshoe directly in the center of the wall above the bed. A yellow trunk with brass latches and the black-painted initials F.V. in Old English italic was pushed up against one wall. That about cleared it for the inventory. What kind of life was she living here? *Trixie Belden and the Box Canyon Mystery?* Jesus H. Christ. His feet tangled in a mound of mashed aluminum cans, and he tripped, just barely catching himself on the pulled-out sofa bed.

"You drink a lot of soda."

She scooped the cans into a grocery sack. "Hannah's."

"The dog drinks soda?"

"No, she collects cans for recycling. I buy her tinned dog food with it, otherwise with our budget it's strictly dry kibble." She gathered up the blanket and wrapped it around his shoulders. It smelled strongly of horse. "This will help to take off the chill." She pumped water at the basin into a battered aluminum coffeepot and set it on the butane burner.

"You really enjoy pulling my leg. A dog who collects cans."

"Swear to God. She won't play Frisbee, ball, fetch, any of the usual dog nonsense. One day she brought me a Coke can, and I gave her a reward. You'd be surprised what you can do with simple reinforcement. Hannah had a hard go of it until we hooked up. She tries to pull her weight, and I try to do my best by her."

He looked down at the shepherd, who was nosing an old enamel pot half-filled with chow but still keeping an eye on him. "A dog with the Puritan work ethic."

She smiled, exposing the chipped tooth. "Maybe so. Anyhow, I like the way you make it sound. Feeling warmer?"

"A little. Were you planning to show up at all?"

She cocked her head and stared at him for a full minute, her mouth drawn in a straight line. "You don't know me, Professor, so you can take that nasty tone out of your voice. I generally keep my word. I got hung up at my other job, and I forgot you. That's all."

"Your other job?"

"Teaching kids to ride horses."

A horse bum. Terrific.

"What do you do?"

"I teach, too. Folklore, the old myths. Junior college kids— a few older students returning to school."

She smiled. "Like 'How the Elephant Got His Trunk'?"

"Not exactly. That's more in the line of fables, though we do cross over from time to time. Myths deal more directly with creation stories, the rulers of the heavens, sky, sea, and underworld—how the mortals who became entangled with the gods made out."

"Not all that well, I guess?"

"Well, usually not. My shirt?"

"It's just out back. I'll get it." She went out the front door—the only door, Hank noted—a homemade plywood affair with the shimmy of dampness turning the elevated grain furry. It had a simple hook-and-eye latch on the inside. Wouldn't keep out a determined visitor, but the dog might. Hannah lifted her head and fixed him with a wary stare. Those coal black eyes were unreadable. He didn't move beyond his helpless shivering.

Chloe returned, shutting the door against a wind that had come up icy. In her hand were the remains of his shirt, torn, muddied, shredded ivory cotton and a few buttons, all of it chewed beyond repair. She was grim faced. "Hannah did a real number on it. Funny, she usually leaves the laundry alone." She placed the fabric on the counter. "Look. I'll pay you for it, but I can't do it all at once. Let me write you an IOU. And you can check with Phil, my word's good."

He felt ridiculous taking money from this impoverished woman whose idea of luxury was a butane burner and a dime-store oil lamp. "It's just a shirt. I have others. Maybe we should forget the entire episode."

"Oh, no. It was my fault, and I want to pay for it."

She turned her back to him and set out two tall Ball glass jars. His grandmother used to have those, back when he was a kid. After the homemade piccalilli was gone, she might fill the jars with prickly pear jelly or iced tea with a sprig of mint from her herb garden. She'd lived in the Arizona desert long before it became fashionable to do so. He remembered bright, still mornings and her weathered face smiling at him across the breakfast table. Outside, long-armed cacti and the cackle of a passing roadrunner over rocks so red he wondered if he cracked them open they might bleed. His father hadn't approved of drinking from jars, or of the desert as Hank's playground, but they'd sent him there for almost a year when he was four or five and his sister Annie was dying, and many a summer after she was gone. His grandmother's odd ways were a source of childhood fascination to him. It had been years since he'd thought about those jars. How he'd cried when she grew ill and no longer remembered him. He wasn't allowed to go along when his parents shut up the house. His first experience with death had been Annie's, but she was a faint memory. Then Nana was gone—no funeral, just no longer there. She'd been wise. She would have understood this woman before him, would have known exactly how to speak to her without saying the wrong thing.

He became acutely aware of his need to pee. There was no bathroom to the place, no real accoutrements to elevate it above storeroom or broom closet, though it had a true floor; he could feel the support joists squeak beneath his feet. But it was obviously her home, and she must have encountered the same pressing need. Across from the counter shelf there was a chipped iron sink with an old-fashioned pump handle that worked; he'd seen her draw the water for the cocoa, so they were hooked up to a water line somewhere. Maybe out there in the woods, an outhouse? How did one ask? One didn't.

He crossed his legs on the fold-out couch. A turned-back corner of the sleeping bag lining he sat on featured cowboys and Indians involved in an endless chase. He saw a pair of riding boots set out on a sheet of newspaper on the floor; next to them, rags and a tin of boot-black. He felt her watching him assess the place, and her dignity scared him in places that had moments earlier been numb with cold. They stared at each other.

He saw in the plain face a fierce humility, as frankly exposed as the cow skull that hung on the wallboard. A large rock doubled as a doorstop, and a five-gallon jar next to it was filled with the dog's kibble. Every material object in this room had a practical application. He remembered her scarred back outside Phil Green's office and felt the itch of excitement stir below his belt. Why? Right now, he needed to pee, then revive under a hot shower, and collapse into his own bed. A microwaved Stouffer's macaroni-and-cheese dinner and a glass of Chablis, comfort food to numb this day into memory. He didn't need a woman, didn't need two hours up a tree to round out his life. But he wanted to stay. If he dropped the shirt and left, she would resurrect it, study the possibilities, and find a use for torn fabric. She was that kind of person. He wanted to know what she would do with it—of what use it could possibly be to her. Suddenly the interior of the cabin shifted for him. The cow skull, placed strategically to cover the patched gypsum. Simple but deliberate positioning, like centering the horseshoe. Some people might go so far as to call it art.

"Thus far I've been a jerk—sorry."

She set the powdered cocoa packets onto the counter and smiled. "I don't get a lot of visitors."

"Would you believe I'm pleased to be among the invited?"

She stood still, buttoned to the chin in her denim jacket. The sleeves were rolled up to elbow length, and a faded blue turtleneck peeked out of her collar. He wondered what else she was wearing, whether her flesh was as chilled as his was, and what it might feel like to touch her. "Water takes its own sweet time to boil, doesn't it?" she said.

If he didn't urinate soon, his bladder might burst.

She nodded her head toward the window. "Creek's up because of the rain. Hear it? What a great sound, water hurrying over rocks."

He winced. All too well he could hear the rushing water, which reminded him of his own pressing need. He could slip outside, use the excuse of taking a look at the creek. What about the dog?

"Hey, listen, if you need to pee, go find a rock. I'll hold the dog."

"If you don't mind my asking, What do you do?"

She laughed. "You ask a lot of questions, Professor. There's a portable on the way into the compound. It's my last stop at night and first one in the morning. I keep a bedpan thing outdoors for emergencies. I've pretty much trained my body to be patient." She opened the door. "Go on. Your cocoa will still be here when you get back."

He slipped out the door behind her house. There were man-size boulders down by the creek, and he walked toward them, noting her clothesline strung between two oak trees, where his shirt had died in the jaws of the white beast. Better the shirt than me. Unzipped and standing there in the cold dark, he looked down at his penis in his hands. How completely transparent a man he was. She knew just by looking at him. Knew exactly what he was thinking, as if there were a trapdoor that opened into his predictable brain and a neon display therein, broadcasting his rudimentary thoughts. What in the hell was he doing here, stuck, hungry, cold, unable to move his car, not even the shirt as a reward for all his trouble? He needed the intervention of the gods to get himself free of this one. Wind blew down his neck and he shivered, shut his eyes, and listened to the hiss of his urine dousing the ground underfoot. People were fooling themselves if they thought there was such a thing as progress. Man was indeed small and utterly dismissable compared to the earth.

The sweet cocoa stung his lips. Outside the window he could make out the shadowy outline of the shepherd standing guard. Chloe came over and stood by him. She stared out into the trees.

"See that oak there, the one with the deformed lower branches? A great horned owl comes to it most every night. Not this early, though. She's something. Devils Hannah so bad she misses her beauty sleep."

"What about you?"

"Oh, I can sleep through anything. I only seem to need about five hours, though. Which is good, since I work two jobs."

She had a small but sturdy frame beneath all those clothes, and he remembered the pared-down version of her in the café, the real thing in the hallway outside his office. Her blue jeans were worn nearly smooth, her legs stuffed into knee-high policeman boots that amplified her steps and flattered her shapely calves. Hank abandoned the half-drunk cocoa on top of the orange-crate end table.

"All done?"

"I'll finish it in a minute." He moved away from the window, closing the distance between them in a few steps that echoed on the bare floor. His heart beat as if he had committed a felony. This near, he was aware of her femaleness tenfold. No warpaint or perfume for allure, just the honest smell of a woman who'd put in a full day's work. He didn't see any shower outside. What did she do for washing up? Drag in an old copper washtub, fill it one steaming pot of water at a time? Washcloth, plain soap, scrubbed-pink heated flesh: they were ablutions of the sort that drummed images into his mind he knew had no business being there. What could he say? He hardly knew her, other than to perceive she was masterfully adept at choosing a hearty breakfast, diminishing his wardrobe, and making him want to kiss her.

"You look like you have something on your mind, Professor."

"I wish you'd call me Hank."

"Hank."

"After this is over, would you consider going out with me?"

"Out? You mean like a restaurant, the movies?" She said the words as if rolling them over on her tongue to identify something antique or obsolete. "You've been out of this a long time, haven't you?"

"Not all that long."

She moved closer to him. Moonlight from the window shot through her hair, turning the blond momentarily to silver, aging her thirty years. She still looked good. She would age well. "You're a fairly handsome man. I might consider it."

"Fairly handsome? Am I to take that as a compliment?" He watched her hand find the tear in the front of his sweater and press the ragged edges together as if assessing repairs. His mother had bought it for him last Christmas. It was durable enough for teaching classes, but apparently not when it came to guard dogs. He would have to mention that to Land's End. Shaker-knit cotton, easily replaceable, thirty-two bucks. He caught her fingers and felt the calluses on her palm. How curious, and compelling, to hold a woman's hand and find the skin tougher than your own. "You're unlike any woman I've ever met."

"Is that so?" She looked him square in the face, unsmiling. "Kiss me," she said. "I know you want to. Go on, let's find out where we're headed." She tilted her chin.

Open brown eyes gave permission. Just like that. Do it. She didn't look away when he bent to her face. All the way down to her lips he was thinking, There have to be logical reasons why not to do this. Think harder, Hank. It is nine-thirty on a school night and here you stand, holed up in some canyon shack with no phone, no heat. You haven't eaten since breakfast, and what about your car, hood-deep in muck? Outside, a white wolf stands sentry, and here before you is a woman who has wrecked your wardrobe and can apparently read your every thought. But if you walk out that door now, you will turn forty-three, forty-four, and all the way up to eighty, regretting not kissing the horse girl in the canyon shack on that cold January evening when you lost your car to the earth. He pressed his mouth to hers. There was a thin ridge of dried cocoa in the corner of her lips. His tongue began there, tentatively tracing the contour of her full upper lip. Her mouth was still, as if listening to all his had to say. Just when he grew fearful that she was merely enduring him, and he began to pull back, she answered his kiss with her own. Her tongue was small, hot, and sweet, and it moved deliberately. When she slid it in between his lips, he felt each nerve ending leap upright. They stood there a while, touching each other in nonthreatening places, all that clothing between them, two disparate strangers gathering courage, shivering, saying hello in the old common language.

Six months ago, when Hank regrettably allowed Karleen to coax him into her Mondrian designer sheets and pillowcases, she'd handed him a beribboned wicker basket filled with individually packaged condoms; some—though he really didn't want verification—were supposed to glow in the dark, others purported to be mint flavored. She'd executed the maneuver in a blasé fashion, much as he imagined Chloe at the Wedler Brothers Café might pass packets of saltines to accompany a bowl of chowder. The condoms were manufactured in assorted colors now, with various textures and hides to them, though he'd read the books: plain or nubbed, it didn't matter to women. He'd laughed at Karleen's preparedness at the time; she'd countered with a bit of secretarial wisdom: *Remember the ant and grasshopper?* Now, as Hank Oliver sat on the sofa bed watching Chloe remove her denim jacket, he wished he'd had the foresight to pocket a few of Karleen's stockpile. Here came the boots: one, two, and underneath them gray men's socks with a red stripe, socks she tucked into the boots as if embarrassed they were hers. Dammit, Karleen didn't need that many, and he, foolishly, had fiddled his way into this season quite empty handed.

The transistor radio hummed sad Hawaiian guitar, he couldn't make out the lyrics—another somebody-done-somebody-wrong song. Presage? Omen? The fire she'd laid in the oil-barrel wood stove was starting to put out some heat, thank God. She was down to her underwear now, the plain, garden-variety white cotton kind, nothing fancy, yet nothing could be more alluring than the honest truth of her body, the hard ridges of her stomach muscles as she bent to shove the boots under the bed, the swell of breasts threatening to spill from the bra cups. She turned toward him, her profile chiseled and stark in the shadows. "You're still dressed. Did I miss a cue?"

"We need to talk."

"Sure." She settled herself Indian-style in the center of the bed, and the springs of the cheap mattress creaked. "You going to tell me you have a wooden leg?"

"Nothing like that." He ached to touch her skin. It was gleaming in the lamplight. Beneath the bra her nipples were pressing against the cotton, and he wanted to palm them, kiss them, study up close what looked fascinating from far away. "It's more what I don't have."

She took a corner of the blanket for her feet. "You're afraid I'll give you some kind of disease? I don't blame you. Wonder if in the next few years people will start carrying doctors' affidavits. I have one on my horse, to prove he's up to date on his vaccines when I take him to shows. Well, when I used to take him to shows."

"It isn't solely my concern. What about you? Aren't you worried?"

She shook her head and stuck a leg out from beneath the blanket, poking a toe into his belt loop. "Last man I slept with was a board-certified veterinarian who pretty much screens skirts for a living. He always used rubbers. That was well over a year ago. If it makes you feel any safer, I tend to do this about once every other decade." She worked the toe through his belt loop and tugged.

"Aren't you wondering?"

She laughed. "You couldn't kiss like that and be contagious."

"Kiss like what?"

"Careful. Honest. Like a guy whose candidates always lose."

"A year is a long time. Don't you get lonely?"

She shrugged, and he watched her breasts lift and drop ever so slightly with the flexing of muscle. "You mean horny. Don't you think sex is kind of overrated? I used to think I wasn't any good at it. Then I figured out it took more than just slapping bodies together. So I'd rather do without than feel crummy after."

Hank lay down next to her in the dark, still fully dressed. He stared at his Rockport Pro-Walkers, muddy and ruined from the tree adventure, but the laces still double-knotted from morning. "You have a lovely body."

She leaned up on one elbow and reached through the sweater tear to locate his shirt buttons. "I'll bet you do, too. Guess I'll never find out until I get past the armor. Want to help me?"

To Hank it felt like a long, slow dance, one he'd forgotten all the steps to. But that didn't matter; she could lead. There was the vague recollection of a time before all this, his job, the faces of students, their uncorrected papers that tried to make the most of the least effort, the moment he felt the wheels of the Honda sink into mud all the way to the axle. Then the tentative kiss at the window, and the twisted branches outside, his sanctuary oak, which an owl called home. His own hesitation seemed absurd in the midst of this very promising present. Clothes all gone now. The slight wind through the makeshift cabin lifted each hair on his body. Not a cold wind, exactly; the wood stove was cooking. Strong arms circled his chest. He reached up behind her and fumbled with the bra; where was the catch? She guided his hand back to the front. "Here, it undoes in the middle. Right here." Sure hands traveled and parted his thighs, creating a space in which to fit her own body. He opened his eyes and studied her above him, the angle of arm connecting to one hand which was parting the lips of her labia, positioning herself to allow him to enter. It was happening so quickly. He drew one hand up, touched his thumb to the moist delta of flesh between her legs, was both shocked and entranced at her readiness. He could feel her blood pulse under the skin he touched and was afraid he would come before they began to move.

She reached for his hand and drew it to her mouth, tasting herself, which caused the blood in his pelvis to throb painfully down the length of his shaft. He would come. He had to look away. Think of mathematics. First her left leg, then the right one, straddling him, corralling him beneath her muscles. Sixteen times eight point two was. . .

She rocked over him, letting the head of his penis graze her. "You like this?"

He made a sound, inarticulate, quickly covered by her kiss.

"Good. Then hush."

With a single calculated pitch forward she guided him inside her, arched her back, breathed out harshly, then settled her body down, nestling her face into his neck, where she closed her teeth gently on his whiskery flesh. He felt the tips of her breasts press into his chest, and his hands cradled the sides of them, the impossibly soft flesh. He tried thinking how afraid he'd been, hugging the hard branches of the oak tree. He pictured his department chairman with his ingratiating Cook Islands tan and that silly gold chain he wore around his wattled neck. From there, he visualized shower mold. A hideous polyester sports jacket he'd worn in high school that had cost him the affection of a plain girl who admired his brain. Herb Alpert and the Tijuana Brass, that awful, awful music. Day-old trout in sunlight. Anything to make time stand still, to keep him from crossing the threshold of inevitability. But she knew that too, and showed him no mercy, digging her heels in as if he were just another horse to be broken, his cock straining to spill free inside her narrow passage, she softly laughing when he felt his eyes roll back and the shudder travel down the entire length of his body. Blinded by his release, somehow for the first time in years, he sensed the primal notion that he was *home*.

Out of his near sleep, he felt her rise up again, rock to life on what was left of his dwindling erection, her hips rolling and insistent until she came, too, crying out. Her cry was unearthly in the small room, part confusion, part bewilderment, part angry loss and sudden recognition. Her arms and legs tightened around him again, the heat of her body nearly stinging. He didn't move, didn't reach down to help her, she didn't seem to want or require anything beyond that. Let her find the way. Then a smaller shudder coursed through her, and she cried out again, her second orgasm acknowledged by the howl and scratch of the dog outside the door.

She fell forward on him and sighed. "Oh, Hannah, just quit!"

He could feel the fluid of his ejaculation leak from her onto his thighs, gluing them together. She yawned loudly in his ear and drew the sleeping bag over them. He was afraid to sleep, afraid not to, and wondered briefly if he was dreaming her, the cabin, the entire evening.

He woke once in the night. It was still dark out. She was not in the bed. She sat on the counter, knees drawn up to her chin, feet pigeoned inward. She held a lit cigarette, the blue smoke making a nimbus around her head. He watched as she smoked the cigarette down to the filter and dropped it into the basin. He could hear it sizzle out in the sink water. The mattress underneath him was dotted with dampness and particularly lumpy in the region of his left shoulder. He lay there silently and watched her take and dampen a scrap of his torn shirt under the pump handle, then reach down between her legs to clean herself. He had never seen a woman do that before; he just assumed they took showers, some nondescript and utterly private ritual men weren't allowed to witness. She blotted herself and rinsed the rag out, folded it over the sink edge, and shivered once before returning to the bed. Slowly, she edged in so as not to disturb him, but he turned and let her know he was awake.

"I was watching you."

A gritty scream tore through the silence, and the dog let out a yip. Hank scrambled to his feet, his rekindled erection wobbling in front of him like a cardboard sword. "Jesus, what was that?"

She laughed and pointed to the window. In the branches, he could see the outline of the owl silhouetted in the tree and settling into familiar territory. Hank had the distinct impression it was looking directly at him.

Three hours of sleep gave the dawn a psychedelic sheen. The bare oak's branches dripped dew, and the creek that sounded so loud in the night proved to be no more than ankle high when he walked down to inspect it. Her idea of breakfast? *I think there's an apple around here somewhere.* She was businesslike as they worked to extricate his car, backing her truck up, checking the hitch twice. Hank felt like he'd camped out, though he knew that twenty minutes of driving would deliver him to his old world. He listened to the sucking sounds of wet mud reluctant to give up the grip on his bargain Kleber tires. Chloe hung her head out the window of the old Chevy truck and watched, rocking the Honda free inch by sluggish inch. It went so slowly that Hank was ready to give it up, hitch a ride into town with her, and call a towing service, but she wouldn't hear of it, and soon enough the earth groaned and his Honda reemerged, looking as if it had been down in the trenches for an entire world war.

"Now!" she called, and he set the planking beneath the wheels before he unlatched the tow hitch.

"It's done."

She circled the truck around and yawned, then whistled for the dog. Hannah made a low noise in her throat—a warning—as she passed by Hank, then navigated the leap into the truck bed. He thought better of attempting to pet her. *She's letting me know who's in charge, and how much she does not appreciate sleeping outdoors while a stranger sleeps in the warm bed.* He watched them go down the road until they were out of sight—a white dog and a girl in an old truck. He was lightheaded with hunger, yet every cell in his body felt gratified.

Chloe waved. No words, just a gloved hand and the crooked smile he had already memorized. They hadn't talked much this morning, hadn't even decided on a time to get together again. The wind hit his neck and he drew his collar up. She was gone, the highway had her.

Asa Carver made it into the office first for once. Hank performed a quick room check, but neither the new Mrs. Carver nor the old one was here, so that wasn't the reason.

"Morning, Asa." He smiled at his colleague and set his breakfast down on the desk top: fresh blueberry muffins from the bakery, a wedge of sharp cheddar from the deli next door, and an extra large cup of cocoa with marshmallows already melting into a sugary suspension on the surface. The cocoa he'd gotten downstairs in the snack shop from a sleepy cashier who'd undercharged him forty cents, and who said, "Well, la ti da," when he told her so.

Carver smirked. "Powerful hunger, Oliver?"

"So?"

"Did I say anything?"

It was happening—that uncontrollable grin spreading over his face—and Asa Carver would take this to the mat. "Oh, hell," Hank said. "I am hungry, hungrier than I've been in years."

Carver reached across the desk and helped himself to a muffin. The blueberries were fat explosions driven into the risen dough. Carver broke open a muffin and deposited an entire pat of butter inside, then licked his fingertips, one by one. "Okay," he said. "I want to hear every detail. Length, Duration. Her favorite position. Moaning, screaming, that stuff doesn't interest me, but the rest does, you lucky bastard, and you'd better not leave anything out."

The muffin Hank held warmed his hand just as her breath had. He thought for a moment how her hair spilled down into his face as she straddled him, with just that soap-and-water scent that would forever after remind him of her. He could taste the spicy tang of her skin from their collective exertions, and recall that moment when he was wonderfully confused as to where her skin left off and his own began. The hollow of her collarbone; why hadn't he told her how superbly she was constructed? The cold water cat-bath they'd shared this morning that ended them up right where they'd begun, and made him feel weak and spent just remembering. He was determined to keep her to himself, Asa's prurient interest be damned. "Well," he said. "I don't tell tales out of school, but I'll give you a nibble. She drives a truck."

Asa's laughter echoed in the hallway. Hank liked the sound of it.

CHAPTER

11

Oh, the trouble with sex wasn't that it made you lazy and thick tongued, though it did both those things all right. Chloe hung her apron on the deer horns above the pay phone after her shift and headed out to her truck before Kit could come by and catch her. No, it wasn't anything quite so simple. What it did do that was truly dangerous was make you lose the necessary edge for survival. It made you nicer than it was safe to be, and preoccupied with the oily peacefulness spreading through your hips, slowing your life down to a *mañana* tempo. Worst of all, it opened that dreaming doorway to a hopeful future, and hadn't she been wise and slammed that one shut after Fats died? An eight-hour shift and she'd screwed up six orders, one of them that lady mayor who'd lately taken a shine to Rich's black bean soup— a new record. The mayor politely insisted it was fine, she liked the vegetable just as well, but after she left, Rich let Chloe have it in spades, and she did what she had to do—she stood there like a three-legged cow and took in his acid sermon because she needed his money more than she needed her pride.

"Read your contract, Morgan. Waitresses are not allowed to think.

Just leave your brain in the back room and smile at the rich people. Now, you want to go back and ask table three *one more fucking time* whether it's sunny side up or scrambled, or should I send Lita?" Lita, quaking behind the register like a kicked pup, would she even last the week?

Waitresses *weren't* allowed to think, and that was a pretty good idea, because the longer you thought about a job like this, the less you could stand having to get up each morning and do it again. The truth was, last night was muddying up her judgment, so she couldn't exactly tell Rich where to take his egg orders when it was her fault. A lovely aspect to hindsight, that; about as useful as getting gut shot and coming to the slow, painful understanding that you were going to die anyway, it was just a matter of time and place, and the circling birds' welcoming committee.

She turned left onto the boulevard and was immediately swallowed up in a tangle of cars. No one was going faster than fifteen miles per hour, for the apparent reason that there were too many people on the planet, and while all of them wanted to live within bicycling distance of the beach, none of them actually wanted to be caught dead working the pedals.

It dogged her every day, the exhaust fumes and the million-dollar asphalt beneath expensive cars covering up honest dirt. Sometimes when the city crews were replacing pipes, they would cut down into the dirt, and the primary oxide both shocked and delighted her. Fossils were coffined in the road just eight inches beneath the blacktop, forgotten. Sometimes she found them in Hughville, broken remains of calcified clamshell, even that far inland. She wished she were back in the canyon, where a walk through rocks and cacti worked better than good dope for letting you forget a city existed, and sometimes netted you a potsherd in the process, a piece of dull brown clay that once held somebody's breakfast.

A sleepy Hannah rode shotgun today, her chin resting on the open window as she surveyed the passing cars. Chloe eyed her sorrowful muzzle and gave her ruff a friendly scratch. "Bones Jones, old pal, how about a kiss for your friend in crime?"

The dog sighed and moved closer to the window. Jealous of Hank having spent the night, that's what it was. She was getting old and wasn't happy with a cold night in the wild. The silent treatment was most effective when she wanted to drive a point home. Chloe would stop and buy her some prime rib bones from her butcher friend in El Toro; that would ease her peevishness. Then they would take a sundown walk through the canyon, up past the creek and to the cliff side, sit and watch the sun collapse onto the hills, spilling its brief display of color before the blue dark took over, share a beer like the old days, the two of them alone, as well matched as a team of shires.

What of the slumber party guest? Chloe smiled to herself. He was something. Muscles ached with that rare pleasure of sexual exertion, the best kind of aches to have. Good sex made you foolish, toned up the muscles, but stunned the brainpan. Those small nuggets of memory gleamed in her consciousness. A college professor—good lord, she could hear Fats laughing from the grave at the very idea of it. And he was so polite, good-looking, too. Now that she had a firm grip on getting her life back in control, it would be a shame to ruin it over some guy. Still and yet. Earnest, upright, a solid, considerate lover. Last night took place in the dark, suffused with mood and intention long before they hit the sleeping bag. It had made her shiver, though the wood stove was stoked and ticking. *Just stop.* What they did wouldn't survive examination in the light of day, would shrivel up what happened like an albino newt exposed to sunlight. No, good stuff was doomed to hide in the dark places. Such sweetness, likely never to be repeated. Better that way. She'd probably scared him off with her moves anyhow. Run back to that college, gotten himself an Rx for penicillin—just in case—wouldn't go lending his clothes out any more, that's for sure. But oh, those flashes—this morning, his body above hers, his face so focused the pleasure gave him a grimace. What if she saw him again—just supposing. Could she handle another complication?

Gabe would be the first to point out how foolish it was to entertain the idea. Lying in his arms in the back office all those months, he'd confided in her, treated her to his personal philosophy of wisdom when it came to the school of love. "Chloe, you aren't like other women."

"How's that? I've got the same number of appendages and orifices."

"That's true, and let me go on record as saying they're downright lovely. But trust me, you wouldn't be happy tied down, milking yourself dry to feed the barnacles children all become, no matter how good you treat them. Or living off some guy's paycheck. It'd drain you."

"Doesn't seem to bother Cynthia."

He shook his head. "Sister, you don't know the half of it. That woman nets over thirty-five grand a year just in residuals from her trust fund. That's her play money. If it wasn't for that money and most of mine, I might add, she'd be out my door so fast scouting some other poor bastard with a Mercedes you'd think one of those Midwestern tornadoes had passed through. Just my luck she fancies horses. We leave each other alone except when it comes to raising those daughters we were foolish enough to conceive."

He'd shown her their school pictures. They were beautiful girls—faces a little pouty, russet hair, and big, sleepy hazel eyes surrounded by thick lashes, eyes the same color as Gabe's. "Nobody said I had to stop working or breed if I got myself a partner."

He stroked her blond hair back and bared her neck, then spent a while dizzying her with those kisses that came close to art for all they lacked in heartfelt emotion. "Hell, I don't know, you're like the last honest one of the breed. I've convinced myself you were put on earth to walk alone, and now I'd hate to see anyone try and cage you."

"Guess I'd better hightail it out of here then."

A tug on her shirttail, followed by smooth fingers tallying every rib. "Doesn't mean you can't shower a lucky few along the way with attention."

There was more than a certain amount of truth to what he said, sure, but she had been around the block before him, and loved Fats all Fats would allow. After he died, what it boiled down to was one lonely hike. Hannah helped. The horses, too. People *could* mesh lives. Didn't have to be marriage necessarily, just togetherness. Maybe companionship was what it was all about. Maybe not. Maybe the kind of blindness brought on by multiple orgasm caused the whole institution to be invented in the first place, because something that powerful. . . it was natural to want to own it, recall it, press on it whenever you wanted to feel good. Fats used to say: "Darlin', you can whip a mean horse into a cowering kind of obedience, but sometimes you take away more than the vice."

Something to that effect. How scary to think his words were fading from memory. He never spoke much. But if Chloe did something that pleased him—cleared a five-foot fence on the Canadian thoroughbred, or took the trouble to hunt up sweet basil and fresh oregano to make him homemade spaghetti sauce—he might laugh out of pleasure, deep and rumbling, causing the pearl snaps on his shirt to flash and jiggle. He favored fat cigars and the ever-present smell of gin—*that's my juniper berries*—would filter up through the smoke and laughter. His hands, the left one broken so many times the fingers lay crooked, and his only ring, that mother-big hunk of Bisbee turquoise set in a silver horseshoe. This April he would be dead two years. The idea drove a fist into her sternum. Some people had Jesus, and some others believed in the reincarnation of souls, as if the human spirit were nothing more than recycled gases, but Chloe believed only in the here and now: what she could feel beneath her fingertips, between her legs, and thumping hard in her heart.

Hank. Such an old-fashioned name for a man with college degrees. What business did she have sleeping with him like that, no more than a torn shirt and a cup of store-bought cocoa mix to go by? He was a walking plot to an old movie starring Jimmy Stewart. In this movie nobody took out the garbage or got a yeast infection or had credit card companies breathing down her neck for unavailable sums of *dinero*. When she was a girl she used to dream about that kind of stability, ache for arms to hold her on the long first nights when she didn't dare toss or turn in one of the new foster homes, just lie there praying for enough of her own self to imprint on the sheets to make them feel comfortable. *Be careful. You are not an easy child. Walk alone. Darlin', you can whip the meanest horse into a cowering obedience, but you lose. . . .*

Hannah snapped at a passing insect, and Chloe hung her arm out the window to signal a left turn. The blinkers on the truck didn't work, hadn't in a decade. Not that anyone paid attention in this traffic anyway; it was a free-for-all when a space opened in one of the lanes and a power game not to let anyone in, because to be nice meant you were fair game.

Set your priorities, girl. When was your last menstrual cycle? So sporadic she couldn't remember, so scratch that worry off. Gabe said she was too malnourished to support the delicate balance required for the monthly release of an egg, *but that didn't mean not to be careful*. Especially now that working at Wedler's she ate a regular meal every day, and she could tolerate raw vegetables again. Hannah could get downright tubby off the scraps Kit was sneaking her. She'd buy a package of condoms and stick them in the glove box. Think ahead, if there was a next time. Abortions cost money, more than the professor's shirt, you could bet the farm on that. Damn it all, she wouldn't be pregnant, she'd will it away, she'd never have children. Women could do that. They had the power to create life and the power to deny it as well. The shirt had to be replaced. She'd buy one, tell him, yeah, sure, sex was nice, one heck of a party hat, and you did it, buddy, you made me smile, but time to get real, back to work for both of us, good-bye, *sayonara, vaya con* whatever you believe in, Professor Folklore. Then back to work. That was all there was to life, really, work, and if it made you happy, you were lucky to have it. She wouldn't get rich off the horses, but she would get by just fine, thank you, she and Hannah.

So why did her bones ache and her very skin feel like an envelope for a hive of angry bees? Fucking town, fucking traffic, *fucking*—get to the truth of it. Goddamn that shirt. She hit the gas, cut across four lanes of traffic, and took the freeway exit to the mall.

Inside her canvas bag, the shirt label rested in her wallet. She found a parking space with a shade tree and cracked the window for Hannah. "Don't you go working that door handle," she warned. "Stay in the cab or some Big Canyon housewife will think you're a rare white coyote and try to make a coat out of you."

Chloe tucked her T-shirt into her jeans and ran her fingers through her hair, twisting it into a knot at the base of her neck. Though she hated them, she slipped on sunglasses someone had left at the diner, because the mall with its designer clothing stores and jewelry shops always made her feel the need to become invisible. She took a breath and braced her weight against the heavy glass doors to step inside that other world. Cooled air and Muzak blared through the bright sunlight directed through skylights onto the crowds. Forty-foot palms abounded, and impossibly green ferns rested in sterile dirt no weed could ever hope to penetrate. There was a motor-driven waterfall gushing over what looked like the rippled corrugated metal used to anchor Thin Set when laying bricks—arty. Someone had thrown pennies into the pool, the old make-a-wish, but what kinds of wishes could a fountain like that possibly grant? People moved by in droves, blank-faced and clutching bags, three or four to each arm. Three-thirty in the afternoon. It was after Christmas, way after. What was going on? Was she the only person who worked for a living?

She stopped to look in the windows of an art gallery. Not much to fall in love with, but there was a Charlie Russell oil of three tired cowboys on buckskin horses, the yellow dust of a desert storm swirling at their feet. In the background of the canvas, a notch-eared palomino wearing a rope halter was being ponied back to camp. The damaged ear reminded her of Amánte, one of her geldings off the old lesson string she'd been forced to sell. One by one, she found the best homes she could secure, and told herself not to look back. Amánte was lesson-sour and aging, past twenty, not much to look at. What's that ding in his ear? kids would ask, and she'd weave fables for them: He used to belong to a big-game hunter, and that's where he'd lay his shotgun, you know, like a sight. Really? Oh, sure. Absolutely. She'd let him go for one-fifty, plus the Circle Y saddle. It was the only one that fit his touchy back. She could have gotten two or three hundred for the saddle alone. The man who bought him kept assuring her he was picking out a first horse for his daughter—wanted something bullet proof— but she didn't trust anything at that stage of the game and cried herself to sleep at night wondering if it might not have been kinder to make an X and put a bullet through the horse's skull. Saying good-bye was like abandoning a retarded child in the middle of traffic. Amánte knew. He never minded loading into a trailer before, but this time he turned his head and stared back at her, whinnying all the way down the drive onto the highway. He knew.

Her throat closed up. She wanted to buy that painting so that she could secrete it away in a closet where no one else could see the nicked ear accusing, *You left me when you said you wouldn't.*

A pale young man in an expensively tailored tan suit brushed against her arm. "Western art is a wise investment. Would you like to see some Remington bronzes? Reproductions, of course, but still worth consideration."

Already he had turned away from the Russell. He didn't feel anything when he looked at the painting. He didn't notice the tears welling in her dark eyes, or the shame she couldn't dismiss. Already he was dividing up his commission: this much for the car payment, this much for the condo, this much for the cocaine that got him through the week.

"You ever been on a horse?"

"Excuse me?"

"Riding. Horseback."

He looked at her, confused, then smiled. "Russells are expensive, but certainly one way to approach a serious collection."

She pointed to the saddle girth in the painting. "See the way he painted that, and the bridle, how the horse's mouth isn't yanked up by the bit, just wrinkled, the way the cowboy's hands give a little slack to the reins? That man knew about horses. You couldn't know that if you didn't ride them."

"How interesting. Well, he was a vanguard as far as colors went. I find that quite compelling in his work. Did you know some of the early Western film scenes were patterned off specific paintings of his? Isn't that just astonishing?"

Sure it was, considering most Westerns were about as phony as election year speeches. She didn't ask the price. It would be one of those amounts with an elephant's nest of zeros. She set her gaze and marched through the storefront, past the splattery Leroy Neiman sports figures and the starving Flavia urchins and beggars. Bypassing the slick fossilized marble front of Bally shoes and the granite mouth of Tiffany's, she stood before Nordstrom's—three solid floors of inventory capped by skylights and stained glass. Likely as not, the men's department had this shirt or one of its near cousins.

"Eighty, ninety bucks," the snub-nosed clerk informed her, flicking a thumbnail on the edge of the label. "You want me to throw this in the trash for you?"

"No, I want it back."

"Oh. Really? Here. That particular men's line is one of our finest, but the shirt you're describing we haven't carried for six months. Can I show you something similar?"

"If it won't cost me to look."

He led her to one of those torso mannequins, square breasted and tapering to a waist as narrow as her own. It wore a cream-colored silk shirt that closely resembled the one Hannah'd eaten. Her attentive clerk quickly laid a paisley tie across it. "Smashing, don't you agree?"

"The material's different."

"It's sand-washed silk—the latest fabric."

"Does this store have a layaway policy?"

He squinted as if he had been stung. "Credit department is on the third floor."

"Got it," Chloe whispered back to him. "Write me up a slip or something. This one's near enough to what I want."

He did, all the chitchat suddenly dissipated. She had thirty-seven dollars in her wallet left over from the fifty in tips for the week. If she put a third toward the shirt, she would have to get by on next to nothing until her paycheck. Gas tank was full, she'd done that this morning, and it would last until Monday. She could take Hannah out on the trail this weekend and let her hunt up cans. Ask Kit to pay her for a block of lessons up front. Robbing Peter and lying to Paul, but it would be the first step toward distancing those tender hands. She scouted the floor for the stairway; she didn't like the feel or smell of elevators.

She wasn't the only one buying on time; in front of her an older couple held hands, waiting patiently for their turn behind three young giggling girls. The man's hand rested in the small of the woman's back. Chloe looked at the wedding ring the man wore. It was softly scuffed, as much a part of his finger as the knuckle.

Margaret and Ben Gilpin behaved like that well into their sixties when Ben died. Chloe watched her final set of foster parents in the kitchen, mornings she'd come down for breakfast, dressed for the public high school in the most neutral clothing she could muster from Margaret's ideas of high school fashion. Ben made the coffee. He set out the tiny calico pitcher of cream for his wife and the saccharin tablets in the medicine bottle. You're not fat, he'd say, but Margaret faithfully used the tablets instead of sugar. She bought Ben English muffins and a special brand of marmalade that came from the deli, imported from Scotland. Just like that man's hand on his wife's back, they were small acts of kindness that contributed to the comfort of the household. There was passion, too, Ben's hand patting Margaret's behind as she stood at the counter stuffing pork chops with the chopped apples and bread crumbs he loved. Some nights when she was supposed to be studying, she'd hear Nat Cole on the stereo and catch them dancing in the living room, all the lights turned off, they knew their way around the room so well. She'd watch from the stairway, her chin resting on the curved banister, wondering how in creation they could still find the courage to make love when death had robbed them of their children. They held on to each other as if love were an offering they alone had discovered, infinite in possibilities.

Her senior year they said okay to her working afternoons at the stables so long as she kept her grades up, and that meant above C's. When the failing notice for Civics and Economics arrived, Ben took Chloe for a drive in the turquoise Apache. They drove in silence, Ben rubbing his chin once in a while but not looking her way. Chloe said nothing until he threw the transmission into park and shut off the key. They were in the parking lot of the county courthouse.

"Ben, are you going to have me arrested for failing Social Studies?"

Spring air wafted through the old truck's cab. Ben didn't play the radio. Chloe looked the county courthouse over, one of an anonymous gray cluster of buildings connected by walkways. Around the corner was Orangewood, which despite the brick-and-glass exterior, still felt like home.

Ben said, "You're smart, and you've never crapped out on us in school before. I'm just wondering if this doesn't have something to do with finding out where you came from." He reached beneath the seat and brought out an envelope. "Now, I've got some papers from Orangewood, and the picture that was in your file. You're nearly eighteen and you have a right to them."

Her heart hurt; the muscle was stoning her.

"I'm mixing this all up, aren't I? If you want to find out, I know how to help you, and this is the place to begin."

"I'll pull the grade up, Ben. Put the papers back where they were."

"Sooner or later—"

"Later, all right?"

Lawyers and secretaries moved purposefully across the walkways in the noontime rush for lunch between court cases. Ben waited, the papers in his lap. Chloe waited, fear bristling the hair on her arms, adrenaline flooding every pore until she felt hot enough to levitate. Finally she took the photograph from him. It was of a sober-faced two-year-old sitting on top of an old Shetland pony, one of those photos everyone had taken as kids; a man brought the pony door to door and posed you, your mother paid him money. Some weeks later he came back around again minus the pony, with a sepia eight-by-ten made personal with hand-tinting. Here, the painter had done a careful job on the red bandanna, but gotten her eyes wrong. He'd painted them blue instead of leaving them brown.

"Most everything was blacked out on the papers I saw," Ben said. "But from what I could make out, her first name is Belle. If you ever want to know more, all you have to do is ask. Margaret and I've discussed it, and we understand that it's natural you'd want to know. So don't you go worry about hurting us, you hear?"

Ben's bare face did it to her. That crewneck white T-shirt and zip-up Windbreaker jacket. She cried noisily, like that two-year-old must have when she was left off at the Children's Home later that same year. The crying scared her when it wouldn't stop. She grabbed Ben's hand. "Help me," she said between sobs. "I can't get my breath."

"Here now," he said, becoming very businesslike with a handkerchief. "Let's see what we can do." He held on to her for awhile, one big arm around her shoulders, beefy hand patting her awkwardly. "Let's take a little walk."

He locked up the truck and made her walk three laps around the park while they drank regular Cokes. "A good snort of sugar will settle most shock. Learned that in the Pacific, when I went to fight for this country." He pointed out small birds and squirrels racing through the shrubbery. "Sometimes I think we got it all wrong, kid. Take those crit- ters in the bushes—they sure look happy to me. Maybe we just live too long. Maybe that's the problem."

"Ben?"

"Yes?"

"You've been a great father to me."

"I tried to give you breathing room."

"You did that, and more."

When she was back in control, he handed her the keys to the Apache. "Here," he said. "It's all yours. I was going to give it to you anyway. Now's as good a time as any. Happy graduation, early."

That was when he'd bought the motor home to retire in. He drove it to work. Ben Gilpin drove short hauls for Elder's Meat Markets, a small chain that specialized in servicing restaurants and delis. The trucks were painted a deep burgundy with gold-leaf letters on the side and a phone number. When Chloe stopped by the bowling alley to buy cigarettes from the vending machine on the way home from school, she saw his truck parked outside and looked in to see if he were catching a quick afternoon game or a beer. He was kissing a dyed-auburn barmaid across the wet bartop. Her lacquered fingernails wove through his thick hair like giant pink lice.

"Always tell the truth," he'd told Chloe the day she walked into their home. "I'm not saying it will get you out of trouble if what you've done merits punishment, but in the end, folks will respect you for hav- ing the guts to say it, and you'll respect yourself."

The elderly couple standing at the front of the line now arranged to have their packages sent to Florida, where, they took great pains explaining to the clerk, they had seven grandchildren, four in college, one—uttered in hushed tones usually reserved for the priesthood— *pre-med.*

What was a wedding ring anyway? A piece of metal hammered into a circle that could just as easily be melted down into money.

"I want to buy this shirt," Chloe said when it was her turn.

"How do you want to pay for it?"

She fanned out her tip money as if it were a Reno jackpot. "Same way I do everything. One week at a time."

* * *

The note was nailed to her door, right through the center of the yellow lined paper. Three words: *See me. Hugh.*

She took it down with shaking fingers. Rent all paid, could he kick her out just like that? He could. He had done it before, when people got rowdy or arrested. She'd been quiet. Kept everything neat. Cut the brush back from the cabin without being asked, trucked her trash out to the dumpster at the stables. Hannah hadn't bitten anyone. No guests besides the professor. That was it. She dropped her stuff inside on the unmade bed and let Hannah take a long drink from her water bowl. She made the bed up tight, tucking the corners of the sleeping bag and fluffing the single pillow up as much as it would fluff. She swept the floor clean. Hannah looked at the broom curiously. "Relax, I'm not going to hit you. We'll take the long way," she told the dog, "and pretend it's just a walk we're taking for as long as we can."

His barn home loomed like a mansion on the small hill up from the main road of "Hughville," as the press liked to refer to the compound. Back in the eighties, Hugh started painting the woodwork, but the passage of years weathered the exterior back to its original cedar, grayed now to driftwood. Woodsmoke poured out of the chimney. The curtains were drawn. Hannah whined. "I agree one hundred percent," Chloe said, "but it's always best to face the music." She rapped sharply on the door.

Hugh Nichols dressed Western—XXXX Stetson, Circle T shirts, and Wranglers bunched up over Justin Ropers—the genuine cowboy's boot. Like a politician out to befriend the prairie, he never said a harsh word, just pushed with that big smile until his foe got the jitters and tripped up all by himself. His graying hair was slicked back, and the laugh lines in his face were etched half an inch deep, but they were hard lines that contained as much rage as they did laughter. No Rolex glittered from his tanned wrist, just an old Timex with a cracked crystal he swore was the most reliable watch he'd ever owned. He didn't look wealthy. Two hundred thirty-six acres of the canyons belonged to him, though, deeded outright from his father, and he held no paper on so much as one square inch of it. Owed only the taxes, which for largely undeveloped land were manageable. T. S. Winters, Winter-Haven Homes, and the Stroud Ranch Company each had master-planned communities designed for his acreage down to the blueprints and miniature models, just waiting for Hugh Nichols to slip, meet with an unfortunate accident, or outright give in to greed. He sat tight, but he wasn't silent. Any chance he could, he shot his mouth off about the land rapers and the lack of consideration for the working man, the few remaining wild animals, and topped the heap with a cherry—saving the environment. He got a lot of press. It drove the developers to maniacal measures. They came down on him hard, in the form of harassment from the county health department, sending social workers in to take a look at the tenants' children, several private investigators working on finding dirt in his past. There'd been some threats. He'd been accused of defamation of character when he'd called the county supervisor a third-world toady—he'd run against him as a write-in candidate twice, and lost. While he likened his renters in Hughville to the family he never had, the press waffled back and forth, not quite sure how to see him. An activist working for the homeless seemed too good to be true, but a slumlord profiteering from the meager rents he charged, well, that was hardly news in this county.

Hugh stroked the broad skull of his Irish setter, Gillian, who stood by his side. He invited Chloe in. "You unhappy here, darling?"

She held on to the glass of iced tea he insisted she take and stood by the wood stove, a Swedish job, pretty red lacquer but not terribly efficient in terms of heat. "No, Hugh, just the opposite."

He stared at her, his black eyes looking her up and down.

She shifted her weight from one foot to the other. "I pay you my rent in cash, so it can't be that I bounced a check. What'd I do wrong? You going to tell me?"

"Nothing, sweetheart." He laughed. "I know you had a visitor last night."

She colored. "I won't deny it."

"I have my spies out. They keep me posted. You want to stay to supper? Chilies rellenos. Stuffed and ready to go. Course, you have to fry them. My cook quit on me."

"Sure. I can do that. I'd like to."

He waved her toward the kitchen, then followed. Gillian stretched out by the fire, her red fur shining like oil paint. Hannah waited outside on the step where Chloe had left her; she wasn't quite sure she liked Gillian, and Chloe didn't want to find out.

The chilies were stuffed, breaded, and ready for frying. The cast-iron skillet was oiled up, ready. It looked like Edith had gotten pissed off and left halfway through dinner preparations. Chloe wasn't going to ask what about. She was going to cook up the chilies, unfold Hugh's napkin, tuck it into his collar, and listen closely to whatever he wanted to say. "You mind if I switch on the radio?"

"Hell, no. I Super-glued the tuner right to KIK," he said. "Saves time. No sense arguing over music."

"That's one way to look at it." Chloe fried the chilies and sliced up a papaya somebody had left on the counter. There was a basket of eggs, too, from which she extracted whites for the rellenos. One or another of the families here kept a few laying hens. Unlike the rest of them, Hugh had electricity, a real refrigerator, and the electric stove. Uptown. She put the remaining eggs away in the refrigerator, set the spare yolks into a small bowl for Gillian. There was a half gallon of milk in there, some orange juice, bagels, plain yogurt. No beer, no wine. Good, if Hugh fell off the wagon, she didn't want to be around. She served up the chilies on his pretty stoneware plates and unfolded the napkins. "Wash your hands," she said. He did.

They ate the chilies. Chloe took one, ate slowly, sipped the iced tea when her tongue felt like a live flame in her mouth. Hugh wolfed three, toyed with a fourth, tried to interest Gillian in it, but it was clear the dog had been hoodwinked by Mexican food before.

"What do you think?" Hugh asked. "Can a dog be that smart?"

"I think a dog can definitely be that smart."

"Seen Wesley lately?"

"Couple days ago. He looks exactly the same."

"Blue plaid shirt and the old trout bolo tie?"

"That's about right."

"He ask you to marry him?"

She smiled.

"You should, you know."

"Everyone around here seems to want me married off more than I do. It's a funny thing."

He looked at his mangled chili and mashed some runny cheese with the tines of his fork.

"What's the trouble, Hugh?"

"I've pissed some people off again, shooting off my big mouth."

"Tell me something new."

His eyes were wary now. "I'm afraid this time they might come after me."

"What did you do?"

"Nothing I can go into. Better you don't know. Forewarned is forearmed. That's all I'm going to say. Keep your door latched."

The chili sat hard in her stomach. "What kind of trouble are you talking?"

"Probably nothing. Just best you keep your ears up. Now about this visitor. Anybody I know?"

"Just a mistake I fell in lust with for about eight hours."

He chuckled. "Well, we're all a little guilty of that now and again. Keeps life interesting. Say, he ride? Coyote hunt coming up. We can always use new blood."

"I don't think so."

"Then he's not for you. Smart girl, Chloe."

"I think I'm a little too old to fit in the girl category anymore, Hugh, but thanks for making my day. Let me do up these dishes."

He didn't argue. Went back to his BarcaLounger by the fireplace and stared into the flames. Chloe squirted the Ivory liquid into the sink and sank her hands into the hot water. Forget diamonds, Hawaii vacations and dinner out; luxury was hot, soapy water. She wished she could duck into the bathroom and take a shower, but would never ask such a favor of Hugh. That wouldn't be fair to the others. She took showers at the college sometimes, early in the morning when the locker room was empty, otherwise she made do with cold water and a washcloth. Hugh was dozing now. She dried the plates and stacked them on the countertop where they'd been when she came in. No reason to get Edith more riled up, thinking another woman had been in her kitchen. Edith took good care of him. She worked as a nurse in the emergency room saving the lost causes and then came home to bigger problems. Before Edith, there were Valerie, Suzanne, and one other whose name she'd forgotten. Chloe shook some Science Diet into a bowl for Gillian, added the yolks, and watched the dog nervously grab a few chunks and race right back to Hugh's side. That was a purebred for you, insecure and skittery.

Hannah led the way home, her white plumed tail as good as any flashlight. There was a fair moon, too, three-quarters silver shining down on the earth. Chloe took her time through the back trails, hugging her arms to herself, craning her neck to make out the stars in the night sky. No matter what dire nonsense Hugh spewed, she had her job, a tank of gas in the Apache, a good dog, and one lame horse she loved—a full house. She spied the cabin through the small grove of oaks. A feather of smoke rose from the chimney. Hannah's hackles went up. Chloe froze. He was back, that professor. In her house. He'd come back.

He was asleep in her bed, his naked shoulders pale and childlike above the edge of the sleeping bag. She willed her breath to be quiet, took a few minutes to study him, taking off her jacket, hanging it on the peg by the door. He had the fire stoked up so high it felt as if they were braising in here. His clothes were folded neatly on the foot of the bed. Socks rolled up inside his shoes into perfect balls. Honestly. He'd come bearing gifts, apparently; laid out on the counter was a whole barbecued chicken wrapped in supermarket plastic, a tub of potato salad, a bottle of some pale wine, and a corkscrew—corkscrew wine— probably he knew all about wine, what went with what, what didn't; cared about it, too. There was a package of chocolate cookies, a Stanley thermos still warm to the touch, an old soft blanket that looked like it might be cashmere, a new down pillow—that had to cost some major bucks—and a case of canned food for Hannah, tall cans of supermarket Pedigree. There was also a round of sharp cheddar from Trader Joe's, fresh-ground coffee in a silver bag, some croissants, and a jar of hard, coffee-flavored candies. Jesus, was he always this hungry? He certainly slept like the dead.

She stacked the foods away, folded the bags, worried about the chicken and the potato salad spoiling, finally wrapped them in several layers of newspaper, tucked the bundle into an old milk box outside, and put a couple of bricks on top to keep Hannah from investigating. When she shut the door, he was sitting up in her bed, awake, smiling.

"Hello," she said. "I don't recall inviting you back."

"You didn't." He pulled back the covers. She could see his body now, much clearer than she had last night. It was nice enough to look at, not too hairy, lean, a little soft in places, but not where his penis emerged from the tufts of reddish pubic hair. Not there. There it was arced upward in definite hardness. She looked at it, then up at his face.

"Will you come here?" he asked. He waited for her answer, but didn't once look away or down, held her eyes with his own. All the shyness was gone. "Will you?"

Trouble on the horizon, as Hugh intimated—well, it never seemed that far behind. At any moment it could reach right out like the fist of God and shake up your life like it was a cheap *maraca*. Well, if you shook it yourself, you could make your own music.

CHAPTER

12

"If I get to pick when I have to die," Chloe said, "now would be my first choice."

"Why?"

She pressed a finger to Hank's chest, turning the damp hair around her finger. "Tell me it gets any better than this."

"Let me show you." Hank pulled one of her hands up behind her as if she were his prisoner. Her free hand splayed out on the mattress, keeping her balance. His weight anchored her naked body beneath his. "Don't talk," he said, and covered her mouth with his.

After a dizzying number of athletic positions that each offered their own sweet distinction, they now lay across the thin mattress, heads leaning over the edge, bodies completely spent, lungs sucking cool air where it rose upward from the wooden floor. His cock was still inside her, but only technically, diminishing and retreating millimeter by millimeter. Their tandem breathing slowed from ragged gasps to smaller inhalations with each passing moment.

She'd begged him—*Come in that way—I like it—need* it was more like the truth—but few other words passed between them since she'd said yes. It was all movement. Her legs bent outward into triangles; his hand grasping her flank to draw her into him; both of them standing on the cold floor as he bent her over; her breasts filling his hands; the slow drag of his tongue on her shuddering thighs. The bedsprings' sweet rusty song creaked like an elderly cricket. She'd asked him to push, harder; he'd countered—Don't want to hurt you—but she hissed—Just do it, hurry—and he evolved from the gentle, cautious lover of the night before to the barely contained one of this evening. Then, at the last, he fairly pounded his orgasm into her. She could feel each thrust bruising her cervix. Wanted that. Wanted it hard and tee-tering on the edge of painful. Needed to feel each smack against her body to believe it was real. And once he quit staring at her and began to concentrate on his own pleasure, she felt unbridled, and free to move. Everything real dissolved into the hazy periphery—smoky wood stove, the abject howls of Hannah, displaced by a stern command to the floor, the memory of other hands on her body—Fats, Gabe, the barely remembered others, all gone, replaced with the rapid blossom-ing of white heat that began so small in that tiny knot of clitoral flesh Hank reached down to stroke. It wasn't hard work after all, it just took the courage to ask, the willingness to face the fear of what she knew she needed. She came against the press of his fingers, a solid wave of rippling muscle and raked breath. Only afterward, when he released her arm, did she feel the small aches of strained, well-oiled muscles, the press of his hand against her damp flesh. She was a little ashamed then to have forgotten him so entirely, but he didn't seem to notice. Kissed her neck and said, "Well, my goodness." Made her smile.

Now he pulled her close. They fell back onto the mattress on their sides, stunned heaps of exhausted flesh. Reaching down, she pulled the sleeping bag up over them. They lay quietly together, feeling the minutes tick off against their cooling flesh.

"So where's my movie date?" she asked when words would come out orderly. "Where's my dinner out?"

His voice warmed her ear. "Didn't I bring you dinner?"

"With enough leftovers to last until April."

"Now I suppose I'm to be punished for getting carried away."

"Hannah will get lazy."

"It's my resolute intention to win that dog over to my side."

She smiled. "We'll just have to ask Hannah about that."

"Chloe?"

"Yes, sir."

"Nothing. Just the sound of your name. What's your middle name?"

She breathed into the pillow. "Don't have one. Just the first and the last."

"Your birthday, then."

"Don't know."

"Sex this good kills brain cells."

"Maybe slaps them around a bit. Seriously, I don't know. My last set of foster parents insisted I pick a date, any date. So I took August thirteenth."

"Foster parents."

She tapped her finger across his lips. "Don't try and fool me. You've probably been quizzing Phil Green like some sleazy game-show host. Know all about me."

"I might have asked a few things. Nothing quite so bad as you make it sound. Why August thirteenth?"

She rolled away from him and stared up at the ceiling. "It's a long month. No major holidays. Thirteen gets a bad rap. It seemed like a good date." She yawned loudly, twice. "Breaks things up."

Hank pulled her hair back and traced her collarbone with his fingertip. "Can I take you out to dinner on August thirteenth?"

"I don't know. It's a long way off. You might change your mind."

"I won't change my mind."

"I might have plans."

"My plan is to keep you busy enough from now until then that I become your plan."

"Oh, really? That busy?"

"Yes. Here." He cupped her breast with his palm. She felt the sated flesh begin to arouse again. "And here." He palmed her sticky thigh. "Movies. Restaurants. Dinners. Et cetera."

She sighed. "Hannah and me. We're both a little gun shy."

"So we'll go slowly."

"Will you tell me about what you teach?" she asked. "I don't know much about mythology. Is it *dios y relampagos*, like Constantina blames for all her bad luck?"

"Who's she?"

"The wife of a friend of mine. She's always making charms and crossing herself." Chloe yawned again. "She's going to have a baby."

"I'll tell you a little bit."

She turned her head and his mouth was at her ear.

"That owl outside your window? There's at least seventy separate legends about him. Birds are never just birds in most cultures."

"How so?"

"Depending on who you listen to, they can be considered a harbinger of evil or a blessing. Egyptians believe the vulture to be a sign of fertility, and the owl to represent stillbirth, or possibly death."

"Sounds like they got that one backwards."

"Maybe, but if you ask the Yucatán Indians, you get an entirely different response. To them the owl was a household figure, entirely female. Representing fertility. Power."

"Did it help with the dishes? I'm kidding. Go on."

"Shall we keep on with birds?"

"Okay. Hawks, crows, cranes, ravens; I see them all from time to time when I'm out there riding on the trail. Tell me their stories."

He did, drifting into a sleepy lecture. Beneath his arm, she listened for as long as she could, lulled by his voice humming against her ear.

They settled into sleep together—no false starts into the darkness interrupted by jerking muscle spasms, nothing but a swift kick from two tired bodies who had worked out the kinks of several years in a few hours. Hank swiftly entered a dream where a brace of white horses galloped in unison, pulling an empty chariot over a plain of clouds in a cerulean sky. Lovely animals. Sweet breath of timothy, shining coats, and impossibly curled manes over arched necks. He would go wherever they went. Just to follow like a wastrel seemed ambition aplenty.

Chloe dreamed her recurring dream of steep hills, the one where she worked hard to ascend the rocky earth only to slip at the apex to the rubbled bottom, shins bloody, and her breath knocked out of her rib cage. She had to try again, or whatever was in pursuit would find her. Then she cleared a hill and surfaced in a small, dark forest with the clear lapping of a spring-fed creek covering her dark hooves. Her dappled hide blended into the aspens quaking in the sunlight. There were no words, just the sense of drinking deeply with a rough tongue at the shimmering water. Smooth mossy stones lined the bottom. Darting silver fish wove the current like fine thread. Skating insects dented the water's surface, chasing each other from sunlight to shadow. Her belly was heavy with the fawn she carried. No alarming scents nearby, not a one. If she needed to, she could rest awhile here, even sleep. It was good earth. There was shelter. It was safe.

The rain stopped just after sunrise, as if it couldn't compete with the sun. The highway asphalt steamed as Chloe drove Hank down the narrow streets to the library in Silverado where he'd parked his Honda.

"You college types always park near a library?"

He got out of the truck and came around to her side. "It does lend a sense of the familiar."

She chuckled. "If you lose your nerve, you run in and commune with the Dewey decimal system?"

"Library of Congress now. They switched."

"Whatever. You walked all the way from here? That's a couple of miles, Professor."

"I was an Eagle Scout. I wanted to see you."

"Well, you saw me." She folded her arms on the window edge and watched him search his pockets for keys. "I find this interesting. Here I know what kind of sounds you make when you come, all your little sexual secrets, but I don't know how old you are, where you live, whether you have any brothers or sisters. Don't you think that's strange?" Hannah's face was pressed against the rear window, making big slobbery smears on the glass. "Hannah, for Christ's sake quit."

He took her hand through the open window. "I'm forty-two. I live in the beautiful city of Irvine, in a condominium that is virtually indistinguishable from its neighbors. No brothers. I had a sister who died when she was seven, and I was five. Her name was Annie. I don't remember her, though I do have a picture of us together. I loved my grandmother, my mother's mother, who lived in Northern Arizona, and taught me to shoot a rifle, and also how to make jam. My elderly parents live in a retirement community a little south of here. My mother does needlepoint. My father is a dreadful golfer. My favorite color is blue. May I see you again tonight?"

"No."

He shoved his hands into his jacket pockets and sighed. "How about next Friday—we could have dinner out. Lots of people do that on Fridays, you know. It doesn't mean anything except the hungry enjoy a little company as they get fed." He reeled her in by the shoulders. "Please?"

"Fridays I work late at the stables. I have six horses in training to exercise. Lessons to give. I'm there early all day Saturday and Sunday, and so tired when I get home I flop into what's left of my bed. Weekends are workdays for me. Always."

"I could come watch you. I enjoy horses."

"I get nervous when I know someone's watching me."

"You didn't seem nervous last night."

"Shows what you know. Let's take a little break until say, next Monday? Maybe you could get a few things done at home."

"I'm caught up, really."

"For starters you could try changing your oil and filter. That poor car smokes. How long has it been?"

"I have no idea. I let the garage take care of it."

"And they probably charge you upwards of forty bucks. Jesus. It's not that hard to do, honestly. Don't you worry about your engine?"

"You can do it if you like. Or you can teach me how. Will you let me kiss you good-bye?"

She ran her hands through her hair. "Against my better judgment."

They kissed. Thief—he had her heart right there in his pocket. She ought to charge him. Ought to take the money and stuff it into a coffee can to ease her woes when the day came that he treated her heart the same as he did his car's engine—shabbily, taking for granted it would always turn over when he put his hand to it.

That kiss escorted her through the morning. When a small grease fire broke out in the kitchen, she whistled the refrain to "Don't It Make My Brown Eyes Blue" and let Rich rage all by his lonesome. She took Lita out back for a cigarette and found out she was divorced twice, with three boys nearly grown up, one in the navy and two at various colleges. They made a pact to stand united against Rich's mood swings. Wasn't anybody's fault but his own he forgot to clean the pit. She collected twenty-eight dollars in tips, nearly twice the usual. Now she could afford to gas up the truck, lay fifteen aside toward the cream silk shirt. She felt all right, maybe even a smidgen proud, if that wouldn't jinx anything, rap wood. Last night Hank had planted a smile on her face. The smile elevated her from plain, tough girl to self-assured woman. Customers didn't know exactly what they found so alluring about that smile, but they were laying down dollar bills and plenty of quarters.

One storm and a week later, the bridle trails were dry enough for travel. They were no longer lazy circling miles behind the metal barn dotted with prickly pear and scrub oak, eucalyptus and buckthorn, shattered granite and an abundance of leave-her-right-there rock. In some cases the old trails were firmly blocked by barbed wire and rail fencing, in others sheared off to a bright red wound of earth leveled for impending development. Chloe paid little mind to these fences. She dismantled them like an archaeologist, careful to disturb as little as possible, and put them back up on her way out. Developers' markers she considered fair game. She swung her body down in an agile arc to uproot fluorescent flags from trees so often that Absalom would squeeze up close to them without her leg cue, like an old milk horse with a twenty-year route fixed in his mind.

"You could get in trouble for doing that," Kit said. "That's like stealing."

"More like justice." Chloe undid a lipstick-pink belt from an old half-dead oak. She tied the streamer alongside three others on Absalom's throatlatch. "Parade pony," she said. "Now we have to gallop to get the full effect."

"I don't think we exactly *need* to gallop," Kit said warily

"No, but the horses do. You see, Kit?" Chloe kept Absalom in check, Elmer pinned alongside, so that the old gelding wouldn't get any ideas about turning tail for home. "Horses have to get out and blast once in awhile. Just like people. Helps them to remember they're capable. Rejuvenates the spirit."

"Like shopping for earrings?" Kit offered.

"Somewhat. Maybe more like singing." She remembered Hank's cries in her ear the last time they were together, as if something were loose inside him, something difficult to own.

"We could sing," Kit insisted. "I know a shitload of show tunes. Wilhelmina wanted to be a singer once. You want to do side one of *South Pacific*?"

"I can't speak for you, but my singing would spook these horses."

They crested the small canyon. Ahead of them five miles of flat graded fire road led to Old Camp, Chloe's personal favorite of the canyon trails, blocked off to keep the range cattle from straying. The story went that the trail had been a favorite of outlaws in the days of the settlers, before Stroud Ranch weaseled it out from under the Mexicans. Along the way there was a small lake, usually dry, but this time of year it would be deep enough to attract all manner of bird and animal life. Chloe stilled Absalom for a moment, turned to look back over the cliff. From the top of the hill the valley spread out with grace, like God's upturned palm. The bulldozers hadn't made it down that far yet and she hoped they never would. Along the streambed two families of deer were visible. She nudged Kit. Kit liked that—baby animals with their mothers. She'd like running the horses, too, once she relaxed. Only her fourth lesson, but for this trail ride Chloe had put her in a big Western saddle. She'd only let her run on the flat. Old Elmer was capable of a short blast at best. Worst-case scenario: If she fell, it would be into soft dirt. Kit wasn't happy about it, but she was wearing her regulation helmet and the long-sleeved jacket Chloe insisted on. It wasn't more than four feet to the ground off Elmer anyway, but she took no chances.

Beneath her Absalom's trot fairly danced with anticipation, sensing what was ahead. "You'll see, Kit. This is about the most fun you can have without boys, I swear on all your mother's Indian gods. The only thing I can compare it to is a real good kiss. Now shorten up your reins and take hold of his mane with your free hand. Heads up—you don't want him staring at the ground, do you? Ready?"

"No!" Her voice sang out, dwindling away beneath the sound of hooves. Beneath them, the deer startled and disappeared into the brush.

She cued Absalom for a right lead. Buted up, he moved like a circus horse, a slow, deep rocking-horse canter that Chloe held in check until she was certain Kit was under control, then allowed him to extend into a decent gallop along the fire road. He pressed his dark neck forward and snorted through those huge, comma-shaped nostrils to sieve the air. The plastic ties whipped through the air. Chloe rose up in her stirrups so that she hovered above her old Crump saddle, feeling the whistle of wind between the leather and her many-times-mended chaps. Elmer looked a little choppy at the canter, but his heart was in the chase. Hannah ran alongside, pinning her ears back to some dim memory of long-ago escape. We'll run long and hard, and with luck, the horses will appreciate their suppers, Hannah will sleep through the night, and Kit will be too exhausted to lift more than a forkful of dinner. She'd show Kit how to measure and mix grain for Elmer tonight. He deserved a fat scoop of sweet feed as a reward for playing by the rules. The blue dusk was coming up, filtering through the forest, daubing away the skeletal framework of expensive homes being built on the ridge above them. They didn't matter. The sound of hooves thudding into earth was as grounding as a drumbeat. She wondered what Hank was up to at this moment—did he play racquetball after he finished teaching those college kids which god threw what terrible curse on this or that mortal? Did he watch specials on public television, sitting on a clean white couch and drinking more of that corkscrew wine? Maybe he read the *Wall Street Journal*, or Shakespeare. He'd kept his word— stayed away for a week—was he at this very moment—please God, no—back at her place again, waiting for an encore? Absalom stumbled, and she clung to his neck, caught herself, and slowed him down to a trot. Elmer, eager to please, slowed too.

"Oh, my God," Kit said, her breath wheezing. "Oh, my God. When can we do it again? When?"

"Look," Chloe whispered, smiling. At the edge of the lake an enormous pale bird stood and lifted wings that spanned a good four feet. "I'm no bird expert, but I'd swear that's a crane. It's beautiful, isn't it?"

"So?" Kit said. "Big deal. Some extra large bird gets lost."

"Someone told me this Indian legend about cranes. Supposedly, they're messengers to the spirit world, and when you see one, it means they're considering taking you along."

"Who told you that?" Kit said. "Your *boyfriend*? My dad told me some guy's been nosing around you at the restaurant."

Chloe didn't answer.

Kit threw her head back and screamed, and the bird startled, then shook its huge wings into a gangly flight.

Absalom shied, and Chloe had to reach up to grab his neck to quiet him. "Jesus, Kit. Why'd you do that?" she asked. "Why?"

"Big fucking deal," Kit answered. "It's just some damn bird."

"Who has just as much right as you do to be on this trail."

"Sorry."

She patted her horse's neck. Kit had been doing so well.

They walked the horses single file up the skinny trail that led to the back entrance to the stables. It would be dark when they returned, and both horses needed cooling down and serious grooming before they got their dinner. Abruptly, Absalom leapt sideways and crowhopped up the hillside. "Easy," Chloe said.

"What the hell got into him?"

"Maybe your yelling."

"I said I was sorry."

"He probably picked up a stone. Hang on, I'm going to dismount and take a look." She gathered her reins and led him back to the trail. Her boot stepped into something squishy. She knelt and wrinkled her nose at the meaty scent. It was the recent remains of a cow, backbone protruding from the tough red hide. The head was missing, severed neatly at the neck where white bone jutted up and tendons curled into a purplish knot. Surrounding the corpse was a mess of congealed stinking blood that Hannah immediately rolled in, the ultimate dog perfume.

"Aw, Hannah, don't." Too late.

"What is it?" Kit demanded. "Should I get down, too?"

"Stay on Elmer." Chloe tried to push the carcass to the side of the trail, but it was too heavy and not yet completely stiff. Her boot unearthed a roiling mass of organs and insects. She thought she might lose it then, but she held it in, turned Absalom's head away, and coughed until the gag reflex left her.

"Somebody killed that cow on purpose," Kit said. "Why the fuck would somebody do that?"

Chloe mounted her horse and they rode up the trail in silence. "We don't know for sure, Kit. Maybe it died all by itself." She wanted to believe that. Tried it out a couple ways in her mind.

"So where's its head? Huh? Can you tell me that? Is this what those weenies who worship Satan do? Kill a defenseless cow?"

All night the dead cow haunted her. It was windy following what the radio insisted was the "last rain of the season, folks. Spring is just around the bend." Forty degrees outside and before morning the temperature would drop low enough to frost the bare trees. Branches scratched the cabin and kept waking her up. She'd had a late-night feast on take-out food—sharing the last of the chicken with Hannah—tucking the bones into a napkin on the countertop to throw away in the morning. She finished off the meal with a slab of cheese and one of those coffee candies Hank had left, brushed her teeth at the sink, rinsed her toothbrush, and put it into its case. She fell asleep, almost dulled into dreamlessness by her full stomach.

A short pass of light across her face woke her. She had less than a minute to separate it from dreams into a reasonable explanation before the door flew open, ripping the cheap lock from the wood frame. She pulled the sleeping bag to her nakedness and tried to focus into the waving flashlight beam. Hannah dived, snarling, for the light. Chloe cried out for her to stop, but over her own voice she heard the yelp of animal pain as the flashlight came down hard on Hannah's muzzle and silenced her.

"You—on your feet!" the voice insisted, and she stumbled from the bed without question, clutching the bedding to her body.

She couldn't see him. The urge to run overtook reason and she lunged forward into the darkness toward the voice. Hannah whined in pain. "What the fuck did you do to my dog? Who are you? What do you want?"

She felt his hand grab her upper arm and roughly twist her away from him. Then she heard the crackle of police radio and struggled against his weight to keep her balance. "Hannah!" she cried, and heard the scrabble of toenails against the wooden floor.

"Stand still," he said. "Jesus. H. Christ, stop pushing me or I'll have to deck you."

The hell she would. She dropped the sleeping bag and shoved with all her weight against the stranger's hands. She wound up her right arm and sent a fist toward his cheek. It didn't catch him square, though, dammit. He reeled backward but managed to hang onto her.

"Hannah! Where are you?"

The man pushed back, one well-trained shove that sent Chloe pivoting on her right leg, slamming into the trunk, losing her balance entirely, and going toward the floor. She heard the snick of bone in her ankle and knew dully before the pain registered that it was broken, that she wouldn't be able to get back up.

"Hannah," she said from the floor, but even without benefit of light, she knew her dog was gone.

Now he said, "Police. Just stay where you are."

She did. Others came, with larger flashlights. One of them held a battery-powered lantern that lit the room in a dirty yellow glare that stung her eyes. They were deputies from the sheriff's department. Dark jackets and holstered guns were this evening's costume. Most of them looked to be right around Hank's age, save for the one who had pushed her; he had to have been nineteen or twenty years old, no more than a boy. He stood there pointing his flashlight at her, tracking her eyes, making certain the light kept her blinded. He was breathing as excitedly as if he had just finished a satisfying bout of energetic sex. She didn't like that. Didn't like the way he looked at her. The asshole had smacked her dog with no provocation. Her full bladder wanted to burst, but that discomfort was a distant cousin to the fire in her ankle.

"Nice ass," one of the older cops said as he entered the cabin. "You want to tell us what happened here, Elliot?"

The boy's face turned cool. "What could I do? She sicced her attack dog on me. I think it was a pit bull. Fucker ran away. Then she tried to deck me." He rubbed his side. "I think the bitch might have cracked my rib."

"We'll get you an X ray."

Chloe studied their faces and made no move to cover herself. Her twisted ankle was in another county. Bare ass on the wood floor and she wasn't even cold. *Trouble on the horizon.* It was weeks ago that Hugh had tried to warn her. What if Hank had been here? What was this all about? Hannah. Oh, Hannah. Run fast. Don't come back, girl. A man who'd use a flashlight on your skull would have no hesitation about a shotgun.

A woman officer entered the cabin. She had a kind face, mouth set hard as if she found this job less than pleasant. She took a look at Chloe and made a sound of disgust deep in her throat. "You're a bunch of sadistic jackals," she said, and they laughed. She bent to Chloe. "Let's get you up and some clothes on."

"I want to know where the fuck my dog is!"

"No need to get excited. Take my arm."

Chloe slapped her away. "Look, he broke my door down and hit my dog! She's licensed, I was sleeping, this is my house. What the hell is going on here? Am I under arrest or what?"

"Your house!" the boy scoffed. "Squatter's cabin tapped into the county water line, no sanitation services, you name it."

"Calm down, Elliot."

"It's true!"

"We're not here for that."

"This time."

The woman officer sat back on her heels. "There's been a drug bust. I'm afraid Hughville is being shut down. We're taking everyone in for questioning. You included. You might want to keep your mouth shut for the time being."

"But I didn't do anything!"

She read Chloe her rights from the Miranda card. The officers went through her things, upending the gallon jars of dog food and grain onto the floor. Down went the chicken bones into the goulash they created.

"Could you please pick the bones up? An animal could choke on those things. Please?"

They ignored her. It was no longer her house, her things, at all.

They opened her clothes box, and the dark-haired one lifted a pair of her purple underpants up by a finger for the others to see. "Well, well," he said, as if it were a misdemeanor to own colored undergarments. Chloe shook with rage. When he kicked in the latch of her trunk, she screamed.

"Let that alone! God damn you sons of bitches, get out of my house!"

"Something in here to hide?"

The men gathered around the trunk and riffled through the contents. "Just a bunch of ribbons," the one who'd pushed her said. "Trophies and ribbons and a bunch of old pictures of some old geezer riding horses. Letters and pictures. Nothing important."

They fluttered from his hands into the growing pile of refuse. Nothing important. Fats Valentine's legacy was in that trunk. Every last memento of their time together now lay in a heap underfoot.

"You want to get her into the wagon with the others?" the dark-haired one said, "or are we going to take all night?"

"Aren't you going to let her get dressed?" the woman asked. "Get a robe, at least?"

He lit a cigarette and flung the match out the hole where the door had been into the darkness. "For Christ's sake, Jeanette, she probably doesn't own a robe. Just get her into the truck. Quit with giving me the lip, *comprende*?"

Chloe clutched at the sleeping bag as they pulled her to her feet. "My ankle," she said softly. "I think it's broken."

The boy who'd hit Hannah circled it with his palm and squeezed. Chloe saw a palette of white lights and felt bile rise in her throat

"Looks all right to me."

She felt his hands slide down her backside, brush needlessly against her breasts.

CHAPTER

13

Kathryn Price's fuchsia-and-black aerobics top and tights clung to her body like a wet suit. One of her legs draped over the chair in front of her. Her thigh was tensed like a joint of particularly high-grade meat. A shameless New Age seal, Hank thought, catching himself looking. With a practiced impassivity, he managed not to respond to his students' designed-to-provoke attire. They wore miniskirts and cropped shirts the approximate size of postage stamps; bralessness was *de rigueur*, all that power-of-my-sex posturing at the junior college level. When he heard of on-campus assaults, read the sad details in the school newspaper, made the obligatory announcements to classes about not walking alone to parking lots, he wanted nothing more than to herd the girls together and cover them so completely no one would go after that hopeful flesh and damage them. But it was a touchy subject; one wrong word and you were subject to feminist diatribe, turned into a blubbering chauvinist defending your own well-meaning words. He shook his head, passed the paper on Medusa back to Kathryn. He'd given her a B+. It would have been an A paper except for her indulgent lapse into free verse at the very end. *This is a conclusion?* he had pencilled in the margin. "I liked what you said about the snakes," he told her. "Very original thinking."

She grinned at him. "Mr. Oliver?"

"Yes?"

She pointed to his midsection. "Did you know your shirt's unbuttoned right there in the middle, three whole buttons?"

He blushed like a fool and felt the heat spread down his neck. "So it is. Thank you for pointing that out."

She laughed. Gentle Cora had overdone her paper, as usual. Painfully typed on an old manual, and footnotes! Good lord, they were accurate, and done according to the MLA style sheet, but it was work beyond junior college expectations, and he waffled between telling her to move on to university and worrying about his own dwindling enrollment. William Strauss hadn't turned in a paper, and neither he nor Carlos was present today. Wherever Will was, Hank hoped he wasn't out biting the heads off bunnies or piercing yet another hole in his beleaguered ear. Odds were the paper would surface in his mailbox with an inventive excuse, pleading for mercy. Whatever his classroom persona, William cared about his grades—pulled solid A's. Hank worried more about Carlos. The boy had hinted about money difficulties, so maybe he'd gotten a job. Larry Kolanoski's paper—where're the nitroglycerin tablets—had come in on time and had obviously been typed by someone else, for it was without typos, but wading through Larry's *whoa, dude,* semantics was as pleasing as it had been pulling his Honda from the Hughville muck that first visit. His students—he looked at them in their Formica chairs, chatting carelessly among themselves, eating potato chips, and swigging down soda as if it might empower their blood for the battles of adulthood. At their age he had been alienated from such ease.

He studied his books and took long walks by himself in the foothills in back of his parents' house, his pale skin frying in the California summer, only lizards and occasional quail for company. Summer evenings, he'd climb the trees up behind the Greek Theater and listen to the live music wavering through the night air, never dreaming he could simply have invited a girl, purchased tickets, belonged to the crowd. He was a loner. In his parents' house—where they ate dinner on TV trays in front of the Magnavox watching Huntley and Brinkley—there had been a certain amount of comfort and trustworthiness that the newsmen would be there night after night. Now? Now he wanted to take Chloe everywhere he went, see the sameness of his world made new through her eyes—as corny as that sounded—grow used to her laughter, watch her at work, delivering plates or training horses, whatever she would allow him. He dreaded weekends, when she wouldn't see him at all, and became anxious for the workweek to begin, when she would see him. *Hold on, there, Hank. It will keep.* Wasn't it just his luck?

The coward's way out—he showed them a videotape of Joseph Campbell being interviewed by Moyers on public television instead of lecturing. He tried not to do that too often, didn't want to earn the reputation of being a slacker whose classes were easy to sleep through, though Larry Kolanoski could undoubtedly sleep through jackhammering. It didn't appear to be drugs. The boy just looked tired and underfed. Probably spent his lunch money on surfboard wax. He had the same dark circles under his eyes that Chloe did, the morning he'd seen her outside his office when Phil's mare died, as if all-nighters were a regular part of his itinerary. Hank had the Intro class after this one, where he just needed to pass back a few more papers, and then he thought he might stop off and see the colt, try to detect if Phil was making any headway with his motherless child. It wasn't as if he had anything else to do this Friday; Chloe'd been firm again, and he knew it would do no good to argue with her. *Well, Joe Campbell, Mr. Follow Your Bliss, what do you do when your bliss says sorry?*

He folded his arms across the desktop and wished he were back in the ramshackle cabin in her foldout bed and more specifically, deep inside her. Their lovemaking made life seem worthwhile. Had he been a polite fool all these years, fretting over women's pleasure before his own? With Chloe, things unfolded rather simply, astonishingly. Up there on the screen Joseph smiled broadly and related the Irish tale of the prince of the Lonesome Isle, going after bottles of holy water to heal his ailing queen of Erin. Campbell's grin grew lusty as he moved past the shaggy pony driving the Prince unharmed through the forest of poison trees. He nearly cackled describing the twelve beautiful maidens. But it was a holy business that drew the man to his chair's edge as he described the queen of Tubber Tintye, reclining on her golden couch, surrounded by the well of fire and the prince's determined leap. *Upon my word, I'll rest here awhile.* "The prototype of grace," Campbell said. "Mother, sister, mistress or bride, the answer to every hero's quest. . . ." and he held his hand palm up, as if the mystery was thoroughly beyond his understanding as a mortal man. Campbell had died less than two months later, heart failure. At the moment of departure, did how really matter?

Asa Carver opened the classroom door, and the entire class looked up into the sudden burst of sunlight. He waved Hank over.

Hank met him at the door. "Keep on with the video," he told the class. "I'll be right back."

They stood outside in the covered breezeway. Wind tossed eucalyptus branches overhead, and seed pods smacked the cement with regularity. The air was cool. "What is it, Asa?"

"I saw your girlfriend."

"What girlfriend?"

"Don't be coy. The Valkyrie."

"Here on campus? Is she with Phil?"

"No, on the news, Henry. Channel seven."

"You yanked me out of class, Asa."

"I'm serious. I went to Fedco on my lunch hour and looked at wide screens, but I didn't buy one, dammit. Lost my *cojones* when I thought of Bethany's reaction. Anyway, she's been arrested. The whole town up there got raided. In the words of the authoritative Christine Lund,'alleged drug bust.'"

Adrenaline shot through his limbs. "Chloe doesn't use drugs."

Asa shrugged. "What can I tell you, buddy? I was there when she changed clothes, too. I'm a washout when it comes to anniversaries, but I never forget a breast."

"She was naked?"

"It was a scene right out of Bosch, the police unloading them in the county transfer in the dead of night. They threw some kind of sheet over her, but not before America's viewers got a peek. Guess they went in when everyone was asleep. Hey, where were you, anyway? Thought you two were an item now."

Hank started to walk toward the parking lot, but Asa stopped him. "You're teaching a class, remember? You'd better finish it or cancel. Otherwise they'll have your ass."

"You're right." He went back to the classroom door, placed his hand on the knob, and felt the cool steel beneath it.

He let them out forty minutes early. Shoved a big fat discussion topic like the hero's quest down their throats and then cut them loose until Monday, when they would have forgotten everything except which parties they'd attended over the weekend. Didn't bother to assign reading or to remind them of the next paper due. He gathered his briefcase and went to the department office to request a cancel notice for the rest of the day.

Judi, a senior secretary covering three departments, was a pal of Karleen's and eyed him warily. "Oliver. I know you. I've worked here twelve years, but I don't remember ever writing one of these for you. What is it? A family emergency?"

A pipeline straight to Karleen, whatever he said. "Emergency root canal," he told her, tapping his cheek.

She gave him a sympathetic smile. "God, those things hurt like original sin, don't they?"

In his office, he took the battered Yellow Pages down from the shelf and found listings for the sheriff's department and the county facility. Hughville was on unincorporated land, where jurisdiction got a little fuzzy. He started dialing.

Yes, she was in the jail. Yes, he could post bail. Four hundred dollars. Four hundred dollars? The charge was assault. Assault? Assault with what? I don't really know, sir. Come on, a weapon or what? I think she struck an officer. Hit a cop? Well, different terminology for the same sort of offense. Yes, they'd take a personal check for the amount if he had proper ID. What was this about her being on TV with no clothes—We have no information in that regard, sir, but it couldn't hurt to bring her a few things. Couldn't hurt. Was she hurt? Had she been injured? Not that I'm aware of, sir. Not that you're aware of? Christ! Does that mean she might be? I really have no information in that regard, sir. No, he couldn't go out to Hughville to get her things; the compound was taped off, and all the cabins' contents were being impounded for evidence. What the hell kind of evidence is dog food and some mended bridles, I'd like to know? Sir, if you're going to use that tone of voice perhaps we'd better terminate this conversation. No, wait, please. We're very busy here. Sorry, I'm truly sorry. It's just that I've never done this kind of thing before. Well, sooner or later we all get some experience, don't we? I suppose so. There are others waiting. And release takes awhile. You want to come on down? But why arrest Chloe? Sir, I just don't have an answer for you. Can you at least give me directions?. . . .

There was a J.C. Penney's that had seen better days just off the main boulevard near the college. Hank rushed in, found the women's department and stood there surrounded by so many types of clothing in sizes both complex and discouraging that he felt panic rising like floodwaters. He fingered a few blouses to hide his uneasiness and went back to men's, found a lemon-yellow assortment of sweatshirts and pants, and chose one of each, size small, $12.99 each piece, a bargain. Underwear? How was he supposed to know what size she wore? Momentarily he was overcome by the memory of the span of her hips in his hands, the arc of her legs, the muscled flesh beneath his lips. Maybe they would give her underwear. Yes, jail had to be civilized enough to stock underwear. Jail. My God. Chloe.

The reception area of the county jail reminded him of the Price Club discount store, where he sometimes went to buy film and laundry soap and usually managed to dump another hundred dollars on unnecessary incidentals—once, a five-pound bag of Jelly Bellys he ended up giving to Karleen—*Oh God, Hank, how did you know I just love these you big sweetie come here. . . .* When you wanted a large item, tires, new speakers, a circular saw, you were issued a ticket and had to wait at a counter for someone willing to fetch it. Here people anxious to be waited on were milling around, nobody looking too closely at anyone else: *I don't have to shop here, I'm slumming.* Hank studied the glass doors reinforced with wire mesh that presumably led deeper into the bowels of the building, to the cells where prisoners were kept. There were two sets of doors, similar to storm doors up in the snow country—he'd always meant to learn to ski—the walls were painted a harsh yellow-orange; he wished he'd chosen a softer color of sweats. But it was too late, they had been duly examined, turned inside and out by the matron who took them from him. She removed all the labels, returned the price tags and pins and small bits of nylon string to Hank. He'd looked at them stupidly for several minutes before he shoved them into his pocket rather than litter the floor of the lobby. You'd think they'd at least have a trash can, but no, crumpled *People* magazines and cigarette butts, ratty vinyl furniture.

A young girl was crying by the window, and Hank wanted to go to her, to ask her what was the matter, but thought better of getting involved. She left with a tough-looking redhead he supposed was her mother, who grabbed the kid's elbow and wrenched her along toward the exit, stopping only to light a cigarette and flip off the entire building in one succinct gesture of human frustration. He sat finally on a butt-sprung tan couch and studied the detritus the girl had left behind. A half-eaten bag of caramel corn, its wrapping folded down, a *National Enquirer* with La Liz on the cover, overweight again and bedecked in likewise obese jewelry. Was the violet stone amethyst or was it garnet? There was a child's toy on the floor, an animal-decal-covered wheel with a pull string that seemed to be stuck halfway out, grimy from constant jerking. The room gave off the rancid stench of fear and bad news. He put his head into his hands and scrubbed at his face, trying to erase the oily gleam his skin took on when he was nervous. He waited, watching the clock tick off minutes, then an hour, people coming and going, sometimes a joyful reunion when they received their loved one in exchange for bail, sometimes leaving empty handed with a guard on one arm and a set frown. *Bliss, Joe. Bliss.*

Nearly three hours after he'd arrived, the matron brought her out. This wasn't his Chloe. This disheveled barefoot limping creature in traffic-light-yellow sweats was somebody else. She wouldn't look at him. She kept her eyes on the spattered brown linoleum as if looking for something she'd dropped.

The desk clerk handed Hank a receipt for his check. "Good luck," she said.

Out of habit, he whispered, "Thanks."

Chloe was standing right where the matron had left her.

He put his arm around her. She leaned against him to keep her balance. "Are you okay?" he asked.

She didn't answer. He looked down at the floor she seemed to find so fascinating and saw her right foot splayed out oddly. "Jesus, are you hurt?"

She nodded.

"You are." Those bastards had broken her ankle. Fury fueled him. He scooped her up and carried her to the doors and would have liked nothing better than to kick out one foot like John Wayne, but the doors opened automatically. He waited until they opened and carried her, not very dramatically, to his car.

In the emergency room, their intern was a young East Indian woman, very patient, overworked, and tired. She called Hank over to show him the X rays. "See the fractures?" she said in English that lilted as if it were studded with pearls. "One, two, three. These two are greenstick, but this one is bigger. When the bone twists as it breaks, a spiral fracture results. They heal slowly, and sometimes surgery is indicated. Six weeks in the cast, then six more in a walking cast. Minimum. Your wife?"

"My girlfriend." It was the first time he'd said the word, claimed ownership.

"She is mute?"

He shook his head. "No. She's had a terrible shock."

"Take her home and put her to bed. Tomorrow, call the orthopedist on this card and make an appointment. I'll write you a prescription for the pain pills. She wouldn't let us give her a shot, but in a few hours she will be feeling quite differently, let me assure you." She smiled and pressed his hand. "You can trust me on this."

Hank wrote another check. He bought the crutches they insisted she would need, put the icepacks and hospital forms into the Penney's bag. An orderly wheeled Chloe to the Honda.

Over the tops of dark cars in the parking lot, the halogen glow of lights illuminated the outbuildings, county animal shelter among them. He debated. Chloe wasn't talking; she was hugging her arms to her sides and staring down at the floor. Did that mean they'd taken the dog? Sons of bitches, breaking her ankle and letting her sit there untended—had they gone and shot her dog? Hannah wasn't exactly shy when it came to intruders.

"I have to ask about Hannah."

She started to cry.

"Did they take her?"

She shook her head no. "Ran."

It was eight-thirty now, long past the shelter's hours. Surely they didn't leave animals untended. There had to be a kennel attendant.

"You wait in the car," he told her.

There was a slot outside for dropping off animals—just like mail—but these letters were delivered to only one place and didn't leave the building. The smell of disinfectant volleyed with a thick undercurrent of urine. Mournful howls of trapped canines rang in an unearthly chorus. Hank rapped hard at the door. Surely someone was there, but no one came to answer it. He took a dry cleaner's receipt from his billfold and wrote down his name, address, phone numbers at home and work and a description of Hannah. *White German Shepherd mix. Black spot on left ear. Red collar with tags. About eight years old. Will fetch aluminum cans. Don't kill this dog,* he wrote, then underlined it. *I will pay all fines.* Underlined that twice. He stuck it between the front doors of the building, but he didn't think it would help. One look at those snarling jaws and the collar would be conveniently "lost," and for the first time in her life Hannah would be moved to the head of the class. He thought about later, after some time had passed, adopting a puppy, but knew without asking that Chloe would never go for it.

Back in the car, he grasped her shoulders. "We'll find her. Tomorrow we'll hit every shelter in the county."

Fresh tears. Hank held on. At the very least, this seemed like an improvement on the terrible silence.

At his insistence she took a pain pill in the parking lot of the drugstore, washed down with a sip of Seven-up. By the time they reached his place, she was slumped against his shoulder, groggy. He parked in his slot, studied her for awhile, noting the inconsolably beautiful face that emerged from the haggard one. Women could do that; sometimes through the deepest grief they emerged looking regal and proud. Jackie Kennedy, after Dallas. Every news photo he'd ever seen of Coretta King. He had a picture of his mother that always beguiled him—she was dressed in a black sheath, standing on the side of a road, her hands on his small shoulders—it had been taken in the Badlands. From the date on the back of the photo he concluded that Annie had only been dead a few months, yet here was his mother looking hauntingly beautiful, presumably pulled together enough to go on a vacation.

He left the crutches in the car; they could get them in the morning. He helped her out of the car and carried her to the condo. It was late, but it was also Friday night, and he could feel the eyes of his neighbors peering out from their kitchen windows.

Carrying Chloe up the stairs to his bedroom, he had to stop and rest twice. "Lord, how much do you weigh?"

"One thirty, when I'm in fighting trim. Probably one twenty now."

"Must be the cast."

She roused enough to ask him a few questions. "How much did it cost, Hank? How much was the bail?"

"Don't worry about it."

"I want to know how much I owe you."

"I'll take it out of your hide."

"Where are we?"

"My place."

"I wish I could see more of it. My eyes won't stay open. I never should have taken that pill."

"You can see it tomorrow. Actually, it's kind of a wreck right now. Beer cans all over the place. Lingerie, dirty magazines."

She struggled in his arms. "What?"

"I was trying to make you laugh. Go to sleep."

He laid her down in his bed, on top of teal blue sheets he'd gotten on sale two years ago, and put a throw pillow under her cast. Place the injured limb above the heart, as per Red Cross instructions. The fiberglass was off-white, still warm as it cured into the hardness that would heal the one, two, three fractures; her bruised toes peeking out the end were dirty and smeared with plaster bits. He wet a washcloth and cleaned them off gently, set the cloth down on the nightstand, and watched her settle into his bed.

"You want a drink of water? Anything?"

"Just the last day and a half back."

"I'm sorry, baby."

She gave a dry laugh. "I've never been anybody's baby."

"Well, tonight you're mine. Think you can sleep now?"

"Probably."

She shut her brown eyes and turned her face from him, but not before he caught sight of fresh tears glistening in the corners of her eyelids. She was here, in his bed. Something he'd wanted, argued for, and now gotten. But at what price? He wondered if he should call the restaurant, the stables she referred to. Tomorrow. He'd do everything tomorrow. Find a lost dog. A substitute teacher for her riding lessons. A Kelly Girl waitress, if there were such an animal, whatever it took. Get her a lawyer.

She cried out in her sleep, and he took her hands in his. "You're okay, Chloe. You're here with me."

Her hand slid from his as she fell back into sleep. There in the dark of the room he'd grown to ignore, he felt his universe execute a groaning shift off its axis. Her presence altered everything—caused the Joseph Cornell prints to appear cluttered and pretentious, the Eadweard Muybridge photos to reduce themselves to stilted assessments of human grace. His John LeCarré books sat thick and dull on his bookshelves, alphabetical by title, looking as pompous as rhetoric on long-dead subjects. He had, in sequence, every issue of *Parabola* since the late seventies, but in truth he couldn't recall what lay between their covers. He wondered if she would stay for awhile, or possibly longer. He had never imagined such a thing possible before; sharing these quarters with a woman, this woman. On impulse, he knelt alongside the bed and gently pressed his face to her chest. He could hear her heart, beating steadily through the screaming yellow fleece, a survivor's heart, right there beneath the breast he had held in his hand a few weeks ago. Now he cupped it gently, felt ashamed at himself for doing such a thing while she slept. He knew he should get up, eat something, go sleep on the couch, for Christ's sake, let her alone after the last twenty-four hours, but just like that first night, seeing the owl outside the window at her place when he hadn't wanted to move for fear it would disappear, he stayed where he was. When he was a kid and saw rainbows reflecting through the kitchen window at his grandmother's, he would signal her to come over and the two of them would stand there and watch until the Arizona sun shifted and the colors raced away, set free in the dry mountain air. Sundogs, she had called them. Spirit puppies whose territory bridged earth and heaven. Dust motes, his father said, when Hank tried to explain the phenomenon to him. Either way, they existed, and Hank had developed a lifelong fascination with the naming of things, fearful that if he did not do so, did not call what he loved to himself in a specific and finite way, did not hold it, he would lose everything.

CHAPTER 14

Hank tried but couldn't name another teacher he knew, male or female, who would be out there in the dirt, a trash sack tied around a broken ankle, leaning on a cane and barking orders to students less than twenty-four hours after getting out of jail. Following arrest, he'd expect to find his colleagues in any number of places—Santa Anita, betting on maiden two-year-olds, or rinsing their troubles in the El Torito Grill bar, scouting up a decent lawyer. Chloe's singular concession was allowing him to drive her to these second-rate stables, a decision she seemed to base upon expediency, nothing more, since during the raid her truck had been impounded along with everything else.

"Take some time off," he urged her. "You don't have to prove anything."

"Hell, I already missed a whole day of work," she said. "The way things are going, does it look like I can afford to miss any more?" She had on a pair of his ancient Levi's—*Think about it, Hank, why go and wreck a new pair?*—he'd cut down the seam to allow for the passage of the cast. She was wearing one of his T-shirts, the infamous yellow sweatshirt over that, and had her hair pulled back in a ponytail by the rubber band from the morning newspaper. Whatever unpleasantness the night held, it had been postponed; now was a new day and business as usual.

The sturdy lesson horses weren't much to look at. When you came right down to it, horses resembled camels once the thoroughbred sheen was removed. Unkempt and ordinary, her camels behaved themselves in the corral—*working arena*, she'd informed him—moving in a circle, nose to tail, cantering when asked, chastised if they didn't, taking turns hopping the shabby painted jumps as if they lived to please the woman who stood in the center. She possessed authority here. He leaned his elbows against the wobbly chest-high fence. Peeling flakes of amber paint and graying wood stuck to his shirtsleeves. He kept his mouth shut. If he passed this test, she might allow him to feed her a hamburger at noon. Then again, best not count on it.

Young women in skin-tight riding pants passed through leading horses, sporting buckets and sacks of carrots. The March weather held up, sunny but cool. In a few weeks it would be vernal equinox, and the sun would move over the equator, shifting winds and blowing current pressures away. Over the tops of oaks he had a clear view of Saddleback and blue sky broken only by a few power lines. He'd hiked out here years ago. One of the canyons had a waterfall that ran when they got decent rain. Back in Modjeska Canyon, there was a viewing station, where dozens of hummingbirds came to feed from red glass bottles the rangers hung from trees. He'd taken his mother there, maybe fifteen years back, so she could sit and watch her favorite birds up close. Now highway traffic emitted a constant hum, muted only by the stand of oak trees that separated the stables from the highway. When the county supervisors got their way, a freeway would replace the winding two-way road, the commuters would have a straight shot from Mission Viejo to Orange, and the stables would be a memory.

Kit Wedler was Chloe's stable brat this Saturday, running bridles and saddles in and out of the tack shed with surprising speed. When Chloe introduced Hank to her, the chubby redhead looked him up, down, and sideways, taking inventory.

"Hank's a friend," Chloe'd said.

Kit dismissed that notion with a terse "Right."

Which meant she thought they were fucking, which they were, which was none of her business. Hank considered taking out his wallet to show her his California Teacher's Credit Union identification. Listen, young lady, I have an account here, I'm not some cowboy opportunist with his eye on your teacher's jeans. Kit possessed that bullshit-proof demeanor of youth. If he had sported Oxford robes and four dozen sheepskins, she would have still answered, "Right." He was after her teacher's ass; he was a stranger here.

He watched her fill buckets from the faucet on the small deck outside the storeroom and office. "Want a hand?"

"And watch you pop your first blister? Give me a royal break."

He raised his hands. "Mercy. I just asked to help."

"Do I look like I need help?" She went back to her chores, racing from the trash cans full of grain, cussing like a seasoned barmaid at skittering mice, measuring out coffee cans full of various feed with her tongue stuck out of the corner of her mouth. Like the horses, she worked as if driven. She was horse crazy—this, penance for some adolescent sin. Maybe Chloe gave her extra lessons in exchange for the chores. A Black Beauty scenario, soon to be displaced by some awkward teenage boy with acne. Childish as it was, it chafed—Chloe allowed Kit to exclaim over her injury and to drape her in hugs—he was expected to remain detached and anonymous. He paid her bail, drove her places. He stood at the railing and wished he smoked cigarettes. He'd ridden horses at his grandmother's, an old pinto pony named Chances, loaned to her for the summer by a friend on the reservation. Mornings he'd saddle up and wander until the sun got too hot, when the willful pony would turn and trot home, fueled by his own laziness. He wished he had paid closer attention at summer camp when he endured his weeks of riding lessons, instead of looking forward to riflery and canoeing. He didn't know one saddle from the other. The straps and buckles were many and mysterious. If Kit had agreed to his offer she would have had to spend precious time reeducating him. She was leading two horses up from the pasture now, striped lead ropes clenched in her chubby hands. With that red hair and pout, she reminded him of a cranky sprite, one capable of nasty magic. He turned back to watch Chloe.

When a thin black cowboy offered her the cane she now leaned on, he too gave Hank the eye. Hey, I bailed her out, he wanted to say. I donated the jeans. That's also my trash sack, a premium Hefty, not some cheap generic, in case anybody's wondering.

A curly-coated mutt and what looked like a spotted dingo nosed around his ankles. Since his question in the car, they hadn't spoken out loud about Hannah. Chloe'd wept in the night, but wouldn't talk about it when the sun rose.

"Desmond Morris believes that a lost dog will circle widely until he finds a familiar scent," Hank said over orange juice that morning.

"Desmond Morris. He work at the college, too?"

"No, he's a writer. He's written a number of books on behavior."

"You've read a lot of books. Have you ever had a dog?"

"When I was a kid. A rotten beagle who ate my oil paints and left technicolor droppings all over the yard for a week."

That had made her smile. Chloe wasn't up to hoping, but he stacked his chips next to Morris. Perhaps Hannah was circling even now above the hills behind the stable, through the many canyons and old trails that had for the moment escaped development. Probably there were creeks she knew of where she could at least get clean water. An old dog didn't stand much of a chance against mountain lions or off-road vehicles. He pictured her in the middle of nowhere, amassing a pile of aluminum cans, waiting for Chloe to return to praise her.

He hiked up the slight hill through the breezeway stalls and went to the pay phone outside the barn office. With a pocketful of change, he called information to get the numbers of the animal shelters between here and Irvine. He pressed the buttons and gave his spiel three times. "White German Shepherd with a spotted, torn ear. Collar and tags. Answers to Hannah, doesn't like strangers."

The shelters were a washout. The few who halfway promised to keep an eye out also informed them that the personnel turnover was faster than a major league spitball, so don't go getting your hopes up. By the midafternoon lull, Hank noticed Chloe had bitten her nails down to the quick.

"Here's an idea," he said. "Let's run past Hughville and take a look. Maybe she came back."

"I'm ass deep in alligators already, Hank. I don't want to piss the police off any more than I already have."

"We can just drive by."

"I don't want to get in any more trouble."

"Don't you want to collect your things?"

"There wasn't that much there. Besides, they're ruined."

"Chloe, did you really hit that policeman?"

She lit a cigarette borrowed from one of the stablehands. "He was a fucking Boy Scout dressed in a cop costume."

"Whom you hit."

"Anyone who goes after my animals without provocation is asking to have his ass quartered."

"Open or closed fist?"

"I don't remember. Why?"

"Nothing. Forget it." But he was worried about the consequences in the courtroom. That tough face, held together by the wobbling cotter pin of swear words worked on him, but how would a courtroom full of strangers feel? "You could stay in the car."

"I'm telling you, she wouldn't be there." Chloe folded her arms across her chest and stared out at nothing. "She's miles away by now. I know Hannah." She left him and went to greet the next batch of students, lifting the cane to wave hello.

It was Saturday morning, when he'd normally finish the *Times* and grade a few papers, but this Saturday morning he'd helped her wash with a new bar of Irish Spring and a washcloth he'd bought only because it came with the set of charcoal gray bath towels. She leaned over the basin, naked and unembarrassed, lathering herself, limbs, breasts, crotch, anyplace she could reach. He did her back and helped her sponge off. "Can I wear some of your underwear?" she'd asked, and he went digging through his dresser drawers for shrunken T-shirts and briefs with halfway decent elastic. If *Esquire* was running out of ideas to make their models look sexy, here was one angle they could certainly implement with a measure of success. She bent over the counter and brushed her teeth. Chloe, seeing him behind her in the mirror, turned and laughed, her mouth outlined in foamy ice blue Crest. "For Christ's sake, Hank, take a breath! How am I going to get downstairs if you pass out on me?" Then, softer, "It doesn't take much to get your motor started, does it?"

So he'd fixed her breakfast—doughnuts zapped to warm in the microwave, sliced bananas, oranges. Brewed Kona coffee he'd never opened—a gift when his parents had gone to Hawaii a year back, just before Iris was diagnosed with cancer. He shredded his Levi's for her. Pinned them up the side every two inches with two-inch-long safety pins his mother had bought for him—*Now, Henry, you never know when these might come in handy, just put them in a drawer for later.* He did that. On the way to the stables they stopped at Mervyn's for a bra (Jockey, 34B), women's underpants, plain cotton, white, three pairs of socks, and tennis shoes. Impractical, she insisted, because she could only wear one shoe, obviously. Well, are you going to go to work barefoot? She steered him away from the expensive brands. *These here are twice the price, now what's the good of that, I ask you?*

They fit better, he said hopefully. She poked a crutch tip at him and he capitulated. *Fine, they're your feet, get whatever you want.* She wouldn't let him buy any more than that, insisted she'd get her stuff out of the compound eventually, the police couldn't keep her clothes, could they? Maybe they could. Nevertheless, he noted her sizes in the blank pages of his Week at a Glance while her back was turned at the register. Never again would he be stuck clueless as to what kind or size of underwear she wore, jail, bail, or upcoming court date, when in all probability she would require a decent dress, stockings, good shoes, the whole nine yards.

She was coated with a light layer of dust by afternoon. When a nasty-looking Appaloosa got out of hand and sidestepped the foot-and-a-half-high jump a little girl asked him to take, Chloe signaled them both to the center of the ring. Immediately the horse started shaking, from mule ears down to horseshoes, penitent, but Chloe wasn't buying the routine. After holding the reins of the criminal and seeing the rider safely to the ground, she pulled herself right up onto his back with her arms. That took decent upper body strength, more than he had. Her wrapped cast stuck out comically but no one laughed. While she ordered the beast through his paces, insisting he back up, turn every which way, and execute a few jumps to her liking, it seemed as if the whole stables ground to a halt to watch her. The cast didn't trouble her much. She rode the rangy little horse out of his nasty mood, never using the riding crop once, but Hank could tell the horse never forgot for an instant that it was in her hand. After a dozen circles the fractious horse began to move fluidly, and the two of them reached for each gait as one unit. Pure grace flowed from the canter, where before the rank attitude had kept it choppy. Beneath her, muscles stretched and rocked slinkily, as if set free. She collected the reins and sat back in the saddle and they came to a smooth halt, not a misstep or stumble. At Hank's side, Kit mumbled, "See that? A leg in each corner," then turned and hurried off. Chloe reached down to pat the horse's neck and spoke in his ear. Only when faced with her dismount did she look around uncertainly. Hank slid under the fence and went to her, caught her in his arms, and helped her to the ground.

"Downright gallant," she whispered into his ear. "You trying to get all these little girls to fall in love with you?"

"I wouldn't say no to some intense affection."

She gave him a playful smack; then he was ordered back to the fence. More girls in tight pants. So many perfect bottoms in one place. All those well-developed leg muscles. Something he could tell Asa come Monday.

When dusk fell and the bridles and saddles had been scrubbed down, dried, polished to Chloe's standards, and set away into the sheds on their individual racks, she was finally finished with her workday. He watched her tally up checks and cash, enter them into her ledger—a pink spiral-bound notebook with considerable water damage rippling the pages—deduct 10 percent of her take and put that into an envelope for the stable owners. He could read upside down; she wasn't in the red, but within a hairbreadth of breaking even.

"Why do you do this?"

"What do you mean?"

"There are easier ways to get along. Why not learn to type and go be someone's secretary?"

"This is honest work. Here I get to be my own boss. I hate typewriters."

"It's backbreaking work."

"Which I happen to be pretty good at. I have to put this envelope in the safe up at the barn," she said. "On the way, you maybe want to meet my horse? Or are you too tired? God, I'm sorry, you probably aren't used to this. We can go."

"No, no. I'm fine." His bones were lead weights surrounded by damp tissue paper. Windburned and gritty, he'd undertake the Boston marathon rather than wimp out on her now. "Lead the way. As long as your leg's up to it, I'm game."

"Well, the check has to be delivered."

They drove the Honda partway up the dirt road.

"Pull over here and stop."

She took him to stall 72, in what she explained was the breezeway barn, a corrugated metal roof covering twenty-four stalls on each side. The upside of horsetown. Here the pens were roomier; a horse could trot around a little, roll over, lie down. The horses each had individual feeders filled up with green chunks of compressed hay. They shared a watering device that swiveled between the bars and filled with fresh water when a tongue pressed a metal bar in the center. In the lower stalls he'd seen filled trash cans with thin scummy coatings of moss on the surface. The horses didn't seem to mind. He watched her unlatch the gate and slip inside. The horse dropped his nose once to give her a nod, made a low noise in his throat that sounded more like a grumble of pleasure than a warning, then continued eating.

"He doesn't sound as if he wants to be disturbed."

"That's just saying hello." She shut her eyes and put her arms over his neck, whose arched crest sported a shining black mane. He watched her trace the muscles in his neck down to his wide breast with fingertips, as if she were reading him like Braille. The horse lifted his massive head from the feeder and nuzzled her neck, dropping mangled bits of hay onto the sweatshirt, down her neck, and throughout her hair. She shivered. The smile that covered her face left him in awe. Hank had seen Chloe grin, bark a short laugh now and again, cry out in passion, and once in his car wail in grief and rage, but then only briefly, and immediately postscript it with a stammer of apology. She'd wept into his pillows over a dog she couldn't speak of directly when the sun rose. But right here there was history, intimacy, relationship.

Nothing he'd done in the nine weeks they'd been together came close to this. Not pay her bail, buy her tennis shoes, or bring her to climax.

"What's her name?"

"He. Absalom."

"Like the Faulkner novel?"

"Guess so. I didn't name him."

"Who did?"

A jet from the marine base passing overhead rattled the corrugated aluminum roof. Chloe waited until it was gone before she answered.

"A man." Her voice was soft, tentative.

"Who was he?"

"His name was Fats Valentine." She pointed to the small heart on the animal's upper rear leg. Whereas he was an otherwise unbroken dark brown—*bay*, Chloe informed him—this heart consisted of whitish hairs fixed somewhat lopsided, as if he'd resisted the tattoo. "See here? His freeze-brand? The little heart. All Fats' horses had them. Have them," she corrected herself. "He's dead now, but there's still some horses."

"I'm sorry."

"Yeah. He broke and trained Ab, and when I got the money together, I bought him. I wish I had a cigarette. Don't suppose you'd spring for the cigarette machine?"

"I might. Be nice to me."

"I'm nice to you, goddammit."

"He's a lovely animal."

She brightened. "He is, isn't he? He has a great heart. He would jump off a cliff if I asked him, give up his life in an instant. Funny thing is, I might have to put him down."

"Down?"

"You know, down, mercy killing."

"Why?"

"His legs. He has navicular disease pretty bad. And a horse that can't work for his board, well, let's just say it's impractical to feed him."

Hank put his hand through the bars meaning to pet the doomed horse, but got his fingers nipped for the effort. "Hey! That hurt." He rubbed his fingers, feeling for broken skin.

"I tell them not to, but the stable brats feed him sugar cubes. They all think he's Black Beauty reincarnated. He thought you might have a goody for him. Carrots for fingers." She reached for the injured finger and gave it a kiss.

"Your animals don't seem to like me." Christ, Hannah. "Sorry. I didn't mean to bring that up."

She slipped back out and latched the gate. "Don't even worry about it. Maybe she'll survive the highway. Maybe she'll be back. You want to go eat?"

That was supposed to be his line. All day he'd had visions—quiet dinner, a glass of wine, scenic drive through the hills while the sun set—a bit late for that now. Finish up in his bedroom where he would try his best to cheer up her flesh and relieve his own pressures—all of which she managed to skew, quite naturally, in her own straightforward, rather unremarkable way of stating the obvious. "You've been on your feet for hours. Maybe you'd rather pick something up and take it back with us."

"Sure, grab a hamburger, whatever you want."

He drove down the canyon highway and took the turnoff toward Hughville. At first Chloe didn't seem to notice, then she sat upright. "Where are we going, Hank?"

"Just a drive by. No one can arrest us for that."

She slid down in the seat. "This is stupid. Even I know better than this."

He made the left toward the compound, then saw the sheriff's sawhorses, the yellow tape. He waved to the deputy who turned around at his headlights, made a U-turn and edged back onto the narrow road.

"What did you see?" she asked.

"Nothing that would help." He reached for her shoulder. "You like onions and pickles on your hamburger?"

"Whatever. I'm not that hungry."

Not hungry enough to eat all her sandwich and half of his, a cup of potato salad, both dill pickles, and sigh as she bit into one of the half-dozen croissants he'd bought for morning. So what. She'd worked hard enough to afford the calories. Most women he'd dated picked at food as if it were unseemly to have an appetite; required behavior to waste a twenty-dollar entrée so long as they weren't paying.

With the aid of the cowboy's cane she managed the stairs all by herself, though it took nearly ten minutes. When she got to the top, she voiced doubt about getting down unassisted. "Up is okay. Up I can handle. Maybe I need glasses. Downstairs just looks so damn far away from up here. And steep."

"Try it right now if you want to. I'll spot you all the way down in case you lose your footing."

There on the carpeted landing she shook her head and stripped off her dusty clothes, let them drop, and held out her arms. "You are such a polite man, Henry Oliver. It's a wonder you ever get laid."

Lame horse, lost dog, court case pending, she gave up all her worries in his bed, let him investigate her body like a kid playing detective. "You smell wonderful."

"I smell like a team of mules. I wish you'd at least let me get up and brush my teeth."

"Not a chance." He held back, kissing conventional places in utterly conventional ways, prolonging the instant when their bodies would shift into high gear from this humming idle. He ran his hands down her belly and legs, stopping at the top of the cast, fingering the fiberglass where her knee stopped and the mending apparatus began. One, two, three fractures. He hefted the weight of it in his hand. "Does it hurt?"

"What?"

"I'm curious. I never made love to a woman with a broken bone."

"But you're going to."

He smiled. "I am."

She rubbed her palm across his chin. "When you do all that other stuff I can't even feel it."

"But otherwise—it hurts?"

For a moment her face clouded. "Yeah, like somebody shot me."

"All day?"

She nodded.

"Well, Christ, why didn't you say so? I had the prescription for your pain pills filled."

"I like a clear head when I'm working. Horses are stupid, but they outweigh me. No sense in giving them an advantage."

He leaned against her, resting his head on her shoulder. "If I were in your position I'd be outraged. But you just turn a little to the left and keep on going. I can't quite fathom it."

She ran her knuckles across his cheek. He could feel a day's worth of whiskers bristle under her fingers. "Much as I hate to own up to it, I'm pretty fair at handling trouble. I've had a lifetime to get used to that. Orangewood, foster parents. All that stuff."

"But jail?"

"Maybe they'll drop the whole thing. Slap Hugh with six more fines and forget about me. What good's it do me to worry? Still have to pay my bills. Keep on working. Head down and all that. Believe me, I've been through worse than this."

"No to the pill, then?"

She smiled, but it was a tired smile. "No. If I can't brush my teeth, I guess it's just yes to you."

He stood up and took a long look at her lying naked on his bed. She didn't grab for the sheets or turn her face away in shyness. He knelt at the bedside and reached for her, beginning at her feet and moving north, became distracted by the V of her pubic hair, the neat way he could cup the entire area in his palm, how it fit as if made to be framed in his hand. With his thumbs, he parted the two halves and bent his face down to taste her there, felt her hands reach down to push him away, mutter an argument about washing up. He grabbed her wrists, thin for such a strong woman, pinned them both in his right hand and anchored himself across her; she couldn't move. "Hank, don't."

He lifted his face. "You like it."

"Sometimes I do, but not right now."

Her wrists pressed against his fingers, then slackened. He felt her pulse fluttering and loosened his grip a little, but kept his mouth on her, decisively exploring.

"Hank. Hank, come on."

He kept on; she quit fighting. Now he was sure she was content to hold on for the ride. He worked his tongue over her flesh in earnest, exploring and rolling the inner folds between his lips, lightly tapping the clitoris with the tip of his tongue. When her breathing quickened, her whole body focused into a singular taut muscle ending between her legs. It was difficult not to move over her, enter the tight, damp passage roughly when he felt her so ready, arching up to meet him. This time he wanted to take her this way, all the way to orgasm, under his control, guided by his moves. He pressed his tongue in deeper, and felt her squirm beneath him. Didn't like that, couldn't move away. His hand was a lock, the cast a weight. She was beginning to like it, in spite of any misgivings. He tried different rhythms, assorted movements, cataloging the cries she made—whimpers, begging, gasps, low throaty grunts that echoed a sympathetic ache in his balls.

"Hank," she cried, but he wouldn't stop, not until he found a way to move his tongue that sent her stiff-legged and arched, suspended into another dimension where horses ran soundly and lost dogs were found, and money—Christ, what was money when you had this? Nothing, nothing at all, nothing. When she came, the cry was just the beginning, the sound of a clay bell, an O tone so pure he wanted to stop and listen. It ran slipshod over his pretentious decorating, spoke volumes to the newlywed neighbors who were probably simmering in another unpleasant aftermath. He lifted his damp mouth and smiled; she was in tears.

Hank reeled himself in and moved up the mattress to lie next to her. In the windowlight he could see the small rosy rash erupt on her upper chest. The accomplishment made him feel stupidly proud. Spots he planted; he owned her for however brief a time that might be. He slid his swollen cock inside her. So tight, so wet, he moved only once, possibly half that again, before giving up the gentleman's notion of trying to hold back and didn't apologize for any of it—the small hurt it caused or the haste.

Sometime later, she found her voice. "Wasn't fair."

"Tell me you didn't like it."

Her damp cheek turned away from his face.

"I heard you come. What I did sent you someplace else, somewhere far away."

After a minute she said, "Maybe I wasn't ready to go there. You could have asked me before you went ahead and bought me that one-way ticket. What you did, Hank. Some people might put a nasty name to it. You might have listened to me."

He gave it some thought under his allocation of sheet. Knew better than to touch her now. "I won't let things get out of hand again, I promise."

She wiped her face. "Could you get me a washcloth?"

"Sure." He pulled out of her. In the bathroom he switched on the light and took clean towels from the cupboard beneath the sink. He ran the faucet over one and glanced up at his sorry face in the mirror. A streak of blood swathed his cheek and stained his mustache. He touched the drying blood as if it were warpaint, some kind of ancient initiation rite in a flush of male pride. But he'd paid a high price for it when the animal had gone cold beneath his knife. He splashed his face and rinsed the towel under the faucet until the water ran clear. Well, she wasn't pregnant, and she sounded as if she might forgive him. When he opened the door and the light arced out in the bedroom, he was surprised she was still there in his bed.

"I had this crazy idea you might leave me."

She stubbed out one of her cigarettes into a saucer on the night table. "Where would I go?"

CHAPTER

15

I hope you're practicing safe sex with that goofy teacher," Kit said, mining ice with her straw for the dregs of her Diet Cherry Coke. "But why anyone would voluntarily allow one of those fossilized hunks of dinosaur *caca* to pork them is beyond me."

Chloe smiled across the tabletop. The restaurant was closed and the tables were cleaned. She could go home in a few minutes, as soon as Hank came to get her. "What a colorful way to describe sex."

"No! Wait," Kit said. "Don't tell me. I've got my pathetic suspicions, but that's not the same as saying I really want them confirmed. Let me be innocent for another week and a half, okay?"

"Whatever you say."

"Did you bring the picture?"

Chloe got up and took her purse from underneath the counter top, came back to the table and handed Kit a manila envelope. Inside was the picture of herself on the ancient pony—her only baby picture. It had come out of the safe deposit box this morning, along with her birth certificate, with her parents' names and her actual date of birth blacked out as they had been all along. Even such minimal proof of her existence was necessary to apply for another drivers' license. The old one had somehow disappeared in the Hughville bust, and though she knew her number by heart and the computer confirmed it, the DMV insisted on another form of ID. Hank's lawyer wanted copies of everything, receipts for whatever she had to replace—ammunition. She sat down.

"That's really you?" Kit marveled. "God, you're so little. You look so sad. Do you remember any of it? Your mom? What she looked like or anything?"

"I know her first name. Belle. That's all." She ran a thumbnail across the photograph's creases—fractures, she thought. Her childhood.

Kit waved her hands. "Hello? Chloe? Can we finish the interview now or are you going to stare out the window thinking about boning that professor some more?"

"It's been a rough month. Staring feels like an accomplishment."

"Any word on Hannah?"

"Nothing yet. We keep looking."

Kit pointed her straw across the booth at Chloe. A single bead of Coke dripped onto the tabletop, and out of habit, Chloe blotted it into a napkin. "Tell me your life didn't start to crank out of whack as soon as you met Mr. Geekface. Go on, convince me."

Chloe sighed. She'd agreed to help Kit with her assignment for this semester's elective, Journalism. Assignment: The Eyewitness Memoir. Interview a role model and outline her life objectively in a feature story. Don't forget the five W's and the all-important H. Hank was none of her business. Where in the hell did she find these W's—Dr. Joyce Brothers? The paper was probably due tomorrow. Role model, my ass. Why the girl couldn't have chosen her grandmother. . . but after a quick inventory of Kit's immediate family, Chloe knew without question she was the most dependable female Kit had ever encountered, familial or otherwise, and that included the animal world. Yet aiding and abetting a seventh-grader in the delusion that hers was a life to aspire to was just plain wrong. She could feel Rich's stony glare peering out from the kitchen. Probably he had spy equipment set up in the napkin dispensers and was only pretending to be cleaning. He hated cleaning, hence the small fires that broke out on the average of once a week, precipitating his rages. What was he doing back there?

Kit tapped her yellow pencil against her notebook paper. "So don't even answer me. Like I give one-sixteenth of a monkey's shit."

"Monkey shit? What are we talking about?"

"Jeez! I hope you concentrate more when you're with the horses, or you'll get stomped."

"Kit, lighten up. I'm tired. I have things on my mind."

She blushed. "Sorry. Okay, I already know about Orangewood and your foster parents. When you lived there did you make a bunch of close friends? And do you guys, like, keep in touch forever now, like sorority sisters or something?"

How to go back? Open that creaking door and the dark mouth of her past loomed out—no lamps for sale nearby. "Close friendship wasn't encouraged, Kit. Kids came and went. Most left within a few months at the longest. I was an exception."

"Really? Guy, that is rough. What about weekends? Did you go on field trips and to Disneyland and all that free stuff they give to poor kids? Was it totally embarrassing or fun?"

Chloe took a moment organizing her words. "You have to remember this was twenty years ago," she said, softly. "It wasn't popular to help the quote-unquote disadvantaged, not that it really is much today, either. Once a year the Kiwanis or the Elks did a circus thing for us. I got into it when I was young. But as I grew older, it was the same thing year after year, a bunch of drunks finding an excuse to ride miniature motorcycles around like fools. Relieving their collective guilt in one lump sum, that's all. Sure, a few tattered elephants whipped into lifting a leg to amuse the kiddies, sick horses that should have been put down, not asked to rear up on cue, but kids are smarter than anyone gives them credit for; you know that. They see through nonsense. We did have a color TV, and that was kind of great, but all the best shows were on Saturdays and we weren't allowed to watch then." She made a face. "Saturdays. Never mind all that shit. Here and now's what matters. Ask me what it's like to be homeless and finally get yourself squared away only to have it ripped out from under. Ask me a horse question. Or how to soothe a customer when I've refilled his tea with coffee. That's what my life's about, not Orangewood."

"What about these Saturdays?"

Chloe folded her arms across her chest. "Jesus, Kit. You could work for the IRS."

"Come on, tell me, please? I just know this might be the one detail I need to make my story ultra-cool. Please?"

"You'll probably get an F on this, and Rich will fry my ass up in the grease pit."

"Ninety-nine percent of the kids don't even do their homework. This'll be an A paper, styling. I might even pass seventh grade."

"You'd better pass seventh grade or I'll take it personally."

"Chill out. I will." Kit poised her pencil. "Ready."

"All right. Saturdays were a hot item thought up by some Simon Legree who never had to live through one. We couldn't wait for Saturdays, because there was always a group of people who would come visit the home and think about adopting a kid. Like the Animal Shelter, in a way, checking out the puppies. So we were dressed up, told to smile, pushed into this whole competitive thing about who could be the most charming—you know, be the perfect child. They could take you home for the weekend and bring you back Sunday night, a trial run. Pancakes, your own bedroom, a shower without a guard and ten million girls looking to see if your breasts had started to grow. And there was always the possibility that if they liked you the situation might turn permanent."

"So how many times did you go with someone like that? Were they rich and stuff? Did you get to go swimming in kidney-shaped pools?"

"I never liked the water much. Let's just say I didn't drown."

Kit's eyes widened. "No way! So you're saying you didn't ever get picked? Not once?"

"No." A handful of dirty chain-link fence in her fingers. Shiny cars driving away to suburbs that rivaled any Disneyland adventure. *Not that one. Not the skinny blond girl. Her hair's too straight, that dress doesn't fit right. Doesn't she ever smile?* "I wasn't what you might call outstanding in the charm department. The whole ordeal kind of left a sour taste in my mouth. Pancakes!" She shuddered. "You know, to this day I can serve them up, but I can't eat them."

Kit dropped her straw in mid-suck. "That is just A-one fucked up, Chloe, and you have to admit that's the only word that fits the circumstance."

"Well, it's a white man's thinking. But don't put that in your paper or your teacher will be on the phone to Rich in a heartbeat."

"God, give me a tiny bit of credit, will you?"

"I do, Kit. Can't help it. That stuff gets me riled up. It's in the past where I like it. It's not easy to go nosing around."

"Did you ever go looking for Belle—your real mom?"

"No, I didn't *go looking* for her. I don't play the lottery, either."

"Why not?"

"'Cause it's a misery business. What I am is here in my own two shoes, Katherine Wedler. Well, one shoe and a walking cast."

"How much longer till you get it off?"

Chloe grimaced. "Would you believe a whole month more, thanks to Hank's fancy-ass orthopedic doctor who says they set it wrong in the first place? I've already had it on a month! I should have got your dad to saw it off with his Makita."

Kit pressed the ends of the straw between two fingers and smiled slyly. "So. You've been in our garage, too?"

Exasperated, Chloe reached across the table and took the girl's chin into her hands and gave it a shake. "When I fixed the Jacuzzi filter, I needed a fucking screwdriver. Quit making my life out to be a soap opera, okay?"

"My, my. Such language." Kit drew hearts in the margin of her notebook paper. "You really are in love with that weenie Hank, aren't you?"

Chloe looked out the window at the steady stream of cars passing by, then closer in, where a bird was yanking sphagnum moss from a hanging fuchsia plant out front. Rich's attempt at increasing curb appeal was a home-improvement bonanza for city birds in springtime. "It pains me to consider such an idea."

"Then that means you are, or almost."

Chloe took a moment to consider Kit's words before responding. "When it comes to love I'm sure about two things—my good-for-nothing horse, and Hannah, wherever she may be. Those two shapes fit together, sort of like puzzle pieces inside my heart. Not much room otherwise. No geekface professors, no errant cowboys."

"That's all?"

"Go easy on me, Kit. Love's expensive. Doesn't have to mean that you'll stop being my best friend."

Over in the corner, Lita was counting out the day's take into the bags for the bank. Chloe winked at her and Lita smiled back, her crooked half-grin born of seasoned motherhood.

"You shouldn't kid about a thing like that."

"Who said I was kidding?"

Kit balked. "But best friends tell each other the truth, goddammit. Best friends do right by each other."

"Don't I always make you wear your helmet when we're riding?"

Rich brought out a tray bearing a cup of soup for each of them. "Here. Free samples."

"What are these little floating things on the top?"

"For Christ's sake, Kit. Just try it."

"Dad. If I find out there's squid in here, I'll puke."

He waved the spoons, then set them down. "I'd give a hundred bucks to the first person who can find me a woman who isn't a smart-mouthed cynic. What we have here is soup. There's chicken broth in it, and some goddamn shredded turkey breast and cracked peppercorns and sliced-up corn tortilla with fresh son-of-a-bitching cilantro. If you don't want to try it, just say so."

Lita came over and sat down with them. "Let me try it, Rich. I think it looks wonderful." She smiled at him, then looked down at the soup, blushing. Rich twisted his frown back into his normal straight line. A smile wrestled beneath, hoping to come out, but he managed to contain it.

Kit said, "Eveybody's always ragging on teenagers about responsibility, but it seems to me all you people over thirty seem to think about is fucking. Excuse me, I have to make some important phone calls."

She slid out of the booth and marched to the pay phone.

"Where the hell did all that come from?" Rich asked. "Chloe, what are you filling her head with?"

Lita set her spoon down and pressed his hand. "Honey, if you don't know, I really can't think how to explain it to you."

Chloe laughed out loud and smacked the table with her hand. All the little tortilla strips trembled in their broth.

Rich rubbed his chin. "All I know is one minute it's Barbies and the next she's a badge-carrying hormonal shrew. I suppose it's time to start dropping Midol in with her vitamins."

Chloe took a sip of the soup. "Good, but I think it could use a hair more spice. How about you throw in a couple jalapeños?"

Rich gathered the cups onto the tray. "Jalapeños. Jalapeños. Don't start telling me how to cook, too, Little Miss Getting-It-Every-Night." He lifted his tray and sped toward the kitchen.

Lita and Chloe looked at each other. Chloe said, "I told you this would be an interesting place to work."

Lita smoothed an unfurling napkin and stuck it back into the dispenser's chrome jaws. "I've been thinking I might want to sleep with our cook."

"I wondered when you would recognize his unique form of courtship. You want some advice?"

"Anything. I've been celibate for six years, except for my dreams, and as promising as those are, they fade out into blackness at the important part."

Chloe waved her hand. "Not to worry, Lita. That part comes back to you pretty quick. But stay out of the Jacuzzi for awhile—just till you set down the ground rules, if you can. Something about those bubbles, I don't know."

"Oh?"

"It makes the next morning rather interesting. Sorry to say, I speak from experience, but that happened way back when, before I came to work for him. Probably he doesn't even remember."

"I doubt it," Lita said. "He looks at you that way."

"What way?"

"Oh, you know. The usual. Baffled, bewildered, utterly enraged that someone else has your attention."

"Lita, he looks at every woman that way. He took a rough spill off Willie. Are you sure you want to climb on?"

"Kit's a sweet girl, Chloe."

"No argument there."

"She needs a mom."

"Well, Rich does, too. If you're up to it, I wish you every last bit of luck available."

Hank arrived fifteen minutes later. He walked in the back way now, familiar, nodded to Rich, who was slicing jalapeños on the cutting board and waved back with the knife, a wheel of bright green pepper stuck on the blade's surface. He said hello to Kit, who didn't say hello back. She bent closer to the phone, cupping her hand around the mouthpiece as if what she was up to were top secret and no one over the age of sixteen could possibly understand. Lita was always gracious to him. She smiled and held up the coffeepot, which Hank always politely declined.

Chloe sat in the booth counting her tips, taking in the little scene with all its various characters. We're like a soap opera, she thought. Drama at every intersection. No wonder Kit's so busy trying to fit us to one another. She tried to unravel what Kit had said—in love with him, or almost—was she? She was fond of Hank, that was the term, *fond*. The word fit right beneath his mustache and most nights her mouth fit right over his. His body on hers, his fingers inside her, his cock, his lapping tongue, sometimes it scared her that she couldn't seem to get enough. But love? Love was the arched neck of Absalom, his quick canter below her at the minute press of her calf muscle; it was Hannah's head resting on her knee, the two of them bonded without speaking the same language, in their shack in the canyon. Love did not have an IOU a mile long connected to it. Love was not awaiting a twice-postponed court date for assault, and dependent on somebody else's tricky lawyer playing expensive games with the DA.

"It's early," he said, just standing there, looking at her. "You want to go somewhere or straight home?"

He never forced pancakes on her, though sometimes he pushed her into sex she wasn't entirely ready for. There was a swimming pool in the condominium complex, not kidney-shaped, as was the vogue in the fifties, like every kid at Orangewood drew into pictures with stubby crayons on miles of rolled out butcher paper—*Someday I'm going to have me one with a high dive and a slide and a Coke machine you don't even need a quarter for*—but one long, blue-tiled sensible, shallow rectangle for executing laps to harden the body. While Hank swam, Chloe sat in a webbed chair, her cast resting on the arm of another chair, her body wrapped in his towel. Overhead, the late afternoon sun gently warmed her as it gained strength for the summer. She watched his pale arms slice easily through the water's surface. His willowy butterfly stroke made her heart dance, his underwater turns, fluid as an otter's, never failed to surprise and delight her. When he finished, he'd stand over her and shake his head like a dog, dousing her in a hundred cooling drops of water, then bend down to kiss each one away. It was comfortable there with him in his place, as comfortable as anywhere could be without Hannah and her own things, as long as she didn't think about it too hard. "Home," she said.

But they didn't go straight home, they stopped in at the shelters between here and there as they often did, and were led back to the wire-and-cement kennels where dogs howled in primal fear. Hank brought along a giant box of Milk Bones for the occasion, and they doled them out one by one when the shelter attendants would allow. Despite their minimal rations, some of the dogs would no longer take them—they would go hungry rather than trust another outstretched human hand. She was starting to recognize them. Most were big dogs, shepherd mixes, clumsy Labs cut liberally with terrier, producing that wiry, curly-tailed large mutt that no one wanted to adopt. They weren't cute; they were rangy loose-jointed mongrels who needed a place to run, something to guard or protect—jobs, tasks, a reason for living, someone to live alongside. Occasionally they came across a purebred Great Dane or handsome Saint Bernard—money dogs, their muzzles screaming pedigree, careful breeding, show ring. Chloe sat down to pet them through the mesh and wished she could take them home. Sometimes they licked her hands with sorrowful dignity. Her hip joints ached for these animals who would never run free, never rejoin the hierarchy of herds humans had so successfully bred them out of recognizing. She could not allow herself the luxury of loving them. She sat in the car after these awkward missions, seething. Her lack of courage humiliated her as much as the dogs' imprisonment, but the truth was, in the end none of them was Hannah.

Chloe stood at the sink doing the dinner dishes by hand. There was an automatic dishwasher Hank pointed out on a daily basis, but she never trusted it to clean the dishes properly. The feel of her hands in the sudsy water was too familiar a pleasure to forgo, especially since she was still limited to makeshift bathing. She stood at the sink naked, her body rosy from post-dinner fooling around, a panacea rapidly turning to habit following the shelter forays. They'd done it right there, leaning over the sink with the blinds pulled halfway down; I'm getting adventurous in my old age, Hank had said. You make me want to add one more location to my life list. Let me get a condom. No, she said, you won't need one. She finished him off in her mouth, laughing when he had to grab the counter to keep his balance. She told him, Listen, if you keep on breathing like that you're going to hyperventilate. He ran his thumb across her glistening lips, kissed her for the thrill of tasting himself, caught his breath, stammered, *What have you done to me?* Now he sprinted downstairs in his running shorts, bringing her a shirt.

"I will admit a certain amount of trepidation in offering this to you given your history with men's clothes."

"But what else can go wrong?"

"It was a joke."

"Inside I'm laughing like a hyena." She let him help her into it, rolled up the sleeves and turned back to the dishes.

He cupped her buttocks with his hands, pressed himself into her, kissed her neck. "I'm just going to do a quick five miles. Then I have to grade those tests, so I'll be back early."

"Whatever happened to guys who fall asleep after? It's dark out."

"There are streetlights."

"I can see them. Just be careful."

He hesitated in the doorway. "You seem far away tonight. If you'd rather, I'll stay."

"No. I'm fine. Go run."

"You want the stereo on?"

"Yeah, that would be great."

"I'll get it on my way out."

She heard the door shut, and shortly after, Willie Nelson's *Stardust* album began in a spasm of violin. Hank wasn't so academic that he didn't possess one single country music record, even if it was old Hoagy Carmichael tunes; he also claimed ownership of a Chet Atkins Christmas album. The music was melancholy, heartbreakingly aimed toward an evening where you might as well open a bottle of bourbon and settle down to drench your troubles. Hugh'd called several times, bleating apologies into her ear. A deal had been struck, and all the charges had been dropped—all except hers. They were making an example of her, Jack Dodge said, it would never stick. What did he know—what did Hugh know? He'd sounded drunk. What a great idea. She made herself a drink, two fingers of Glenfiddich. She added one ice cube and drank a good first swallow down, washing away the salty taste of Hank and replacing it with the medicine of scotch. If dogs crawled off into bushes to die, they were at least close to the earth. If Hannah was dead, hopefully the end had come mercifully quick, say a truck tire, leaving her brains embedded in the asphalt like a map. They weren't so near the college that she had to worry about the biology department. Besides, researchers favored small dogs, didn't they? It cost less to feed them, took less space to house them, and it was easier to dispose of them when they died. If it came to a lab, she supposed she could stand that, too, if they just put her down right away to reassemble her bones for study. She could stand anything but those stories of product testers dropping detergent onto a dog's forced-open eyes, or slow starvation and the encircling scavengers. Her hand curved automatically in just the shape of the dog's head, and she quickly put it to the glass. Still she could feel the knot of skull, the coarse white hair and the one dark-tipped ear, velvety under her thumb. She could see Hannah's dark-eyed stare of protection. The edges of her soul crackled inside, crisp as burned paper. Wes McNelly'd been carted away once, reemerging two months later sober and down to business. Maybe she should call him up and ask how much a person could hold before they broke down. What were the signs and symptoms of breaking down? Did you stand naked doing dishes like a fool in the middle of a "planned community" whose rocky boulders out front on the greenbelt were composed of wire and plaster? Did you throw yourself into a professor's bed with no thought about the future? Was it the utter stubbornness that finally did you in? Kit's probing nagged—*Saturdays*—Ben Gilpin that day in the courthouse parking lot—*her name is Belle*—Belle, a tinkling chime, who gave her daughter away, well, just go and ring that one somewhere else, why don't you, honey? Don't need you, don't need anyone. Next week she would meet with Hank's lawyer, but this time go *into* the courthouse with its individual hearing rooms and the whole Perry Mason routine—do you solemnly swear—swear what? Chloe tucked her good leg up flamingo-style until it rested on the top of the new walking cast. It was a semigraceful move, and about as athletic as the orthopedic doctor allowed her to get. If he knew about the horses, he would have forbidden her outright, but then he didn't have to rely on them to make a living. Men loved to make decisions that affected how you lived your life. Well, none of this was getting the dishes done. She sighed and ran the hot water over the fried chicken remains in the skillet. The scotch was doing its work—the backs of her knees felt like racetracks somebody'd just done time trials on, smoking, gas-streaked concrete. She lifted her glass to the kitchen window. It was terrible what it had done to the Indians, but God bless alcohol.

She expected Hank when the front door opened, but it was a female voice calling out, "Yoo-hoo! Hank? Are you there?"

A gray-haired woman, medium-tall, dressed in a nice suit of clothes, a persimmon jacket and skirt, an expensive pebbled leather purse over her shoulder, stood before her. She had Hank's smile beneath skin so pale it was almost translucent. If it hadn't been for her years with Fats, Chloe might not have recognized the semipallor of chronic illness right away. Liver, or something fallow in the gut. Whoever she was, she wasn't well in a big way. But her long silver hair tidied up in a bun belied the facts. Despite the doctor's news, she was still handsome and she knew it.

"Well, I'm glad to see my son has finally gotten himself a cleaning person. He's frightfully busy, teaching all those classes. But my dear, you're working so late and your little leg, why it's broken, isn't it? That can't be much good up and down these stairs."

Even with Willie wailing in the background—*those stardust memories, the memories of love's refrain*—music didn't help to smooth this wrinkle. Chloe dried her hands on the clean dish towel she'd set out. Her cheek was taut where the semen had dried; probably it didn't show but it felt as obvious as a sailor's tattoo. Slut, she could have washed up, put on some pants, but no, the shirt wasn't even buttoned and she was standing here drinking his liquor to boot.

"I'm not the cleaning lady."

"No, I can see quite clearly now that you're not." After a pause, Hank's mother forced a smile, extended a hand, and Chloe made herself forget where her own hands had been minutes earlier. She reached out and shook like a good dog because that was what civilized people did.

They sat down at the kitchen table.

"I'm sorry there isn't any coffee. We keep forgetting to go to the market. Can I make you some tea?"

A quick glance at Chloe's libation, then a terse shake of the head, no. The woman wasn't going anywhere. She wanted Hank's assurance this entire interlude was a one-night mistake and she wasn't going to leave until she got what she'd come for.

"My name's Chloe Morgan."

"Iris Oliver."

Like she didn't think I knew his last name. "It's nice to meet you, ma'am."

There was a stack of bills on the tabletop. Hank had been paying them when he decided he'd rather fool around, then go for a run. The lawyer's invoice was on top. Pay in advance, of course. Bills weren't going anywhere, he'd said. I'll pay them when I get back. Her name was on the bill. Right there, in capital letters, next to the charge of assault. Chloe gathered it into the pile and straightened it, face down. Now only the envelopes screamed out utilities, water, she uses them, too! Iris didn't miss a trick, her eyes tracked Chloe's movements and came to rest on her face.

"It's odd Hank never mentioned you."

"Seems that way."

"How long have you two. . ."

There was no need for her to finish the sentence. "Not long. A couple of months."

"Well, we're all just so busy with our lives. I suppose that's it."

"Right."

"Will my son be back soon?"

"He said just a few miles. Are you sure I can't get you something?"

"Oh, no. I'm fine." Now her voice was downright merry. "How ever did you hurt your leg, dear?"

The old game of Truth or Dare. *I was arrested almost two months weeks ago in that so-called drug bust, which according to your son's lawyer now appears engineered by the construction industry as a ruse to gain access to the last ranchland in the county. I struck a junior deputy and he pushed me, and this is the little memento he gave me to remember him by.*

"I slipped. Sounds phony, doesn't it? But the doctor told me that ninety percent of all breaks are due to simple falls like mine."

"You must have weak bones. Have you tried a calcium supplement?"

"This is the first bone I've broken in my life."

"How old are you, if you don't mind my asking?"

"Thirty-three."

It was the same age as Jesus's last one on earth. Chloe felt her thirty-third year to be shaping up about the same way, too.

"And what is it that you do?"

"I train horses, Iris. I also wait tables in a small café for halfway decent tips."

"And?"

"And then I sleep with your son, and I'd say that just about covers it, wouldn't you?"

She nodded gravely. "Yes, I believe you're right."

Call her what you like, the woman had grace. They stared at each other for a while. Chloe knew from experience, in the initial stages of training animals, it was important not to look away first, because the animal took that as a sign of submission. After that it was hard to regain the upper hand, let alone a shred of respect. It hurt her to keep on staring at the steel blue eyes, but she did it. Finally Iris smiled and looked down at her hands.

"Tea would be lovely, but maybe I should get it, considering your leg."

"And why don't I get the clothes out of the laundry while we're waiting?"

"Sounds perfect."

Chloe hustled out of the kitchen as fast as the cast would allow, pulling the shirttail close under her behind as she went up the stairs. End of round one. There weren't any clear losers at this point.

CHAPTER

16

Absolutely a lawsuit is in order," Jack Dodge said across the rosewood desk with its multitude of mysterious black accessories.

"You can't just get them to give me a fine or something?"

The old man smiled first at Hank, then turned to Chloe. "Young lady, I'm here to do what I can—in this case, help you avoid Armageddon."

"Sounds expensive."

"Don't think about money," Hank said. "Think about your future."

"My future when? Ten minutes from now? Ten days?"

"How about ten years?" Dodge said quietly. "You have a choice—a felonious record with at best a half-life of thirty years, or a deserved cash settlement, the latter being of course, our optimum result."

"What's likely?"

Dodge smiled, his store-bought tan complementing his capped teeth and expensive clothing but failing to erase the sixty-odd years of won and lost cases from his face. "Both sides drop their charges and go on with business as usual."

"With your pocket growing a little fatter because of it."

Hank sighed. "Chloe, don't be that way."

Jack waved a hand. "That's all right, Hank. She's correct. I do get paid. I'm paid well, Ms. Morgan, because I'm worth it. The kind of mischief we're dealing with doesn't erase cheaply."

She got up from her chair. "Excuse me. I need a drink of water."

Dodge reached for one of the buttons on his telephone. "Sit tight. I'll buzz Robin to bring you some. What's your preference? Calistoga or Vittel?"

"If it's all the same to you, I'll have the kind comes out of a fucking faucet."

"Fine. There's a drinking fountain in the hallway. If you don't mind, I'd like a word alone with Hank."

She looked at each of them in turn. Hank sighed. "I'll just be a second."

"All right." Her gait made her clumsy and gangly. The heavy cast wouldn't allow for a smooth escape, but she managed. The heavy brass doors opened out into the hush of offices where carpet, wood paneling, corporate art, and tastefully dressed secretaries blurred in her quick passage.

Hank looked back at Dodge. "She's a touch independent."

Jack Dodge leaned back in his chair. "Have you done a background check on this girl, Henry?"

"Don't be absurd. I don't investigate the women I date."

He fanned a sheaf of papers across the desk. "Well, I do. All my clients as well. Can't be too careful, not in this county."

Hank's palms felt damp. "What did you find? Is there something in there that I should know?"

"Oh, nothing too surprising. This is a copy. Here. Take it. Read it at your leisure. It occurs to me how much more successful marriage might be if we all started out with a set of papers like these. Of course, it might also put me out of business."

"I don't want the thing, Jack."

"Take it. You paid for it." He tossed the file across the desk.

Hank reached out to keep it from falling to the floor.

"What can it hurt to know these few things? It's like a résumé, not government secrets, Henry. Take the file."

He didn't want to. But it was a force of habit—whether he'd liked it or not, he'd always followed Jack's advice—*Put your money into this mutual fund; follow that stock option*—he'd been a good attorney. He took the file, stowed it inside his briefcase next to a lecture on Lares and Penates, the household gods. Immediately he felt guilt deliver a rabbit kick to his sternum, but he didn't give the papers back.

Dodge began cleaning his thumbnail with a paper clip. Hank had known him his whole life—Uncle Jack—had caught his first fish—a pearl gray flounder that looked as if it had been assembled by Picasso—with Jack at his elbow—*Reel the son of a bitch in, boy, that's the way! We'll fry her up for dinner. But I don't like fish. Can't I throw it back?* Jack's elbow in his ribs. *Gotta learn to like it, son. That's what women taste like.* Smoky laughter, the sting of sea spray in his face, Henry senior's leering grin. Murdering fish and making dirty jokes was as close as men got to the rites of manhood. But Jack was wrong, women didn't taste like that, they tasted sweet, a little horsey in Chloe's case, not unpleasant. Jack put together a small will for Hank when he bought the condo. Under its terms, it went to his parents should anything happen. Family—up to now there hadn't been anyone else to consider.

Dodge set the clip down, studied his fingers. "I'll say this much. Your sweetheart certainly brought herself up out of the gutter. Given her start, I find that impressive. You know about the Children's Home, I presume?"

"It's been mentioned. I don't press."

"I find it interesting, that's all. Now don't get that look. No matter what, we're going to the mat with this thing. Ten to one they drop the charges once they hear from me, or make something stick on Hugh Nichols."

"Was he dealing drugs?"

"Certainly not. Don't be naive. They simply want to diminish the man's credibility. This is not about drugs, it's never been about drugs. It's about the land, Henry. If the old goat would let go with grace they'd probably name the development after him, let him grand-marshal the Swallows parade every year until he's pushing sod."

"He owns the land, Jack."

"When has that ever mattered in this country?"

"Chloe said there've been continual threats, and constant hassling of the tenants by Social Services. These are people who used to be homeless. The way I see it, Nichols is doing them and the county a favor."

"Substandard domiciles, lack of adequate plumbing and sanitation. Some might call that exploitation of the poor."

Hank felt his face heating up. "Whatever it is, it got Chloe off the streets. She was safe there until the police went after her. Broke her goddamn leg, Jack. In three places. I took her to my orthopedist, and he said it was a nasty break—had to reset it."

Dodge was quiet for a few moments. "We'll certainly use that if we have to. You kept the bills, didn't you?"

"Of course. It's like the King case, isn't it? Only on a smaller scale."

Jack nodded. "Don't think that won't be in the minds of the jurors. We'd better acquit her, or we'll have a miniriot on our hands."

"You really think it will go to trial?"

"When cops are involved, it's usual."

Hank shook his head. "Christ."

"Nothing's happened yet, Hank. Let's just hold tight."

"I'll try."

"That Nichols is a character, don't you agree? It makes you wonder what this place was like a hundred years ago. The old cowboy fantasy, wide-open spaces, outlaws. This girl of yours, she lands you pretty close to living it, doesn't she, horses and all?"

"Her horse bites me."

Dodge laughed. "Oh, that's priceless. Your father must be having apoplexy."

"He hasn't met her yet. Just my mother."

"And what did Iris think?"

"They were polishing their spears when I walked in and found them together at my kitchen table."

"They're both formidable women."

"True. Maybe they'll settle down to being friendly enemies. Not that I can hope for much more."

"Iris doing well?"

Hank showed Dodge crossed fingers. "She goes to the doctor every couple months, and they run a battery of tests. So far, she's holding."

"Let's be frank. You going to marry this one?"

"Marry? I hardly think the word's in her vocabulary."

"If that's what you're after, you could knock her up."

"Oh, sure. Brilliant idea, Jack."

"You think only women hold the cards on that sort of thing?"

Hank stood up. "No way. I like kids, but I'm not ready to sacrifice one in exchange for a wife."

"But you've thought about it."

"Christ, I've thought about Katharine Ross and Rosanna Arquette. But that doesn't mean I joined their fan clubs."

Dodge stood up and went to the beveled glass window behind his desk. "Take a look out there. Fifty's peeking over the hilltop, Henry. You want to be able to throw a ball to your own kids."

Hank looked at the oil paintings on the walls: Seattle Slew, Risen Star. Dodge fancied racehorses, but he was an armchair observer, too busy to attend the races in person.

Dodge came over to Hank's chair and extended his hand for a shake. Business concluded. "Well, it's your concern. Mine are settled and making me a grandpa every five years, it seems. At least I know where my money's going. Do me a favor and just dress your cowgirl in a nice navy blue suit for the hearing. Nothing low cut, but keep the skirt short enough so that the judge can see the cast, and make sure she walks in on the crutches. I'll take care of getting the doctor's statement. Incidentally, you might wash her mouth out with soap first, too."

"I admire her vocabulary. She calls the shots like she sees them."

Jack Dodge winked. "When most of us wouldn't say shit if we had a mouthful. Admit it. She's got you by the short ones."

Hank smiled. "It's a possibility. But have I got her?"

"Ah, well, that's the eternal question, isn't it, son?"

The men smiled at each other. Between them they shared a history that included much of Hank's childhood. Now Chloe's defense added to the timetable of carvings. "Thanks, Jack."

"You'll get my bill." He rubbed his palms. "I'm looking forward to this. It's been a long time since I shot pool with the sheriff's department."

* * *

Hank dropped Chloe at work. She was quiet all the way into town. He kept the speedometer on the fifty-five mark, let all the other cars hiss past him. Even with the leg cast, she could draw herself up into a folded smallness in the passenger seat. If he reminded her to use her seat belt, she turned her face to the window, not hearing. Yet if he took her to bed, she would open right up. Flesh to flesh, there were no defenses she considered worth hiding behind. He wanted her seventeen times a day; he thought about it too much. Tonight, when they were ready to quit this sticky day, he knew he would turn to her again. Fishhook through the heart, calluses on the dick, brain out the window.

"May I take you out to dinner?" he asked as he let the car idle by the back-alley entrance to Wedler Brothers.

"I need to go check on Absalom tonight."

"So we can eat out there somewhere. You pick. Find a steakhouse, and throw my heart into shock with some red meat."

She gave him a half smile. "Anywhere I want?"

He nodded. "What are you standing out here for? Get your sweet behind in there and start hustling coffee."

"What a mistake it was to introduce you to Rich. See you later, Hank. Teach them the truth today."

"Always do—the way I know it."

He looked back once before he put the Honda in gear and drove onto the boulevard. The coffee shop was tucked into a string of older shops, their stucco exteriors crumbling in the corrosive sea air that traveled up the boulevard from the peninsula. It wasn't the greatest part of town. There were rundown trailer parks and a few cheap motels, a Mr. Goodwrench, and a host of shade-tree mechanics offering cut-rate tune-ups. The homeless stood on curbs in the speeding traffic holding signs reading "Will work for food." In a few years, if the city kept on with the current redevelopment plan, everything here would be razed and replaced with something else, a cheap but trendy adobe look, maybe, something already disintegrating before the stringers dried out. He had no idea where Chloe would be then, or whether he might even know her. It was hard on her to look beyond each day toward the future, to make plans, and he couldn't quite understand it. The way life happened, the future nearly always took care of itself.

Asa Carver sought Hank out while he was having lunch in the school cafeteria. "Hey, buddy. Haven't seen you in a while."

"Hey, yourself. What brings you to eat here? I thought your new Mrs. packed you a lunch."

"She slept in today." Asa crumbled crackers into his minestrone until it resembled sienna pablum.

Hank watched him stir the mess, then looked away. A work-study student was watering the pale ferns in the planter near the windows. "Don't tell me you're going to eat that."

"Eventually. You shouldn't have skipped the department meeting."

"I had to take Chloe to the lawyer's."

Asa tsked. "Hank and his bad girl—everybody's intrigued. How's that going?"

"It's going."

"Anyway, you were missed."

"As if anything new was discussed. Whose textbook budget gets axed this year? How come we can spend a hundred dollars on a football helmet and not one dime for a guest lecturer? What poor fool's contract won't be renewed?"

Asa set his spoon down on his napkin. "Try yours."

"That's mildly amusing. A good beat, but you can't dance to it. I'd give it a four."

"I'm serious. You and Phil Green, Alec in Fine Arts, and all the part-timers in English. The women are hopping mad. They're making the old order pick up a comp class each, the newest ones two each, and the only faculty they're hiring for fall is ESL."

Hank set his tuna sandwich down on the sturdy ironware alongside the nest of potato chips he knew he shouldn't be eating anyway. The dill pickle had turned them green and soggy. Salt was bad for the heart. "They can't fire me. I've been here too many years."

"But they can cut you back, buddy. That's the rumor. Can you make it on half pay, quarter pay? Will you go sell cars at Theodore Robins to make up the difference?"

"The union won't let it happen."

"It has nothing to do with the union. This is enrollment figures, budget cuts—we're talking Sacramento. They'd reassign you if there was a secondary specialty on your credential. Get this. They might give Green a karate class. Can you beat that—a fucking karate class!"

"Well, he is a black belt." Hank watched Asa chew his soup. English Composition versus Folklore and Mythology. The logic was as clean as exposed bone. Years of frugal living amounted to his ample savings. Still, talk didn't mean walk—it would probably never happen. Maybe he'd make a few calls—just to be on the safe side—there were other junior colleges in the area. The MLA Bulletin was in the library if the pink slip was in his future. His mind blurred over—he wondered what soup was on at Wedler's, how much Chloe made in tips, whether Dodge was in a four-star haunt parrying with a fellow attorney, their BMWs and Mercedes parked outside, glistening with layers of hand-rubbed wax, grinning chrome.

"Where are you, Oliver? Are you okay on this?"

"Sure. I have to go. Office hours." He got up and walked toward the door, leaving his unbused tray behind, the first time he'd done that in years.

Only Kathryn Price came in to see him. She was cheerful, half of her plain blond hair drawn up into a high ponytail, her jeans rolled at the cuffs, a smiling, timeless example of coed who could be dropped into any decade from 1940 on.

"Hey there, Mr. Oliver." She sat in the ratty overstuffed chair at Asa's desk, as if being invited was a formality she'd left behind in Texas. "I came to see about borrowing your book on Campbell. That was such a great videotape you showed a while back, and the library's lost the book and. . . Jesus, what's troubling you? You look as miserable as one of William Strauss's earlobes."

"Do I?" He smiled. "I had a disagreeable tuna sandwich for lunch. Let me get the book for you." He turned and took it from the book-shelf, then handed it across the desk.

Kathryn chattered on gaily about her term paper. Hank saw her lips move, registered nothing beyond how full and pretty they were, how a kind word from a student like her had lifted many a day from the curb along the gutter. Next semester she would be sitting in some other professor's office, just as excitedly sharing her progress.

Chloe went over her horse like a safecracker, using a stethoscope to study heartbeat and gut sounds. She shoved a monstrous greased glass thermometer up the beast's rectum so far Hank felt his own buttocks tighten, even if the horse didn't seem to mind. After five minutes, she wiped the smeary Vaseline across the horse's rear, read the thermometer and shook it down.

"Normal," she pronounced, as if she'd wished it otherwise. "Well, we'll fix him up a bran mash and just see what happens."

"What's so terribly wrong? He's just standing there."

"That's it, Hank. He's got a feeder of cubes and he could care less. Otherwise, he's a vacuum. It's not like Absalom to go off his feed without a reason." She palmed a handful of sweet feed, oats and corn mixed with molasses, toward the horse's dark muzzle. He nosed them with slight interest, but let the bulk of them drop to the stall floor. "I wish he'd snap out of it."

Hank hauled the buckets for her, emptying thermoses of hot water into bran that closely resembled the stuff he poured into his morning cereal. Chloe stirred, and steam rose from the batter. He watched her trickle unsulfured molasses over the top like tarry icing. This the horse took, as if he had been holding out on them for the good stuff.

While she was tidying up Absalom, Hank took the tack box and grain back to the shed. He passed dozens of horses, all dedicatedly chomping away at their suppers. Such important names for such ordinary-looking animals—Boom's Hallelujah, Nancy B.'s Comet, Bailey's Irish Cream. Whatever happened to Pardner and Red and Banjo? Mr. Ed? Why couldn't a horse skip a meal now and again if he felt like it? Hay could get boring, even pressed into those neat little cubes. What was the big deal? The stable goat crossed in front of him—apparently running loose was a way of life. The small horns looked innocent, but he'd seen one of the stable hands get popped onto his ass by the creature, so he gave it a wide berth.

The hills rising up behind the stables were green this time of year, bright long grasses and deeper green where cacti bloomed with waxy white flowers, soon to be replaced by the plum-colored fruit Chloe told him the grooms gathered to make a cheap but potent wine. Tiny wildflowers bloomed as if ushering in spring. He wondered if Chloe might take him out on those trails someday—if he could take a look at them through her eyes—come September, if Asa was right, there'd be time for anything. He could do any number of things besides teach. And hopefully Dodge would see to it that Chloe could join him. He needed to call his mother, touch base. Ought to explain to her about Chloe, how it was, meet the two of them for supper and smooth the waters down a bit, introduce Henry senior eventually. Maybe next week, when things were a little calmer, after he'd talked to some people at school—learned whether Asa's message had been just a rumble of thunder or actual fact.

She wanted to go to a bar in San Juan, where there was food and drink, live music, and old friends. "We need some music to cheer us up," she said. "Plus, it's about time I introduce you around. You've already got this reputation as my savior." She leaned over and kissed his neck. "They'll be checking for your halo, Hank."

"Will I pass muster?"

"Likely they'd have to see you ride before they let you into the club."

"I can ride a horse."

She looked surprised.

"That's right, I can. I can do several things that might surprise you."

The Swallows Inn was crowded with slumming yuppies and old timers, a smattering of the Harley-Davidson wanna-be crowd who worked regular jobs until five, then did a Cinderella metamorphosis into black leather and chains. Out front, the place was plastered with fliers advertising the upcoming March parade, and contests for predicting the date the swallows would return, notices for the three-day rodeo. There were want ads for used motor homes and hardly used horse trailers. Inside, back toward the dance floor, three old cowboys whistled and waved as Chloe came through the door. Hank took hold of her arm.

"Come on," she said. "Don't lose heart now."

She made the introductions: Wesley McNelly, Francisco Montoya, Gabriel Hubbard, DVM. Francisco chattered low in Spanish—*Who is this guy? Looks like a carpet salesman to me. He treating you right, Chloe?*

Hank wanted to answer him in his own passable Spanish but knew he'd learn more if he played dumb. A barmaid wearing a toy holster set brought beer for them. Gabriel Hubbard gave her a possessive squeeze, and she patiently removed his hand.

"Come on, Tracy, be nice," he said, and she set the shooters of tequila for the others down with exasperated patience. "Tracy goes to graduate school, don't you, darlin'?"

She took his money. "Just to pass the time until I get to come here."

Gabe said, "It gives her an attitude, you know?"

Hank smiled faintly.

Chloe ordered them rare steaks and home fries, turned to Hank and said, "Trust me, you're gonna love it."

He wanted to. But when the Lonesome Prairie Band struck up a swing tune, cast and all her protestations be damned, Wesley McNelly took her out to the dance floor and Hank was left alone with two strangers, both of whom were smiling and staring at him expectantly. It was an alien landscape. He made himself sip his beer, cut small bites of steak, and chew them twenty times each.

"Hard to believe she can dance with that cast on," Gabe said. "Seems there's nothing in this world that can down our Chloe for long."

"I'm well aware of that."

The vet held his gaze steady. "I bet you are."

Then it was Francisco's turn to dance with her. While he guided her slowly through a handicapped version of the two-step, Wesley buddied up to Hank. "What's your line, Hank?"

"I teach over at the junior college."

"Teaching. Now there's a noble profession. What's your field?"

"Folklore and mythology."

Wesley squinted. "I'm not sure I follow. Does that mean the little stories?"

"In a way."

"There a lot of call for that nowadays?"

Hank swallowed down the last of his beer. All intellectual arguments were sieves to piss beer through. "Actually, it looks like next term I'm going to be fired."

Gabe clapped him on the back. "Well, why didn't you say so right off?" He nabbed the waitress on a pass to the bar. "Tracy, bring the professor here a shooter and a chase, will you? Got something to celebrate."

Wesley grinned, Gabe grinned, Hank drank his drink, trying to locate a grin inside the alcohol to go along with them.

On the wall before him hung a mounted deerhead with marble eyes and fourteen points of horn sporting a ball player's cap, a horseshoe, a peach-colored brassiere. The art was of the Miller HighLife glowing clock variety—bears palming struggling salmon in everlasting waterfalls. Any blank wall space was filled in with rude signs, crude jokes, notices. A clock that said "No drinking until after five" turned a single second hand; every number it passed was a big, red, and not terribly surprising five. Hank drank his shooter, the next one Wesley bought for him, switched back to beer over their protests, and ate but never tasted the steak, his palate numbed by alcohol. Chloe reappeared from time to time, grabbed a bite of her dinner, her face animated and her conversation a whisper under the throbbing music.

The singer in Lonesome Prairie was well past fifty, a chrome-white platinum blond with a black velvet ribbon tied around her crepey neck. Her dress featured ruffles that made Hank think of circus clowns in whiteface. When she took a break and went off to smoke a cigarette at the bar, the boys in the band launched into an instrumental version of "Amarillo by Morning." Wesley McNelly stood up and accepted the fiddle player's offer of his violin. He set the instrument beneath his chin and began sawing notes into conical piles of longing, each flat and sharp slicing like a razor into the smoke-filled room. It was more than a decent rendition; the man was gifted. Hank saw tears welling up in Chloe's eyes. Francisco patted her hand. *No te triste, mi amiga.* Gabe Hubbard lifted her up off the barstool and danced her across the floor, his pelvis thrust into hers, driving her out of her mood and into the dance. Only a man who'd been her lover could do that and not get slapped. He had that funny, hunched-over cowboy stance to his dancing, formal from the hands up, but decidedly intimate from the belt buckle on down. She kept her brown eyes on Wesley, let her head rest on Gabe's shoulder.

Hank felt the alcohol lending everything a fun-house angle. He sobered up, made his way through the dancers and cut in, Gabe backing away, hands up as if Hank held out a gun. "She's all yours, buddy."

He didn't know those steps the other men used, but what was so wrong with a box step? Her cast thumping on the wooden floor, she danced the last dance with Hank. When the bartender hollered out last call, Tracy balled up her apron and threw it at Gabe, smiling.

"I told you college wasn't ever going to be enough to satisfy you," he said, chasing her across the floor until they both disappeared into the back room. Hank went to pay the check, but found it had been taken care of by Gabe Hubbard.

A few minutes later Gabe reappeared. "I can't let you pay for our meal," Hank said.

"Relax. Someday you might be able to return a favor."

Hank didn't like the way he looked at Chloe when he said it. He liked it even less when the big man scooped her up and carried her out to the Honda.

"She give you good mileage?" Wesley asked.

For a moment Hank thought he'd meant Chloe. "I beg your pardon?"

"Don't get riled. I'm talking about your car, son."

"Decent." Its smallness was made more obvious alongside the king cabs and double-axled trucks. Fuck them. None of these men was taking her home. He was. That counted for something.

She came out of the bathroom in an old T-shirt of his that didn't cover much. The triangle of pubic hair showing was the tail end of a heart. It glistened with water from her cat-bath. She limped over to the bed, yawned, and stretched her hands above her head. He looked at her belly, the breasts that defined the T-shirt in profile.

"I had a good time tonight. Why didn't you? Tell me, Hank. I know you're mad at me, but I don't know what I did wrong."

"Nothing. We're just extremely different people."

"On the surface, maybe. Inside we're a lot alike."

"Hardly."

"You'd better help me out here. I think I'm losing you."

"What a funny way to put it."

"Now you're scaring me."

He pushed her back onto the mattress, kissed her hard, pressed her legs apart, inched two fingers inside her, bent close and whispered in her ear. "You like this?"

She gasped. "I might, if you give me a minute to catch up."

"You like it. You like it more than any woman I've ever met. You want me right now?"

She pushed at his wrist with her hands. "What is the matter with you? It's late. You're drunk and you're heavy. Get off me."

He wrestled her down, jabbed at her with his cock.

She went limp. "Go on, if that's all you're after. Be my guest. Treat me like landfill. Dump your load and drive off."

His erection immediately went limp, and he jerked away from her, pressed her knees back together with trembling hands, and stood up.

Her voice punctured the dark. "I don't understand. You're curious about my friends, you kept on saying you wanted into that world. So I take you there. Why's three old buddies of mine dancing me through my troubles so goddamn threatening? I'm here in your bed, aren't I?"

"Our lives are too different, Chloe. I don't see how we can make it."

She was quiet. "If that's what you believe, no amount of argument from me will convince you."

He watched her get up and pull on the yellow sweatpants he'd brought to her in jail. She said, "You want me to sleep in the other room? I can be gone tomorrow."

"I don't want that."

"Then what? You have to tell me where this is going."

What did you say when you were a soon-to-be-unemployed teacher, when your own jealousy made you turn on the person you loved best? Once said, words didn't fit back on the tongue. Like devils set loose, they ran from one conclusion to the next, fearless of the havoc they wreaked. "I know you slept with that vet."

She turned back the covers and got into the bed, patting his space for him to join her. When he settled down onto the pillow, she nestled herself inside his arm, the length of her body flush with his, the cast making a tent of the sheet and blanket. He felt her breathing, even and calm, though her skin was tense. She laid her head across his heart, and he could feel each beat sending its rampant code of testosterone defensiveness into her cheekbone. He smoothed her hair with his other hand. It was soft and thick under his fingers in the darkness.

"I slept with Gabe, all right, but not for the reasons you think. It was a while ago. Sometimes we do stuff to get by, Hank. It shames me to say it, but Gabe was one of those times I had a choice that wasn't much of a choice. I won't deny it."

If he had been less drunk, less guilty, he might have taken her in a close embrace and told her for the first time that he loved her, that he didn't care what her past held, then sealed what the saying of those words meant with lovemaking, but he didn't—couldn't.

The first phone call came at three-fifteen, waking them both up from a sound sleep.

"My mother," Hank said, lurching for the phone.

"Absalom," Chloe said, climbing over him.

But it was no one, no one who would identify himself, either to Hank or to Chloe, who tried Spanish, thinking it was one of the stable hands with bad news, the shy boys who spoke deferentially to anyone they didn't know well, fearful of immigration at every turn.

The line was too quiet, as if somebody on the other end needed to hear one of them say a frantic hello to get through the rest of the night. After they hung up, Hank and Chloe lay together in the bed, too jittery for sleep, too tense for speculation. Chloe gave up around four and went downstairs to make coffee. Hank followed.

"You want some toast?"

"Am I forgiven for last night?"

She turned from the counter and pointed a finger. "You promise to stay out of the tequila?"

"I do. I feel awful."

"I'm glad."

"Thanks so much."

"Well, you brought it on yourself."

"What do you make of that phone call we had last night?"

"One of your old girlfriends?" She handed him a cup. The streetlights shone outside the windows, and it was still too early for the newspaper.

CHAPTER

17

Y ou look like you're in a real bad mood. Are you on your period? I get horrible right before my period. I cry and eat way too much chocolate and then I throw up. Oh, my god. Are you *not* on your period?"

Chloe gripped the steering wheel. "Kit, honestly."

"Listen, how am I supposed to know if you're being conscientious? People get pregnant all the time."

"Well, I don't."

"Still."

"Trust me, it's not that. Some jerkoff is getting his kicks by calling Hank all hours of the night. I can't sleep and it's pissing me off."

"How weird. Who do you think it is?"

"I don't know. One of his old girlfriends, most likely. Jesus, I hope he gets a new phone number soon. I'm about done in."

"You could move. Me and my dad have two extra bedrooms. If you lived with us we could be together almost all the time."

Chloe stopped the truck in front of the box stalls a little quicker than she had planned to. Ropes, boots, and Kit's purse slid to the floor. "You're not the one who's calling, are you?"

Kit's face turned red. "Of course not! Fucking A, Chloe! How could you even think it?"

"Sorry. I'm so tired I suspect everybody. Hey, what'd you get on your interview project? I'm dying to know."

Kit stayed tight lipped. "Hasn't been graded yet."

"Will you let me know when it is?"

"Maybe." She opened her door.

"Goddammit, Kit, wait." The girl flew out of the cab in a huff, biting the tips off carrots before passing them randomly through the open stall doors. Chloe could see a dozen muzzles lean out hopefully. The horses knew Kit. Her gentle hands and quiet talk had won them over; the carrots were frosting.

Chloe bent to the truck's floor and loaded up her arms with the newly purchased ropes and a packet of herbal salts Wes included. It was some kind of neon pink appetite enhancer, and he bet her a longneck Coors it would work on Absalom. Just mix it in with his chow and stand back, he said. Ab had eaten yesterday, but only a quarter of his feed, then looked sour again. Maybe it was time to call Gabe.

"Chloe!" Kit's scream echoed through the barn.

She dropped the ropes in the dirt and ran as fast as her plastered leg would allow.

"He's cast!" she cried, unlatching the stall door.

"Quiet down, Kit. We'll get him up. Won't do him any good if we start getting hysterical." She gently eased the girl out the stall door, took a quick inventory of the entire situation. Ab was down on his left side. The feeder was full of hay cubes. There were two piles of manure, easily hours old, nothing so odd looking about them that it should cause the dark horse to colic. Moreover, he wasn't writhing like his gut hurt, he was lying still, his breathing labored, his chest lathered as if he had been run hard and not cooled down properly. She checked his vitals, nothing too off the mark. She tried all her usual tricks, but he didn't want to get up. As a last resort, she felt the laminae of each hoof, but just as she expected, they were cool.

Kit's voice trembled. "In my horse book it says they can die from laying down. Is that right?"

Chloe nodded.

"Here, boy, have a carrot." Kit waved one in front of Ab's face, but he was past carrots.

"Over by the pay phone there's a list of telephone numbers. Dr. Hubbard. Can you call him for me, Kit? Tell him to drop everything and come right away. And tell Francisco I need him to help me get Ab up."

"Sure. I'm already there."

"You need a quarter?"

"I got one."

When Kit was gone, Chloe settled herself down next to her horse. She lifted his head, brushed it clean of shavings and dirt, and cradled it in her arms, touching the fine bones and cartilage that formed the Roman nose she'd brushed nearly every day of her life for the last seventeen years. His nostrils, lightly tinged on the edges with pink, flexed open and shut as breath sieved in and out of his lungs. She knew the anatomy of a horse so well she could have taken a stick and drawn the respiratory system in the dirt, but she didn't know what was wrong with him.

Last night he'd been a little twitchy in the forequarters, but not overly so. She'd haltered him and walked him up and down the breezeway. He'd seemed nervous—he was a thoroughbred—sometimes all it took to get him riled was the wind changing direction. He'd managed to get out of his stall once or twice, rip his chest up good on barbed wire, founder in the grain shed, but never before had he taken this kind of dive. She looked up. All around them his neighbors stood watching. Animals knew. Their senses weren't daunted by human convention. If one of their species was headed for the exit door, they either gave him a wide berth or formed a circle of support. She stared at their questioning muzzles and wished she could ask them what had taken place in the last twelve hours. As soon as the excitement of Chloe's arrival subsided, back they went to eating their cubes, drinking great draughts of water, and snorting out morning greetings.

Kit came running back, her red hair streaming out behind her. "He's on his way right now. I told them it was you and he got on the phone himself."

"Thanks. Francisco?"

Kit frowned. "He's down at the gelding pasture. They tore the fence out last night. But he's coming."

"Good."

Kit pressed her face into the stall bars and kicked the dirt with her riding boot. "Chloe? Can I come in there and sit with you?"

"I don't know if that's such a good idea, honey. We don't know what might happen next."

"I just want to hold a hoof."

"All right. But as soon as Gabe's truck gets here, you have to stay out of the way, okay?"

"Okay." She brought a dandy brush in with her, and ran it lightly over the horse's flank, then gathered his tail in her lap and untangled the long hairs, brushing them until they were shiny, separating them into smaller bundles to make dozens of tiny plaits. Chloe watched her stubby fingers work, heard her humming some Top Forty tune to herself like a lonesome five-year-old playing with her dolls. Even without a vet's diagnosis she knew that her horse was dying, that no matter what trick Gabe pulled out of his truck, it was happening. Absalom was twenty-one, old for a thoroughbred. He'd had a full life, the navicular disease was pressing on her to make a decision anyway. Maybe it was a myth, that business about childhood being a happy time, hers wasn't; Kit's could serve as proof that things weren't getting better. This time she didn't have to ask Hank what the gods had to say about that, she'd looked over his shoulder and read enough of his lecture notes to know. Half the time the sons of bitches were changing their kids into goats, the other half burning them up in the sun. Hubris, he called it. He said that was what separated mortals from gods. At some point she'd have to call to let him know what was happening. In a couple of days they were going to court. He'd badgered her all week about getting a dress, and she agreed to go shopping tonight just to get out of the few hours she spent in the house. The phone calls were driving them both to screaming fits; if they took the receiver off the hook at night, it would ring first thing in the morning like a knee-jerk reflex. Nobody there, just the listener, the two of them taking turns blaming each other for some twisted fool's shenanigans—and she'd accused Kit, well, that wouldn't be forgotten in a hurry. None of this would. She missed her shack in Hughville. Running water cost money, and solitude exacted its own price, but it had been a rare and fine time. She guessed Hannah was dead now, it had been so long. Funny, she didn't feel dead to her heart, not the way Fats did.

Here, next to the horse he'd broken and trained, she was flooded with memories. Fats was back, right here in this stall, squatting down on the heels of his worn black Justin Ropers, examining a horse he'd birthed, gentled, and seen master third-level dressage, been offered ten thousand dollars for on more than one occasion, but saved to give freely to Chloe, whom he once loved.

Tell me what to do, she begged. *You're the expert. Horses die all the time, you used to tell me. Make my heart believe it.* Beyond the breezeway she could hear crows calling to each other. Bright sunshine cast long shadows angling down from the aluminum roof. Rangy hens passed silently through the stalls looking for dropped grain. She reached over and picked some shavings out of her grimy cast.

Gabe's truck eased slowly through the breezeway, and the hens scattered. He had the door open before he came to a complete stop.

She saw him grab a batch of syringes and a box of medicines before he came inside. At the stall door, he looked at Absalom before he looked at her. He was never more gorgeous than when he was humbled by work. Tending a mare through a difficult delivery, his face would focus inward, determined to set aside any notion of statistics just to see that baby into the world. Putting down an aged horse, his hands were quiet and considerate, soothing; the honest portion of his soul shone through no matter what a bastard he was with women. This morning he wore a dryer-rumpled, clean white T-shirt stretched over his muscular chest, Wrangler jeans pulled on with no belt, probably no underwear beneath that. For a rich man he was simple. His work boots were muddy. He met her glance shiftily. He knew something she didn't, something that confirmed her worst suspicions without him saying a word.

He nodded hello. "Chloe, Kit."

"Hey, Dr. Hubbard."

"Gabe."

"I'll get us some Cokes," Kit said, and slipped out the stall door.

"Just tell me right out, Gabe. I can take it."

"Let me get this in first." He found a vein and started an IV of Ringers. He went back to the truck and gloved up, took a plastic sack and dumped all the cubes from the feeder into it, removed his gloves and tossed them into the sack, sealed the top, tagged it, and set the sack inside the truck. When that was done, he came over and sat down next to her, taking her arm and freeing her splayed fingers from the horse's neck. He stroked her hand.

"We have to get him up," she said. "Francisco's coming."

"I've had a busy couple of days. We lost one at Serrano the same way, there's two down at the fairgrounds and one out in Norco I heard of that died before the vet could get there. Rumors of places as far away as Bakersfield having the same kind of trouble."

"What kind of trouble?"

He shook his head. "Nobody's sure. Could be a virus. There's some speculation about contaminated feed. As of today all the hay cubes are being recalled."

She waved a hand toward the other horses. "Nobody else's sick, and they're all eating the same shit. I don't buy it."

"The early necropsies show some evidence that way."

She looked down at the horse's head in her lap. His eyes were shut; he breathed, but not as easily as before. "Save my horse, Gabe," she said quietly.

He showed her a vial. "This stuff's worth more than my truck. I got it Air Express from the CDC this morning. If you're willing to gamble, I'll give it to him, but it hasn't worked on anybody yet."

"What is it?"

"A hurry-up antiserum to a trace strain of botulism found in one of the dead horses."

"If it's an antitoxin why won't it work?"

"Because it seems like by the time the horse goes down it's too late for it." He drew up several syringes and injected them into the tubing of the IV.

All day people gathered, stood silent outside the stall, came and went, nobody saying anything beyond a soft hello. The grooms hurried wheelbarrows from stall to stall, taking back the hay cubes and replacing them with flakes. Somebody brought Chloe a hamburger, but she set it aside and Rabbit, the curly-coated stable mutt, finished it and spent the rest of the day guarding the stall as if it were his personal duty. The stable owners raced back and forth talking on cellular telephones, baled hay was unloaded and stacked into a twenty-foot square, and the hens immediately tried to roost on top. It seemed as though nearly everybody had gotten the news about the feed and had come out to check their horses. People Chloe hadn't seen in years came by. Some young girls, students she'd taught, and their friends were crying. That was okay, they were just putting a voice to what everyone felt. Kit herded them off, looking fierce. How she could have accused her of the phone calls was beyond reasoning.

"I'm here for the duration, Chloe," Gabe said. "We'll sit this through together, but when he's had enough, I want your promise you'll let me send him home, not let him suffer."

She nodded, her fingers numb from the constant stroking.

At sixteen Chloe Morgan fit into size three blue jeans. Her butt was barely two man-size handfuls of flesh, her calves muscled tight in the stovepipe legs, just aching to grip the barrel of a horse, any horse. When Ben and Margaret gave her the go-ahead for a part-time job, she was at Whistler's Stables the following afternoon. The only work Eddie Whistler had available was mucking stalls, and he raised some doubts as to whether she'd hold up.

"You just try me," she said. "One week. If I don't pan out, fire me. But if I can keep up, I get to keep the job."

She was built for hard work, and her muscles sang under the weight of the pitchfork. After three days, she'd learned enough Spanish to play a fair hand of poker with the boys and she'd caught the attention of the lone trainer, a broken-down racetrack man named Fats Valentine. Once he'd been legendary for matching horse to rider on the show circuit between California and New Mexico. He'd lived high, driven Italian cars, and weathered his share of the successes, partying with team Leone, Shoe, some big names. But the horse world favored the young. Drugs and alcohol splashed like cheap cologne. The down times, nobody wanted to be his friend. A succession of three wives had left him, taking the cars and the cash. He'd screwed up more than his share, and the last down time, he stayed too long trying to balance a diet of gin with a comeback, and sunk for good. Small-time training was all he was capable of handling. He was forty-seven the year Chloe came to work at Whistler's; she was a few months shy of seventeen. He took one look at her rough-and-ready style, pulling a rocking-horse canter out of an old half-Arab, half-Morgan gelding she was allowed to exercise on her time off, and his heart beat hard against the wave of gin in which it floated.

"Just might make a rider out of that one," he said to his cronies, a continual parade of men he owed or who owed him money neither would ever be able to pay. "Check out her leg, boys. Look at that flexion."

By way of the grooms, Chloe heard his compliments repeated, peppered with the insinuation that the old man was really after her body. They danced around each other for a few weeks in that testing manner Chloe'd learned in various foster homes; distance a man's interest and you won't jeopardize the situation.

One rainy Saturday when lessons were canceled, Fats called her over in the barn and showed her Absalom, then a greenbroke four-year-old. He was beautiful in the way most thoroughbreds are, long back, perfect neck, chiseled features, shining body-clipped coat, and polished hooves, an ebony angel among the ruins of a third-rate operation. The girl who'd been showing him in halter classes was leaving for college in the fall.

"Who you going to put with him?" Chloe asked.

"You," Fats answered, taking a puff on his cigar.

"Right. What do I have to do? Suck your dick?"

He laughed so hard he got into a fit of choking. Chloe went glowering back to her stalls and filled up the wheelbarrows with steaming piles of manure in double time. At six o'clock she settled down in a box stall with her history book beside an old paint mare named Sheila to wait for her ride home. The rain beat its tune against the metal roof. She hated history, but Ben held the threat above her head, anything below a C, *adios* job. Sheila was excellent company. She didn't care about due process or constitutional amendments. It wouldn't be so bad to own an old horse. Sheila'd never rear up on you nor spook, not even if you lit a string of Mexican firecrackers underneath her. You could ride her all day, right across traffic. Dependable. After awhile Chloe realized Fats was standing in the aisle, watching her.

She kept her face in her book. "I got friends in these Mexican boys," she told him. "They're pretty handy with knives. You try anything on me and you'll be singing the high notes, buster."

"You don't trust any man, do you?"

"Give me one good reason why I should."

"Because a few of us are good guys."

"Well, you know what they say. For the money, there's nothing like a gelding."

"Ouch. Don't be so quick to cut. You're missing out on a whole world of good times."

"Sure, I'm going to end up pregnant with some lifetime brat just so a guy can get his rocks off. No thanks." She scoffed. "Get lost. I have to pass history or I can't even ride, and that's the one thing I want to do."

"Want doesn't even enter into the equation, darlin'. You *have* to ride. With you it isn't even a question of want. But you're wasting your time with nags like Sheila. You can't learn anything on an easy horse. You need a challenge."

She shut the book. "I'll say one thing for you, mister, you're not above dangling a long line."

"Well, you know where my trailer is. Come see me if you want to ride the thoroughbred. Maybe we can work something out."

Then he was gone, his cheap cigar smoke with him, the gravelly voice just an echo in the barn. Had she dreamed him? That night as she lay in bed she wasn't thinking of American history, she was seeing herself in a full riding habit, all new stuff, atop a fine saddle and fixed to that thoroughbred: Absalom's Dancing Irish. Word was his line went clear back to Northern Dancer, but as Francisco said, probably if you pricked him with a pin all the famous blood would leak out in two seconds. She didn't sleep at all, copied the answers to the test from a spectacled boy who had the hots for her, and managed a B–. Ben was thrilled; he gave her twenty-five dollars as a reward. She took the money to Mr. Valentine and asked for as many lessons as it would buy her. He thought about it for a half an hour, during which time she mentally rehearsed several apologies that bordered on groveling. Then he walked by and said, Okay, five lessons, but you have to groom all the summer shows for my regular students and we start tonight, after I finish group lessons. Find yourself boots, a helmet, and have the horse saddled and bridled and in the ring when I get here. She thanked him soberly, went into the portable toilet, and threw up her lunch.

"*Embarazada, chica?*" Francisco and the Mexican boys teased.

"*Mocosos!*" She chased them around the barn, grinning stupidly. "You *vatos* just cut it out," she told them, unable to stop her stupid grin. "Just *cayense!*"

They were inseparable, the blond girl and the dark bay horse. *That Chloe Morgan's better than a goddamn billboard,* Eddie Whistler said. *People see her riding Black Beauty around town and follow her, just to see where they're headed.* And that had brought him a ton of new business. She was there before school for morning turnout, there when the vet came to do Ab's shots, there when the farrier was out to see to his feet, personally mucked out his stall and brought him his feed, carefully adding trace elements and vitamins in mathematics she hadn't heretofore understood.

Out in the ring, Fats would stand in the center and holler at her: *Position yourself, you ride like a sack of old laundry. Straighten that back! You trying to hide your tits? Act proud you're endowed! Drop your heels, you ain't riding bareback now. Slow down, you think you're on a fucking motorcycle? Slack up on the reins, Chloe, Jesus, I'd hate to be your boyfriend if you hold on that hard.* She glowered and did everything he said. Along the rail the Mexicans and Eddie Whistler stood watching and laughing, everybody garnering the maximum entertainment from the Fats and Chloe show, talking long odds, taking bets on who'd get mad and walk out of the ring first. Nearly always it was Chloe, leading the bay horse properly, calmly, each stomp of her boots packing rage into the arena sand, but every once in a while it was Valentine, lighting up a cigar, his face suffused to a port wine with anger, muttering, *You can't teach anything that hardheaded, Lord God, what a mistake.*

Absalom learned fast, Chloe a little more slowly. By the following summer she was showing in her first equitation classes, baby hunter, green over the low fences, winning everything, pressuring Fats to let her start Absalom in pre-first-level dressage. Fats slowed down his drinking. He got regular haircuts. On Chloe's high school graduation day he declined an invitation to the ceremony, but the stablehands went, hair slicked down, over their worn jeans, clean white shirts, the creases where the pins had been stuck still showing. Eddie Whistler went too and lived up to his name, letting go with a big-city taxi-raising toot when the principal announced her name. Eddie gave her a silver necklace with a horseshoe charm; Chloe got tears in her eyes, kissed his whiskery cheek, embarrassing him so badly that his hands shook. Francisco gave her a bunch of wildflowers. Back at the barn, Fats had a gift for her, too: a brand new Hermès saddle and girth.

"You stole that son of a bitch," she said, handing it back. "I don't want it. I'm nearly eighteen. All my life I've been stuck in institutions. No hot saddle is about to make me add jail to the list."

He took out his wallet and showed her the receipt. He'd gotten a hefty discount—he still had connections—but it was paid in full and it still cost a fair chunk of money. No one had ever given her such a present. On the back of the cantle a small brass nameplate bore her name in cursive script: Chloe Morgan. In the cool June air, Chloe stood before him in her jeans and a sweatshirt, the silver horseshoe and chain glittering between her small breasts. She had a blister on her left foot from the high heels Margaret bought her to wear to the graduation ceremony. They and the dress were in the back of Ben's truck, the rebuilt Chevy Apache. She told her foster parents she was going to the school graduation party, an overnight do at Disneyland—they locked you in and you rode the Matterhorn bobsleds until you never wanted to see a mountain or a roller coaster again—*Sounds like fun, Sweetheart, go on and have a good time. Here's twenty bucks for snacks and souvenirs.* She pocketed the money for lessons, and she came here as she had intended to all along. A whole night alone with the horse, no timetables, now that was a party. She rode Absalom in the dark, and Fats came out of the trailer to watch her. He leaned against the arena railing, the glowing tip of his cigar and the occasional flash of uplifted pint bottle defining him. An hour before dawn she and Fats were cantering on the damp sand at Huntington State Beach, laughing through a couple of beers at the way the horses pawed the breakwater.

Fats was a fine rider. He'd done some trick riding as a kid on the rodeo circuit, polished up his equitation during a brief marriage to an Alabama deb whose father raised Arabs before the breed was spoiled. When they stopped to rest, he reached over to give Chloe a friendly kiss, and though she was terrified, it was she who made the fatal turn of her face to meet his lips. She'd thought it over for months, how illogical it was to be attracted to a gray-haired drunk who smoked cigars and had a potbelly, how boys her own age were after her all the time, the Mexicans sometimes got into fistfights over her, and she'd kissed Francisco often enough to know she liked him, and kissing— but it was Fats she dreamed about—always. The breathy electricity inside that kiss surprised them both.

"I am old enough to be your goddamned daddy," he said.

"Well, I never had one, but I guess you are that old. Still, you don't kiss like it."

He pointed a finger. "One foolish kiss in the moonlight don't mean spit. You'll be getting your hopes up for a house with a picket fence and rug rats. I've been through that more times than I care to recall. It don't work, it will never work, and I don't want it."

"I don't care," she said. "I just want to be your friend."

"My friend."

"Your *close* friend."

They argued about that for a good ten minutes, then agreed to race across the sand to Pacific Coast Highway. Absalom snorted and pranced in the sea air, and Chloe gripped his mane with her right hand, leaned forward, squeezed her eyes shut, and gave him his cue. As Absalom exploded into a full gallop, she thought how she should have bet money on the race. Fats would bet on just about anything. It was a fair race. Both horses were in good shape and near the same age. Still, just as she knew she would, she won.

"We gave it a fair trial, Chloe. Now let go. He's suffering."

It had been that time a long while ago. They both knew it. Chloe motioned for Kit to come inside the stall. The girl grasped her outstretched hand. "What do you need? You name it and I'll get it." Tears overflowed and streaked her plump cheeks.

It took her a minute to find her voice, and when she did it was reedy. "It's time to say good-bye, Kit."

"No." Kit pulled away. "No. I don't want to."

Chloe pulled her back. "Don't be scared. You don't have to stay, I won't make you. But he was your friend, too. You were good to him. You were a part of his life. If you say good-bye now it won't hurt so much later on."

Kit looked around as if one of the bystanders might tip the vote.

"Like with your mom, Kit."

"Don't bring that up. It's not fair to bring that up. Let go of me!"

"Please."

She scooted in next to Chloe, put her arm around her shoulders, and together the two of them made her shaking hand press down onto Absalom's neckflesh. Kit's hand was clammy from wiping tears, Absalom's neck was damp from sweat. Chloe held Kit's hand and made her pull it once through the short black hair. When she lifted her hand, four tracks from Kit's fingers stayed behind in the lather.

"I thought someday I might get good enough to ride you," Kit said. "You are the most beautiful horse I ever—"

Her words choked off in her throat. She pulled her hand free from Chloe's and ran out of the stall.

"Chloe?" Gabe said.

She nodded. "Every day of my life was a way of saying I love you to this beast. I never expected it to last even half this long. Send him home, Gabe. Do it quick."

The silver needle pierced the intravenous tubing and the barbiturates penetrated the horse's bloodstream. He breathed for a time, then, after one long body-racking shudder, he no longer breathed. His body fluids released into the cedar shavings. Chloe hugged Gabe to her, laid Absalom's head down into the shavings, and stood up with Gabe's help. One of the stable hands came inside and covered Absalom's body with an old cooler blanket. Chloe looked back. The embroidery glinted in the flashlight glow. On the side of the blanket were two stitched oranges and the cursive lettering *champion*.

Gabe removed his doctoring tools and tossed them into the back of his truck.

Chloe said, "Did I have lessons to give tonight? I can't remember."

"Diane took them for you," somebody answered.

"Maybe I'll go on home."

Gabe put an arm around her and thrust his hand into her right jeans pocket, removing her car keys. "You go on and take a little walk and then you come back here. We're not quite finished."

Numbly she did as he said, Kit leading her along. Alone inside the portable toilet, she stared up at the blue plastic walls. No tears would come. She threw up the Coke Kit had bought her, rinsed out her mouth with the hose outside, and walked back to Gabe, dragging the ankle cast in the dirt.

Midway between her truck and the breezeway stalls, Gabe stood with Casper and Billy, two of the rent string horses saddled up with full Western tack. They were rangy quarter horses, nothing much to look at, but sound and dependable, or they never would have lasted as rent horses. "Get on," he said, indicating Billy.

"I should wait for the knacker," she said. "He'll want money."

"It's taken care of."

"And Kit, I'm supposed to get her home."

"She already called her dad. You're flat out of excuses. Mount this horse, Morgan."

She bit a thumbnail, looked back toward the breezeway to where his truck was still parked at a crazy angle. She whispered, "I don't ever want to ride again."

"You get back in the car after somebody blindsides you, honey. The first thing you do is get back behind the wheel and drive. This is the good doctor talking to you."

"You're a veterinarian."

"Only difference between horse medicine and people medicine is the goddamn labels they glue on the prescription bottles. I stitched up your shoulder, didn't I, when the tendon was showing, and it works. I've shot more penicillin into your butt than any white-coated M.D. It's a matter of opinion, but I'd say it looks like I did right by you."

She put a foot into the stirrup, and he hefted her behind, sending her the rest of the way up. Billy, always one for the moment, whinnied a spine-rippling hello.

Gabe led the way, taking them up a steep incline and off-trail to the fire road leading to the Old Camp trail. In the dark Chloe rode carefully, concentrating on each footfall. They went five miles at a walk, down into the forest floor where the last of the winter rains still shone from the creekbed, washing the smooth stones to a gray roundness. They were mounded up as if they had been hand fashioned, bright clay circles, a child's architecture. Out of the thickest oak and eucalyptus trees they rode into the fire road proper and stopped at a cattle trough to allow the horses to drink. Just past here was where she and Kit had found the dead cow, but she couldn't make out any carcass now. Coyotes might have dragged it into the underbrush, and turkey buzzards had probably set to recycling it. Gabe tapped her shoulder and she saw the outline of a barn owl resting on a tree stump. It stood so still it could have been carved of wood, but when a rein buckle rang against the horse trough, the bird took flight, its head turning nearly three hundred and sixty degrees. Then with that strange vertical lift of stubby body that flung it into the darkness, it was part of the night sky, one dark motion.

Gabe set Casper in an extended trot down the length of the fire road, forcing Chloe to follow. Billy had a stumpy gait, and if you didn't post his trot, the next day the only thing you moved was your finger on the heating pad switch. Then Gabe went off through the brush, and Chloe lost sight of him. Billy set to whinnying again, that old call-and-response communication peculiar to horses. Each whinny resounded in her tailbone. Chloe called out in the darkness, "Gabe! Goddammit, this isn't funny. Where are you?"

"Right here, come on up."

Following his voice, she cut a series of switchbacks into the steep hillside, cursing Gabe's path. She hated hills, everyone knew that; she'd ride on the flat all day if she had the choice. There was a perfectly good trail on the other side of the hill that inclined slowly, but no, had to be this way or not at all—men. Hills made her fearful. There was always that primal urge to throw herself over the edge. It came from nowhere, insisting she follow. She was out of breath and scared to her marrow by the time she found him, standing one foot up on a rock outcropping, smoking a cigarette. She dismounted, unhooked one side of the reins from the bit, and let the rein drop; Billy was trained to ground-tie, and he wouldn't stray now that he stood next to his friend.

"Mother of God, that view's about as ugly as a goat's ass," Gabe said, pointing his cigarette down toward the flashing city lights—pink, purple, lemon yellow, green. "I can't remember when I've last been in pitch blackness. They'll be putting a K Mart up here next."

She slapped his face. "I could have broken my neck coming up that cliff. Why didn't you wait for me?"

He shrugged off the slap. "I figured taking the hard way might cause you to start caring about your life again."

She balled up her fist and sent it toward his smart mouth; he caught it easily and held her at the wrist.

"You go on and beat the living shit from me if that's what it takes to make you feel better. You can hit on me till the sun comes up. Here, I'm letting go now. Start hitting."

She let her hands drop. Gabe pulled her close and sat them both down against that rock while the horses nickered nervously at her noise. He stroked her damp hair back from her face and waited for the tears to empty.

An hour later, neither she nor Gabe had a dry sleeve left to wipe her face on.

"You just save it all up for a lifetime and then cry one time, is that the plan?"

She pulled away from the strong arms. "I'm going to be fine now."

Gabe gave her thigh a pat. "Good. You had me worried."

"Gabe? Why don't we take off our clothes and make each other happy? We've done it before—we sure know how."

She heard his sharp intake of breath—he was tempted. There was nothing like the practiced hands of Gabe Hubbard for inducing temporary amnesia. He could make the body sing. He knew her. She knew him. It wouldn't have to mean anything more than that. The gaping exit wound left by Ab needed a long bridge of bandages to stretch across it, and this could be the first one. He nuzzled her neck, kissed her mouth open, undid her shirt buttons clear down to her navel, and stroked a breast, groaning when she arched her upper body to meet his hands. But he stopped her hand when it slipped inside the waistband of his jeans. She'd assumed right—no underwear—just the furry slate of his belly.

"What's wrong?"

"I can't."

"You've been after me for a year. Why not now, when I need it?"

"It just isn't right, Chloe. Someday you and I have got to face the facts."

"But we're great together." She wove the tip of her tongue between his fingers. "We fit like dovetailed cedar, you always said."

"Yeah, we did. But there's a few more pieces to consider now. This professor, for instance."

"Don't talk—just be here with me now."

He tucked her breast back into its bra cup and pulled the two halves of her shirt together.

"Please. I'm begging now."

He took her face in his hands. "Chloe, Chloe. Tomorrow's going to be a world of hurt no matter what we do with our genitals tonight. You can feel bad about one thing or you can feel bad about fifty, it's up to you."

She laughed, and the sound came out flinty and bitter. "Don't tell me the old skirt chaser's growing a conscience."

"Hell, my daughters are growing it for me. Would you believe Cynthia had to fly over to Scottsdale and walk Nancy through an abortion last month? She's only fourteen, for Christ's sake. What do these kids think they're doing, fucking at fourteen?"

"Same as us, Gabe. Just trying to get through the night."

He smiled. "I told you a ride was just what you needed. You go home and saddle up that professor. Send him to the moon. That man loves you big time."

"Oh, for Christ's sake."

"What's the matter? Doesn't he like sex?"

"He likes it."

"Thank God."

The horses moved urgently through the darkness, flushing rabbits and mice from the trail. They wanted their stalls and routine back. Night rides were for war parties.

"I know he's at peace," Chloe said when they were leaning back in their saddles, coming down the last hill to the stables, "but I have a hard time imagining life without Absalom."

"He was your last tie with Fats. That's got to hurt."

"Well, no doubt there's that to consider. But it's more. He was my longest steady relationship, you know—like a marriage."

"So get yourself another horse."

She shook her head no and cleared her throat. "There's a million horses in California, but there won't ever be another Absalom."

"Not unless you're doing the training."

Now she was quiet.

"Penny for them, Morgan."

"Not worth a penny."

"Tell me anyway."

"You never let up on me, do you?"

"Only because I love you."

She was quiet. Love—that was the problem. Not that she wasn't capable of returning it, but uncertain as to whether or not she ever wanted to open herself up like that again, to love anything as completely and so recklessly as she had that horse.

Gabe tossed her car keys over and Chloe caught them in her fingers. "That's why I'm through fucking you on hillsides, sweetheart." He swung Casper wide and took the last fifty feet of trail at a hard gallop.

The sting of fresh tears seared her eyes. She bent forward and laid her head against Billy's neck, taking a deep breath of hard-worked horseflesh. He didn't smell the same as Ab—horses each had an individual particular scent—but the smell of any horse was comforting. She gave him a loose rein, and he trotted right up to his stall, whinnying to his buddies, *Here I am, I'm home, we made it back, guys.*

Francisco was unsaddling Casper. Gabe's truck was gone. Kit had gone home with her dad, and the stablehands who lived on the premises were tucked into trailers for the night. She allowed herself one glance back through the breezeway. Down at stall number 72 the blanket was folded neatly over the rails, a corner of it waving like a small tattered flag in the night breeze.

CHAPTER

18

Absalom's dead."

Dragged upward from sleep, Hank slowly became aware that he wasn't dreaming; it was Chloe on the edge of the bed, the glow from the bathroom light igniting her hair. She was a smeary mess from crown to cast, perfumed with horse, her features chiseled sharp in the semidarkness.

"What?" He roused to one elbow. All night he'd waited for her to come home to go shop for the dress. Furious, he'd gotten into the Glenfiddich and drunk himself into a slow boil. Around eleven, he quit trying to wait up and went to bed. He'd called the stables countless times and gotten that idiot recording in the phony Western drawl: *Sorry we missed ya, pardner!* Undoubtedly that meant everyone was out drinking at Cook's Corner, a local roadhouse Chloe pointed out on one of their drives. She and a bunch of other horse people had ridden down there on Absalom's twenty-first birthday and bought him a beer. On Sundays the place was a dazzling sheen of motorcycle chrome— the weekend Hell's Angels again. He'd called there, too, but no one had seen her. Every time he hung up, the phone rang back: the listener, punishing him for using his own phone.

"He's dead."

He echoed her words. "Dead?"

She swiped at her eyes. "Gabe thinks it was poisoned feed—supposedly botulism—how come if the sons of bitches suspected this a week ago, they didn't pull the feed then? How many horses had to die first? Why mine?"

Hank pushed the covers back, sat up and laid his head against her shoulder, then wrapped his arms around her. He pressed his body against her from behind, one hand pulling away the denim jacket, the other pulling her close. "Shh," he soothed. "Come here."

She stayed stiff in his arms. She did not like to be comforted the way other women seemed to and elbowed him away. "Shit, it's not your fault."

"He was your horse and you loved him. Can't I be sorry?"

"Guess I can't stop you."

"He had a good long life."

"I know that, too."

"You've been through a mile of shit this year. I don't know how you manage. Wish you'd let me help."

She reached back to stroke his neck. To Hank the gesture felt absent-minded, the reflex of an old woman mired in loss but so used to comforting the move came naturally. The room was quiet, fairly dark, save for the outdoor lighting bleeding through the miniblinds. Chloe often complained that it kept her from sleeping deeply—*They have this place lit up like a sentry post at a goddamn prison; how ever do you manage to sleep?*—*I just do,* he'd said, not ever really considering what she meant until this moment. The bedside telephone rang. Neither of them jumped at the noise, they knew it was the listener. It rang seven times, then Chloe picked it up.

"Whoever the fuck you are, we're two regular people here, and we work for a living. Give us a break, will you? Call during the daytime hours. Just leave us the night." She slammed the phone down.

Hank rubbed his face. "The phone company said it was a bad idea to talk to them. That we shouldn't anger them."

"Oh, fuck the phone company. How much good have they been to us yet?"

"They said they'd get the tap on next week."

"By next week we're liable to have murdered each other."

She got up and went to the bathroom, pulling the door shut behind her. Hank heard the water running, stop, then imagined she was stripped down, washing those parts of her body she could reach, swiping at others, her bathing still jerry-rigged due to the cast. The arrest, the dog, and now her horse. Why didn't she trust him? Should he offer to buy her a new horse? Not right away, certainly. How much could they cost? For a simple woman she was getting to be rather expensive. He exhaled into his palm, turned, then lay back down in the bed. First he would buy her a dress, and they would have a day in court.

"This is a great dress for somebody's Aunt Gladys," she said. "Why can't we go to a thrift shop and get me a disposable dress? It's not like I'd be wearing it more than one time. I'm not exactly a dress type of person."

"So I've noticed."

She gave him a pleading look: *Can we get out of here?* But he was definite. If it took all day, he would find her the dress that would tip the entire courtroom in her favor.

All the department stores met with Chloe's indignant smirk. *Look at these prices!* One by one, they were summarily dismissed. Hank nodded, steered her onto the successive doorways without comment. Then they found a small dress shop with a saddle in the display window—southwestern hype was seemed to be at an all-time high—Chloe stopped to look the saddle over.

"That's a nice saddle. Looks hand-tooled. I'd buy it if they were selling."

Hank looked at the saddle. It seemed to be in fairly decent shape, it didn't have a great deal of silver on it, but what there was was polished to a high sheen. "Why don't we go inside?"

"I'm tired of shopping."

"You can ask about the saddle. I'll look at the dresses." He could tell her leg was aching; she had that pinched mouth, but she wouldn't so much as reach for a Tylenol. Eventually she'd cave in—he'd wait her out.

"Last one."

He made the rounds of the racks with the salesclerk while Chloe chatted up the manager.

"What did you have in mind?" the clerk wanted to know.

He fingered the dresses in front of him. "Something conservative, with a fairly short skirt." He blushed. "That didn't come out right. She's not an easy woman to dress." He stammered and opened his hands. "Help me out here. I'm drowning."

The girl had a tattoo of an Indian chief on her shoulder. She laughed. "If it were up to men to dress us, which thank God it isn't, we'd all be wearing Laura Ashley high-collared dresses with Frederick's of Hollywood's nasties underneath. You guys think we don't have your numbers, but we do."

She started pulling hangers from various racks. Hank stood by the scarf rack, astonished at the price tags, wondering what one did with a ninety-dollar scarf nowadays.

The clerk returned with two outfits—a navy suit with white piping in a western cut, made fancy by the ruffled jacket hem. He shook his head. "I don't know."

"Give it a chance. See it on her first."

The other dress was dusty pink, with tea-colored lace running up and down the front. It had a dropped waist and hung on the wire hanger as if it were so much sacking. Like some turn-of-the-century prairie woman's Sunday best, the dress had a timeless charm to it. Hank fingered the lace. The clerk smiled. He knew if Chloe put that dress on it would transform her. He also knew she would have to be talked into it. He cleared his throat.

"I know," the salesgirl said. "Like it was made for her."

"Still, it's not exactly right for the occasion."

"Let me just set it aside so you can think about it."

She knew her business better than a bait-and-switch used-car salesman. He knew he would buy the dress, regardless of Chloe's yammering.

The blue suit performed its job nicely. She looked sedate but trim, the ruffle met the tapering skirt which proclaimed *Oh! Poor Me!* at precisely the top of the cast. Add the crutches and Marvin Mitchelson couldn't have put her together any better. Dodge would cackle with approval. Hank didn't listen to any of Chloe's protestations—price and practicality be damned—he went ahead and bought her a small white purse and shoes to go with the suit. He bought the pink dress, too, even after she refused to try it on, and sighed when Chloe closed a deal on the window-display saddle.

"It's a perfectly fine saddle," she said. "I have an old show saddle with a broken tree that would look even better in her window. I can use hers, she can use mine. It's not about money. It's barter, Hank, plain and simple."

"And here I stand with my silly toy dollars. Do I get to buy us lunch?"

She took his arm and leaned her shoulder into his. "Two dresses, a purse I'll never use, one shoe I can't wear, and you won't drive home to make sandwiches."

He ordered antipasto and an artichoke-and-prosciutto pizza from the outdoor Italian place. The sun was at their backs, pleasantly warm as it filtered through the tall glass windows. Chloe drank water; he allowed himself a glass of red wine and let the muddy darkness of last night slide from his tongue.

Chloe gave him a look. "What if we just leave town right this minute?"

"Where are we going to go?"

"You're the one with the atlas in his bookshelf. How about Europe?"

He played along. "Where would we go first?"

"I'd like to see Vienna."

"Vienna? That's interesting. Most people want the British Isles the first time around. The security of the language and all that."

"Are you kidding? The Spanish Riding School—seeing the Lippizaners perform the airs above the ground?"

"Everyone in your life comes second behind those horses, don't they?"

"Kind of."

"Will you get another horse?"

She tore off a piece of crust and held it between her fingers. "Eventually, probably. When I find the right one. Gabe says I should start with a yearling, train it all the way up myself, but I don't know. That takes a lot of time, a real commitment. I'll have to see."

"You're so calm."

"What do you mean?"

He waved a hand. He didn't want to say the name of her horse aloud. "Your losses."

She made a steeple with two hands and rested her chin on top of it. "They're here, all right, burning inside me like little lumps of coal. But I learned a long time ago that it won't bring anybody back if I kneel down and make a religion out of grief."

She was quiet for a few moments, the smile fading slowly from her face. The fountain nearby spilled its perfect columns of chlorinated water. Ferns grew green and lush in the nearby marble planter. Hank said, "Have you ever thought about looking for your parents?"

"Have you been talking to Kit?"

"Not really."

"Good. She's young and full of ideas about a fairy-tale ending around the corner, waiting on me to stumble into it. No, I haven't. Why should I feel beholden to the accident of growing in some woman's womb because she got unlucky? You tell me."

He reached across the table and took her hand, stroking the palm lightly. "I'd say your conception was extraordinarily lucky for me."

She studied her plate for a few minutes, then looked up into his face. Her brown eyes were wet, threatening to shred her tough exterior. "Hank, we're in a public place. Quit trying to get laid."

It was no big thing for him to dress in a suit and tie, but he marveled at the change in Chloe. She had her hair tucked up in a knot at the back of her head, and was yanking at her necklace. "I hate pearls."

"No one's going to know they're imitation."

"I don't care if they're real, they just feel like they're choking me. You shouldn't have bought them."

"Hush. I think I can afford twenty dollars for fake pearls. You look terrific. Is there any way I can get you in a dress again without involving the legal system?"

She maneuvered the crutches down the wide hallways. "I wouldn't go betting the farm."

"Well, isn't that just my luck."

"I feel like a pig on roller skates using these stupid crutches."

"Humor your lawyer. Dodge knows what he's talking about."

"*Your* lawyer."

"Chloe, he's yours, too."

"Hank?"

"What?"

"Is this going to be like Judge Wapner or what?"

He laughed. "Trust me. A courtroom looks like any other room in a city building. Quiet and boring, decorated by a Republican plagued by hemorrhoids."

He waited for her to negotiate the corner. The floors were slick amber marble. As they turned, he saw the assembled group waiting for her outside the courtroom—the veterinarian she'd slept with, the cadre of stablehands, Wesley McNelly dressed in a threadbare suit topped with a cream-colored cowboy hat, Rich Wedler of the café, his daughter, Kit. There were several other faces he didn't recognize, and the lone gentleman with the leathery face who towered over them could be none other than Hugh Nichols, the reason for Chloe's displacement and broken leg. She was mad at him—wouldn't take his phone calls, wouldn't accept his apology for the mess. There was a handful of reporters, too, cameras and light meters held high as they angled their best shots. None of that surprised him, though it seemed to move Chloe greatly. She had to stop and gather herself, and asked Hank to pass her a Kleenex. Don't let her cry, he begged silently to whichever sullen gods were half listening, help her keep it together for a few hours longer.

Asa Carver was there, too. He stood off to the side of the crowd, his face smirking. As soon as he spotted Hank, he shouldered his way out from behind a group of well-wishers and demanded an introduction.

"Asa, what a surprise."

"I don't know why. You're completely close-mouthed about this whole affair. I suppose I could wait for the papers, but I didn't have classes this morning."

"I see. Chloe? This is Professor Carver, English literature and composition. Don't let him kiss you."

"Why? Is he rabid?" Chloe shook his hand and let Kit Wedler dominate her attention. "You guys," she said. "You all should be at work."

Kit handed her a dark braided bracelet. Chloe asked Hank to fasten it onto her wrist.

"It's very clever, Kit," he said. "Did you make it yourself?"

"Yeah, I did."

"What is it? Elephant hair for good luck?"

"No. It's a braid from Absalom's tail. I only cut a little bit off. God, I hope you're not mad. Don't be mad, Chloe. It didn't hurt him or anything. Honest. I thought you would like it."

Chloe's face threatened to crumple for an instant. "It's better luck than any gold charm," she said, and gave the girl a hug.

The massive oak doors were shut, so the group waited outside them. Sunlight was deflected from these hallways by ceiling-high tinted windows designed to impart a feeling of spaciousness, but all the glass panels accomplished was to make the building feel like an expensively decorated, airless hamster cage.

Jack Dodge emerged from behind the courtroom doors, his face nearly broken in two by that fisherman's grin. "Who wants to go to an early lunch?" he asked. "After a last-minute conference behind the judge's doors, the sheriff's department has dropped all charges and agreed to pay all Ms. Morgan's medical expenses, plus a small sum for her trouble." He kissed Chloe's cheek. "Cheer up, girl. We got what we wished for. As of half an hour ago, you're cleared of all charges."

"So what was the last half hour about?" Hank asked.

He threw his hands up. "Planning a little expedition down to Cabo in June. His honor and I share a deep love for marlin."

Chloe said, "That's it?"

"That's it."

"I don't have to get up there and swear? No probation officer?"

"None of that."

"They can't change their minds?"

"Trust me."

"I could go back to Hughville if I wanted to?"

"Absolutely."

"God, I never expected this. Thank you."

She let out a hoot of joy. Hank took the crutches from her and watched as the crowd spread the good news. Photographers snapped.

Anyone was fair game, but they were after the good stuff. When they caught her in an embrace with Hugh Nichols, the silver bolo tie at his neck throwing reflected light into a star shaped blur, Hank knew he was witnessing the turn of all these months. From this moment forward, nothing would ever be like it had been. She was free to go, and go she would. Reporters pressed questions on everyone. *How do you know the defendant? Do you support the slow-growth initiative? What role do you think Stroud Ranch played in this arrest? Were any drugs actually found on the compound? How do you feel about the proposed highway extension?*

Rich Wedler clamped a hand over Kit's mouth before she could answer. "Hey, you guys want a statement for your six o'clock broadcast? Here's one. Take your cameras and tape recorders and insert them up past the transverse colon. That just about covers it for all of us, *comprende?*"

Asa grinned. "Fun crowd, Oliver. You going to buy yourself a pair of cowboy boots with silver toe clips?"

"I might if the soles are by Reebok."

"You're the main topic of conversation in the department, you know. Gilded rumor, sprouting wings."

"No doubt."

"Have you heard from the powers that be?"

"You mean regarding my contract?"

"Phil Green did. He gets two classes for fall. Karate's one of them. Says he's going to try the high school."

Hank sighed. "Nothing firm yet. But I've been thinking I might take an unpaid leave. "

Asa pressed his arm. "Jesus, why do that now? You want to make it easy for them?"

Hank shrugged. He hadn't known for certain that he would until that moment, and couldn't have explained why if a gun were put to his temple. He just knew, as he heard Dodge assure Chloe she was cleared, that he was leaving the college, even if it meant he had to pump gas to make his house payments. Asa could go back and spit that out into the rumor mill.

"I'll let you know when I figure it out," he promised. "Don't worry. Maybe they'll give some young female my half of the office space."

"Hank, don't be crazy."

"What's crazy about leaving everything secure in your life?"

Phillip Green had Chloe now. The tall cowboy lifted her up into his arms, and she gave the reporters the thumbs-up sign. Evening paper, Hank thought. I've no doubt that one will make the front page.

Over a table for seventeen at Olamendi's, they made a raffish group, drinking too many pitchers of margaritas, eating off each other's plates, and listening to Hugh Nichols, frustrated by missing an opportunity to testify in the courtroom, orate one of his trademark speeches against the powers responsible for the nightmarish last few weeks.

He tapped his glass with his spoon and rose up to his full height, just a few minutes over six feet, but to Hank he looked much taller. McNelly groaned. "Keep it brief, Nichols. I don't want my digestion of these fine chilies disturbed by your gas."

"Button it, McNelly. I have something important to say."

"God knows it won't keep till we finish our coffee."

Nichols shook his head. "No, it won't. And I can't think of any place on earth where it's getting harder to believe in the American way than it is right here in this county. Goddamn—what do we got that needs fixing? Winters that can't be beat, there's jobs aplenty—granted, not that many of them too promising—but jobs all the same, just for the asking. Well, I'll tell you. Aside from that we got a handful of fine people, quite a few of which are sitting right here at this table. I wish they'd breed like savages and repopulate this county with more of their kind, that's one of my dreams. Flush out the yuppies, the builders, and take the hippie environmentalists along with them. Add in a few decent head of horseflesh and roping cows, what more could a man ask? I challenge each and every one of you to tell me.

"I've seen a world of changes come over this county in the last twenty years, and I can count on one finger how many of those changes I stand behind. It's not much of a world to bring babies into when a thing like this can happen on your own land."

Land stolen from the Mexicans, Hank thought, swirling his margarita slush, but it wouldn't do to point that out now.

"Well, you all know my feelings on that. Let me read you what Charlie Russell said about the land." He undid a pearly snap and pulled a folded sheet of paper from his breast pocket. After he found his reading glasses, he cleared his throat and read.

"'In my book a pioneer is a man who turned all the grass upside down, strung bob-wire over the dust that was left, poisoned the water and cut down the trees, killed the Indian who owned the land and called it progress. If I had my way the land here would be like God made it, and none of you sons of bitches would be here at all.'" He folded the paper and put it back into his pocket. There was a chorus of laughter.

"But it's true," Nichols said. "Once we were cowboys, but by God, now we're the Indians! Chloe Morgan is the finest kind of human being I know. I'd trust her with my life, my bank account, and my dog, and those of you who know me know those words don't come easy out of this old body. She's pure-dee grade A, and that comes from knowing her, not just the time she spent keeping my old friend, Fats Valentine, alive way past what he deserved. We all owe her for that, but I owe her more for standing up and fighting back when this last little fiasco got dumped on my land. She's not afraid to smack a bad guy, boys." He lifted his glass. "To Chloe."

There were cheers. They all lifted their glasses, from Edith Nichols in her nurse's uniform drinking iced tea down to Kit Wedler, whose glass sported Diet Coke with a pastel pink umbrella. Francisco started in singing "Cattle Call," and most of the men joined in. The high-pitched notes sung a cappella struck a primal chord. Chloe, visibly shaky, pressed her hand over her mouth. Hank touched the small of her back, then whispered, "Are you all right?"

She scooted her chair back. "Fine. Bless you all. I have got to be alone for just a minute." She left the table, headed for the ladies room, Kit Wedler following. The men finished the song.

The waiter brought their check, and Jack Dodge took it—Hank protested. "Jack, look at all these people. It's got to be a heck of a bill. Let's pass the hat."

He wouldn't allow it. "Hank, let me do this."

One by one they trickled away. Asa waved from the end of the table, pointing at his watch. Phillip Green was deep into a conversation with Wes McNelly; they had ballpoint pens out and were bent over the tablecloth, sketching away. Rich Wedler and Gabe Hubbard stood up and Hank walked over to them.

"Thank you for coming today," he said.

The men gave him half smiles.

"All of you showing up meant a great deal to her."

Rich Wedler cleared his throat. "This part's turned out fine. I'm just a little curious what you plan on doing now."

"Excuse me?"

"Now that Chloe's free to go."

"She's always been free to go, Rich."

Gabe looked across the room. "Rich, let it alone."

"Let what alone?" Hank tried hard to make sense of this. "Frankly, it pisses me off, you barking in my face like her Dutch uncle. She can do what she wants."

Rich said, "Listen, pal, twenty-five people turn out for her court hearing, take off work. I closed my fucking restaurant. That's merely a fraction of the representation behind her. You hurt her, you answer to the whole enchilada, get it?"

"For Christ's sake, where were you when she needed bail money and a lawyer?"

Martin Luther King be damned, the truth was no gateway to freedom, but it did earn Hank a black eye. He felt the small rush of wind behind Rich's fist and the initial impact of his knuckles as he instinctively ducked, allowing the punch to graze his jaw, slide upward, and introduce itself to the occipital bone of his brow. Then he was witness to those universally shared secrets—a cartoon array of stars and circling planets, needle-bright slivers of silver and sagging painful violets—until Gabe Hubbard laid him down on the floor, feeling his head for damages.

"He may not look like much now," Gabe said, shaking ice from his drink into a napkin for Hank to use as a compress, "but Wedler was a bantam featherweight awhile back. You're lucky he only got a little Western on you. If he'd wanted to, he could have used your ass to mop the john."

"Remind me to send him a thank-you note," Hank said, squinting into the icy napkin. "I'll have it delivered by tank."

Gabe patted him back down to a sitting position. "Just hold on there, professor. Hey, somebody want to get this guy a shot of Turkey?" He whispered to Hank, "Finest painkiller on earth."

Kit reappeared, kicked her father in the shin. "Asshole!" she said. "Why do you always have to go and hit people? Just once, couldn't you count to ten first?"

Rich looked sorry. He glanced Hank's way and shrugged.

Hank stared back, surprised by Kit's defense.

"By the way," Kit continued. "Dr. Hubbard, did you bring your doctor bag? I think Chloe could use a Valium."

Hank picked up his mail; the notice was there in a small, plain envelope bearing the college's logo, a puny-rayed small orange sun. It didn't bother to disguise itself or try to fool anyone into thinking it was a health insurance premium increase. Karleen turned sharply away from Hank and kept her back turned. No offers of home movies and the basket of protectionary goodies this time. News traveled fast. He called out to her.

"Karleen."

She flashed him a big phony smile. "Not too many more papers left to grade, eh, Professor?"

It was a low shot he ignored. "We're still friends."

"Are we?"

"I thought so."

"It all depends of your definition of the word."

"I'm to be punished because I met someone, is that it?"

"This someone—would she be a blond, horsey someone, recently let out of the pokey?"

He laughed. "The pokey?"

She flushed. Her face was tired. No amount of makeup would cover her weariness. She lowered her voice. "Why, Hank? Why someone like her when you could have someone decent?"

Her hand was perfectly soft. Probably she slept with unguents applied to her skin, plastic gloves. "She's more than decent, Karleen."

"Are you in love with her?"

Hank was quiet a minute.

Karleen reached up and touched his brow. "Did she give you the black eye?"

"No."

"Thank God. Are you or aren't you?"

"I am."

She folded her arms across her chest. Hank had seen his mother do that, his grandmother, too. Chloe spent the drive home from the jail with her arms locked across her breasts. Whenever a woman adopted that pose he knew it meant trouble. *I am holding it right inside here, buster, and you'd better not say anything to make me let it go or you'll be sorry.* Karleen. Who could spend a lifetime with a woman who indulged in baby talk during foreplay? How would that play when she was into her seventies?

She blinked furiously to keep the tears dammed up behind her thick lashes.

"Why does it matter to you what I do now?"

"Because you're one of the good guys, Hank. I guess I had hope for you."

Karleen in her china cat-face earrings. She tried so hard to make the labels work for her—Liz Claiborne sweater sets, Italian shoes—she never looked comfortable in any of it. She looked as tired as he felt, and it occurred to him there was a reason for her fatigue—late-night phone calls just to throw a few darts. A pink slip, a social slip, more than likely they were related. He leaned across the counter that separated them and told her what had started in the bottom of his heart and worked its way up all day. "Karleen, mind your own goddamn business."

William Strauss showed up for office hours. Gone was the parade of steel studs and skulls in his earlobes, also noticeably absent was the shock of spiked hair. He sported what Hank's father used to call a "regular boy's haircut," dreadful words to hear from a barber. Like a marine recruit, he looked scared and resigned to wherever this new look might take him. He handed Hank a yellow drop card. All his other classes were signed off except Mythology II.

Hank accepted the slip, gestured to an empty chair, and waited for William to sit down. "What's going on, William? You were pulling a solid A in my class, I'll wager in your other classes as well."

The boy shrugged. "It's not my idea, believe me. Hey, who hammered your eye?"

"Just like Wotan, I made an exchange for a shot of wisdom."

"Does it hurt?"

"Like God hit me with his hammer. Whose idea, then, if it wasn't yours?"

The boy leaned back, balancing the chair on two legs. "My dad. He's completely wigged out. Bought some chunk of fucking wilderness in the middle of nowhere, Wyoming, and I'm supposed to pick up and move out there with him so we can buck hay together. You know, the whole father-son number."

"Excuse me?"

"He went into 'guy therapy' after his latest divorce and thinks he's personally discovered male bonding."

Hank smiled. "That will probably pass. But what about college?"

"There's a JC about seventy miles away. Maybe after a few months of pitching steer manure around he'll be ready to quit the gentleman farmer routine and start traveling again. He'll fall in rabid lust with some bimbo and leave me to clean up what's left. That's his pattern, anyway."

"What about your mom?"

The boy threw his hands up. "Which one? Hallmark adores me on Mother's Day."

"Would you like me to talk to your father?"

William looked shocked. "You? What would you say?"

"That you're bright and capable and deserve the chance to finish school where you are now."

"Rumor is you're not even going to be back in the fall."

Hank shook his head. "There are always other teachers, William."

"You were a good teacher. You shouldn't quit."

"Thank you. I'm not quitting. I just might have to take a vacation from it, not a whole lot different from yours."

Now William smiled. "You going to beat drums in the woods?"

"Not exactly."

"I gave you a hard time in class."

"No harder than anyone else."

"It was a good class, but you were a little weak on the brutal legends."

"Sorry."

"Those legends were the best, you know, all the eye-for-an-eye stuff. It helped me a lot, when my parents broke up, you know, to read all that shit about vengeance. I mean, so it was made up, so what, it still helped." William shoved his hands into his Levi's pockets. "Thanks anyway, you know, for the offer."

"No problem. You want me to sign this?"

"Yeah."

Hank signed the form, handed it back. He watched the boy leave his office, his shoulder blades making wings against his white T-shirt. William, removed from his cyberpunk cohorts, William without Metallica on the headphones. William in undomesticated Wyoming, his days beginning with the first ribbon of dawn striping the sky and the cries of hungry animals waiting to be fed. His father might be a lost cause, but a little solitude away from the city might just do some good for this boy. Stripped of his black clothing and painful jewelry, he was showing signs that already a Protean transformation was in progress. Hank would miss his quick wit and how artfully he deviled Kathryn Price. Who was he kidding—he would miss all of them if he left—when he left. He reached into his briefcase for the class rosters in order to take William's name off the list. Out with it came the file Jack Dodge had pressed on him, the paper clip awry and Chloe's name leering out in boldface. With the horse dying, the hurried shopping trip, and court, he'd forgotten the papers completely. He fingered his sore brow as he read.

Chloe Morgan. No middle initial. Year of birth, 1957, date, August 11; how odd that she was only two days off with her guess. Attending physician, Padraic O'Reilly, M.D. Hank imagined a young intern with a head of flaming red hair catching her, gleeful at the birth process, not yet dunned by overwork and tragedy, fear of malpractice suits. All babies looked alike at birth, didn't they, pink, bald, and squealing— probably he couldn't have picked Chloe out from a dozen others. Dodge had gone sleuthing—here was the story of her coming to live at Orangewood, her mother's forfeiture of parental rights, the succession of foster homes that Chloe the child endured—so many names it had to be an error—but Hank knew it wasn't. Allegations of child abuse from two homes they'd placed her in. Didn't anyone look out for her? A psychological report—bad attitude—predictions of trouble. Then a bio on the Gilpins, the last ones who'd taken her in and raised her until she was eighteen—was eighteen grown up? Could a kid like William Strauss be called an adult? Her high school graduation pic ture—straight blond hair parted down the middle, no lipstick, no heavy eye makeup, but the hard edge was there behind the sweater and forced smile. She looked slightly dangerous, and he felt his pulse quicken because she *was* dangerous, the most dangerous thing that had ever happened to him, and also the most amazing. The memory of all the time they'd spent in his bed howled through his bones like a hot, dirty Santa Ana wind, tightening his flesh. Never was it enough to have her once, roll over, and go to sleep. Most mornings he woke sore and chapped, his cock rising like a tired recruit, blind but eager to go back inside again. He looked at the picture. Even when she wasn't smiling, there was the faint hope in her face that at any moment she might change her mind.

Her legal offenses included several parking tickets she never both-ered to pay—including a recent one from the college—some juvenile nonsense supposedly "sealed" from her record, but Dodge's cash-green trowel had pried that loose. She'd briefly shacked up with a twenty-four-year-old when she was fifteen, and the guy'd been arrested for panhan-dling; Chloe'd been accused of shoplifting groceries; the store owner took pity and let her go. Did Hank know what it was like to be hungry? His parents had always been a half step behind him; *Now, dear, do you need anything? Here's some money, no, just take it. Can we get you a new stereo? Son, why don't you apply here to school—try this class—business is a good choice, study business.* His largest rebellion had been mythology—choosing to spend his time explaining the "little stories," as Wes McNelly referred to them. He'd never dealt with police other than the occasional speeding ticket; he wrote a check to the court and forgot all about it. He was green, just as Rich Wedler intimated. She might leave him.

The personal stuff bit hard. County-funded abortion at age six-teen—what possible reason did anyone need to know that? Who was responsible for getting her knocked up—this Fats Valentine character she seemed to rank up there with Jesus? Did he go along, hold her hand, or just shrug "tough luck," and let her walk alone? Medical records—she'd been in the hospital twice, once for the "procedure," once following a rape. At that sight of those words, something went hollow inside him. When he imagined her savaged, dragging herself to the emergency room to be prodded for evidence, stitched up in those places . . . the hollowness turned to sour rage, and he had to set the file aside. He walked to the window—Asa's visual strip—and tried to see past the stucco buildings where the eucalyptus trees slowly swayed in the afternoon breeze. There was no clear view anywhere—the college was a haphazard maze of buildings that grew out of no particular plan. Had he the power, he would have swept them away with a stroke of his hand, cleared a path from here to the ocean. Start over. It was possible to learn too much about a person. You could read their history like some detailed résumé and enlighten yourself as to the actual events of their life, but for every truth, a larger mystery remained separate, unexplored, inviolate. You could never know a person, not completely, not even if you made love to them five times a day. Rich Wedler was waiting for him to drop her; that vet had slept with her; a dozen of those men had looked at him over the lunch table as if he were slumming, wondering when he'd grow bored and discard her. She would leave him. Jack Dodge investigated the women he dated. Hank Oliver? Once in a lifetime, he fell in love with one, whether he deserved her or not. He shoved the papers into the file and loaded the whole mess into his briefcase.

"What we have here is a story about famine and greed," Hank explained. "It comes from the Karok Indians, which no doubt, all of you who've read your text, already know in some detail. But look at it also as a story of transformation. When the greedy father fishes for his family, rather than share equally with his wife and children, he eats the fish himself and carries home the tail, explaining to his children and wife that hungry beggars stopped him along the way, and all that he now has left to share is the tail.

"Now, rather than allow this duplicity to continue, his smart wife sets a trap for him, and catches him in the act of feeding himself first. What happens then is quite interesting in terms of the Indian myths and legends, because they seem rather universally to punish such betrayal, but punish most eloquently, as if to approach metaphor. As the man reaches out to touch his children, they each turn into lilies and plants, his wife—a pine tree. Finally, he is turned into a small bird that can only feed on mosses, and there his transformation ends. But interestingly, his wife and children go on to be made into baskets used in various celebratory dances. On one hand, it's a straightforward tale with a moral," he went on, "and teaches the consequences of lying. But additionally, it speaks of the concept 'to be of use.' Any reactions?"

His students looked at him, blankly or fascinated, sometimes it was difficult to discern which. Maybe his swollen eye was more interesting than the Karoks. If he quit this job, he was walking into a future with no certainties—Chloe—equally as uncertain whether she would stay. But the budgetary foot was in his backside, nudging. He didn't want to stay where he wasn't wanted. If he kept the news from her, he was a coward, unworthy, the cheapest kind of bastard alive, a moss-sucker. Maybe now that her trouble was over she wouldn't want to stay with him—maybe she'd walled up that avenue long ago. All he wanted to do was love her, live with her, watch her smile at him in the half light of evening, feel her body up close to his own, hold on.

Twice a student asked him to repeat what he'd just said, and he stopped dead in his tracks—all the memorized lectures were dismissed from his head—as if they had been wiped clean from the cells. He had to go to his briefcase and refer to notes for the first time in years. He found the answer there, the faded precise typing he'd done his first couple of years of teaching—how he'd cared then, how much he'd wanted to give. Now, well, there were the occasional good days, but mostly he looked forward to his paycheck.

"But Mr. Oliver, I still don't get it. The Greeks were kind of amoral themselves, and the Norse gods were even worse."

"No argument there."

"I thought the Native Americans might lighten up a little. Why couldn't the wife forgive her husband? I mean, he was just hungry. It wasn't like he didn't bring his children anything."

"Gods were vengeful," he said. "They didn't just provide explanations for the unexplainable phenomena, they also had to teach consequences. Whenever mortals stole or lied, they were punished."

CHAPTER

19

Just who are your people?" Iris Oliver asked Chloe over the rim of her fluted wineglass, shimmering with the pale Chablis.

"I don't know. Regular people, I guess." After Chloe asked the waiter for burgundy, they'd all ordered white wine, including Hank. What did it matter—white wine tasted like mule pee. She could get her mouth around a glass of something dark, red was supposed to build up your blood, and besides, hadn't she felt a little weak lately, a little run down? The trouble was this wine tasted a little metallic, which figured for rich restaurants, screw up the simplest things and charge double for them. Why ever had she agreed to dinner? *They're my parents, Chloe. I couldn't exactly say no.* Sure, you could. Just tell them we had to go to court this week. That we're tired. That you want to spend the night in bed with your girlfriend, seeing what it's like to make love to her without a court case hanging over her head. *Chloe. . .* They were polite, but they squinted at her as if she were a necessary border town to be crossed on the way to some spiffy little villa complete with servants.

"Surely you're on good terms with them?"

Chloe took another sip and set the glass down, shining like a dark jewel on the linen tablecloth.

"What I meant was, I suspect they're just some regular people. You see, I didn't grow up with them."

Hank's father set his menu down. He wore steel gray glasses and a pale blue seersucker sport coat, one of those white belts with the swanky gold buckles made from a valuable coin. "Oh?"

"I had a fine set of foster parents, though. Ben and Margaret Gilpin. They used to live right here in town, near the fairgrounds. Ben was an independent trucker, and Margaret worked at the hospital, volunteering, over twenty years. Ben's dead now, heart failure, and Margaret moved to the Florida Keys to be near her sister. I'm local weed—I went to high school here, studied 4-H and agricultural business, got fixated on horses. Listen to me going on—you ask a simple question and I give you the history of the universe—Hank's probably told you all this anyway."

"No," Iris said. "He hasn't told us anything."

"Well, then," Chloe said, smiling at Hank. "I guess they weren't wasted words."

Henry patted Chloe's hand. "Poor girl," he said. "Such a sad beginning."

"I'm fine." She kept her voice even. "It was all just fine."

"Don't you think we should order?" Hank asked. "It's getting late, and you two have a long drive."

"Nonsense," Henry said. "There's time for another glass of wine. Chloe? Would you pour? Or are you one of those feminists who insist men do for themselves?" He laughed, a great hollow booming that turned heads in the restaurant. "Hank, is there a smudge on your brow? Or is that a bruise?"

"It's the lighting in here. Dad, really, don't start in on women's rights." Hank started to reach for the carafe, but Chloe intercepted it.

"I don't hold much with labels," she said. "As far as I'm concerned, you all can take back the vote for all the good it's done women. I haven't voted since I was twenty years old. Nobody real exciting to vote for, is there?" She smiled, tilted the carafe, and poured the old man his wine.

He looked a little put out but drank it anyway.

"My father used to work for the Republican party," Hank explained quietly. "Voting's one of his pet causes."

Chloe laughed. "Well, open mouth, insert broken foot," she said. "I'm sorry. Those of us in the blue-collar world have a slightly different outlook on the voting thing."

"There's civic duty to consider," Iris threw in.

"Sure," Chloe said. "If you have time left over after working fifteen hours a day, you can feel a little bit civic."

"Hank votes in every election," his father persisted. "You should, too."

"And basically what happens is you and I cancel each other's votes, Dad. Let Chloe be. Between your questions and court, she's had a tough week."

She kicked him beneath the table.

"Court? Did you get a traffic ticket?" Iris asked. "Honestly, the police hand them out to all the wrong people. You should have seen this man on the freeway tonight, he nearly forced us off the road. And not a day passes that someone doesn't give us a rude hand gesture, if you know what I mean. There's so much crazy driving it plain scares me."

Hank buttered half of his roll. "It wasn't traffic. The thing with Hugh Nichols's land—Hughville. Chloe was involved when the police raid went down. Thanks to American justice, it's all cleared up now." He leaned across the table and lifted his glass. "To the American way," he said. "Long may it wave."

She bent her head, embarrassed. "Hank, stop it."

"No," Henry said. "Hank's right. Let's all lift a glass in honor of America." The candlelight glinted off his lenses, and Chloe tried to read his thoughts. She couldn't, but she knew the man was looking at her as hard as she was looking at him.

Iris sipped her wine. "Broken leg, court? Your life's rather dramatic, isn't it?"

"Lately. Most of the time it's just plain work."

"I quit working when I married," Iris said. "I wanted to stay home. I think that's right."

"I don't think I could ever quit working," Chloe said. "I'd miss the horses too much."

"I used to bet the horses," Henry said.

"Did you win in the money?"

"Not often. How about you—you ever bet the horses?"

"I don't bet, and I don't hold much with racing, either. I'm not saying all of the industry, but most of it fosters pretty sleazy treatment of animals." She remembered him suddenly, from the diner. "Decaf and dry toast," she said.

"Beg pardon?"

"The Wedler Brothers Café—I'm sure I've waited on you."

Chloe felt Hank's hand squeeze her leg under the table.

"Now I remember. You used to come in and watch the exercise show. You know, in the mornings."

"I'm sorry?"

"Dad, Chloe waits tables at that little restaurant on the highway," Hank said. "The one with the cinnamon buns you love."

"Oh, well, certainly," Henry said, coloring. "I've been a customer there several times in the past."

Iris said, "Customer? Henry, no wonder your blood pressure won't come down if you're sneaking pastry."

"Not recently, dear. Chloe will back me up, won't you, sweetie?" He winked.

"The last time you were both there," she said. "Decaf and dry toast, and something about the cream not being fresh. Listen, I don't want to start a fight. Maybe we should go back to talking about horses."

"Great idea." Hank raised his hand for the waiter.

Chloe studied her wineglass and felt Iris's eyes on her, seeking answers to questions no one would dare voice.

"So you waitress," Henry said.

"We make good, affordable food," Chloe said. "People have to eat."

Everyone smiled. Henry senior reached across the table and patted Chloe's hand. As soon as she was politely able, she withdrew it and placed it in her lap.

"Are you a student at the college where Hank teaches?" Henry said. "Is that where you two met?"

"We met there. But I don't go to college."

"Hughville—is that the place that's always in the newspaper?"

"Tell me again about Grandmother's place," Hank said suddenly. "Is anyone living there now?"

Iris turned her gaze from Chloe. "The Greers look in on it once a month, Hank, you know that. I suppose one of these days we ought to consider selling it."

"Not just yet, I hope. I've been thinking of taking a vacation there this summer."

Henry senior laid down his salad fork. "That's absurd, son. There's no electricity. You have to pump the water by hand—use an outhouse out back."

Chloe smiled. "Sounds pretty grim. Where is it, Hank?"

"Northern Arizona. Red-rock country, on the edge of the Navajo reservation. As you come into town there's a gas station where they give you a free piece of cherry pie with every fill-up."

"No kidding? Your grandmother's place?"

"My mother's mom," he said. "She's gone now. She taught school on the reservation for forty years. Mom grew up there. I used to spend summers with my grandmother."

"Oh, Hank, that was forever ago."

"Why do you always belittle that time, Mom? You grew up know-ing another culture. They let you come to the blessings and dances they won't even let anthropologists see. I wish you'd write down what you remember."

Iris shrugged. "It's all so long ago I've probably forgotten every-thing important. Who would want to hear about it, anyway?"

"Some of us would."

Chloe eyed Iris's silver bracelet, a horned ram's head with turquoise eyes. "That's beautiful. Did your mother give you that?"

Iris's hand clamped involuntarily over the bracelet. "Yes."

Chloe drew back the outstretched finger that had been on its way to touch the bracelet. "I'm allergic to silver," she said. "Makes me break out in a rash clear up to my elbow. Actually, I don't wear jewelry at all. It's too easy to catch a ring or something and break a finger when I'm working around the horses."

Henry said, "It sounds like dangerous work. Is that how you hurt your leg?"

Chloe sighed. Iris had recognized the lie she told back in Hank's kitchen; she'd said as much to Henry. She was a smart woman. They were after answers. Well, it was nuts to keep doing this tango with the truth when sooner or later it would come out wearing a neon party dress. Hank, toying with his watercress salad, wasn't going to give her any help. "My leg was broken in three places when an overeager junior deputy with the sheriff's department threw me to the floor in the raid on Hughville. It was in all the papers. Probably you saw me on television. I was the one almost wearing a blanket."

The waiter chose that particular moment of stunned silence to appear tableside, deliver in his perfect actor's tenor the daily specials, tease a little about the dessert tray, and fawn pretentiously over Iris's jewelry. "I just think Santa Fe's the darlingest town," he said. "Plus it has all those, you know, high energy centers? If I can't get a part in the soaps, I might go there this spring and live in a cave."

Chloe listened to what they ordered. You could glean an entire personality from menu choices. Iris wanted broiled skinless chicken breast and a baked potato, hold the sour cream, a single pat of diet margarine. No special sauces, no raw vegetables, a cup of plain chicken bouillon, not soup. Henry senior wanted the prime rib, the sixteen-ounce steak, the double rack of baby back ribs, wanted the whole she-bang, but opted for the orange roughy with lemon, rice pilaf, and stir-fried squash medley to Iris's obvious approval. Hank, her Hank, shocked them all.

"Filet mignon, rare."

"Rare, sir?" the waiter repeated.

"I want it cold, raw, and mooing in the middle," he said and upended his wine glass and finished it, "or I'll send it back. Could you refill this with the house red when you get a moment?"

Chloe had to bite her lip to keep from losing it entirely. Iris and Henry senior were stuttering into their rolls. "I'm not all that hungry," she told the waiter. "But I have this craving for chicken-fried steak. Don't suppose you guys make that?"

"Sorry," the waiter said. He went over the specials again, and she chose the catfish. Raw steak and bottom fish—the Olivers were confused—well, the hell with them. Time was, Fats would drive all night for fried cat at the El Molino Outpost on the Pete Kitchen Ranch in Patagonia, Arizona, yapping all the way about the taste of the buttery fish, then be too drunk and tired to eat any when they arrived. Chloe'd developed a taste for it, a knack for driving long distances with an unconscious seatmate, snacking off his foil-wrapped leftovers while he snored away a state's worth of miles.

She smiled when the plate was placed in front of her and said thanks to the waiter. The no-nonsense aroma of fish surrounded by lemon wedges tickled her nose, brought back a few good memories. She lifted her fork over the flaky fish. Hank gave out a groan when he saw his enormous steak overlapping the edges of the plate. He'd drunk too much on an empty stomach, and Iris and Henry were being very quiet.

"I am so damn hungry," he said, slicing through the meat. "Everything looks good—including you." He leaned over and kissed Chloe's cheek, a big sloppy smack that spoke of a deeper familiarity. Iris looked away; Henry grinned, but it was a smile that disapproved. They ate their dinners in silence. The stiffness got into every forkful—Chloe couldn't finish even half her plate.

She insisted on driving the Honda home to Irvine. Hank meandered into and out of subjects, sadly apologizing that his condition forbade them spending the rest of the evening working the kinks out of each other in bed. Chloe rubbed his arm; bless his heart, did he really think the strained silences the evening had invoked would disappear in the rush of orgasm? In the ladies room at the restaurant, Iris had tagged along and stood by the vanity, watching Chloe run a comb through her hair.

"That's a beautiful dress," she said. "Pink's your color. And the cut becomes your figure. Wherever did you find it?"

Chloe looked into the mirror. "Hank picked it out."

"My son has good taste."

Chloe stopped the comb, turned and faced Iris. The powdered cheeks were flaccid. Wine had rosied them up, but age and illness were pulling them down. "I'm happy to hear you say that, Mrs. Oliver."

Iris placed a hand on Chloe's wrist. "I'm an old woman, Chloe. I've had half my intestines taken from me, thanks to cancer. During my life, I've buried my only daughter and endured a philandering husband who suddenly wants to be my best friend, now that he's getting too old to chase women. Hank's the most precious thing I have."

"Have?" she echoed. "You make it sound like you own him."

"You'll understand when you have a child. There's a bond that can never be broken. And somehow you've gotten him to do the one thing I never could."

"What's that?"

"Relax, and be himself."

Chloe chuckled. "I think you're exaggerating. Hank's always himself."

"Not around us. He's very careful. I'd hate to see him get hurt if you're not in this for the long run."

"I don't know what you mean."

Iris released her wrist. Little heat phantoms rose up from Chloe's skin. "Don't evade the issue," she said. "You have to know my son is in love with you."

"Love?" Chloe's laugh grew flinty. "Maybe a heavy state of like. I get your point, Iris. You don't have to worry, I'm not planning on marrying your baby."

"I can see that," Iris said. "That's what has me worried."

When she got Hank into bed, he woke up, revived by his car nap and eager to make love.

"Not now," she said as she pulled away to her side of the bed.

"Don't turn me away, Chloe."

"I'm tired, Hank. Court this week, now your parents—Jesus—where does Iris get her lines? She really approves of me, doesn't she? The cardinal sin of ordering catfish. How long before you're forgiven for eating a goddamn steak? I'm worn down to my bones. I don't like you when you drink too much. You act stupid and guilty around your parents."

But he didn't let go, he kept after her, kissing her, murmuring as he moved himself to straddle her. He hadn't heard a word she said. She went slack underneath him. He reached down to guide his penis inside her, but as she could feel him jabbing blindly at her, hitting her thigh, her behind, she realized the poor fool wasn't even erect.

"Hank, you're pushing a rope."

He tried a while longer, then clung to her, broke down crying into her hair in a big damp huff of sour wine breath.

Over his shoulder she said, "Maybe Iris is onto something. Remind me never to feed you red meat again."

She reached over his back to shut off the light. Hank's tears were slowing now. During large gaps of time in between his intakes of breath she could feel him deciding whether to speak to her or not.

"You're getting awfully heavy," she told him.

He rolled away. "I've lied to you."

She pulled the covers back up to her chin. "Wouldn't be the first time a man did that."

"This is different."

Her stomach tightened. "What? I can deal with just about anything except you suddenly having a boyfriend."

"No, no. You're way off track here." He twisted the sheets away, stumbling from the bed, naked. Nothing looked sillier than a half-drunk naked man, half aroused. She turned to watch him. If every woman on earth took a picture of her man in that state and showed it to him when he was sober, maybe there was a chance for world peace. He turned on the light. He brought his briefcase into the middle of the bed, unlatched the top and dumped the contents out. "Read this."

She looked at the mass of papers and files. "What? You found some myth that turns me into a toadstool?"

He took an envelope from the file folder.

"What's that?"

"A letter from the department, cutting back my class load from four to none for fall," he said, laughing bitterly. "If I'm a good boy, if the war proves profitable, maybe I can come back in the spring."

"Oh, Hank. My God. I'm sorry."

"Hey, not to worry. I'll find another job. I was afraid you'd leave if I told you. Will you? I still don't know that you won't."

"What in the devil are you talking about?"

He left the room, wrapping a towel around his waist and lumbering down the stairs. She heard the clatter in the kitchen; he was making a cup of tea to sit on top of the steak and wine; he'd be one of God's favored dogs if he could keep it all down. She fingered the envelope. It was Hank's mail—she started to put the papers in order. Here were his lecture notes for class—some wild story about a coyote named Trickster. She opened the envelope from his school and read the brief message that his job was being eliminated due to budgetary concerns. When she got her settlement from the court—ten thousand dollars, Jack had said—she could pay him back everything he'd spent on her, that would help. On another file folder she saw her name. Jack Dodge's letterhead inside. She glanced over the pages, her heart thudding. Birth records. A list of the names of the foster homes she'd shuffled through. Doctor visits, the abortion she'd kept a secret from the Gilpins. All the low points of her life, remanded to crisp, white paper. How did Dodge get these records? What was Hank doing with them? Some of this shit wasn't even true. She hadn't had a *bad attitude* in the foster homes, she just got tired of the fathers thinking since she wasn't blood kin, that meant they could do whatever they wanted to her, including using her for fun and games in the bedroom. And the shoplifting thing—if they supposedly dropped the charges, how come it was here in print? She hung her head at the hospital records. Rape. A single word didn't quite cover the experience. She remembered bright hot lights overhead, the clatter of metal instruments on a tray, and the intern's low whistle as he measured her bruises. *Well, at least you gave him one heck of a fight, didn't you, honey?* Nobody needed to know these things about her. Just how did somebody go about gathering that kind of information—what right had they? This was what separated her from Hank and his mother's remark—*your people*—she had a blacked-out birth certificate and a private investigator's dossier. She took the file and the letter and went downstairs to Hank in his oak-and-glass kitchen. "You weak son of a bitch," she said. "How could you keep this from me?"

He looked at her for one moment, his face crumpling. "Cowardice," he said. "I love you."

"I'm not talking about your job." She threw the file across the table. The folder tipped his mug, splattering all over him and the tabletop. He sat still, dripping.

"You had me investigated! That's not love. If you wanted to know anything, all you ever had to do was ask me. Have I ever told you one single lie? Ever? No. But you've told me a few, more than a few, it seems."

"It wasn't me—"

She pointed a finger. "Don't. Don't say another word." She crossed the oak flooring, went to the knife rack, and selected the largest one, the one with the serrated edge and eight-inch handle, went back to the table where Hank sat and yanked a chair out, set her cast leg on it, and began sawing down the fiberglass.

"Don't," Hank said. "You're supposed to keep it on until they do the next X-rays. Come on, Chloe. Don't damage your leg because of me. I'll drive you to the hospital if you want it off that badly, but don't hurt yourself because I'm an asshole. Don't."

"I need out of this cast and out of this house. I'm going back where I belong."

"Don't go. It's early. We can talk. Things will be clearer in the morning."

She kept sawing, stopping only to tear off a chunk of file folder to stuff in between her leg and the cast. She nicked herself once with the knife, let the blood run into the cast, and fifteen minutes later her face was dripping with sweat but she could wedge her thumbs in between the two halves of the cast, crack it, and pull her leg free. Her bare skin felt odd in the air, felt as pale and hairy as it looked, the calf muscle shrunken so much smaller than it used to be she wanted to cry. How would she ever leg a horse properly again? She shoved the chair aside and put her weight on the leg, but a dark green insinuating son-of-a-bitch pain shot up her leg and made her reel, grabbing the chair for balance; she nearly passed out.

Hank was on his feet in a heartbeat, catching her. "Chloe," he called. The phone rang.

He waffled back and forth between her and the phone.

She gripped the chair back to steady herself. "By all means, answer the goddamn phone. Talk to our anonymous friend. Am I going anywhere?"

"What the hell do you want?" he screamed, and Chloe thought for a second he was speaking to her, but no, it he'd said it into the receiver, then listened a while, then mumbled, "I'm terribly sorry. Just a moment."

"I don't want to talk to anyone!" Chloe yelled back at him, sickened by the sudden notion that maybe all those calls had come from her mother, her real mother, who had given her up years ago, like a sack of too-small clothes someone else might find a use for. No. She wouldn't talk to her. Ever. She batted at the phone. Hank caught her wrist.

"It's the county," he said. "They've found Hannah."

"Hannah? Hannah? Is she alive?"

He held the receiver to her ear.

She grasped the knife. "A pencil, some paper," she stammered, and he took the phone back, wrote down the numbers, said thank you and good-bye.

For a fraction of a second they were okay, two slightly broken in lovers holding onto each other in the hum of an upper-middle-class kitchen. There were clean dish towels with blue edge trim folded across the shining oven door, sparkling copper-bottomed pans hanging from a ceiling rack right within reach, a bottle of lemon-scented Joy with the cap properly pressed closed on the edge of the sink.

Chloe threw the knife down, and Hank leapt back. It stuck into the hardwood floor before falling flat. "Sorry," she said, but the word was charged, a piece of slag in her throat. She gripped the chair back and looked at him, still holding the telephone receiver in his hand.

After a moment he hung it up. "People make the biggest mistakes in the name of love," he said. "It wasn't my idea, it was just something Jack did." He picked up the knife and set it on the countertop. "I'll drive you to get your dog," he said. "After that, I won't interfere. . . ." His voice trailed off.

They weren't fools at the shelter; they kept Hannah housed in a far corner behind eight-foot chain-link. A battered sign attached to her cage read "Vicious—Will Bite." Inside, the pacing dog was barely reminiscent of the white shepherd Chloe had loved and lost—here instead was a gruel-colored, matted, cowering mass of bony limbs, muzzled, eyes wary. Chloe braced herself with her cane and squatted down as much as the sore leg would allow. "Hannah? Old girl? Remember me?"

Hannah lunged at the chain-link twice, jaws snarling inside the muzzle. Chloe didn't move, even when the chain came within millimeters of her face. "It's okay, it's okay," she repeated levelly.

The dog moved back, circled, reached out with her snout, and tested the stranger's scent through the muzzle. Then she tried hard to funnel her mouth into an O to howl, but the best she could manage were muffled cries. She pawed the muzzle furiously, flung herself at the chain-link again, but now in earnest to get it open and abolish the barrier between them. "That's right, I'm here," Chloe said. "I've come to take you home. We'll both go home. Yes, we will."

"Hannah?" Hank took two steps forward, but Chloe raised the cane between them.

"Stay back."

Hank stood next to the kennel attendant. Hannah was home from her long journey, but she had come to see only one person, and it wasn't him.

"You can open her cage now," Chloe said.

"You're sure?" the handler said.

"She'll be fine."

He opened the lock, and Hannah flung herself at Chloe. Down they went in a pile, Chloe rubbing the ruff of Hannah's neck, Hannah's face butting in between limbs to deposit a lick wherever she could dart her caged tongue, the cane clattering to the cement, Hannah's bladder letting go, Chloe grinning through it all despite the fact that the big dog had just showered her liberally with urine.

"God knows why," the kennel attendant said to Hank, who stood aside, watching the phenomenon.

Chloe unbuckled the muzzle, and Hannah barked hoarsely twice, then doused her with kisses.

"One of you want to come up front and check on the bill? She's only been with us four hours, but she's still managed to destroy a fair amount of county property."

"How much damage?" Chloe asked.

"Never mind," Hank said. "I'll take care of it."

"I'll pay you back every dime, Hank, no matter how long it takes."

She sat in the back seat of the Honda with the dog, making soothing sounds, brushing her fingers through the matted fur. Hank drove soberly; the wine at the restaurant was in the distant past.

"How do you suppose she managed all this time?"

"She's like me," Chloe answered. "Even when everybody else quits on her, she gets up and keeps going."

"I would never quit on you."

"You did the minute you took those papers."

"Jack Dodge had your background checked. I knew nothing about it."

"But you read them all the same."

Hank didn't answer. It was true. She washed Hannah in the tub, used a whole bottle of Paul Mitchell shampoo, and clogged up the drain several times. They stepped back from the tub while the dog shook herself.

"My God," Hank said. "She's so thin."

"She'll gain it back. Where have you been?" Chloe asked her, over and over, and received only the woofing cries of *Here I am now* as an answer.

Hank tried to help with a towel, but Chloe said she could handle it. She used the hair dryer until it overheated and quit. She gave up, both she and Hank so wet and grimy they were shivering. Hannah tentatively took to exploring the house, fascinated with the stairway for some reason, going up and down the carpeted steps and pausing to howl into the spaces she hadn't gotten brave enough to enter. Chloe hugged herself.

Hank stripped off his T-shirt and sweatpants, turned on the water. "Let's take a shower," he said. "Just to get warm. I won't try anything, not even to wash your back."

She steadied herself, taking hold of the countertop.

"Listen, you're not that secure on your leg yet, and let's face it, we both reek."

"Keep the shower door open so Hannah can see me," she said.

"I will." He helped her over to the tub, got her to a sitting position, then took the clothes she handed out to him and set them on the sink.

She was tired; the turquoise tile swam before her eyes. She sat down in the back of the tub while Hank stood near the shower head, washing his long body with short, hard, businesslike strokes, anxiously glancing back at her now and then. He handed her the soap and turned his back.

"You can turn around, Hank. I'm not going to bite you."

"I'd rather not."

"Why?"

"Whatever's wrong between us, well, nobody's explained that to my penis."

She finished washing, rinsing herself with the facecloth. "Turn the water off."

He reached out and twisted the knobs until the water stopped. Then he stood there, his back to her, dripping.

"Hank, turn around."

His pale skin was beaded with moisture. Down the flat of his chest to the curving arc of his erection he placed a hand to cover himself up. "I'll get out."

She reached out to him, touching his ankle. He looked down at her hand. Finally he knelt in the tub, facing her, water streaming off his face, his hair. His face was tense.

"Nothing's changed how I feel," he began.

She placed her fingers over his mouth. "Don't spoil it by talking. Don't waste a minute of this by mouthing some worn-out words that don't mean shit compared to this."

"What are you saying?"

"You know what I'm saying. Come inside me. Fuck me, make the hurt go away."

It was no good—the tubs were small in this complex—just like the rest of the town, three-quarter scale looked like a great idea on a blueprint, but when you fitted actual lives inside the lines it didn't quite fly. He helped her out of the tub, scooped up her wet body, and took her to the bed, the sheets knotted beneath them. He wasn't half-anything now. He knelt between her legs, entered her; she rose up to meet him, her eyes shut tight. Hannah cruised by and barked once, then climbed up on the bed and curled up, watching. Chloe held onto Hank's shoulders, tucked her chin in the hollow of shoulder where it fit best, wrapped her legs around his thighs, melded herself as much as she could to his body, taking every thrust of his and sending back her own strenuous echo. She was a strong woman; if her leg had been healed she could have lifted Hank up as easily as he did her. The sound of their slapping flesh resounded in her ears. They slowed down together, as if they had each arrived at the same swift conclusion that this was the last time, and it might be wisest to savor each moment, memorize each finger's placement. They moved slowly against each other, hips rolling in cadence, holding back sensation deliberately, trying so hard not to feel anything too wonderful that they were both biting their lips when orgasm came, first to Chloe, who clutched at Hank as she started to heat up and cry out, consequently flipping whatever switch it was that made him come, just a half second behind her, shouting her name into the hollow of her collarbone, moving against her long after he was finished. She lay there holding on, feeling him arch and rock, feeling the fluids run between them, nothing separating them but their ridiculous complicated minds—whoever said man was a domesticated animal was being sadly optimistic. She didn't want to move, or to think. Hank was breathing quietly into her hair. Hannah butted her damp nose at Hank's buttocks and he jumped, and then he was no longer inside her.

Chloe started to get up.

Hank said, "I want to say that they're just pieces of paper. That it doesn't matter what's written on them, that I don't care. But we both know differently."

She stood by the bed looking away.

"You met my parents. My father categorizes everything—nuts, bolts, grocery receipts, emotions—all the same to him. When I was thirteen years old I took a girl from school to a dance. My father's parting words? 'Keep it in your pants, son.'" He rubbed his face. "So, you see, Chloe, it doesn't take a Brahman to make me understand the power of the written or the spoken word. Words are powerful; sometimes they change everything, permanently. But they can be overcome. It's your past. You have to face it, and I have to face up to sneaking learning things you might have told me in time, had I been patient. Screw Jack Dodge, he probably has his paper boy investigated. I'll do anything for you, whatever it takes to make you smile again. I don't want to lose you."

"This isn't about doing anything. I need my life back."

"I thought this was your life."

"No, it's your life, Hank. Mine's back in that canyon, with the pump handle for getting water, and no electricity, and the fold-out bed. I want my stuff, Hank. My crummy, third-rate belongings and my memories. Can't you see?"

He shook his head.

She took his face in her hands and kissed the planes where the tears streaked down from his eyes. When he shut his eyes, she kissed them too, lightly running the tip of her tongue over the eyelids, feeling the smooth globe of eye beneath, wondering what it saw staring up into the top of his skull. She held on to him until he was asleep, then she got up, dressed herself leaning on the cane, motioned to Hannah, and the two of them went, Hannah hanging her head out the passenger side window of the Apache, all that lost time erased for her in the familiarity of her old space. She relaxed, probably recognized the way home before Chloe herself did.

It was a quick trip. They exited the freeway at Lake Forest, drove ten miles past the sprawling developments, and finally left the city lights behind to enter the canyon roads.

A few of the old barns were flattened, new lumber shining pink as skin against the rubble. The hills were still covered with the green grassy plants of early June, which gave the impression this was fecund land, but in a few weeks the sun would burn it to cracked amber. Fire warnings would go up, those billboards that beseeched cigarette smokers to wait a few more miles before lighting up. Hugh and the boys would be moving his small herd of range cattle to his ranch up north, two or three days of work that nearly always ended with Hugh and the Stroud Ranch people on the front page of the newspaper again—a full-color photo of the rustic cowboy life juxtaposed with the Disneyesque drawings of what this land could be, developed by the grand vision. A crossing deer leapt in front of her truck, and Chloe swerved, cutting into the oncoming lane, instantly thanking God she was alone on this road. She braked to a stop, shooting an arm out protectively to shield Hannah. Hannah gripped the seat with her paws, and they watched as the deer disappeared into the brush, white tail giving a final snap up in the darkness. She pulled back into her own lane, her heart beating hard. She patted

Hannah, checked her rearview mirror, then drove on, past the corner bar with the motorcycles parked out front, past the stables where Absalom had lived, and died, and then made a right into the road to Hughville. She slowed the truck down as she came to the first of the back roads. The voices were here again, *Sister. . . other people's lives* crowding into and over her own. *Excuse me, Ma'am. . . .* Saddleback was a small mountain; she'd climbed it three or four times herself and stood breathless at the top looking down across the wide span of land that ended at the ocean. She knew whales moved along this coastline, same as they had all those years ago, when the Indians had stood in the same place and looked to the sea with a feeling of pride and companionship. Every year the whales came back this way. She felt a part of that same process, that migration. All of them, the travelers through here who kept on moving across the land, the ones who stopped when they hit the edge of something, sought out space to call their own. It was important to foster independence. If you stayed in one place too long you grew sour, people started trying to regulate who owned what, land, ocean, birds, people. Migration—that was what it was all about. The oak trees to her left were nobody's back when covered wagons and men on horseback stopped under their shade, they were nobody's now, though Hugh Nichols held paper that made them his, allowed him to cut or water as he saw fit, and would eventually be the developers', when Hugh wore out. She stopped the truck and pressed a hand to her face. Her skin felt hot, almost feverish. Too much had pressed in on her in too short a while to make any of it understandable. Peace would come back to her. Kit seemed to think if she learned about the past, maybe went after finding her mother, there were answers there, too. Chloe didn't think so. Look what going after her past had done—she and Hank were finished. She sighed, glanced down the winding road to stand of elderly oaks. There, in the shadows of the trees, stood a young girl in a flowered sunbonnet, her smiling face looking out toward this desert land, as she hovered a foot above the highway. Whatever was there to smile at? Why wasn't she tucked into her grave, sleeping her deserved peace? Maybe moving here had set her free, and she hadn't died in full sun, running her tongue over cracked lips, rambling over the memories of another home. *Nunca seremos vencidos. Este nina. . .* For Christ's sake, I'm tired, talk to me in English. . . . *You have to go on. For the children. . .* Then she was gone, the flower print of her bonnet phantoms the eye conjured out of exhaustion. Come back here, Chloe implored the girl, the others. You're all supposed to be dead, gone, part of the past, but you're here with me, so you must have something to tell me. She saw only trees, night sky, the blue-black broken by a few smudges of clouds. Everything was sleeping, from Hank in his bed down to the smallest insects straddling the leaves. She cut the motor, and her ears throbbed with the silence.

Hannah trotted ahead of her to the cabin. Whatever wreckage they encountered, Chloe knew it was right to come back. It *was* her place. There was no money owed; she paid her rent, trucked out her trash, and Hugh let her be unless he wanted to deliver a monologue.

Hannah came loping back with a crushed A & W root beer can, which she dropped at Chloe's feet. "Oh, good girl," she said, patting her, and tucked the can into her jacket pocket with trembling fingers. The cabin was there. There was yellow police-line tape everywhere, somebody—Francisco's daughter?—had tied it around tree trunks, rocks, whatever was big enough to hold a bow was decorated. She smiled. The door had been replaced on new shining brass hinges; even in the dark she could see the repair work. Inside—she was afraid to look—what if someone else lived there now? Hannah barked. Chloe opened the door. Her house was in order, as much as broken, trampled things could ever be put in order.

She sat down on the folded-up couch bed. Fingerprint dust smudged the turquoise vinyl. Her footlocker, likewise; the lid torn completely from its cheap hinges, but someone had carefully packed the ribbons, letters, and pictures back inside the bottom half. The gallon jars she'd kept for storing food were gone, but someone had left a gallon bucket, a new glass oil lamp, a fifty-pound sack of dog food inside a larger plastic bag, and a couple of glasses for drinking.

She found a matchbook in her pocket, set the aluminum can on the counter, and lit the lamp. When the sputtering wick caught and settled into smooth flame, she replaced the glass chimney and set it down on an orange crate, watching the light fill her small room.

So it wasn't a town house in an all-new city. There wasn't any dish-washer, or a stereo cassette player, or even a flush toilet, but it was home: hers. Hannah butted her head against Chloe's knee, laid her head down there, and huffed. "You're welcome," Chloe said, and took out the letters from her footlocker and began to read.

CHAPTER

20

C ome ride fence with me," Hugh Nichols called out as Chloe came around the front of her cabin the next morning, her hands full of wadded-up yellow police tape destined for the Dumpster. She squinted up at him. The sky was just beginning to lighten, and the oak leaves fluttered in the breeze. "You don't have to leave for work yet, and I could use another set of eyes." He threw her the reins of Ringer, an old buckskin with a white rope burn around his neck.

She caught them and whistled for Hannah.

"Well, I see the mutt's done traveling."

"Yeah. Late last night county called and said they had her. She ripped things up a bit down there. That's my dog. Another bill I owe, but I'm glad to have her back." She ruffled the dog's fur, then turned and pulled herself up using the horn of the saddle.

"That's a good way to end up on your can," Hugh said. "I'm surprised your doc would cut the cast off if your leg wasn't ready to do its old job."

"Well, Hugh, I kind of went to the kitchen-knife doctor. Just couldn't hack the plaster prison one more second."

"And the other prison, too, it seems. Unless you got the professor inside there, a-tied down to your bed." He laughed hard. "Won't forget to water him now and again, will you?"

"He's not here, Hugh."

"Too bad. I was growing fond of the fellow. Teach him to ride, he might make a halfway decent partner for you."

"I'm not interested in a new partner. Hannah'll do."

Hugh reined Lucky, his Appaloosa gelding, to the left, and they started up the hills. "Chloe, you're good at just about everything that you do, save lying."

She felt her face redden. "I'm not lying."

He laughed again. "You might not know it, but you are."

"I'm not, goddammit. That whole deal was just one of those mistakes that seem like a good idea when you get your pants down."

"True enough, lather anything up with a liberal dose of springtime libido, it'll seem just about logical."

"For awhile, anyway."

Hugh smiled. "Don't beat yourself up over it. You're human, like the rest of us fools. Now let's ride fence."

"What are we after?"

"Edith's breachy mare, what else? Good-for-nothing palomino. Odds are she's by the apple trees, working herself into colic, so let's take the long way around and get to her last. Maybe with luck she'll choke on something."

"You don't mean that."

"Maybe I don't, but I sure mind getting booted out of a warm bed to chase that fool horse every other day."

They rode their horses at a walk for nearly an hour before they found any wire down, and when they did, a long wisp of bloody horse tail was caught in the break. Hugh cursed softly.

"The hair's yellow."

"Of course it is. The Steve McQueen maneuver. None of my other horses are that dumb. Why she had to have that horse—I had a nice little paint all picked out for her, but no, didn't she just have to have Trigger's sister!"

He prattled on, but Chloe only heard bits of what he said, as if he were the lightest rain she had to pass through on her way somewhere else. The sky was bright now. It had a yellowish cast to it, not the usual blue. As they moved into summer, the blue seemed to fade. Each glistening tree limb they rode under would soon dry in the early sun.

She was sorry about Hank, even sorry about last night's sex; one hell of a memorable way to say *adios*, but it wasn't fair. It bit into her heart like heroin did, maybe. She'd never been one for drugs or booze—just watching Fats drink had soured her—but she could well imagine stealing car radios to feel that good again, even if it lasted only a moment. She felt tired, puffy, and drawn thin all at the same time. Her head ached from too little sleep. Across her belly, her old jeans cut tight. She reached inside her waistband and undid the button. The cook must have slipped with the salt shaker when he was breading that catfish. Three meals a day made you get lazy. They stopped a moment, and Hugh unbuckled a saddlebag.

"Coffee?"

She saw the chrome flash of thermos, smelled the bracing aroma, and felt her throat close. "No, thanks."

Hugh took a swallow and screwed the cup lid back on, stowed it back in the saddle bag. Maybe she was getting a presummer bug, though it wasn't really the time of year for it. Hannah kept up, her hardy little trot must have carried her more miles than Chloe could imagine. She kept the white dog within sight, wary lest she lose her again.

"Be out of the cabin by noon."

"What?"

"Good. I've got your attention again. I've been talking at you for the last half hour, but you're somewhere else, aren't you?"

"I was listening. I was waiting for you to say something worth answering, that's all."

He shook his head and legged Lucky up ahead. Fats had trained Lucky from a colt. He was a *made* horse when Hugh bought him, and Hugh'd kept him in shape the last twelve years. Forget all the tired Appy jokes, Chloe found the horse handsome, and she felt herself envy Hugh this sound horse—any horse trained by Fats. When they were at the top of the ridge, stepping carefully, granite and shale crumbling beneath the horses' hooves, he spoke again. "There's a few things I've been meaning to say to you about Fats."

"Oh, for God's sake, that about cuts it. I'm turning back."

"Now, hang on a minute. I'm working into it slow."

Her grip on the reins tightened. Hugh had taken them to the spot where she'd stood crying a year ago, finally deciding to scatter Fats's ashes here, a place traversable only by horseback, a place she thought he'd feel most at home. "He's dead and gone, Hugh. Nothing you can say now will accomplish anything unless you're hell-bent on making me cry."

"Stop being dramatic. You women—think it don't pain a man's heart to lose his friend? That you have to sleep with a man to feel the grief when he dies?"

Chloe gave a dry laugh. "Well, it sure can put an edge to it."

"Don't play with my words. Fats was like my big brother. I watched him commit a long, slow suicide. Maybe I was too pissed off at him when he died to feel sad just then. But you never got angry, did you?"

She turned in her saddle to face him. "I forced him to eat when he didn't want to. I drove him kicking and screaming to the hospital a million times. I watched him pickle himself until his skin stank of the stuff. He fucking bled to death all over me. Don't talk to me about anger."

Ahead of them, low brush rustled and Hannah took off at a lope. "Hannah!" Chloe screamed.

Ringer crow-hopped, and Hugh sidled Lucky up next to him. "Easy," he said, pinning the horse with his own. "There's a good boy. Dammit, Chloe, are you looking for a broken neck? Let the dog flush quail, will you? She knows where her supper dish is. She's not going to run off every time you turn your back."

She couldn't speak.

He nosed Lucky forward. "There's some people who would eat me alive for saying so, but I think you and Fats saved each other's lives when you were together. You could have hooked up with somebody who'd use you and throw you out. I see these young girls whoring today, all the drugs and nonsense, well, that's a sensitive subject for me, as you know. My own children consider me something of an embarrassment, think whatever I say is nonsense. But I've been around awhile, and I know money can look downright golden when it's in easy reach. Fats wasn't immune to that. I credit my friend, all he did was love you as much as he knew how. Maybe it wasn't enough, but you gave him your heart and soul, admit it."

"I'm not ashamed to."

The wind blew by them, spreading a fine layer of grit over their faces. Chloe turned her face away. Hugh reached up to secure his hat. "Chloe, you can't sleep with a dead man the rest of your life. You're young. That professor may not ride, but you could teach him. He thinks you hung the moon. Go on back to him. Get yourself knocked up. Give him some good years. Don't hide away in the hills and expect horses and dogs to take up the slack."

"Fuck off, Hugh."

He chuckled. "Such a ladylike mouth. I been trying to for years, darling. But I keep waking up the next day, hard as ever, wanting another go-round."

She rode ahead for the next five miles through the tall grass that grew high on the slanting slope, so steep in places the cattle could reach it only by kneeling. She kept her outside leg on Ringer so he'd pay attention to the uneven ground underfoot. Hugh was one to talk— all those failed marriages under his belt, children who changed their names legally rather than be connected to him. Edith was a casualty herself, and when Hugh's back was turned, she'd been known to do a fair amount of catting.

It was quiet except for nameless birds chattering in the oaks, celebrating the late spring glut of grasses and seeds. No palomino anywhere. Her heart wasn't buried alongside Fats; that was utter horseshit. It's just that it was true love with Fats, love without fear, love from two damaged people who had no expectations other than what might fill the moment. Love didn't bless you but once in a lifetime; it was asking for trouble to think otherwise. What reason was there to explain that to a broken-down old man who got a hard-on listening to the sound of his own voice? Riding fence, my ass—he wanted to get me alone in the middle of nowhere so he could give me a lecture.

She stopped her horse, waiting for Hugh to catch up. "Just because you're older you think you can talk to me like you're my goddamned daddy," she said when he was alongside her, the roll of baling wire bouncing on his saddle horn. "Well, I have news for you, Hugh. Somewhere along the line I had a real daddy. Maybe he didn't stick around and teach me my ABC's, or wrong from right, but nobody—not you, not Fats, not some goofy lying son-of-a-bitch teacher or anyone else—needs to put their two cents in on how I live my life."

Hugh secured the baling wire and nodded. "You been searching down your roots, have you?"

"No. And I don't care to. Say my parents are dead—maybe everybody good is already dead." She stopped to mop the sweat from her face. "Whoever my daddy was, he was my daddy, and I don't need a replacement."

Hugh rubbed his chin, and his lined flesh seemed to sag. "Well, sure. I didn't mean to imply nothing. Sometimes I just get carried away. . . ."

She grabbed his arm. "Aw, Hugh, don't look at me like that. You and Wesley are my favorite people in the whole world. I'd lay down my life for you two. I just want you to get off the subject of Fats, okay?"

Hugh shifted his reins to one hand and scratched his neck. "I guess you'd have no interest in hearing that Hank's back at my place. He's been there half the night. He about begged me to talk to you, sweetie, so I'm talking."

"Christ."

"Whatever happened between you two, he's damn sorry about it and wants to make it up to you."

"Fine. You talk to the bastard." She legged Ringer into a gallop and left Hugh swatting dust.

As she tied Ringer to Hugh's hitching rail, Hannah limped up behind her and sat down, panting. Chloe was so intent on making her slip knot that she didn't notice Pilar, Francisco's daughter, until she tugged at Chloe's jeans.

"Chloe, she's bleeding."

"Who?" Chloe turned away from the horse to look. Pilar pointed a finger at the dog, who held up a dripping paw. "So she is."

Pilar hopped on one foot, clutching a naked baby doll. Chloe stripped tack from the panting horse and set it over the rail, haltered him, and prepared to walk him down until he was cool.

"Aren't you going to take her to *el doctor*?"

Damn Hugh and all men, particularly the one who thought he could wait for her at Hugh's house, and further, that she would come, as if his presence was some almighty magnet. Chloe strained to keep her voice even. No use snapping at an innocent child. "Oh, I don't know. Doesn't seem that bad. Can you find me a long strip of clean rag to tie around her paw?"

"Mama can!" Pilar grinned and ran back to her trailer.

"All right. Let's see what you've done to yourself, Han." Chloe retied Ringer, bent down, and lifted the dog's paw, wiping blood away with her thumb. The cut was jagged, stretching all the way across the palm-shaped pad, probably from a hunk of broken glass, a little deeper than she would have liked to see, but a clean wound. Did it need a stitch? No, it could mend just fine. She turned on the hose and washed it out, then took the clean rag from Pilar, and wrapped up the paw, Red Cross–style, tying the bandage off in a square knot well behind the joint, where she'd have the most difficulty chewing it off.

"No *doctor*?" Pilar said, her brown eyes wide.

She patted the girl's cheek. Pilar was healthy now, but likely she'd remember her winter hospital sojourn for the rest of her life—all those men in white coats who didn't speak her language, her mother's panic, Francisco's rage when the social worker tried to "place" Pilar in custodial care. "Not right now, sweetie. I have to cool the horse out. We'll see, later. *Doctor* Hubbard takes care of Hannah. You know him?"

Pilar put her hands on her hips and did a little bump and grind. "Mama says, Dr. Hubba Hubba." She burst into giggles.

"He has that effect on some women," Chloe said. "But he's just a man, no matter how pleasant he may be to look at. After Ringer's cool, you want to help me get him brushed down and into the corral?"

She could have been offering the girl a porcelain doll in a bridal gown with ten other outfits. "Can I?"

"Sure." Foolish horses, Chloe thought. No, foolish women. Loving horses, it's a disease that has no cure. But horses have men beat. They break your heart all right, the day they fracture a metacarpal or a sesamoid, or unwittingly chow down on bad feed. Sooner or later, you're faced with a big brown eye asking you to make the pain go away, to shut off the lights. In her mind's eye she saw Absalom with braided mane and tail, the glow of Show Sheen defining each muscle. When they entered the show ring, his attitude shifted. He knew how to hold himself, knew who it was important to strut by, knew better than to waste any of what he was mixing things up with strange horses. Fats had taught her to run a thin finger of Vaseline down certain muscles to make a horse more attractive to the judge, but grease wasn't what made him a winner, heart was. Had he ever refused her? He'd earned enough blue ribbons to transform his stall into royal blue wallpaper. Did horses go to heaven? No, they *were* heaven, the only viable piece of it left on earth. She swiped at her eyes, gave Pilar a boost, and lifted her up to ride on Ringer's bare back around the stalls before she led him to the corral. She placed the girl's small hands on the dark mane and clicked her tongue to move the horse forward. She focused on a patch of sky visible between the rotting stall rafters. Rest well, Ab. Let there be timothy, rolled oats, and an abundance of molasses.

"Someday," Pilar said, sitting up straight on the gelding's back, "my papa's going to have his own ranch. And we'll ride all day on strong white horses, and our saddles will have silver *conchos*."

Chloe smiled and rubbed her hand across the girl's small back. "I've no doubt."

"And I'll teach the lessons."

"Maybe I'll take lessons from you," Chloe told her. "Will you teach me to jump the high fences?"

Pilar raised one hand and pointed to the sky, now a cloudless expanse that promised a hot day. "Chloe, I teach you to fly."

"I look forward to it. But right now I've got to go to work, so what do you say we get this pony his oats?"

*   *   *

"You have a couple new students," Diane said when Chloe hung up her keys when she reached the stable office. "A little girl who used to ride hunters at Sycamore under Casey. Wants to be a stable brat in trade for lessons. Guess Dad must have lost his wad in the market and they're scaling down. She's out there drooling over the Hanoverian in the box stalls."

Chloe glanced out the window. The girl was twelve or thirteen, tall and skinny, with long athletic legs fitted into white sueded Harry Halls that cost at least a hundred and fifty big ones. She was built to ride. Her long ponytail flowed over her shoulders. No doubt she spoke the language and rode like a fearless angel, dusting herself off after getting thrown as if it were a small price to pay for communing with the gods. If there was a myth in Hank's books about women and horses, this girl was born to star in it, would have dozens of porcelain statues of horses on a shelf in her room. Looking at her was almost like looking into the past and seeing herself at Whistler's Stable, Fats Valentine just around the corner, waiting to change her life. Of course she'd zero in on the priciest horse; the kid knew her stuff. The only job Chloe had was Kit's, and Kit needed it more than this little princess. "You want her?" she asked Diane.

"Are you kidding?" Diane grinned. "I'll work her wealthy butt down to bone."

"Be my guest. She probably never made her own bed in her life. You said there were a couple? Anybody paying real money?"

Diane smirked.

"What's so funny?"

"Nothing. He's an older guy, kind of cute, really, if you like that pale, bookish type. Brand-new Nocona boots. Woo-woo. At least they're not snakeskin. Says he rode years ago. He sounded halfway humble about it, and he paid for a block in advance."

"A block? Those are the ones I like—the ones with bucks."

"Asked for you, personally. He said he'd take whatever opening you had. I told him to tack up and meet you in the middle arena. He'll fit into that slot in your beginning class unless he's a better rider than he lets on. I gave him Molly."

"Poor old Molly. Gets to break everyone in. Thanks. Remember, the next two that come in, you get first dibs."

Diane nodded, then got up from the warping desk to go talk to the girl in the box stalls. "Hey, Chloe?"

"What?"

"Congratulations about court. We were all pulling for you."

"That's nice to hear."

"And sorry about Absalom. He was a wonder."

Chloe closed her lesson book and looked up. "He was. Thanks. Anybody else lose one?"

"Not that I've heard. They pulled the cubes statewide, and we're about to abandon our twenty-four-hour watch. You know Lorena's bay down at Serrano?"

"Big Fella?"

"Yeah—he pulled through. Dr. Hubbard and his amazing anti-serum. The stuff worked."

"That's great." But it hadn't worked for Absalom. Chloe'd been avoiding looking at that empty stall. Didn't want to keep that appointment with grief. Diane left. Chloe touched the bracelet Kit made her from Absalom's tail. Tight black weaving with a silver catch. There was no bandaging the wound now. She lifted it to her nose and sniffed, hoping to catch a scent of him, but it smelled like soap, the morning ride, coffee grounds from work. She'd simply have to carry his memory inside—why not? It had plenty of company. She lit a cigarette, her first one of the day, and inhaled deeply, allowing the dizzying smoke to travel down into her lungs. Maybe that would relax her, erase the itchy feeling. But it tasted sharp, made her cough, and she tamped the cigarette out on the picnic table outside the office, then tucked it back into her pack. Between the pipe arena and the covered breezeway, Rich was dropping Kit off, his little car shining with a new wax job. Beside him, straddling the gear box, wearing a scarf tied around her hair, sat Lita. She waved. Chloe waved back. Kit hurried over lugging her backpack.

"Sorry I'm late. Trying to get those two to stop smooching in the kitchen, Jesus H. Christ. You'd think they invented sex."

"I'm sure the good Lord had nothing to do with it. We got a full class this morning, Kit, so I want you in the ring. I'd like you to spot my new student, some rich guy in Noconas. Probably been watching old Western movies and wants to *find* himself on horseback. Well, we'll take his money along with everyone else's. He's all yours. Let me know how he chalks up. In exchange, I'll give you another private lesson."

"Can I have it on Midnight?"

"If you think you're up to him."

"I am. Notice anything different?" She twirled around in her rust-colored breeches, her fat rolls defining the spandex.

"You got new pants?"

"Last week! Something else, you dunce. I lost fourteen pounds."

"Really? That's great. That's terrific. How did you do it?"

"I quit eating shit food a hundred years ago and switched to Diet Coke. I was *waiting* for you to notice."

She gave Kit a hug. "I'm sorry, honey. I've been so preoccupied. Hey, listen. You want to say hello to an old friend?" She whistled and Hannah came bounding out of the Apache, where she'd been working her bandage.

"Hannah? Oh, my God! Where were you, girl? Don't you know how worried we were? Get over here and give me a love." Hannah jumped up and planted dusty paws on Kit's T-shirt; Kit took hold of her paws and danced her around. She sat down on the ground and let the dog lick her face, squealing when the dog's tongue tickled her neck.

They were a sight, Chloe thought, watching them cavort and wrestle in the dirt. Kit's ponytail came loose and her red hair made a cloud around her pale, freckled face. Hannah flattened her ears against her head in joy and wagged her tail so furiously her back end was swinging like a kite. If a dog could laugh, she was doing it. No teenage worries about how it looked, or what it might do to her makeup, Kit let the dog kiss and lick her until she was sated. She's too much like me, Chloe thought. Her road's going to be endlessly bumpy, with time-outs only for heartbreak. Still, new breeches and fourteen pounds—the horses were working.

Her leg ached; she rested every other step on the cane, making her way down the slight hill to the middle arena. Her group lesson was waiting: the newly married couple who were convinced riding horses together constituted just about the most romantic notion possible, and elderly May, who had said to Chloe when she signed up, *My husband's just died, but don't bother saying I'm sorry because he was a stingy bastard who stole all my good years. Now that he's buried, I plan to spend the insurance on a little hair-raising fun. My goal's to be the oldest lady jumper in California, think you can help me out?* May was turning out to be a fine rider, but the six-foot fences were still a ways down the line. Sometimes she was just so tired all her students blurred together, and she had to write their names on the palm of her hand to keep track of them. It was important to let them know you remembered them, to ask about personal stuff, no matter how worn out or blue you might be feeling. Part of good teaching was listening to their life stories, listening for what clues they might drop as to what scared them. Damn, she'd forgotten to get the new guy's name from Diane. Kit would just have to ask him.

But there would be no need for that, she saw now, because he was turning in the saddle, making the east corner of the arena as he warmed up Molly, the gentlest, pig-eyed, ugliest strawberry roan God ever put into horseflesh, utterly safe, taller, maybe, but just as bomb-proof as Elmer the pony. She would remember the man's name because more than once she'd cried it out involuntarily, as if her voice might travel into his flesh and lodge there for a lifetime. She'd felt her own tears dampen his shoulder, mingling with his, and realized as they came to rest that they were saying a wordless good-bye.

Hannah and Kit caught up. "Hey, Chloe, isn't that Hank?"

"Yes, goddammit."

"Such language. I thought you were—"

"It's over."

"You want me to tell him to get lost? I can."

"No, no." She was quiet a minute. "He bought new boots and wants to learn to ride."

A wicked glint sparkled from Kit's green eyes. "*I* get to teach him."

Hannah woofed, and Chloe put her on a down command and told her to stay. She sat fifteen feet up from the arena, head resting on her paws, but eyes wary. She wouldn't budge for foot or vehicle traffic, and sneaked nips at the bandage when she could manage it without Chloe noticing.

"Keep your heels down!" Kit ordered Hank, and Chloe smiled, expecting the usual beginner's reaction, wincing and straining. His left ankle had always troubled him—some old Boy Scout hiking injury he'd told her about—and she could imagine it throbbing painfully inside the stiff new boots. Every time he tried to make personal conversation, Kit cut him off with a new command.

"Why isn't Chloe teaching me? I paid for her."

"I'm her assistant," Kit said. "That part comes later, if you're good enough. I have to decide if you're good enough to stay in this class or not. Let's see you move Molly into a jog now."

He did, his hands quiet on the reins, his leg pressure applied deftly, not too much. Molly started up fast, and Hank settled back in his saddle until she found a gentleman's jog, the quietest of gaits, the cowboy's preference for an all-day ride.

Kit shot Chloe a look. *Now what?* Chloe shrugged.

"You say you've ridden before?"

"A long time ago." Hank pressed his lips together and sat the jog for six circles of the arena.

"You can ask her for a lope if you're feeling up to it."

Hank nodded, and Chloe watched him press his outside leg into her barrel, and Molly make a fairly smooth transition into the lope. He held the reins in his right hand, his left resting quietly on his thigh. She reminded May to lift her butt out of the saddle and stole another quick glance at Hank.

About now he should be aching. The least of his worries would be his tender balls; his spine should be feeling jarred into compression that would require a chiropractor to set it right, and his head was supposed to throb painfully in this much sun. That was the way of first lessons; they hurt. If a new student managed to finish one whole hour, he'd remember his sunglasses and not to eat so much breakfast next time—if he came back. That was about all she expected from a first lesson, getting down a few simple ground rules. Hank didn't know any of those rules. He was a natural rider, his long legs draped gracefully in the stirrups, his back straight enough to chalk a plumb line. He was relaxed.

He looked her way across the arena but didn't try to get her attention. He was marking his corners, dropping his inside shoulder, trying to make each turn more fluid than the last one. Molly was flummoxed; she was used to mixed signals, the shrieks of the uninitiated, exercising her constitutional right to dump the unlucky few who vexed her beyond reason. If he gave her ample reason, she might buck, but even if he fell off, Chloe had the uneasy feeling he would get right up, dust himself off, assess his error, and get back in that saddle. Hank loosened his grip on the reins a little and made a decent transition into the trot, circled twice, and slowed into a long-reined walk.

"I feel jerky," he said to Kit. "It's been years. I've forgotten so much."

"You want to try backing through an L?" Kit asked. "Hang on while I set up the cavalettis." She arranged the poles into an L shape and Hank backed Molly through them, bumping one pole twice.

"She's always a little stiff first thing in the morning," Kit said. She shielded her eyes from the glare as Hank circled the arena at a lope. "Don't start showing off! You're supposed to walk."

He lengthened his reins, and Molly obediently slowed.

Kit's voice—was that how she herself sounded to her students—arrogant, pushy? Chloe walked to the center of the ring and got after her couple. They were holding hands across their horses and talking. "Jeff and Cat," she said. "This isn't the 'Newlywed Game.' One of you change directions, and let's see some action besides the hormonal. Figure eights, and I want you to drive into the corners as you cross them, okay?" She moved out of the way and went back to the fence. Hank rounded a corner, then passed by the gate, where Chloe sat on the top rail. "How am I doing?" he asked.

"Nice hands—you ride well."

"Thanks."

"You're welcome." Back he went to Kit, who stopped him and explained how to execute the side pass. Most times, a beginning rider would yank rather than lay the reins across the horse's neck. Sometimes Chloe had to get right up behind them on the horse and show them which was the outside leg and which was the inside before they assimilated the concept that the two worked together in turning a horse. Hank made two wrong moves, shook his head, then had the pass down pat. Molly was in love with his quiet moves.

When his back was turned, Kit turned to Chloe and threw up her hands. "He doesn't do anything wrong!"

"Just let him walk off, I guess."

She was still feeling out of sorts. It wasn't breakfast—she hadn't eaten anything—Hugh'd made her so angry she'd forgotten to grab an apple or anything for lunch. She pressed a hand to her belly as if that might quiet it. Behind her, Hannah had the bandage chewed off now and was tossing it up and down in some grand game of catch as she stayed, technically, on the down command. Terrific.

"We could knock off a little early," Hank was saying, "since this is my first lesson."

"Dream about it," Kit said. "You've still got fifteen minutes left. Around here we give you your money's worth, partner. Trot some more. Trotting's the best thing, boy, it'll develop your seat in no time. A dozen laps of that. Start counting *after* this lap."

Am I that bad? I am. Chloe sent her loving couple off on a stable walk to cool out their horses. They'd gotten half her attention today, and it was pure luck nothing had gone wrong. Now they would go down to Mexico, rent the worst possible string horses on some beach, and probably get pitched into the foaming, romantic sea. They held hands across the horses' backs, separating only to ride around the immovable Hannah. May was jumping her last two-foot-high rail; the grin on her face reached several feet higher than that. She completed her jump and reached down to give her horse a neck pat. Will I be like that when I get old, Chloe wondered, tough, and sharp as some sixty-year-old cheddar? Ten thousand dollars, Jack Dodge had said. *I will get old. Someday Kit will think I'm full of shit and turn on me, or worse yet, outgrow me. I don't know what the hell we're doing on this planet besides hurting each other and burying our best friends.*

At last Hank was allowed to walk Molly off.

"Ten laps cool down, then reverse direction and ten more," Kit said. "Remember to bend her as you go. Those serpentines I showed you, in and out, in and out. Use your leg to tell her, don't rely just on neck-reining. When you're done, we should probably give her a bath since it's such a nice day. I'll show you where the stuff is. Meet me down by the wash racks after you finish your laps, okay? And always dismount when you exit the ring, and remember to close the gate after you." She gave Chloe a wink and slid under the fence.

"I miss you," Hank said when he passed by Chloe at the gate. She tapped Molly's rear end with her cane, and the mare took off in a lope. "Pay attention when you're on horseback," Chloe said. "The horse is a potentially dangerous animal."

He leaned forward slightly and held onto her mane, riding the lope until Molly ran out of gas. "Not half as dangerous as some women."

Chloe let herself down slowly into the sand and unlatched the gate for him.

She looked up into his face, the sober jaw, the little mustache carefully trimmed with the scissors she knew he kept in the drawer next to the bathroom sink. "You're not as tough as you think you are," he said and turned away, got down off Molly, patted her neck, and led her through the gate.

She shut the gate behind him. Probably he believed that saying I love you would solve anything. That didn't surprise her, but the way he rode did. She could never have imagined it, those soft hands so firm but gentle on the reins. From the back he looked like an old hand, and she could imagine him twenty years from now, riding the exact same way, the horse beneath him calm and responsive, the women he passed on trail turning back for a second, maybe even a third glance.

CHAPTER

21

The balance of Hank's silk shirt hardly made a dent in the five one-hundred-dollar bills she took out of the check Dodge gave her—the sheriff's department's monetary apology for her trouble. Before depositing the remainder in a savings account—her first—she asked if she could hold the cash equivalent in her hands. *Ten thousand dollars.* "You know, it probably seems like nothing to you guys, but it feels like I won the lottery," she told the bemused bank manager, who took the single packet of banded bills back into the safe. "Except the money's so clean it looks fake."

Before she had the saleslady box and wrap the shirt, she stuck three hundred fifty dollars inside an envelope, and tucked that into the pocket. She took the package by the college. Holding it under her arm, she walked it by the eucalyptus trees and boxwood shrubs, the gum spots on the asphalt, the flattened empty Dorito bags, the music of student laughter erupting from the classrooms with the bright orange doors. She used her cane to push up those steep stairs to his office and paused a minute to study the closed door before she set the package down. An index card taped to the door bore a neatly typed schedule of his time there, the hours he was in class, his office and home phone numbers. A part of his life that was coming to a close, if what he'd said to her about budget cuts was true. School would be over in a matter of weeks. What would he do then? Get another teaching job far away, sell that Irvine place and disappear from her life entirely? She'd given him the gate; it was stupid to start having second thoughts now. He had office hours any minute, and he'd be the type to show up for them early. She set the box down, smoothed the brown paper once, and went down the second staircase, just in case he was coming up this one. She walked around the Agriculture building to avoid running into him. Three hundred fifty wasn't all he'd spent on her, not by long odds, but paying on your debts was the proper thing to do.

Out by the Agriculture building, three of Phil Green's students were grooming his colt. Two adoring girls were brushing his fuzzy mane, and one lanky Asian boy was frowning at the girls' oohing and aahing. Baby Thunder had grown into most of his features in the last five months. He was starting to get a little studdy—nipping, arching his neck proudly, annoying the few sheep and the single skinny calf housed in the barn. Chloe took a good long look at the legs. Gabe had done all right. He would make a fine saddle horse, once they gelded and taught the beast some manners. Who would Phil get to break and train? Not one of those sixty-day wonders, please God. She'd leave him a note—Vess Quinlan—he was still one of the best, but it would mean moving the baby to Elsinore for the duration. No hurry just yet. The students were starting to look at her, whisper among themselves, maybe remembering her from last year's lecture on horsemanship. She smiled, pushed her cane ahead of her, and went to the truck.

"Customer at your table," Lita said.

Chloe looked up from the misbehaving coffee filter and saw an angry Hank, one fist full of cream silk, the other one sprouting hundred-dollar bills. "You take him, Lita. Looks like he's one hell of a tipper."

Lita set down her icewater pitcher. "No."

"No? What do you mean? I can't ask you to save my ass one time?"

Lita walked past her into the kitchen.

She finished the nonsense with the filter and turned the machine on. Coffee water sprayed the front of her T-shirt. Her T-shirt was soaked. She sighed. Picking up her order pad, she went to the booth Hank had taken, opened her pad to a fresh green page, and waited.

He laid the shirt down and the bills on top of it. "You can't erase us, Chloe."

"You're likely to get a grease spot on that silk, and I paid a lot of money for it. Why don't you pick it up, Hank?"

"This isn't about money or shirts."

The ceiling fans whirred overhead, and Chloe felt dizzy. "Did you want something to eat? If not, maybe you should go."

"I want you back in my life. Sit down at this table with me and let's talk it out."

Rich and Lita stood like a pair of transfixed squirrels, heads peering through the cubby where he took the orders. She gave them the finger and looked back to Hank. His hair had that little cowlick in the back where he'd sometimes forget to brush. The skin around his eyes was lined; he hadn't slept well or much lately.

"The avocado omelet is always a good choice. Filling enough for a light lunch, or a hearty late breakfast. We have a new soup, tortilla, it's real good, but you might want to add a few peppers."

"Chloe, sooner or later you're going to have to trust somebody besides that dead horse trainer."

She pressed her lips together. "I can get you a patty melt, I know you like those."

"That's right—you know what I like, don't you? You like it too. We like each other rather splendidly, I'd venture to say, and it seems foolhardy to let one misunderstanding throw away incredible sex, all those quiet good times, Chloe, goddammit, I can't just stop loving you because you tell me to."

Several men from the city crew turned in their booth to watch. They looked like a singing group, in their orange shirts with the oval name tags. "Patty melt?" she repeated.

Hank sighed, threw up his hands.

She carefully penned the order, sent it back to Rich, and told him to stop gaping. "You're a fool," Lita said. "You make me want to throttle you."

"Both of you mind your own business." She waited on the city workers, busied herself with setting up tables, folding napkins, the whole time feeling Hank's eyes follow her around the small restaurant. The ceiling fans chopped at the static air and blew their stilted conversation into a blended mess of confusion.

She served him the patty melt, brought him a side order of potato salad, a dill pickle, more water. He never reached out once to touch her, and she was thankful, because if he had, she might have broken down like an old jackknife, folded herself into his lap, and cried hard. When she turned the check face down on the table, he laid the money over it, all three hundred fifty dollars.

"Whatever made you think you could buy me off?" he said. And then he was gone, out the door, *adios*, mama.

CHAPTER

22

The bright blue sky was cloudless, quiet, the kind of spring day that advertised summer three weeks before the term's end, dangled it in front of students and caused them to call in bomb threats in order to steal a day at the beach. The sun beat down pleasantly on the back of Hank's neck as he crossed the green quad. Students hailed him and he waved back, a smile playing automatically beneath his twitching mustache, the same as it had for years. Where were earthquakes when you needed them? Angry gods with fists full of lightning bolts? A conflagration was certainly burning in the region of his chest, and the great flood threatened to spill down his face and level him, right there on dry land. She pushed him away because he'd betrayed her trust. He wanted to gut buildings, go after her, scream out her name, and carry her bodily out of that damn café. Instead, he crossed the campus at his usual quick clip, retrieved his mail, miraculously missing Karleen this once, walked back to his office to pick up his notes for his next lecture, and surprised Asa, half asleep on the threadbare office couch.

"What's the trouble?" Hank asked him as he shut the door. "Hangover? Bethany's cooking?"

"Oh, Bethany's cooking, all right," Asa said, scratching his head. "Cooking it up in our bed with some twenty-year-old lifeguard."

Hank paused. "I see."

"No, Oliver, you don't really *see*. Not until you walk in on it and observe your wife's legs wrapped around some tanned guy's bucking ass do you really begin to develop a sense of vision."

"So did you wipe the floor with him?"

"No, I watched them roil around for awhile, then I gave them a round of applause. I swear I could hear a pop when the son of a bitch pulled out of her. Ran like hell, too, right out the door and onto the boardwalk, hugging his little red Speedos in front of his yank. We never should have moved to the beach. Nobody wears clothes."

Hank smiled, opened the file cabinet, and took out his lecture notes. "Did you two work it out?"

Asa lay back down on the couch and rubbed his face. "We argued all night, then she took off for Daddy's, no doubt to tell him what an aging ogre I am. Says she doesn't *know* if she can stop seeing the lifeguard. Says she has *energy* for him, like the guy's some kind of fucking toaster oven, I swear."

"So why aren't you at the beach house?"

Asa smiled. "Apparently my darling frau used most of the rent money for partying with the nose-candy crowd, so we were asked to 'vacate the premises,' as they say. I'm hanging my hat here until the Credit Union opens."

Hank zipped his briefcase shut. "I might be able to help you out in that area, Asa, if the Emerald City isn't too offensive to your sensibilities."

"What about your roommate?"

"Hightailed it back to the campgrounds."

"Jesus, I'm sorry. She take anything of value?"

Hank patted his chest. "Just the old clock. I'll live. You want to bunk at my place?"

"Does it have hot showers and a flush toilet?"

"Plus all those magic boulders."

"Say no more."

Hank pulled out his desk drawer, reached in, then threw Asa his extra keys. "Hey, no girls allowed, okay?"

Asa looked up from the key. "She really got to you."

"I'll reconsider next week. Right now I just want a few days' peace."

"According to the *Mahabharata*, during the endtimes, what we now know as our horizon will transform into a fiery boundary. Picture that if you will—a dozen suns circling our own, boiling the sea down to dry rock. Nowhere on this planet will be life be sustainable. They have lovingly dubbed this phenomenon the 'Samvarkata,' and it's believed it will continue until it has decimated the entire universe. Then, a little like our winter this year, we'll have years of rains leading to floods, until the great watery drink swallows up the universe. Man as we've known him will be one small burp in that last cosmic meal. Meanwhile, Vishnu is oblivious, snoozing deeply in his yogic sleep atop Shesha, the snake, floating on the ghost of the sea. Then, my scholars, comes the time of Patience. For only when the snake awakens will life have a chance to begin again," Hank read. "How about these Hindus? Do they know how to throw an earthquake party?"

"You'd be able to get a rad suntan," Larry Kolanoski said. "Mega UV."

"It's depressing," Kathryn Price said.

Hank set the notes down on his podium. "Which part, Kathryn?"

"All of it. Why does everything have to get destroyed? Why can't mankind learn from its mistakes instead of wrecking the whole planet?"

Hank threw the question to the class. "Anyone have a response to that?"

Gentle Cora raised her hand, then turned to Kathryn. "But it's actually a creation story, don't you see? After the destruction, it all starts over, Vishnu's there—remember—he's the preserver. It's a bit like a forest fire, the reseeding, if you will. On a larger scale, of course."

Kathryn took a hairbrush from her striped purse and ran it through her long hair so hard Hank expected to see sparks rise. "I don't know, Cora. It sounds like none of these clowns ever makes a dime's worth of progress. Just the same old shit, millennium after millennium."

Cora smiled. "Well, it's not a true story."

"Oh, sure. Like it evolved out of nowhere!" Kathryn's dander was up, big time. Hank watched her take a second to assemble her thoughts before she let Cora have it. "It reeks of the history books, don't you think? Birmingham, Chicago, all this Reagan Star Wars shit. When is anyone going to stand up and say Enough?"

Cora set her pencil down and turned to Hank, wanting him to smooth out this potential mess before it began to catch like brushfire. Usually he let these small disagreements blaze and burn out of their own accord. Today anything he said was likely to fall on the debate like dry tinder. "Maybe you're both right," he said. "It does seem hopeless. But it also heralds another chance for a perfect beginning. Wiping the slate clean. I find that kind of exciting, actually."

The class looked back at him blankly. Cora was disgusted with his waffling. He'd let pass a golden opportunity to hammer the Republicans. They may have been students of his subject, still innocents, but they recognized a teacher's absence at fifty paces and were having none of the Indian doctrines today.

"Go get yourself megatans," he told them. "It's a perfect day, and there isn't a fire cloud in sight."

They exited the classroom a little suspiciously—it was a full thirty minutes until the hour—and he stood there after they had gone, shutting his eyes, feeling the room enclose him with its shabby carpeting and never-clean blackboards. Too many words and not enough actions had made their way through this space. Theory and history were fascinating, dense mountains to scale, but it was an ethereal journey made with an invisible pick, nothing ever conquered beyond a concept.

He picked up his briefcase and started toward the offices, then stopped and turned back toward the parking lot. So what if he skipped office hours, left campus early? A black mark next to his name was nothing now. He unlocked the Honda and threw the briefcase in the backseat, where a few wisps of white fur and the odor of unwashed dog remained. He got in and drove to the freeway through the afternoon traffic. To his right one of the last fields of undeveloped land sloped to gentle, rolling hills of green. Over the last few years the space had begun attracting migratory birds. In the winter, dun-colored geese foraged there, their awkward bodies moving in rows over the grasses. Today a small herd of goats clipped weeds. The developers had quit using cattle; there was too much controversy over manure and methane destroying native grasses and altering the food chain. His class had gone badly, and he suspected he'd lost something in there today, some shard of authority that a teacher needed as much to believe in himself as his students did. He envisioned his grandmother's place, a cabin in the red rock—wouldn't do to blow it up any larger than it was—and held it out in front of himself like a focal point to get him through the next few weeks. His chest wall ached, felt as porous as sandstone; he knew the name of that disease: Chloe Morgan. He drove inland, past all five of Irvine's exits, until the turnoff for the Laguna Hills, where the brass globe with the smiling faces turned, in front of World of Freedom.

"Hank, sweetie, what a surprise. Your father's out on the golf course. I wish you'd called."

"I didn't know I was coming until I was halfway here."

Iris gave him a quick embrace, and he felt the fragility of his mother's body. It gave off a slight heat—perhaps she'd been in for chemo again this week. If he asked, she wouldn't say; she'd hedge and change the subject to something she found more pleasant.

"Are you alone?"

He sat down on the sofa. "Yes."

"Do you want a drink? How about a sandwich?"

"Mother, I'm fine." He patted the couch. "Come sit. I want to talk to you."

She smiled, smoothed her skirt, and sat down, hugging a throw pillow to her breast, a doe-eyed lion stitched in ocher and rust threads. Really, she could use some new needlepoint patterns. He would have to look in the Metropolitan Museum catalog and order her a few patterns that weren't so wounded.

He placed his hand over hers, feeling the age-risen veins and thickened bone caused by arthritis. Iris still wore her diamond engagement ring in addition to the heavy band of stones that made up the matching wedding band. They appeared locked into her hand by the enlarged knuckle. She and Hank sat there for an awkward minute, the sound of the radio puffing out a long spiral of Mantovani, so much background noise trying to soothe any potential trouble before it began.

"It was uncomfortable for you that night at the restaurant," she said.

"Well, I didn't help any, drinking so much. It wasn't anyone's best night."

"Your father was up all night afterwards, pacing. He's worried about your relationship with this girl."

"She's a woman, Mother."

Iris smiled. "To Henry she's a girl."

"And God knows Henry's always right."

"Excuse me?"

"Why did you marry my father?" he asked. "You've been together fifty years, but in all that time I've never seen you two kiss or hug. He was always bullying one or the other of us into doing things his way. Making sure his opinions became our opinions. That hasn't changed."

She pulled back sharply. "He's your father, Hank. I won't hear you talk about him that way. What's come over you?"

"I just want to know." He rubbed his temples. All wrong, he'd cut to the heart of it without apologizing to each layer of skin on the journey down. "It's a lot of things. We're all so cautious with each other—even after all these years."

"I'm sure you're imagining that."

"No I'm not. That night at dinner—Chloe babbling on, trying to get us to talk to each other. We never talked. We ate our suppers on TV trays watching the 'Huntley-Brinkley Report.' She grew up alone, without a family, yet she's the warmest thing I've ever met. The three of us—we're always so reserved. Careful. Careful of what?"

Iris set down her pillow and looked toward the window, where several lightcatchers hung on fishing line, spangled with colored glass in the shapes of hummingbirds and seagulls. "You forget what it was like for him—World War II—he was just a boy when he served. It changed him, made him crave security. Henry likes distinct boundaries. He likes to know where everything is going before he takes his first step."

"Is that because of Annie?"

The mention of his dead sister's name gave off its own kind of light, a new penny thrown up into an arc over a dark wishing well. Her picture hung on the wall in a Lalique frame, frosted glass ivy leaves that always made Hank think of her perpetually smiling, locked inside a coffin grown over with ghostly vines, like some princess under a spell.

Iris sighed.

"Mom, I didn't say her name to make you feel sad. It's just that I have so many questions I'm afraid to ask you."

She pressed her hand to her eyes. "Why can't you let the past stay in the past?"

He moved closer. "Because it isn't past. It's right here. There isn't one object in this room that doesn't say her name when I pick it up. I can't remember her. There are these huge gaps I can't fill in. Would you like to know what I do remember? It's not much. Her pink dress with a starched white bow, the feel of her brushing my hair. The doctor coming to visit. I was jealous because he always gave Annie a cherry lollipop. He gave me one, too, later, when he was finished seeing her, but it wasn't cherry."

Iris fingered the pillow trim but wouldn't look up. "She was usually too sick to eat them."

"How long was she ill?"

"Almost a year."

"Why don't I remember that?"

"Because she was in the hospital so much. We shipped you off to Gran's for several months. It wasn't to get rid of you but to spare you the difficult time."

Hank felt the bristles rise. "But don't you see you didn't spare me? You sent me away. I just hurt in a kind of vacuum. That much I do remember."

Iris got up and went into the kitchen. Hank watched her go, the skirt and blouse perfectly ironed, always the matching earrings and bracelet, as if accessorizing her outfits properly would keep all the hard truths away. She had lost her daughter to cancer, nothing on earth could be more difficult, and she had battled her own cancer for more than a year without a single complaint or questioning comparison. After a few minutes, he followed her into the kitchen. Iris stood snipping dead blooms from her potted African violets on the windowsill. She used a pair of nail scissors and gathered the dead flowers into her palm.

"I'd like the keys to Grandmother's place," he said. "I want to stay the summer there, maybe longer."

She stood in front of him, cupping the cuttings. "What about your job?"

"Budget cuts have sort of given me a push to try this."

"Oh, Hank, no."

"Now, don't look so alarmed. I can arrange a sabbatical at half pay. It's due me. But I may as well tell you that I might be leaving there, regardless. Teaching's just not what it used to be. It's time for me to do something else."

"But all your schooling—you can't just throw it away."

"Maybe I'll teach myself to chop wood, train a dog to heel, teach a child how to read. I've lived thriftily, Mom. It's not as if I'll starve."

"But. . ."

"What? Finish what you were going to say."

She stared down at the blossoms still in her hand. "Never mind."

He went to her and held her in his arms. Her smell was the same as it had always been, White Shoulders cologne—*Now don't go buying me perfume that's too strong and much too expensive*—and the simple smell of a woman's hair, natural, not sunk underneath a layer of hair spray or dye, but beneath her smell was the creeping chemistry of mortal flesh fighting to stay alive.

"I ought to have gone years ago," he said over the top of her head. "When it was time for me to break away. I stayed close by all these years because I didn't want my distance to hurt you. Wouldn't you rather see me off now, than not at all?"

"It's because of that woman, isn't it?"

"No, it isn't."

"She's got you turning up this old earth, foolishly throwing your career out the window."

"Mother, it's not Chloe." He stopped and took a deep breath, let it out before he resumed talking. Just saying her name made a kind of wound. "Would that it were. She left me because I was too afraid to trust her with the truth. All my life I've been circling the truth of things, scared to ask questions or open doors. I couldn't look it in the face, and it's cost me dearly. I'll go pump gas if it's the only thing I can do honestly. I just have to get out of here. Can't you see that?"

"Oh, Hank." She threw the flowers into the sink, eggplant-colored strings against the white porcelain. "I sent you away, and you tell me it was a mistake. Now you say you're going—what exactly is the difference, will you tell me? You're still young, you have time and options. I'm working with a fixed amount of time here, and I can't change that, no matter how much I want to."

"We'll talk on the phone, write letters."

What Iris was not saying was what that she might be dead when he returned, if he returned. He knew that, his heart beat the truth of it against his chest wall, and it scared him so he leaned against the counter for support.

Clear lines of tears ran down her cheeks silently, scoring the powder. He wished she would howl out loud, swear at him, order him not to go. She pressed a fingertip to the corners of each eye, willing the tears back. Softly, she added, "Maybe you don't know, but that's where we scattered Annie's ashes. Out on the prairie, when it was ablaze with those yellow flowers. It's never been easy for me to go back there. I feel that somehow we abandoned her."

"You set her free."

"If you had children of your own, you'd know what I mean. Say hello to her for me, will you? Tell her I still remember her."

"I will."

She forced a smile. "Then I'll just go and get you the keys."

She left the room and he looked around at the striped wallpaper, the perky recipe holder fashioned like a parrot, an index card bearing a low-calorie casserole gripped firmly in its beak. They were good people, but losing Annie had damaged them in some irreparable way. It surprised him how much he missed her, the small pink ghost he never got to see grow up. She was present somewhere in all those myths he'd studied down to the bones, in one heaven or another, dancing. It was time for him to stop trying to make up for the random fact of her death. She might have been his close friend at forty-five. He would have been an uncle to her children. Even if she had hated Chloe, she would have been able to convince her to give her flawed brother another chance.

"Here," Iris said, handing over a brass ring of keys. "And take this, too," she added, handing him a shoebox. "Some of Annie's things— pictures. They're yours now. I guess I've been selfish. I'm sorry I kept her from you all those years."

Hank fingered the keys and felt their cold metal chill against his skin. "What will you tell Dad?"

She smiled and gave him a wink. "Don't fret. Nothing until you're safely on your way."

"I love you, Mom."

"I know you do."

"I'll probably be back before Christmas."

Iris paused, then took his elbow, leading him toward the door. "Well, if you're not, you'll send me a card. About Chloe—I'll confess I didn't much like her at first, standing there half naked in your kitchen. I looked at her and thought, Oh, my God, that little tart, what's she done to my boy? Well, she's a sexy thing, there's no denying it. But she's brought something alive in you. You're smiling again. I think you're in love for the first time in your life."

"I wish I could say she felt the same way about me."

She reached up a finger and chucked it under his chin. Her eyes were damp but resigned. "Keep after her. She may yet."

When he was halfway out the door, she called to him. "Because I was pregnant," she said, her smile nearly elfin. "I married him because Annie was on the way. Believe it or not, I was the one who couldn't wait."

Asa's idea of pitching in came to life every Thursday. He surprised Hank with dinner—usually bachelor's chili—two cans of Stagg's mesquite-fired beans splashed in Anchor Steam beer and a loaf of not-quite-stale French bread, chopped onions on the side, grated cheese optional. "Is this the good life or what?" he said as they flipped through the television channels, finally settling as they usually did, on the news.

"Asa, we're starting to develop a routine here. It worries me. Good thing I'm leaving next week."

"Well, I'll miss having someone to talk to. Claire's asked me to see a counselor with her," Asa said. "Wants six months worth of phony-baloney shrink yammer under our collective belts before she'll even consider sleeping with me."

"That sounds reasonable."

"No sex for six months?"

Hank gave him a half smile. "If you're desperate, there's a lady in the mailroom I can introduce you to."

"Not the one with the strange earrings? You?"

"She's really a nice woman. Just a little anxious. Keep her away from the telephone, and she'll be all right." He set down his bowl of chili. "I don't know where it is you got this idea that I'm such a monk. I get around, occasionally."

"Heard from your Valkyrie?"

"She begrudgingly gives me riding lessons on Saturdays. I'm progressing nicely—as far as the horse goes. She sets me a task, and I do my best to excel. I've come to rather appreciate the plight of the student. It's gotten me in good with the horses, but not that far with my teacher. I'll miss her when I go."

"So don't go." Asa ripped another chunk of bread off the loaf and dunked it into his bowl.

"I'm going."

"Phil Green's thinking about having her train Babycakes. I heard him talking in the hall the other day."

Hank listened as Asa went on, the ministrations of the teaching staff were Asa's universe, the one kingdom where he could feel in control. If Claire took him back, which he bet she would, he hoped she'd sink a tether into his groin to keep him from making the same mistakes all over again. And himself? For weeks now he'd had the essentials detailed out on a list—what to take to Arizona, what to leave behind—a few books, sleeping bag, three pots to cook in, his old manual Olivetti, paper. Boxes were everywhere. Always the list ended before he penned her name, the one item he couldn't purchase at the discount store, couldn't fit into a suitcase, couldn't have simply for wanting. On the television screen they were showing footage of the Patriot missiles. Now that the war was over, suddenly everyone was worried about what it had cost. The bright red ribbon of flame whooshed like a kite tail behind the two-million-dollar bomb. It reminded Hank of the *Challenger* accident, that moment of suspension when it was all just a fantastic light show, and everyone stood looking skyward, trying to be impressed and feel proud to be an American, nanoseconds before they became grieving parents and shamed citizens. Her mouth, the smoky voice as she sang along with the country-and-western station on the radio, her rough hands touching objects in this house, his shoulders, his skin. He felt her presence crowd each cell, some slow virus working its dark magic from the heart outward and downward.

Today, in his box outside the office where he collected term papers and late assignments, there had been a large brown envelope, and inside it a copy of Kit Wedler's journalism assignment. *Hank, I got a B+! Isn't that too far fucking out? I know everything's hasta la vista with you guys, but I thought you might like to read it anyway. See you Saturday and remember to keep your heels down! Love ya, Kit.* He'd set it aside; grading final papers was the order of business. But they were done now, and he could savor it until the sun came up, if he wanted to. He took his dishes to the kitchen and loaded them into the dishwasher. His briefcase lay by the sliding glass door, and he picked it up, set it on the crowded table next to newspapers and bills. He unlatched the catches and took out the envelope, laid it down on the table, and went to the refrigerator to get himself a second beer.

"My friend Chloe Morgan . . . " it began, and for a moment Hank marveled at the luxury of those words before he sank himself into the text.

". . . says that she doesn't really have a philosophy about life, but I think she does, because when something needs doing, even if it's a real rank chore and you wish that some other person would magically appear and do it for you, she just goes ahead and gets the job done without complaining. One time I heard her say 'hard work might give you muscles, but it's hard times that make you strong.' I think that she is totally right because my own life hasn't been that great since my mom left, but here I am anyway!

"The thing I like best about Chloe is that even when I am being a total spasmoid pest, she won't ignore me like other adults do. She makes me stop and take a good look at myself and what I've said or done, and usually afterwards I think, hmm, maybe I don't need to do that again!

". . . we have all kinds of adventures, some of which I can't really mention because they sound *way* stupid on paper, but the thing she taught me that I think about the most often is that I can do anything if I face up to it honestly and don't let being scared get me goofed up. She helped me make out a diet that I can live with and so far I've lost twenty-two pounds, halfway there! She taught me to ride horses and now she is teaching me how to be a teacher for other people who want to learn about horses. Chloe has a saying in her office that goes 'the best thing for the inside of a man is the outside of a horse,' by Winston Churchill, a man I never heard of, but whoever he is, it goes for women, too. Now I want to study to be a vet or maybe a trainer. If Chloe still is into horses when I am grown up maybe we could be partners. I hope so. That would be way cool if that happened.

"She had a hard start in life because her mother couldn't take care of her and so she lived with a lot of different families but never got adopted which I think is the saddest thing I ever heard but Chloe says there are way sadder things than that, and that she has a good life and a great dog and some kind people who care about her. But she lives in a kind of rough place and some bad things have happened to her lately. Still she never lets herself get bitter about it because she says she has too much other stuff in her life to love. For example, horses! She knows everything about a horse and can take the most scared person and get them to relax around a horse. It is amazing! She can take the nastiest horse and with time get him to feel all happy again and do what she says without biting and stuff. Why? Because everything she does she does out of love and with respect for that person or that animal. I used to wish she was my mom, because what could be better than having a cool mom who doesn't rag on you, but now I think I am way luckier to have Chloe Morgan as my friend."

Asa came in and set his dishes in the sink. He walked over to the table and pressed a hand to Hank's shoulder. "Why didn't I figure this out before?" he said. "They rule the universe, don't they? And they're just letting us live here."

"You've been an exceptional class," Hank began as he nearly always did on the last day, "one of my best." Then he made his way through a quick recap of which assignments he was returning, his obvious delight in the caliber of the term paper, and then prepared to show a film as a treat and to entice them to further their studies in mythology, some semester in the future when it was offered again as a regular course. "I hope the legends we've discussed here provoked your thinking about your own lives," he said. "Somehow I feel we shortchanged the goddesses a bit, so this film's sort of an attempt to give them a moment in the sun."

He went to the back of the room and threaded the projector with the old sixteen-millimeter reels—someday audiovisual would get around to converting this to videotape. It snagged and he had to remove it and start again. Finally it was ready. "Larry? You want to hit the lights for me?"

The room went dark, and the countdown numbers leapt off the screen into the opening credits. He'd seen the film countless times, always lost himself in other thoughts before the first few minutes were up, but this time he tried to make himself watch. It began with a long sweeping shot of the sea, frothy breakers combing over the dark ocean until the image of horses began to appear, the white foam in the breaking waves became manes, and the narrator explained in his fatuous baritone that the word *mare* and its French equivalent originated from the Sanskrit, *mah*, for mighty. On he rambled, explaining that adding *mah* to *gan*—for birth—formed Morrigan, the transformative goddess who embodied the triple nature so common to women in myths. When they appeared, everything about them occurred in threes: three phases of the moon; three mothers; a maiden, a matron, and a crone; a daughter, mother, and grandmother. Old Morrigan worked her angles. She got around. The black-and-white footage made his students chuckle—the zealous actor portraying Cuchulain, the booming Wagner soundtrack. Larry whipped an imaginary conductor's baton, and even Cora was chuckling. There was one moment in the film Hank found unspeakably sensual. He folded his hands and waited. Here Morrigan bared a shoulder, revealing collarbone and the start of a curving breast as she offered herself to the warrior. Pride made him refuse her love. *I can best thirty men a day—on the battlefield or on the bed!* To make love with her meant he would lose his power. Thus began the mess all men had been in for the last 25,000,000 years. When he further refused to help her in battle, he lost the war without even lifting his sword. *Why is it that men fail the at the simplest of tests?* Hank wondered. *All we have to do is listen and women show us the way. But we insist on making our own way.* Morrigan the horse, Morrigan the raven, Morrigan the crone. She saved Cuchulain's sorry ass, even though he betrayed her, and still he was too blind a fool to praise his luck. *Well, I had my small blessing,* Hank thought. *What I didn't do was respect her magic. I read investigative papers instead of asking her what I wanted to know.* He settled back in his chair, and suddenly the film began to darken as it burned, and he jumped up to shut off the projector.

"Well, fuck," Larry said. "I was just getting into this. You gotta tell us, Professor Oliver, does Sinbad get it on with the babe or what?"

Laughter.

"I'd rather show you the film, Larry, but it looks like this one's cooked."

He opened the door to let out the scorched odor, then crossed to the front of the room and sat down on the table in the front. "Basically, what it boils down to is that man doesn't learn what's good for him until he loses it. Morrigan tried, she gave Cuchulain every chance, but he was stupid and proud."

Kathryn cleared her throat. "Well, stop me if that sounds familiar."

Larry shouted, "Woman, give me a break!"

She made a fist and shook it at him. "I wish I could. I know right where I'd fracture to do the most damage."

Hank waited for their ribbing to cease. Was a romance budding between these two, now that William was out of the picture? "We are all on heroic journeys," he said. "Some of us have more difficult starts to get over than others. Alcoholic parents, foster homes, domestic violence—it's all a kind of mythic journey we spend the rest of our lives figuring out, that's the beauty of myths. We can learn from them about our own lives."

Carlos threw his hands up. "Sure. Easy for you to say. You have a great job and probably own your house. What did you ever have to get over?"

"I was your age once."

"So?"

"So, I went through the same kinds of difficulties you did. Life's not that much different now than when I was growing up."

Larry smacked his desk with a fist. "It is so! Nowadays we have to worry about AIDS everytime we get laid, and there's so many bombs we might as well all commit suicide. There's gangs everywhere, and drive-by shootings, even on the freeway. My cousin OD'ed when he was sixteen years old. Tell me you ever went through anything like that—it's completely different."

The depth of his students' vulnerability often dazed him. It was as if they believed the classroom provided sanctuary, a place to confess and to witness. They knew nothing about him other than his soft-spoken delivery, the fine print he pencilled on their papers. Soon he would be gone, and they would forget him entirely. "Well, in my own case, Larry, it was the death of my older sister, when I was around five. Too young to remember? Everything makes an effect, causes a ripple. The distance my parents put between us so that they would never have to hurt that way again profoundly affected me. It's cost me a lot of years." He paused. "And to put it on a more personal plane, lately it cost me a woman I loved."

Kathryn sighed. "Oh, for God's sake."

"Ms. Price?"

She swung her hair back. Her face was dark. "Really, Mr. Oliver, you're a nice guy. If you know what went wrong, why don't you go after her and just fix it? See, that's the thing with men. They'd rather wait for the woman to make the first move, the second move, all the important moves. Men make the mistake of thinking we think like they do. We're just waiting for one of you to have the balls to ask for what it is you really need."

"Ha!" Larry called out. "What a lie. Would you have gone out with William? That's what *he* really needed."

Kathryn, Larry, Carlos, William. Kit. *Annie*. Everywhere he looked, there were children, telling him what to do. "Have your best summer ever," he told them as he threw papers into his briefcase. "I will never forget this class." His throat was tight, and the words came painfully, blunt instruments bruising his throat. Gentle Cora stood up to give him a hug good-bye. He hugged her back, waved, then beat them out the door for the first time in his life.

CHAPTER

23

He stopped twice on the long drive—once in Needles to gas up, where a Unocal station attendant with a name tag that read "Junior" tried to talk him into buying a new tire.

"You're showing steel on the left rear," he said. "I just happen to have a Michelin inside. Can let you have it for, oh, ninety-five bucks."

"For a single tire? That seems rather steep."

The man looked up, his Ray-Bans reflecting Hank's disbelieving smile. "It'll seem reasonable enough when you have a blowout in the middle of nowhere, buddy."

"I'll take my chances. I have a terrific spare."

Hank finished pumping his unleaded and stood still in the dense, steamy air. The temperature had to be in the high nineties, but the clean swift breeze rushing past his face felt cool. Nobody much lived here—it was an oasis, a rest stop where you could gas up, grab a belly-ful of pancakes at the Teddy Bear Café, then—sufficiently refueled—move on with the map.

In Flagstaff, at the Exxon station, the sign above the pumps read DAN'S: FULL SERVICE WITH A SMILE. No cherry pie, but the petite woman in the cowboy hat who took his credit card was smiling as she approached his car, and more than happy to take a look at his tire. "Looks all right to me. Don't suppose I could talk you into some Indian jewelry," she said, "seeing as you're headed out into the res. Mind what you buy, though. Some of those dealers jack up the silver the second they see a new face. Shop around."

"Thanks, I will." He stretched his muscles and got back in the Honda. Less than an hour to go, and he would be at the cabin. He got groceries before leaving town, some dry milk from a hiking store for his morning cereal, and one of those old-time coffeepots with a percolator. The bright aluminum surface of it made him remember Boy Scouts, the scoutmasters always lugging the pot from the water to the fire, grouchy and squinting until they'd downed a few cups. How soon we come to depend on coffee, he thought. Anything to jump-start the heart into beating another day.

The moment he saw it—crumbling fieldstone walls, once-green composition roof sanded by the weather down to the roofing paper, filthy windows, sagging rail fence that had completely decomposed in places, weedy plants in the front yard, doorless outhouse in back—he knew she would have christened it heaven on earth and set about staking her claim. The nearest neighbor was two miles north. To say it needed work was something of an understatement. Henry senior would have ordered it gutted, sold the land, and forgotten about it in less than a day. Hank circled the perimeter, slowly assessing his plans. Around the cabin's boundary, old pines towered, aromatic, solid witnesses to a childhood he could only recall in fragments. He tried each key in the front door, jiggling the old lock gently, but it took him several tries to get the stiff, aged bolt to turn. He opened the door and ducked through the six-foot opening to a clean, spare room that had seemed much larger to him as a child and found a note from Dave Greer propped on the table. *We'll check in on you in a couple of days, Hank. You might have to work the pump handle a while to get it running. There's lamps and oil in the closet. Joyce and I expect you for Sunday supper.* The cabin consisted of two rooms, the kitchen-living space with the iron sink and wood stove, sagging cupboards, and the bedroom, now empty of furnishings. The matchwood pine ceilings dipped so low that he could reach up and touch them with the flat of his hand. He tore a sheet of newspaper from the copper woodbox by the fireplace and used it to wipe a window clear. Sunlight emerged from the pane as soon as he dropped his hand, creating a warm shaft that puddled a few feet away on the floor. So tired he felt ready to drop, he ran his fingers through it, watching the dust dance in the shaft of light. *Sundogs, spirit puppies, you can reach right out and touch them.* "Hello, Nana," he said aloud. "It's Henry. I'm back."

Several mornings a week Indian kids rode over on rangy bay horses to check on his progress. The crazy white man lugging lumber and roofing materials in the foreign car sometimes invited them to share a cup of lemonade. He made friends with their horses—even offered them his good apples. Mostly he was content to have them watch him hammer and saw. *Mister, what are you doing? I'm repairing my house. No, really. Yes, really. You going to live there? I'm going to try. It snows in the winter, Mister. Then I'd better get this roof fixed, hadn't I?* Very little in the way of the roof was salvageable. He peeled away crumbling shake, and used a putty knife to expose the beam frame. He worked on the roof until midafternoon, then covered it with a plastic tarp weighted down by rocks. When the heavy clouds that gathered near the mountains delivered their offering to the earth, there was nothing to do but stand back. Here weather was respected. When the monsoons came, Hank stood in the doorway, witnessing lightning crackles that lit the dull sky. He got so he could hear the rumble of warning in the distance long before the rain fell. A few times he stood out in the middle of it, shutting his eyes, feeling the water jab at his skin, weigh down his clothing. Sometimes he took a nap in a corner of the cabin, lulled dreamless into his sleeping bag by the heavy thrumming, sleeping as if he'd been hit over the head with a sap.

Frequently he didn't wake until dusk, and then he'd light the lantern and read, or sit on a stump behind the cabin and watch the sky darken completely to black. Maybe the California sky had stars, too, but it must have kept them hidden. Here so many bright white points shone from the night sky that he tried to learn each one's name, and to place them all, as part of his after-dinner chores. Hard work made his body throb with exhaustion, but tired muscles didn't help him sleep. He could feel them toning up from use, see a visible difference in his body. Kit Wedler would have loved it, he mused, placing moleskin over his first set of blisters, soon to be followed by a series of others. He wrote his mother letters, filled his stomach with simple food, tried hard to find peace in the red rocks and wildflowers, but as soon as he lay down in the sleeping bag, he missed Chloe so badly his heartache kept him tossing half the night.

Maybe he would write her a letter—but where did one mail it? In care of Hughville—*Postman: go as far as you can down a dirt road until you sink a wheel, then hoof it until a white dog comes after you, but keep in mind that's nothing compared to the girl.* In care of the restaurant—to Jack Dodge—how about the veterinarian, who danced her so close, who had known the pleasures she was capable of giving—who might know them again? Would she read it, or noting the return address, at once throw it away? He thought of her tough mouth, the grace she ascended to when riding horses, and how beyond all reasonable expectations, she had managed to make a limp and leaning on a cane attractive. She fit by his side in bed, her head tucked into the hollow of his arm, her calloused hand resting on his chest. Simply put, he fit inside her. Most nights he berated himself for his stupidity; other nights he stayed up all hours looking for hair shirts. He slept fitfully, trying hard to take pride in his repair work on the decomposing cabin, quietly troubled that at any moment the whole mess might come tumbling down on his mortal head.

He looked for his sister, Annie, over long expanses of prairie. He stepped carefully across the rocky, pitted earth; the singsong chirp of yellow prairie dogs drifted past him like the jeering taunts of schoolchildren. He saw evidence of their burrows but never caught them out in the open. Bright golden flowers bloomed in wild patches. In their thick centers, a fat throat of dusty brown pollen lay exposed to the wind. Grasshoppers leapt everywhere, covering his boot tips when he walked through the brush. It was so quiet he could hear the sound of the insects constantly chewing, as if they'd learned their lesson and would make it through the snowy winter this time, no matter what. But Annie, like his grandmother, was nowhere to be found. He wanted to believe they both hovered near his shoulder, a mist of energy too important to leave the earth. A faint memory of touch, a soft smell that was gone the minute he tried to name it, a sharp ache inside his chest that lifted—was that Annie, or was it Chloe? He was tired of himself; he didn't want to go back to California, didn't care if he ever taught college again. He watched his skin burn, freckle, then tan up. Daily he drove his body into the cabin repair hard enough to sweat all over. He felt his beard begin to fill in since he'd abandoned his razor, the first time since he was nineteen years old he hadn't scraped it down to the skin. He looked forward to icy cold showers under the hose he'd rigged up on the side of the house, tried his best to fill each hour with an act of purpose and never to let the Indian children see him without a smile on his face.

"You're living like a hermit, Hank," Joyce Greer insisted in the doorway. "Come home with us to supper."

"I'm kind of working on something," he told her, thanking Dave for dropping off his mail. He set his hammer down and wiped his sweaty face with a rag.

"Writing a book, are you?" Joyce craned her neck in the doorway. The Olivetti sat on the table, a blank sheet of paper threaded in the platen.

"Just a few letters."

Dave honked from the pickup. "Let him alone, woman. The man will survive another day without your pot roast."

"Next week, maybe," Hank said, and watched them drive off in the battered old Ford. He threw the letters and bills on the tabletop without looking at them, and finished the hinge on the makeshift cupboard he'd fashioned from scrapwood. The cupboard face shut now, flush with the opening, but it had taken him six tries, and he'd ruined one hinge, forcing it. He set the cupboard into the toggle bolt on the wall and turned the screwdriver until it cranked down tight. He swept up the wood shavings, wiped the tools down with oil, set them in the toolbox, and shut the lid.

For dinner he fixed himself a bowl of cereal, sat and watched the vitamin-infused flakes grow soggy, then pushed it aside, spoon still in it. Earlier, when he'd ripped out dry rotted paneling in the kitchen, he'd found a metal toy behind the wood, a lead soldier atop a stocky three-legged horse. He set it down by the lantern and turned to his mail. The large manila envelope from Asa contained a few bills and a note he didn't feel like reading, but glanced over. *Phil's got Babycakes up for sale, can you believe it? He bought some quarterhorse he's calling Burly. Yippie-ti-yi-yay, Pardner. . . .* There was a postcard from his parents, who were at their fifty-fifth high school reunion, somewhere in Michigan. *Your mother is doing fine.* Reassurances. Nothing between the lines except white space. There was a letter from the college announcing faculty meetings, forwarded, a mistake, assuming he was to be back for classes next term. Look as he might, there was no regular white envelope, hand-addressed in block printing to Hank Oliver.

When they wanted to truly test the mortals, the gods wandered around disguised as beggars. It was always the poor old couple seeking a crust of bread who asked for a mortal's hand, never a youthful magnificent in an ermine robe. If you refused—well, Arachne got turned into a spider, Echo and Narcissus ended up yoked to a life of repetition and reflection.

He remembered watching her in the school arena, once after she'd left him. Her cane hung over the top rail, a length of rope tied to the halter of young Thunder. She moved slowly but surely, convincing the colt to follow, praising him each time he minded her, repeating her actions patiently when he missed her cue. Hank had stood watching, too far back for her to see him, too distant to hear her voice, not that anyone would have noticed him—Phil Green and his students were rapt, the awe spreading over their faces as she turned the skittery colt into her best friend. She knew animals the way he'd hoped to know myths, from a deeper instinct that was integral to her nature. Hannah sat by the fence, waiting. She was always accompanied by the dog, they were part of each other. Chloe in the ring—her quick, sure movements, the colt coming to her side as if he had finally found his teacher, his mother. Phil winking and tipping his cowboy hat, the students fixed—all of it blurred into that great blue sea of otherness that did not matter, could never matter in the way she did—would always matter.

He took a sheet of paper from the box and clicked his pen. He drew a picture of the cabin, the sorry roof, the corral fence—how it would look when he got to that stage. He drew a map of the roads to take off the highway and indicated the few landmarks he now knew.

"Dear Chloe:

"We had a date August 13th—your 'birthday'—remember? I'll come to you, meet you halfway, or you can come here—you might like it—clean skies, no power, just enough rain in the afternoons to validate siestas, plenty of room to ride horses. Sometimes children from the Navajo reservation ride over on ponies, bareback, homemade reins, my God, you should see them, they're fearless. Their horses don't know what to make of carrots. The kids think that's a terrible waste of vegetables. They tease me about my work on the cabin, and tell me I work so hard I'm missing what's important—Father Sky, the summer flowers, the good hard rains. They live in such poverty it breaks my heart. I tank them up on lemonade and cookies, and then they lie, and tell me I'm doing a good job, that yes, everything looks just great.

"Am I? Who can say. Wouldn't you know it, all my schooling and when I need it most, there's no myth for me to call on to say these words. I'm on my own here, Chloe, fumbling through my fingers, trying to say I miss you, I need you, and I want you with me, wherever that has to be. Say you'll come visit me. At least think about it. There's no phone, you can have your own room, I'll sleep in my car, whatever you want.

"Tell Molly I miss her. Say hello to Kit. Think about our good times, and how many more we can make together, looking for lost dogs, facing down the legal system, etc. This is two-step country, lots of bars where they play music just an hour south of here. You could teach me to dance. Think of it as one of those rare opportunities that come along once in a lifetime—the chance to get me away from the library once and for all. Does it sound as if I'm backing my way into asking your forgiveness? I know I'm a coward, but let me tell you, the scariest thing isn't asking you to take me back and hearing you say no, it's wondering if I'll ever hear from you again."

He sealed it inside the envelope, then made out a check to Phil Green. *Give her the horse*, he wrote. *If she asks, you can say it's a gift from a friend.*

CHAPTER

24

C hloe set up the summer riding program at the stables as usual, three groups of rich camp kids Saturday morning, then the teenage boys from the Carlson Youth Ranch for juvenile offenders in the late afternoon. The camp kids, though obnoxious and riding horses only because it was a camp requirement, paid well; the Carlson boys earned good behavior points for the privilege of riding, and them she taught for free. She smiled, complimented, and encouraged her way through three sets of spoiled girls in Camp Kiwah T-shirts, took time out to douse her steaming head with the hose at high noon, had a bite of sandwich, raced out to teach the last group, then worked the boys until sundown. The horses got tired and had to be watered several times. If it hadn't been for Kit there alongside her, she couldn't have managed. By dark she nearly always felt ready to cry, just plain tired-out miserable, too whipped to count her receipts. Summer wasn't even halfway over. Maybe it would never end.

"You should call Hank on the telephone," Kit said one seethingly bright July lunchtime. "The telephone is neutral territory for feuding lovers."

"It's what for who?"

Kit shrugged and sipped her mocha Slim-Fast milkshake. "Just something I read in *Cosmopolitan*. You don't have to try it. But some of us might be getting a little bit tired of watching you pout all the time."

Chloe threw her sandwich to Hannah, who gratefully nosed the bread off the turkey and downed each ingredient in a single separate bite. "I don't pout. I might be in a bit of a bad mood, but I hide it fairly well."

"Don't take my word for it. Ask Francisco. Or my dad. Even Lita the terminally optimistic says so. She's probably making you a crystal charm to wear to improve your *chakras* or something."

Kit's smile was ingratiating. Chloe matched it with one of her own. "Don't you have horses to water?"

Kit tossed her can into the wastebasket. "On my way, master."

Hannah trailed Kit, her tail tucked under her haunches. She didn't want any part of Chloe's bad mood. After she and Kit left the office, Chloe thought about what Kit had said. Maybe she would call him up. What could it hurt? Just be friendly—no fooling around—just hi, how's your mom doing, stuff like that. It had been over a month and a half now—surely they could be civil to one another. She used the tip of her pen to turn the office phone's old rotary phone dial. It rang twice. "Could I talk to Hank, please?"

"Who is this?"

"Chloe Morgan."

"Oh, I see," the voice said. "Well, sorry, doll, but you lost your chance. He moved to Arizona."

"He did?" She stopped drawing circles on the desk blotter. "When?"

"Right after school let out."

"So who are you? His condo-sitter?"

The voice laughed. "This is Asa, his officemate from the college. You remember me—I met you way back in January, and I came to your lunch gathering after court—sang harmony, didn't I? With your fan club. I'm renting the place from him."

She remembered him now. The smart ass who ogled her breasts. "Right. Do you have his address in Arizona?"

"I might be cajoled into parting with it. Listen, I'm alone, you're alone, Hank's five hundred miles away—any chance you might be free for dinner?"

"Oh, piss off," she said, and hung up the phone.

Kit stuck her head in the office door. "By the way, Hannah's limping again."

"She is not."

"Okay. I made it up." Kit let the screen door slam.

There was a sound of brakes outside, then a chorus of screaming childrens' voices. Chloe craned her neck to look out the window and sighed at the sight of the maroon van filled with wriggling girls. "I guess the second group's here," she said. "May as well go earn some money."

Camp funds kept her flush, but she lived for the Carlson youths. When Mark Chapman brought them in the first day, they were wary little *macho* men, strutting up and down, cussing in Spanish, making remarks about her cute behind, about Kit being a tidy mouthful—and it was true—Kit was voluptuous now, her fat melting away, revealing her breasts and the beginnings of a waist. Lita had showed her how to French-braid her hair to keep it out of the way while she worked, and the style showed off Kit's cheekbones. Chloe liked to let the boys mill around awhile so she could study them, get a feel for their personalities. They'd been convicted of more than five misdemeanors apiece, ranging from petty thievery and vandalism to chronic truancy. By the time the court sent them to Mark at the Carlson Ranch, they were in a holding pattern between juvenile hall and committing their first felony, which Mark admitted wasn't a possibility, it was an inevitability and would eventually send them to prison. Most of them would graduate the wrong way, no matter what the ranch did for them. They came from horrific home situations, worse than any of Chloe's foster homes. By fourteen, they had been beaten, molested, gotten on a first-name basis with the juvenile court judges, and labeled incorrigible. Whatever Chloe did for them, she knew it was a Pollyanna notion to expect that six weeks of horses could straighten them out. Learning to ride wasn't a family.

She unlocked the tack shed door and whistled. Mark rounded the boys up. Three tall black boys, with geometric designs shaved into their haircuts; two stocky Mexican boys, with muscled arms and set jaws; one rail-thin white boy with ink-pen tattoos of swastikas carved into his hands—her group lesson. They lined up, and she handed them each a halter and lead rope. "Follow Kit," she told them. "Down the hill there to the pasture. Each of you catch yourself a horse, and bring him back up here to get saddled."

"What?" they exclaimed, nearly in unison.

"I said, catch yourself a horse."

Kit was already showing them the pasture gate. Six tough hombres, instantly humbled, transformed by thousands of pounds of horseflesh into scared children. She shaded her eyes and watched them timidly approach the wily geldings. The horses were sick and tired of camp kids; they wanted to spend the rest of the day eating hay and sleeping. No sooner would one boy lift a halter in hope than the horse would duck his head and turn away. She felt a big smile crack across her face. This was what it was all about.

"You're looking a little tired, Chloe," Mark said. "Is this stuff with my boys too much for you? I wish I could get hold of some money to pay you."

"Not to worry, Mark. It's the best part of my job."

"Have you ever heard of the concept of leisure?"

She sighed and stretched her arms above her head. "What the hell am I going to do with a day off?"

On the second visit, Anton, Marquise, Diego, Aaron, Cordero, and Willie were down to the pasture before she could tell them to go. By the third, they bargained over choices for horses, already having made favorites. From now on all Kit had to do was hold the gate.

"They've been so good I hardly know what to do with them," Mark said. "You ought to write up a grant proposal and get this program federally funded."

"And watch my liability insurance suddenly grow a whole bunch of zeroes after it? No thanks."

The fifth week the boys were mad to gallop those horses. It was like watching an old John Wayne movie, them getting Western. While they moved the horses through their paces, she and Kit spotted three apiece, correcting leg placement, trying to get them to understand the notion of rein length, to *feel* the horse's mouth in between the leather and the nickel bit. They slowed down to a walk when Chloe asked them to, drew hands down to pet neckflesh automatically. Elmer was well-matched to Aaron, the slight white boy. Elmer didn't know from swastikas; all he knew was the boy would never fail to bring him a lump of sugar, to stand quietly and brush him until the gelding's lips started to droop in relaxation.

"Next week we're going on a trail ride," she told them. "We'll go up and down hills, out past the dry lake, and across some pretty country. You boys think you're ready for that?"

A chorus of yeses indicated they were more than ready. But it was also the last lesson, after which they would return to the ranch, and she wouldn't see them again.

She sat on the fence railing while they walked the horses off to cool them. All day there had been the oddest sensation in her belly—a kind of fluttering now and then—as if something small flew inside her, confused, like a moth in a porch light. She placed a hand over her belly as if to quiet it. Too much of that processed lunch meat. She should get back to skipping meals, eating only one a day, but lately she was just so damn hungry. Filling up the empty places with food, like Kit used to, that's what I'm doing. But deeper down, she knew it wasn't that—that it might be something more serious, and she couldn't even say what she feared out loud.

She drove up to Gabe's office that night around ten-thirty. The lights were out, but his truck was there. She touched the hood; cool, he'd been here a while. He never slept much, and she knew he nearly always checked in late in the evening when Cynthia was unconscious in her designer sheets and he was feeling at odds. If he had a patient just out of surgery, or was keeping an eye on some animal he was worried about, he'd sleep there all night on the cot she'd called home for a while. She walked around the building and knocked on the side door.

Gabe opened it. "Hey, stranger. Come on in and bring that cranky blond girl with you."

"Quit trying to impress my dog, Gabe. She remembers your shots."

He ruffled the dog's fur, and she took hold of his arm in her jaws and shook it playfully. "I had a sportsman's lunch with Hugh today. Edith's mare again. I spent two hours stitching her ass back together where she broke through the barbed wire." He patted his stomach. "Got a pastrami sandwich in the bargain, but it seems like three days ago. I'm starving. You hungry?"

"A little. Wire's a bad choice for fencing."

"It's cheap. You might as well get used to it, you'll never convince Hugh to stop using it." He closed the door behind her and gestured toward the kennel area for her to walk ahead. He whistled. "Look at your butt. Mama. I swear you've put on weight, Morgan."

"Shut up. I haven't gained a pound."

"Well, you must have shrunk your jeans then. I'd be glad to give you the field-trip tour, but to what do I owe the honor?"

"Would you take a look at Hannah's foot? Awhile back she stepped on some glass at Hugh's. I picked it out, but it doesn't seem to want to heal."

"Sure."

He took her to the same examining room where he'd first had his way with her. She stood off to the side as he reached down and lifted Hannah to the tabletop. His triceps stretched the fabric of his T-shirt under the seventy pounds of dog, and there was a year-round glow to his skin that bronzed him, not unpleasantly. Hannah trusted his hands, but drew her lips over her teeth when he touched the sore paw. "A few weeks back she started limping on and off. Today she wouldn't stop licking it."

Gabe looked up from the gamy paw. "For God's sake, Chloe, this is infected."

"I had to teach lessons, Gabe. I make my own way, remember?"

"Well, I hope you made yourself a fistful of money, sister, because you're looking at two courses of antibiotics and four or five stitches, after I get in there and dig out the scar tissue, and you'd better keep your fingers crossed it hasn't affected bone. This time I'm going to charge you." He readied his syringes for local anesthetic, then took out the suturing supplies.

Chloe watched him work, his focus so intently on her dog that she could almost love him for being so single-minded. The night Absalom died, he'd said no to her on the side of the mountain, insisted there had to be feelings involved for them to press their bodies together again. Like that old John Conley song—*I only deal in real emotion*—what was this sudden interest in feelings? You loosed them, and Fats died on you or someone like Hank said "I love you," but not before his lawyer had you fucking investigated.

Gabe used a cotton probe to clean the cut. He spoke without looking up from his work. "You're quiet. Something on your mind?"

"Not exactly."

"Oh, God. Here it comes." He straightened, keeping one hand on Hannah. "Are you in trouble again?"

"I've been thinking about my mother."

Gabe stopped probing the cut long enough to look up at her. "That came out of left field. What about her?"

Chloe went to the sink, pressed a hand to the cool metal, ran her fingers across the box of plastic syringe caps. "Maybe she gave me up because she was sixteen years old and married to some clown who beat her."

"If so, that might have been her only choice."

"Maybe she didn't want me at all." Chloe sighed. "I know, all in the past, this is ridiculous. It's just—I've been wondering lately—what if we'd stuck it out together? Would we have done any better?"

"Probably not, so why waste time worrying it?" Hannah whined and Gabe gave her a pat. "Almost done, girl. Chloe, hold her back end, would you?"

She moved to the dog. "Maybe I should look for her, search out the truth, maybe that's what I need."

"Will you be able to live with what you find out?"

A bright pool of blood puddled on the table and the needle flashed silver. She looked away. She could handle the pierce of the needle and the smell of infection, but blood made her queasy.

She crossed her arms across her dog. "You know me too well."

"That's another possibility."

"Gabe?"

"Mm-hmm."

"I have this funny feeling in my belly."

He grinned. "It's probably guilt."

"Oh, fuck you. It's physical, kind of fluttery, you know? And it comes and goes."

"You're not eating that *chorizo* Hugh's always buying down in Mexicali, are you?"

"No. But I'll eat anything else. Smoking tastes bad, and I'm so tired in the morning I feel like a bear in November."

He finished up with Hannah and filled a bottle with purple amoxicillin tablets for Chloe. "One every twelve hours. Finish the whole bottle, then come back, and I'll refill it and take out the stitches."

She nodded.

"Now come over here and let me look at you."

When Hannah was down on the floor chewing up a couple of Pet-Tabs Gabe had given her, Chloe took her place on the table. Gabe unbuttoned the first three buttons of her shirt, pulled the tail out of her jeans and listened to her heart and lungs, front and back. Then he made her lie back, unbuttoned her jeans, and felt around her belly, just below the elastic of her Jockey underwear. "You *have* gained weight."

"I've been eating lunch, that's all."

He reached inside her shirt and cupped her breast.

"For Christ's sake, Gabe, I am not in the mood."

He pushed her back down and told her to shut up. "Your breasts feeling tender, a little swollen?"

"Yeah. You want to rub them for me?"

He smiled. "Not at the moment. When was your last period?"

She put her face in her hands. "I don't know. They haven't been regular for over a year. There was one time awhile back, but it only lasted for a day."

"Nothing since then?"

She shook her head no. "Don't say it. Don't even think it. All day I've been thinking of nothing else, and it's scaring me to death."

He pulled her shirt back down. "Go buy yourself one of those drugstore tests."

She grabbed his T-shirt with both hands, and Hannah started to growl. "I'm not pregnant! Don't you go saying I am."

He held his hands out. "I'm a veterinarian, Chloe. You want a real doctor's opinion, there's a doc in the box off Santa Margarita. Read a *People* magazine while you wait."

"Goddammit, Gabe!"

"Hey, don't swear at me. Did you use protection?"

"Mostly."

"Well, mostly isn't always. It happens every day, darling." He helped her sit up—Chloe not speaking, Gabe using one hand to wipe the counter down, putting the used needles into the disposal tray, the other hand resting on her shoulder. Finally he broke the silence. "If you're feeling life, that fluttering, chances are you're a couple months along. Most women don't feel it until the fourth or fifth month, but Cynthia always felt it in the third, she swore she did. You'd have to decide immediately if you want to abort. Any later it's the saline route, and believe me, that's not pleasant."

The room wasn't that cold, but she started to shiver. Gabe put his arms around her, hugged her to his chest. "Being pregnant isn't the end of the world." He bent his face to hers and kissed her cheek. "Go talk to the professor. He's got an investment." He patted her belly, then took his stethoscope out and pressed down inside her jeans to her belly, moving it until he found a place where he could hear something.

"What are you up to? Can you hear a heartbeat?"

"Even if I could, it'd be deafened by all that racket. Your gut sounds rival any animal's I've heard. If you were a horse, you'd colic, starving yourself like you do. Women." He started to laugh.

She pushed him away.

He took off the stethoscope and set it on the counter. "I'm going to feed you supper, and I won't take no for an answer. Especially if there's a little bandit in there, taking his eats first. Here." He reached into a drawer and handed her a sample vitamin pack. "They're for people, relax. Take one in the middle of the day so you don't get sick from it. It'll pick you up, but don't use it in place of regular meals or you'll puke."

He nuked frozen macaroni and cheese in the microwave in the back room. They ate sitting cross-legged on the floor, listening to the country music station, and Hannah licked the trays clean after she finished a trial-size bag of lamb-and-rice kibble. The kennel was fairly quiet, but sometimes they could hear the *woo-woo* of a malamute Gabe was boarding.

"That dog sounds lonesome," Chloe said.

"Spoiled rotten, that's all. You know, you'd make a terrible mother," he said, sucking on a root-beer Popsicle.

"News flash."

"Boy or girl, the kid would grow up thinking it was half horse."

"What's so wrong with that?"

Gabe laughed. He shut his eyes, the lashes so long and thick she could see why women fell like dominoes at his touch. "Because just like you, the kid would turn out wild and hard-headed, breaking every heart within reach. You want my advice?"

"No, but when has that ever stopped you?"

"Take a chance. If you're pregnant, have this baby. Let that professor take care of you. You've worked hard, Chloe. You've earned a regular life. Just do it." He stuck the Popsicle back into his mouth.

"I take care of myself."

Gabe's face was an odd mixture of puzzlement and hurt. "Since when? You took care of Fats, you mother Kit Wedler, and you fed that lame horse even when you couldn't afford to feed yourself. Try again, sweetheart."

"Oh, Gabe," she said, suddenly feeling her losses mount up. "It still hurts so much. Just like it was yesterday. I can't lose anything else. I just can't."

He set the Popsicle down on his napkin and took her hands in his. "That's the only reason people *have* a baby, Chloe. They take the risk, hoping the joy will outweigh the pain. Don't you get it?"

Chloe didn't answer—couldn't—to say anything would make the possibility of a baby—Hank's and her baby—too real.

Hannah put up her sore paw and howled. Gabe laughed. "See that? The hound's smarter than you'll ever be. She understands me perfectly. And she's telling you to listen."

CHAPTER

25

No matter what grew inside her, tomorrow was a full work-day—but try and tell that to her exhausted body. Worry worked its way into all the muscle groups; her blood jittered like a pot of boiling coffee. She lay there in the dark of the cabin, the smell of spring out-side maddening in her nostrils—wild grasses, the hard tang of sage, a bursting of miniature nameless purple and pink wildflowers on the hillsides. Beneath it all, the fertile damp aroma of mud. She tracked the source of all her trouble back to that night Phil's horse went hooves up. If she hadn't answered the door, hadn't gone down to the college, hadn't been bloodied by Gabe's makeshift delivery, she never would have met Hank, never would have. . .

There came the flutter again. Swift, indecent, and gone as soon as she put her hand to her belly. *Dear Mama, whoever you were, and wher-ever you are: You suppose I'm doomed to repeat your mistakes, even though I grew up with other people? Shall I flush this baby, if it is a baby? Will I end up having to give it up if I don't? Did you even tell the father? How ever did you make up your mind?*

Fats had children somewhere. He didn't talk about them, but

sometimes he'd sent them money. How old were they now? Did they have their own children? They hadn't come to the memorial, she hadn't tried to contact them when she spread the ashes. Chloe'd seen him mail envelopes to Alabama and to some University in Texas, and wondered if she was older than they were, what they would think of their father shacked up with this young girl. Fats had room in his heart for the stable kids. He always found time to stop and squat down, eye to eye with the smallest rider. He admired their bug collections and horse drawings, and oftener than not, one of them sat on his knee while he barked out commands in the lesson ring. Despite the cigar smoke and rough edges, there was some exchange there that came naturally.

She threw off the sleeping bag in the night air. Too hot. The scar on her shoulder blade felt itchy. That accident had laid her open to the bone. *Get your blond ass over the fence,* Fats had insisted, but jumping six feet on an unfamiliar horse, that was pushing fate. She watched the Grand Prix on television in that sports bar in Mission Viejo, but never saw herself in that league. Never. You could admire a thing and not have to do it. Perugina, this money thoroughbred he was brokering, needed a video to show a possible buyer down in Houston. So there they were at night in the arena with Francisco holding the camera and Fats yelling out directions and the horse beneath her trembling. She'd always trusted Fats to know what an animal was capable of and what it was not. She'd gone, and they'd made the fence, technically, landing with the horse's rear legs torn open to the tendons and her shoulder likewise—dislocated, too—the jump in splinters around and in them.

Gabe Hubbard had gone right to work, assembly-line fashion, horse first, getting him stable, Chloe shot full of novocaine, waiting in a daze of blood and gauze.

Fats had been shaken. Couldn't understand how he'd judged so poorly what he knew best. When everyone was repaired he paid Gabe in cash and took off on a weeklong drunk. Chloe took over his lessons, made excuses: *His brother in Georgia's dying of cancer. Again? A different brother, he comes from a big family.* She ate Darvon by the handful and taught until sunset, then lay alone in their bed in the cheap apartment, stitches throbbing, wondering if this would be the time he wouldn't come back, would end up in a twisted heap of metal on the highway for her to come and identify.

When he came home she could sense a change in him. He'd gone beyond tired now, he was out there on the windowsill asking death, May I have this dance? He'd quit drinking, cold. Then he'd start up again, trying to make up for lost time, forgoing pint bottles and upending fifths, four or five of them a week. The first few hospital admissions were more about restraining Fats than healing him. He'd be tied into his room spitting and shitting blood, too weak to withstand the DT's, and some resident would give him a drug to calm him, deluding him into thinking he was well enough to leave. In no time he'd be down the hall, his cowboy hat cocked on his head, his silver belt buckle fastened over those hospital pajamas, catch himself a bus to the nearest bar, find a buddy to buy him the first one. Later on he was too weak to bother tying down and no longer fought the doctors. When they'd accomplish the impossible, bring the tough old bird back from hemorrhaging, no viable platelets in his CBC, he'd open his eyes and start in cursing. *You cheap bitch.* . . . Chloe'd sit there next to his bed, tears scoring her face, deliriously happy they'd saved him for her to love one more day, and there he'd be calling her a cunt, blaming her, saying it's all your fault, you know, why didn't you just let me die?

They were on a first-name basis at county, and they drew the same doctor so many times they were about to start sending each other Christmas cards. *What do we do this time?* he asked, and Chloe said, *Give him his wish. Make him as comfortable as you can without performing any miracles.* He took a full ten days to die. *Alcoholism is the slowest form of suicide*, the doctor told her, early on when they were still trying to get Fats to sit in on an AA meeting. But this marinated horseman wasn't grabbing any intelligent way out. He was riding the dark horse for the full count. There was very little dignity in his pain. One by one, systems shut down, and though she was hoping for uremic poisoning—relatively painless—finally it was the artery to the liver that did him in. When the liver vein shut down, the dirty blood backed up, simple and logical. *Esophageal varices* was the medical term for it, but that put an undeserved dignity to the event, formalized a struggle made entirely of blood and body fluids and human panic. The esophageal artery took over for the liver and ruptured under the strain. He reached for her and tried to cry out, but literally gargled in his own blood. She hooked two fingers into his mouth, trying to clear the passageway, but the blood didn't stop, it just kept flowing. She looked at him, slack jawed, beaded with oily alcoholic sweat, and loved him even though he was bad for her, older than her father, and the whole sex thing, though it wasn't morally right, was really just about two scared people trying to hang on in the dark, not even a quarter as loving as it ought have been. He'd made a choice—the booze, not her—and she'd stood by for those few perfect moments—eager for crumbs. Despite all that, she loved him, even at the moment of his death, as stupid as it seemed, as arbitrary.

She was weeping now, hot tears washing over her face in the dark. She felt Hannah's cool nose press her arm in question. "Thank you, God, for bringing her back to me," she said aloud. "Thank you for not taking her, too." She turned over to stroke the dog. "Thanks for the roof, for getting me out of trouble with the court, and for Fats, no matter if what we did was a sin, because he kept me alive, you know he did, and I guess I had to go through all that to get to this moment, so will you for Christ's sake tell me what I do now?"

Outside her window, the owl took up residence in the tree. Oak branches scraped up against the single pane, and Hannah took off, nosing and scratching the door open so she could investigate. A warm wind blew in; Chloe felt it move across her arms and face. She was alone in her bed, her few possessions spread around her like museum pieces. She held her hands to her stomach and sighed her way into a troubled sleep at last, not even bothering to shut the door.

The morning was an hour off yet when she woke. She went straight to the small brown-paper sack on the windowsill, took out the pregnancy test, and read through the directions. She took the chamberpot from beneath the couch bed and went outside to use it. Hannah barked hello from her place on the creek bank, twitched one spotted ear, then laid her head back down to sleep.

Back inside, Chloe eyedroppered her urine into the test tube and set it back on the counter to wait the hour this test took. The others claimed results in only a matter of minutes, but they were upwards of twenty-five dollars, and this one was eight. Ten minutes—an hour— did it matter how quickly you knew a thing that might take months to happen?

She crawled back into bed and slept, waking two hours later. She got up and stretched, fetched Hannah a bowl of kibble, threw one of the amoxicillin tablets down her throat, and stroked until the dog swallowed. She thought about washing her face. The tube sat in its holder on the counter, right next to the pump. She didn't want this final confirmation, but when she looked, a small gray ring in the bottom of the tube looked back at her. Proof. She left it where it was, dressed in her jeans, threw a T-shirt over her bare breasts, and scrubbed her teeth at the sink. Hannah came up, nosing her leg, sensing adventure. She stroked the dog's head and pointed to the door. They both went outside, moving at a quick pace toward the lightning rock formations on the perimeter of Hugh's property. Chloe kept her head down, looking out for anything else Hannah could get hurt on. They walked two and one-half miles, up a steady incline to the flat rock outcropping where they'd come dozens of times before to watch the sunset. A blue-bellied lizard lay there doing push-ups, warming his cold skin in the shaft of sunlight. Chloe sat down on the rock and Hannah stretched out beside her, ignoring the lizard's quick jettison to a higher, less populated rock. They watched the sun come all the way up, no big gold ball, no fiery tomato, just a cupping of some ordinary god's hands to gently yellow the sky.

Chloe lay back down on the rock and sighed, unbuttoned her jeans. Gabe was right, she had put on weight, just a couple of pounds, but it was pressing the buttons. Was that baby, or was it three meals a day? Her hands gravitated toward her pelvis, reaching inside the jeans to feel the swell of stomach, trying to assess the differences that, no matter how small, she shouldn't have missed. She began to stroke herself, across the belly first, to calm the fear more than awaken the flesh. Gradually, her hand moved lower, parting the folds of skin until she grazed the small bump of her clitoris. The sensation slowly built as her finger darted back and forth, and didn't start out erotic, just an abso-

lutely necessary physical affirmation to convince herself she hadn't
been swallowed up inside that small gray ring and choked to death.
She felt heat begin to rise in her belly, dapple her breasts and throat,
felt it grow like a crack of lightning across a dark sky, arcing, seeking a
target, and did not pull her fingers away. When she came, she made no
sound. Only the barest twitch crossed her face. The hidden muscle
spasms from her womb throbbed, strong and rippling. What did that
do to it—the baby? She quickly pulled her damp hand away and felt
foolish. No laws against your own pleasure, but it was a dull and
momentary gift compared to what two people could accomplish. Hank
had been able to coax miracles from her flesh; he'd left proof of that
inside her. All those years she'd slept around with stablehands and
never once gotten unlucky. *Ain't that the way the luck goes, seems like it
never can be found. . . .* She buttoned her fly halfway and let the sun
bake overhead for a little while until her breathing quieted. Then she
patted Hannah's neck.

She would take her Hermès saddle to Wesley, let him buy it, get
out of horses, start a new life. Use a little of the cash settlement to pay
for an abortion. It was still legal, and women had the choice. It wasn't a
baby yet, just a few swimming cells, a child's drawing of a baby, dark
dots for eyes, finger buds—*Stop*—*don't imagine it.* Surely it wouldn't
take much out of her to cross over a few picketing right-to-lifers, just a
couple of steps of awkwardness, papers to fill out, the exchange of
cash, then feet up in the stirrups, ride 'em, cowgirl. The scrape of the
doctor's scalpel, and then the flowing blood. Freedom.

When Chloe returned to the cabin, Pilar was playing alone in the
shade of the biggest oak tree. At one time that tree had been Hank's
aerie. Pilar had a small red cloth laid out beneath the tree, bits of bark
torn into plate-size chunks, and an acorn cup for each plate. *"Dos
bebidas, por favor,"* she said aloud to an imaginary waiter. She took up
her doll, the acrylic hair wound into greasy ropes, smoothed her doll's
dress down, and held her in her arms, whispering to the doll's glassy
stare with great intensity. Then she lifted her own T-shirt and pressed
the doll's face to her breast. All around her oak trees stood like stubby
guards, their small leaves spangling in the sunlight like sequins.

Chloe moved back silently so as not to disturb the girl's play. She ducked back behind the corner of her house, taking one last look at Pilar, who swung her grinning face upward in the sunshine in a moment of childhood bliss. Constantina had came looking for her and stopped short, directly opposite Chloe, watching her little girl pretend at mothering, a bemused smile across her face. Chloe studied Constantina's huge belly, the way she laid a hand protectively over it, crooning a song Chloe couldn't make out, but singing, all right. *Hija, hija. . . .*

Chloe went inside her shack long enough to grab her keys and motioned silently for Hannah to walk through the woods to the truck. She felt ashamed, with ten thousand dollars sitting in the bank. Constantina and Pilar had no trouble accepting their circumstances, and they lived far less comfortably than she did. I have no mothering instinct, she told herself. *Shit, I can barely keep hold of this dog.*

Wesley was wearing his flannel shirt and the silver trout bolo tie; maybe he slept in them. He was waiting on people, selling some of the wealthy horse folk a few things more than they needed when Chloe came into his store lugging the saddle. He gave her a wink, turned back to his customer, then did a double take.

She nodded and set the saddle down on the counter, then stood looking over his bargain table at the odd pieces of tack he was selling for half price. Old hackamores more people abused than used properly, a mismatched set of English spurs, salt and mineral blocks broken in shipping, but would a horse care? Wes was a good salesman; he took his time and engineered things so the customers thought they were making a reasonable choice, but in the end they bought exactly as he had first advised them, top quality tack and the old brand names that lasted. He rang up the purchases, called out to his stockroom for his helper to load them into the customer's car—brand-new King Cab, Chloe noted—and made his cheerful small talk, calling everyone by name.

"Well," he said when he returned from holding the door for them. "I thought the court was going to pay you some money."

"They did. It's tucked away in the bank. There's other reasons to unload a saddle. This time it's yours for keeps, Wes. I want you to sell it."

He ducked behind the counter and shuffled papers into stacks. "If I do, you can't come crying back to get it because it won't be here."

"I know that."

"What are you going to do when one of your rich little students comes wandering into your arena, lugging your saddle?"

"Grit my teeth, take her money, and teach her some horsemanship."

He cocked his head like a bewildered dog. "You want to come at me again? I thought everything went okay in the courtroom."

"It did. Look, I'm horseless except for a few lesson nags, and maybe it's time to put all this behind me, like you said. If I sell the saddle, I can always get myself a new one, maybe one with less history to it."

"How's your boyfriend feel?"

"Don't give me that. By now you've heard all the news. If not Hugh, then Gabe or Francisco—somebody at the stables."

"All right. I'll give you eight hundred."

"Eight hundred? A grand or I take it back to the truck."

"Eight-fifty. And a month's credit for feed, including hay."

"Deal." They shook hands. He held on to hers, pressed it to his dry lips.

"Maybe I didn't do so well with the game of life, but you're still young, Chloe."

"And?"

"You know what I mean."

"Has Gabe been talking when he shouldn't have?"

"We care about you, that's all."

"Dammit."

"Chloe, I'm a down-home boy. I can piece the truth together nearly as good as my grandmother could patch her quilts."

From a counter display, she picked up a keychain shaped like a snaffle bit and played with it. "So?"

"So if you've got a bun in the oven, I'd hate to see you do a foolish thing you'd regret. I've seen what that can do to a woman. When she isn't sure. It'll haunt you. Think long and hard."

For such a spread-out county, there was no keeping a secret. They might as well have been roommates. She let him count out the bills and kept her lips tight. "You know me better than that, Wesley. When I make a decision, I think it all the way through."

"Be sure you sniff all this one's corners before you do."

"I will." She gave him a hug, held onto his aging body, and felt the strength of his embrace. For all it reminded her of Fats, Wes's love was entirely different. A woman could feel safe there, could sleep dreamless, and wake refreshed, not worried about the contents of the new day. Not one iota of passion, but enough security to make you sleep through the night.

"Hang on any longer, and I won't never turn you loose," he whispered.

She stepped back and looked into his gray eyes. "I love you," she said, and gave him a kiss, right on the lips.

He pressed his hand to his mouth and looked embarrassed.

"After all these years, you're shocked?" She went out the door, where Hannah stood up in the truck bed and wagged her tail.

The Carlson boys rode single file behind her down the steep rocky grade onto the fire road. Billy, the rent string horse she'd chosen, welcomed his position as leader, arched his neck proudly, and kept his footing. Behind the boys, Mark, who tried several excuses to get out of coming along on the ride, begrudgingly rode Casper, Billy's next-door neighbor. From time to time Casper let out shrieking neighs, and Billy answered. Chloe turned her head back to look, and Mark shook his head. "You know, everytime he does that I just about have a heart attack."

The boys laughed. "You're a *wuss*, Chapman," they said, and whatever that meant, Chloe noticed it sure tickled the hell out of Kit, who rode alongside Marquise, the only one still a little insecure about his equitation.

"You're doing great," Kit told him. "Keep your head up. Tonto doesn't need you to watch his feet for him. He's been walking on them for almost twenty-seven years."

It was hot; Chloe could feel the back of her neck getting sunburned. If she didn't watch it, one of these days she would end up a leathery old wattle-necked turkey like Fats. Sunscreen only worked until you sweated it off. She led the boys through the cool forest, where ferns lined the canyon floor and the live oaks' thick branches formed a lacy canopy overhead. Sun peeked through in between branches, yellow as newly ripped plywood. Over the top of this hill there were two ways to go: the fire road into the Whiting Ranch, and the long grade that led to a new housing development, where acres of huge stucco houses with swimming pools and tall iron fences were spreading through the hills. Before long they would multiply; nobody's land was sacred. Maybe Robin Leach was up there right now, dipping jumbo strawberries into French champagne.

She legged Billy to the right along the fire road. Rattlesnakes were likely this time of day. They lay across the road in full sun, soaking up heat. Absalom used to spot them before she did. There'd been times she'd given him a kick to go on, and he'd held his ground, unmoving. She would dismount and check his feet, unbuckle and examine his girth, give up, then, one foot in the stirrup iron, hear the familiar rattle before the snake moved on. She sat back in her saddle and Billy halted.

"Okay, you guys," she said, turning back to view her scraggly line of riders. "This road's five miles long and flat. We're going to lope these horses, and when I say lope, I don't mean gallop. No passing each other, no Lone Ranger bullshit; you're riders now, you're responsible for keeping your animal in hand. We'll blow it out for a mile, then it's back to the trot. Understand?"

Mark sighed and made the sign of the cross on his blue workshirt. The boys nodded. Kit just grinned. Chloe pressed a hand to her belly. Get used to it, kid. Hook up with me, and this is the way it's going to be.

"Stand still, this is a Kodak moment," Kit said, posing each boy standing alongside his horse. Kit snapped pictures of the boys with arms thrown around the necks of their horses. Some of them were tight lipped, a few were sniffling. Marquise looked like an African chief, his black face stern, a gentle hand on the reins. Since mastering the lope, he'd undergone a small transformation.

Anton held up his leftover lunch apple. "Take my picture, Kit," he urged, but wily Tonto reached across and swiped the apple in one clean bite, and Kit howled. "He almost got you that time!"

Willie sat alone on the picnic table, off to the side of the photo session, his face down, shoulders hunched up. Chloe went to him. "You need a cigarette?" she asked.

He looked up at her, surprised. "Chapman will bust me."

"You need one or not?"

"Yeah, I could use one."

She offered her pack, lit it for him with a match. She kept her distance, didn't reach out to touch him. "You're going to miss these horses, aren't you?"

"A little."

She looked away, toward the rows of pipe stalls, where horses stood dozing, slurping from their waterers in the late-afternoon sun. She could hear the highway traffic faintly, ever constant behind the wall of oak trees that grew alongside the stables. "Willie, I'm going to tell you something I'm not going to tell any of the other boys. You have something they don't—that spark it takes to make a rider. That's why it hurts you so bad to say good-bye to them. From here you go back to the ranch. What happens next?"

He shrugged. "I'm supposed to go back to my mom."

"Supposed to?"

"Shit. She's a flaming alkie. Half the time I end up wiping puke off her."

"So take care of her until you're eighteen. It won't kill you. You're a smart guy, Willie."

"No I'm not."

"Listen, if you're smart enough to swipe car stereos, you're smart enough to make the best of a bad situation at home. Try setting yourself a goal, maybe work toward the horses. You stay in school and out of trouble, I might be able to get you a job at a stables."

"No way." Tears glittered in his blue eyes. He knuckled them away, and Chloe stared hard at the new ink-pen tattoo on his wrist.

"The horse world's not that huge. I know a few people."

"Can I write you when I get home?"

"Sure you can. Now hand me that cigarette, here comes Mark."

* * *

Even Kit was crying when the Carlson Ranch van pulled away. Great sobs tore from her chest, and she leaned against Chloe. "Oh, my God. How can you stand this, year after year? I feel like I'm going to die!"

Chloe patted her shoulders. "Kit, get hold of yourself. I can't have you weeping whenever it's time to move somebody on. Those boys were just about in love with you. Don't you know that crying sends men running scared into the sports page? Every single bit of life is out there just waiting to break your heart. You have to hang tough. Now, come on, we have tack to clean, and lessons again in the morning."

"Wait up," Kit said, wiping her face. "I have to get a snot rag from the office. Snot, I'm telling you, one major drawback to crying."

Chloe leaned against the railing where the horses had been tied. The metal bar still held heat from the day, and it was pleasant against her back. She would miss those boys, too. This summer they'd kept her going. Now they would be turned loose back into the big, bad world, and they'd already failed there once. A wave of sudden understanding overcame her, chilling her sunburned skin—*So, Mama, that's why you gave me away, wasn't it? You were afraid of days just like this one.*

The screen door banged twice as Kit came out. She let out a big sigh, then held a white envelope in her hand out to Chloe. "Look what was on your desk," she said. "Looks like somebody in Arizona wrote you a letter."

CHAPTER

26

Of course, he hadn't really expected her to answer his letter, but when August 13, another of those rare, perfect northern Arizona summer days with a temperature that hovered around eighty, and only the lightest of afternoon rains segued into a quiet dusk, Hank couldn't hide his disappointment. The roof was finished, and even without lemonade bribery, the Indian children pronounced it a job well done. It was solid and would hold through winter and well beyond. Despite the darkening sky, he wasn't ready to put the tools away and face down the long night alone in the cabin.

Shirtless and driven, he'd worked double-time getting the corral fence put up, though it was unlikely it would ever again hold anything save a neighboring pony when the Indian children came calling. He'd spent three days on the gate alone—hinges—they looked bafflingly simple until you tried to match the pin to the joint and make the whole business line up. Fixing broken things took unwavering faith and unlimited patience, and he had found plenty of both here with no tempting distractions. By a small miscount in estimating, he had twenty boards left over, but at $5.20 a running foot, he'd find somewhere to use them. Hammer in hand, he drove a few more nails home into the top rail and slipped on the last one, smashing his thumb right above the moon of the nail. He cried out and stuck it in his mouth where it throbbed hard, and stood in the dark, letting the tears flow down his face.

Up the dirt road that led back to town, he heard the rumble of a truck. Please God, he thought, not now, not Joyce Greer offering the everlasting pot roast again. I've been polite, and I'm thankful for my blessings, but I don't know if I have it left in me to be civil, not today. But it *was* a truck, and it was coming his way. He could see headlights now, two small white beacons shining down on him. The truck, like countless others he passed in town, was towing a two-horse trailer behind it. Well, he'd learned the gods had no respect for any mortal timetable; when the mood struck them, they sent a stranger or even came themselves, in such clever disguises you never caught on until the test had been flunked, yanked from your hands, leaving you stinging and sorry. He reached for his shirt, hanging across the fence rail. It didn't cost much to act neighborly, to offer a drink, to take a look at a map. People got lost all the time, and if a small act of human kindness could help them be found, it was the decent thing to do. But there was something familiar about this truck—inside the cab, he could make out the curve of a woman's face, and next to her, the tall pointed ears of a white German shepherd, riding shotgun.

The only myths he knew dealing with second chances ended in sorrow, but this wasn't a myth, this was his life.

He took his thumb out of his mouth and hung his hammer by the claw on the fence post. Take a deep breath, he told himself. *Steady now, and don't go expecting miracles.* He stood by the fence, waiting. However complicated and remarkable the rest of his life was going to be, it was here now, come to claim him.